CW01103073

# The Balance Between

# The Balance Between

PR Moredun

Rookstone
Publishing

First published 2004
by Rookstone Publishing

© 2004 The author

Typeset in Goudy by Wearset Ltd, Boldon, Tyne and Wear
Printed and bound in Great Britain by Creative Print and Design (Wales), Ebbw Vale

All rights reserved. No part of this book may be reprinted or reproduced or utilised in any form or by any electronic, mechanical, or other means, now known or hereafter invented, including photocopying and recording, or in any information storage or retrieval system, without permission in writing from the publishers.

*British Library Cataloguing in Publication Data*
A catalogue record for this book is available from the British Library

ISBN 0 954 71730 9

For Duncan and Edward, who prompted the stories, and for Amanda.

For Eda and Tim, who never wavered in their support. For Stuart, who read the roughest draft and still believed.

For everyone who helped, and everyone who reads it. Thank you.

# Contents

| | | |
|---|---|---:|
| *Prologue* | Evil Beginnings, 1895 | 1 |
| 1 | The Sea Arch, May 1910 | 3 |
| 2 | The Brothers Bandamire | 10 |
| 3 | A Wicked and Cruel Night Out | 29 |
| 4 | Clues, Now and Then | 41 |
| 5 | The Western Tower | 62 |
| 6 | More Questions than Answers | 77 |
| 7 | The Warkrin | 90 |
| 8 | A Surprise in the Dark | 111 |
| 9 | Footprints and Claw Prints | 127 |
| 10 | Abroad in the Land | 140 |
| 11 | The *Parsimony* Paradigm | 154 |
| 12 | Breaking and Entering | 170 |
| 13 | In the Land of the Marked | 188 |
| 14 | Doctored in So Many Ways | 207 |
| 15 | A Line is Drawn | 225 |
| 16 | The Talon Grab | 240 |
| 17 | The Battle of Beadnell Bay | 258 |
| 18 | A Farewell to Arms | 279 |
| 19 | The Truth about Everything | 294 |
| *Epilogue* | Old World, New World | 309 |

*East of England Coast from Holy Island to the Channel*

- Holy Island
- Bamburgh
- Beadnell Bay
- Newcastle
- England
- East Anglia
- Sandringham
- Purbeck
- Cambridge
- Orford Ness
- Felixstowe
- Oxford
- London
- Foulness Island
- River Thames
- Straights of Dover
- Zeebrugge

# Prologue

## Evil Beginnings, 1895

February in the fens. A thin moon had risen early and now the pale crescent slid back towards the horizon, yellowing in the mist that rose in eerie swirls from the dark wetlands. It was as if the ground were exhaling. Somewhere in the emptiness an owl hooted. A little later, a fox barked in reply.

In the distance, a forlorn rank of winter trees marched nowhere, their barren branches thrust upward as if praying to an unseen deity high up in the ink-night sky. Beyond the trees a large stone building reared up. Hollow black windows were set evenly into the walls of an old country mansion. A faint glow stole from a shuttered first-floor window, the only sign of life in the otherwise abandoned dwelling.

Inside, a woman lay huddled beneath a pile of coarse blankets upon an old four-poster bed pushed against the far wall of the cavernous room. A tearful, lonely cry slipped from her lips. She groaned in pain and rolled on her side, flinging the blankets from her body. She was feverish and frightened, her barely clothed body covered in sweat. The feeble lamplight set shadows dancing on the walls. The woman cried out, alone, afraid. She knew her child would be born soon, very soon.

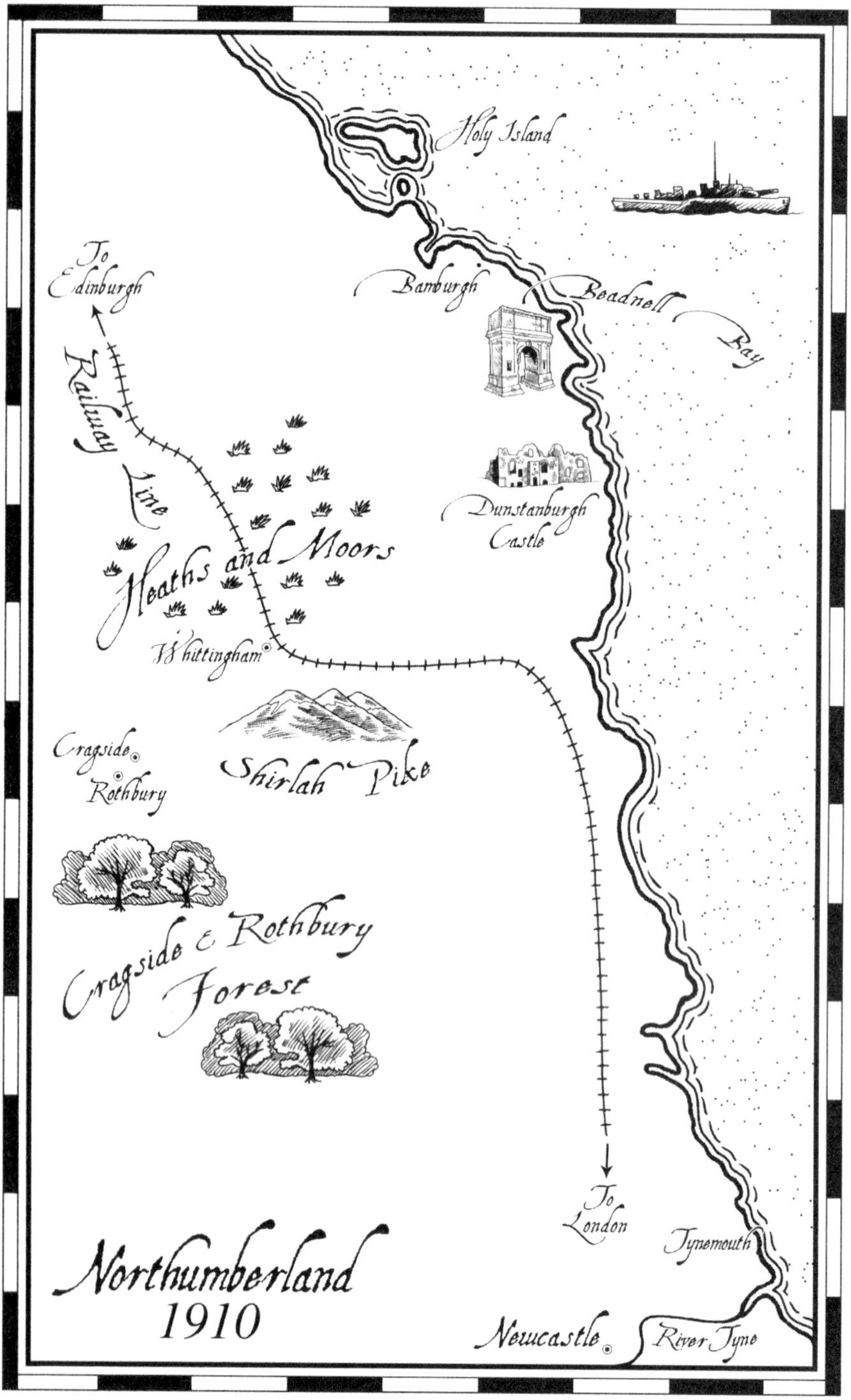

Holy Island
To Edinburgh
Bamburgh
Beadnell Bay
Railway Line
Dunstanburgh Castle
Heaths and Moors
Whittingham
Cragside
Rothbury
Shirlah Pike
Cragside & Rothbury Forest
To London
Tynemouth
Northumberland
1910
Newcastle
River Tyne

# 1

## The Sea Arch, May 1910

James Kinghorn had escaped!

He'd escaped, if only for half term, from the school where last September he had arrived for the first time, a reluctant fourteen-year-old sent to honour a family tradition. Every generation of Kinghorn had despatched a son to Drinkett College (the 'Eton of the North') since Waterloo, and James was not about to let down the family name.

James stood amidst the sand dunes that lined the barren coast of Northumberland in northern England. Wisps of cloud traced across the brilliant blue sky. A crab scuttled into the surf, its claws raised in defiance of marauding seagulls. James spied a small, wretched boat left stranded above the high-water line – its hull planking stoved in, a casualty of a winter gale – and he trudged through the sand to investigate. Inspecting the broken vessel, he imagined himself shipwrecked and alone, on some great adventure.

James's father, Sir Philip Kinghorn, worked in the War Office, although in what capacity James wasn't quite sure, but he was pretty certain it was an important job. Sir Philip had arranged for James to spend the weekend with him and his mother, Lady Jennifer, while Sir Philip attended a naval gunnery demonstration held off the Farne Islands, just up the coast. Today was the day of the demonstration and James, let loose to explore the desolate coastline, was intent on having an adventure of one sort or another.

The distant rumble of gunfire carried on the sea breeze and James turned in the direction of the sound, half expecting to see giant dreadnoughts and battleships on the horizon, sheathed in flames and smoke. Instead he was amazed to see an enormous stone arch standing amidst the dunes only a dozen yards from where he stood. As he looked at the arch it appeared to shimmer and become translucent like a mirage before finally solidifyng into stone. The arch was collosal, towering over him like a leviathan. Set into the archway was a pair of enormous iron gates, chained and padlocked shut. The lock was so large that one of James's fists could easily fit into the keyhole. It was locked tight. James couldn't understand how he'd failed to notice the arch earlier; it was so grand and imposing, and he could see from his footprints that he'd already passed close by the edifice. There was something very peculiar about it.

James walked around the arch and studied it more closely. It was made of great blocks of white marble, smooth to the touch. Across the top, just visible from below, he could make out the words 'Sea Arch' carved faintly into the stone.

James stood wondering what on earth it was there to commemorate. The distant boom of gunfire had faded away now and, except for the gentle rolling of the sea, all was quiet and still.

Suddenly, with a machine-gun stutter, the chain snaked off the gates and fell with a thump to the sand. The unexpected noise made James jump. At the foot of the gates the big lumpy padlock lay sprung, the chain links, each one as big as a man's fist, had cascaded into a haphazard pile that sank into the sand under its own weight. A shiver of suspense ran down James's spine. Only seconds before when he'd looked at the padlock it was secure, the chain tightly wrapped about the central rails of the gates. Now the gates stood ajar. James looked down at the chain and padlock and saw how clean and rust-free they were. He took a step closer, feeling the temptation of the open gates. Then, without a second thought, he slipped between them and was gone!

# 1895

Thomas Hopply broke open his double-barrelled shotgun, checked the cartridges and, hanging the fowling piece in the crook of his arm, waited patiently for the approaching figures. Constable Tauning, the only officer of the law for ten miles in any direction, marched up the drive. Next to the constable, the parish vicar, Reverend Much, kept pace. Behind them, wheeling his cycle, was young Finnigan, the lad who'd raised the alarm.

'Good day to you, Thomas,' called the vicar. Thomas nodded solemnly in reply.

'Good day to you, sir,' said the constable as he removed his helmet and mopped his brow. 'I understand there's a body ...'

'It were me and the lad who found it,' said the gamekeeper. 'The name is Hopply, and I'm gamekeeper on the Purbeck estate.' He swung his arm in a gesture that took in the full sweep of surrounding countryside. 'This here be the estate and that –' he jerked a gnarled and weathered hand over his shoulder '– that be what's left of Purbeck Hall.' He paused, before explaining. 'I've hunted and fished most things, but in all my life I've never seen anything like what's in there.' And with that the gamekeeper fell silent.

Leaving Hopply and the boy standing on the gravel drive, the policeman and vicar climbed the stone steps leading to the once-grand front entrance. The constable shouldered the double doors open. Light flooded into the cavernous hallway and dust swirled at the men's feet like marsh mist. Ahead, a broad staircase climbed up and around in a grand sweep, the dark mahogany banister like a snake hemming in the stone steps. A grimy stained-glass window filled the wall above the stairs, framed with heavy, worn, crimson drapes. Neither man, however, took any notice of the surroundings. They stood in shocked astonishment, gazing at the strange bloodied object that lay in the centre of the hall.

Reverend Much fell trembling to his knees, his hands clasped white as he quavered through the Lord's Prayer. Constable Tauning stepped up and gripped the frightened man's shoulder, shaking him to his senses.

'Reverend, please go at once and send the lad to the nearest railway halt. The Station Manager is to get word through to Divisional Headquarters in Cambridge. Tell him to say –' but there was no point in continuing. The vicar had scrambled to his feet and ran from the building as if Satan was at his heels.

## 1910

James had no idea where he was. One moment he'd been standing on the shoreline in broad daylight, the next he found himself in a clearing surrounded by dense conifer trees, with only a hint of a path threading into the distance. A fresh breeze blew through the trees, carrying the familiar scent of pine. On the horizon the sinking sun, now blood-red, set the tree line into relief. James, troubled at the apparent loss of time, turned to retrace his steps back through the arch, but found his way blocked. The gates stood padlocked and chained!

Beyond the gates he could see the waters breaking on the shoreline. His hands grabbed at the chain, but it was solid and unyielding. Panic welled up in James's chest and he took several deep breaths to calm down.

'This is not happening,' he said to himself. 'Walk around the arch and let's go home.' He rounded the arch, but he didn't find the beach. Instead the forest crowded in on all sides, forming an unbroken wall around the increasingly gloomy glade. James looked at the arch again, trying to rationalise what had happened. The

## The Balance Between

Sea Arch had somehow taken him from the seaside to the middle of a forest, but how? He studied the structure more closely, searching for a clue to explain this bizarre occurrence. He spotted a brass plaque set into the stonework with an inscription on it. It read:

> *The roaring seas are silent now*
> *And secrets are themselves once more*
> *Complete the earth and fill the void*
> *To mark the time when earth was whole*
> *Locked are these gates to keep the vow*
> *To end a world on barren shore*
> *Protect a place to be destroyed*
> *By man's belief, a lack of soul*
>
> *Yet stand a vigil and wait a time*
> *When stranger from the stranger land*
> *Before the gates, behind the sun*
> *Gives passage to the unsouled son*
> *To pass to wild and pass to grime*
> *The places split by sea and sand*
> *Where one is slaved beneath the gun*
> *The other stalked and evil begun*

James looked at the words, but they were too deep and mysterious to make any sense of. He kept looking for another clue, one he could understand. On the far side of the arch he could now see the words, 'Where Westerly?', but they seemed to make no sense either.

Finally, James accepted that he'd have to find another way back to the beach. There was no way back through the magical arch and no one to help. He'd been alone on the beach earlier so it was unlikely he's be rescued by someone on the other side, or his cries for help heard. The sun was disappearing fast. Soon it would be night and he didn't want to be stumbling around the forest in the dark. He'd have to find shelter. He set off at a run, following the path that led from the Sea Arch into the cooling forest, hoping to find safety before night fell.

Daylight abruptly faded as if a curtain had been drawn, plunging the path into gloomy darkness. The tree tops, moving ceaselessly by a light wind, creaked and swished in the strange language of trees. James stumbled over an exposed root and fell, pine needles puncturing his palms. In the dark, he smelled, rather than saw, his own blood. He began to get scared again.

'There's nothing to be afraid of,' he said to himself as he tried to hold his fear in check. 'This path must lead somewhere and somebody will be able to explain where I am and contact mother and father and then I'll get home.' James's words weren't so convincing in the forest gloom. He got to his feet and hurried on.

A smear of daylight lingered in the highest clouds, but there wasn't enough to penetrate into the forest. James could no longer make out the path. The wind grew stronger, whipping the tree tops into a roof of noise. Fear came creeping through the dark pines, fear of the unknown and the unseen. It began to stalk him. James stumbled on, his hands groping at pine branches in the darkness as he tried to hurry. He focused his thoughts on the unseen path, imagining it leading him onwards in an effort to stop himself from panicking.

'All I need is some light,' he told himself, wishing it to happen. 'All I need is some light.' As if in answer to his wish, James found that he could see enough detail around him to pick out the lighter-coloured path from the dark forest floor. Looking up he discovered a cloud of fireflies silently swarming above him, the iridescent glow of their bodies bathing him in a greenish light. As James stood watching, they moved further down the path, lighting the way. James followed. They led him into a clearing, the trees falling back beyond the pool of light. A low stone wall materialised from out of the night, set in ghostly relief. Behind James, back up the valley, a creature howled, sending a shiver down the boy's spine.

He followed the wall until it ended at what looked to be a yard. James stood before a solid wooden door with a heavy door-knocker set into it. He was just about to lift the knocker when the door swung open, revealing a stout figure silhouetted by a fire burning brightly in the hearth.

'Come in, come in. We've been expecting you.'

## ∽ 2 ∽

# The Brothers Bandamire

James stumbled over the threshold, relieved to escape the forest and its dark secrets. He found himself in a long, low-beamed room, an open fireplace on the far wall providing the only light. Thick cords of wood crackled in the grate, sending swirls of sparks up the chimney.

Glancing apprehensively around, James watched his host shoulder the door closed and set a crossbar in place. He spotted a second figure seated by the hearth, almost lost in the flickering shadows. What appeared to be a big animal skin lay stretched across the floor in front of the fire.

'Sit yourself down, sit yourself down,' his host insisted, the voice gruff but friendly. James sank into the nearest seat and felt the warmth of the fire lull his eyes closed. He really could do with a rest. But it wasn't to be, not just yet.

'There'll be plenty of time for that soon enough, young lad,' interrupted his host, who saw James nodding off. 'First we must speak with you. You've quite a pressing schedule and we must be mindful of the circumstances.' James wore a bemused look. 'Your arrival is of interest to many, good and evil,' the dwarf explained.

'Please, sir,' James asked, 'where am I?'

'Well, that's a good question,' chortled his host, now standing

## The Balance Between

by the fire, warming his hands. 'A very good question indeed. With possibly the most difficult answer to understand.'

James waited for his host to continue.

This time the figure seated by the fire spoke: 'We're not far from where you were – but many miles from where you've just been.' James caught sight of the man's gnarled hands. They were large, weather-beaten and powerful looking, the hands of someone used to heavy manual labour. With his eyes growing accustomed to the light, James saw the same characteristics in the man's worn features. Bearded, and riven with creases, it was a strong, determined, yet compassionate face. But it was the eyes that grabbed and held James's attention the most. They were electric, piercing and alive, cobalt blue even in the firelight. It struck James that both of the figures were dwarves. They looked familiar . . .

'Excuse me, sirs. That doesn't exactly help me. You see, I was on the beach between Beadnell and –'

'Dunstanburrrh Castle. Yes, lad, we know,' cut in the dwarf standing by the fire. 'We've been waiting for you.'

'You took your time getting here,' added the second dwarf as he rose and busied himself. Presently, a lamp shone, revealing more of the room. The dwarf came forward and extended his hand to James.

'My name is Solomon Brunel Bandamire,' he said formally as James shook his hand. 'And that is my brother, Bartholomew Shakespeare Bandamire.' He too had amazing eyes, pearlescent grey and set beneath big bushy brows either side of a crooked nose that seemed to burst from his face. A mass of dark hair flecked with streaks of grey gave him a wild look.

Solomon smiled. 'I reckon this young lad has seen us before, Bartholomew,' he called over to his brother.

'It was one of you at the fair!' exclaimed James, and watched as Solomon's smile widened. Danart the Dwarfen King had been a popular sideshow attraction touring the north of England gypsy fairs during the spring.

'Indeed, young sir. And we had occasion to deliver coal to your school, tend to the gardens at your home and even sweep your chimneys! Bartholomew even worked for the local smithy to keep an eye on your family's comings and goings,' Solomon added in triumph.

A perplexed look on James's face hastened the dwarf to explain. 'Don't worry lad,' the dwarf assured. 'We were there to look after you, to watch out for you. We were there under orders.'

'Secret orders,' added Bartholomew with a conspiratorial wink as he laid the table for supper.

'I'd be grateful if you could explain a few more things to me. Where am I and why am I here?' James asked between mouthfuls of stew and dumplings, to which the dwarves readily answered.

'Well, lad, firstly you've made a remarkable journey,' Solomon replied. 'You are in Lauderley Forest and you came here through the portal.'

'What's a portal?' James asked.

'It's a gateway of sorts, a magical device that allows one to travel between the two worlds.'

'Two worlds?' James couldn't help but interrupt.

'Aye,' chipped in Bartholomew. 'Your world and this one, Eldaterra.'

'It means "Old World",' went on Solomon. 'The two worlds are separated by magic. They've been separated deliberately, to keep them apart, to keep the existence of each a secret from the other.'

'But the fact that you've come through the Sea Arch means that you're important ... very important,' said Bartholomew in a serious voice. 'Neither my brother nor I know why you're so important; that's a question the Guild will answer. And that is where we're heading, at their express orders.'

'Please, Mr Bandamire, what is the Guild?'

'The Guild are the wisest and most learned in the land. Those who stand for Good, that is!' Bartholomew replied. 'It was the Guild who ordered us to watch over you and, when the time was right, deliver you to them.'

'And sure enough that's what will happen,' declared Solomon.

'So how long have you been keeping an eye on me?' James asked. The dwarves exchanged glances.

'Twenty-two months,' replied Bartholomew.

'Twenty-two months!' cried James. 'But that's impossible.'

Bartholomew laughed. 'Yes, very nearly. Imagine how hard it's been for two not-so-inconspicuous dwarves to shadow you to northern Italy on your summer holidays. We had to pretend to be travelling monks on a pilgrimage.'

'Not that it helped,' Solomon continued. 'We were obliged to act the part, which included wearing disguises and singing psalms! We've never given so many blessings and bestowed forgiveness on so many strangers!'

'Your religion is astonishing,' Bartholomew added. 'Who'd have believed it could be so powerful, and yet possess no magic whatsoever?'

'Yes,' Solomon agreed. 'Too weak to be anything but words, and yet powerful enough to influence thoughts and deeds of so many people. Strange indeed. But now, getting back to our story, we kept you under constant surveillance. Yet in doing so, we have travelled through the portal many times. And for that to be possible implies that something unprecedented is occurring between the two worlds.'

'These are dark omens and the portents are not good,' said Bartholomew. 'The Guild acts for the Good, but these are troubled times.' Solomon rose from the dinner table. 'We'll learn soon enough what the Guild has in store for you, my lad.'

'But my parents will be wondering what has happened to me. Mother will be worried ...' James began, his voice quavering with concern.

## The Balance Between

'Never fear about your mother, lad,' Solomon reassured. 'Your father will comfort her, and there's a good deal more about your father than either you or we know. You'll be home before they realise you're missing.'

'We start very early tomorrow morning,' continued Bartholomew. 'Your arrival here is not a moment too soon and we must hasten east to the Guild's representative.' A look passed between the two dwarves. 'We'll take a short cut to get there sooner, but the path is not without danger.' James caught the meaning in Bartholomew's voice but said nothing. Instead his attention was caught by a sound from the fireside rug. Slowly it shook itself and stood up, padding silently towards him.

'Don't mind Tempus,' chuckled Solomon, seeing James's astonishment. Tempus was a giant dog, almost as tall as the dwarves. 'He's as gentle as a pussy cat,' Bartholomew added merrily.

James woke in a narrow bunk, a blanket thrown over him. He'd fallen asleep in his clothes. Light streamed through small windows. A few feet away, Tempus sat patiently watching him.

'Good morning, Master James,' Bartholomew called cheerfully. 'We'll have you fed and watered in two ticks and then we'll be off.'

He sat and ate a breakfast of bread and honey washed down with coffee, and then stepped outside. The dwarves were busy making preparations to depart.

'Good morning, Master James,' Solomon said brightly. 'I'm just packing the last of our equipment.' He pointed over towards Bartholomew. 'And he's preparing the traps.'

James watched as Bartholomew dragged the mantrap's jagged metal jaws apart and set the trigger plate.

'That's the last of them out here,' said Bartholomew as he carefully placed the trap in the middle of the path leading directly to the front door. To James's amazement the trap vanished. 'I'll just set the ones inside and then we're done.' He picked up a big, clanking sack and disappeared inside.

'I've taken the liberty of packing a bag for you, Master James,' said Solomon, pointing at a knapsack. It stood next to two mountainous rucksacks. The dwarves would carry these, even though each was practically as big as the brothers. In comparison, James's knapsack looked embarrassingly small.

'We've filled your knapsack with provisions,' advised Solomon, 'though there's plenty more in the other rucksacks. And my brother and I would like you to accept this gift. It may come in handy.' Solomon held up a leather scabbard and drew out a long, sleek double-bladed knife, the polished blade catching the sunlight. 'It's just a dagger, I'm afraid. But we'd feel a lot happier knowing you are able to defend yourself should the need arise.' He sheathed the dagger and passed it to James, who grinned and said thank you.

Stuck, as he was, in a forest in a strange land with two burly dwarves and a giant hound for company, James was reassured to be carrying a weapon. The dagger was fashioned with a stout hilt of bone and a blade at least a foot in length. Engraved patterns wove a long, looping design down each side of the blade.

James fastened the dagger to his belt and picked up the knapsack just as Bartholomew locked the lodge door. James thanked Bartholomew and Solomon again. The brothers bowed deeply and James bowed in return. Then with a whistle from Solomon to Tempus, they set off to meet the Guild.

## 1895

Chief Inspector Corrick rubbed his stubbly chin, deep in thought. He stood in the first-floor room where the body had been found. Apart from the enormous four-poster bed, the room was empty, bare floorboards and cracked plaster echoing policemen's footsteps as they searched for evidence. Various officers and technicians came and went, studying and recording the grisly scene. Out on the landing, Corrick's deputy, Sergeant Smith, was taking statements from witnesses while a photographer and his assistant set up their panoply of equipment and took magnesium-flared photographs.

'I want a photograph showing the details of the wounds,' Corrick called to them.

The bed held the grizzly remains of a female body. On first inspection it appeared as if the corpse had been eaten by scavenging animals, but closer examination suggested that this was the state the murderer had left his victim in. Both the victim's hands bore abrasions, as if she'd tried to ward off her attacker. Corrick sighed. There was something unhuman, diabolical about the way she had died. He sensed something demonic. Turning away, he made a brief entry into his notebook. So far no one had come forward to report a missing person, and the 'thing' downstairs in the entrance hall couldn't be explained, adding to the mystery. Sergeant Smith came into the room. 'Right, sir. I've got the witness statements and their stories corroborate. The reverend was pretty badly shaken by it all. Kept declaring that evil was abroad and it was all the Devil's work. Not very helpful, I'm afraid, sir. Didn't recognise the victim as one from his own parish.'

'Well we can't expect him to know every soul in the parish,' replied Corrick, 'and he's not the only one to think the Devil's involved,' he added.

'Yes, sir.'

'Smith, have a final word with the witnesses before you let them go. Put the *By-Jesus* up them, scare them. We don't want rumours flying about, or every sightseer for miles around will be on the doorstep. Tell them if they gossip we'll arrest them, even Officer Tauning.'

'Very good, sir,' Smith replied before turning and leaving.

A new figure stepped forward and introduced himself.

'Good day, Chief Inspector. My name is Harrington. I'm with the Foreign Office,' the man said as he touched his hat. He was of fair complexion, about the same height and age as Corrick, putting him in his mid-forties, with a slimmer build than the policeman. Corrick marked Harrington as the academic type: glasses, a rather limp handshake, but a keen pair of eyes, bright and impishly alert.

Corrick nodded. 'Yes, I've been expecting you, though I can't see why the Foreign Office is interested in this incident,' he said brusquely. Corrick noted how Harrington's gaze quickly and expertly took in the horrific scene.

Harrington turned back to study the policeman. Corrick's rugged face and brown eyes conveyed intelligence and professionalism, while broad shoulders beneath the gabardine coat hinted at a powerful build. The two men stood, sizing each other up.

'I'm to help you in any way possible,' said Corrick, 'but maybe you can help me as well.' Only something important would drag the Foreign Office into a murder enquiry.

Harrington warmed to the policeman and his directness. 'Yes, perhaps I can help. I'm with the illegal alien department,' he explained. 'It's a small office, no more than a dozen of us, trying to keep tabs on illegal entrants into the country. Refugees, diplomats on the run for fleecing their embassy, requests to look into the affairs of exiles, that sort of thing. You wouldn't believe the stranger aspects of the job,' Harrington elaborated. His eyes flicked back to the murder scene and Corrick caught a glint of hardness in his gaze. Harrington was clearly untroubled by the grisly surroundings.

'As I understand it,' Harrington continued, 'the investigation centres on the death of this woman.'

Corrick couldn't help wondering if Harrington was fishing for information or suggesting the direction the investigation should take. He took Harrington by the elbow and led him back into the corridor. 'Let me tell you what we know so far, and see what you make of it,' he proposed, watching the man's every move.

## 1910

Bartholomew led them through the seemingly endless forest. Ahead, Tempus loped through the trees snuffling the ground and scenting the wind. Though the brothers had shorter legs than James, which meant they had to take three or four steps for every couple of strides James took, they happily bowled along at a considerable pace.

'It'll be a push to reach our destination by nightfall,' said Solomon, 'but we should arrive before the moon is up. Provided, that is, we don't meet any trouble on the way.'

'Trouble?' asked James. 'What sort of trouble?'

'We're not alone out here in these woods. This is a strange land, nothing like the world you come from. And there are forces that may seek to delay or stop us.'

'Which, of course, we have no intention of allowing,' added Bartholomew hastily.

James got the impression that they hadn't explained the situation fully. He let the matter drop, but kept a wary eye.

James now noticed the two brothers were indeed prepared for trouble. Bartholomew carried a long broadsword across his back, partially obscured by his rucksack. Down his side, hidden in the folds of his green travel cloak, the tip of a scabbard jutted out, similar to the dagger James now wore. Looking behind him, James could see the flat profile of an axe head strapped to Solomon's back, no doubt easily reached if called for.

'So where are we heading?' asked James.

Bartholomew pointed down the trail. 'We'll descend this valley, cross the Crashing River by means of a short cut. Then it's on up to the Col.' He pointed upwards. Ranks of pines and firs flanked

*The Balance Between*

the valley walls, into which they had descended. On the far side, the pine trees which soared up a hundred feet or more looked like mere matchsticks set against the vast size of the mountains which hemmed them in.

At length they reached the valley floor, where the river blocked their route. Stone and broken rock lay piled along the river banks. The river rumbled a deep, angry growl and the ground shook. Great boulders rolled along the riverbed. Smaller stones simply flowed like water in the current. A fine spray filled the air and fed the green moss that clung to everything. Impassable, they turned northwards, following the river up-stream. After a while they reached a fallen tree, its lower trunk caught between two mighty stones, much of its length suspended over the river.

'We'll cross here,' called Bartholomew above the din of the torrent. They all shrugged off their packs. The dwarves delved into their rucksacks and began unpacking coils of rope. Tempus leapt nimbly onto the tree, ran along its length, and sprang into the air, sailing over the last stretch of open water to land on the far bank.

'It's easy for him,' Solomon said, nodding towards Tempus. 'Pity it isn't so simple for us,' he added dryly. 'There is a bridge down-stream but we're in a hurry.' He heaved his rucksack onto the trunk. 'Now then James, I'll show you what to do. Pay attention, your life may depend on it,' Solomon commanded. He took a length of rope and tied it securely to the straps of his rucksack. The other end he handed to James. 'I'll carry my pack over. If for any reason I have to let go of it, you'll be able to retrieve it. If you slip, the important thing is to save yourself. This river is so violent that nothing, neither fish nor fiend, can live in it. So be very careful.'

James looked at the stones hurtling along in the current and felt the instant grip of fear. Solomon heaved himself up onto the trunk and walked its length as if it were nothing more than a garden path. At the end he crouched and sprang forward like a giant frog.

Even with the rucksack in his arms, he landed well beyond the water's edge. James felt his knees go weak.

'Now you, James,' Solomon called. James felt Bartholomew give him an encouraging nudge from behind. He tied the rope to the straps of his knapsack just as Solomon had done, and pulled himself up onto the fallen tree. James took slow, deliberate steps. In his whole life he'd never undertaken such a perilous task. Shadowy boulders, as big as shire horses, rolling along the riverbed made his heart pound and the blood surging in his ears drowned out the crashing sound of the torrent below. James shuffled forward, clutching his knapsack to his chest as if it were a life jacket.

He was midway along the trunk when something punched him in the shoulder and he lost his balance. Just as he started to topple, something jerked him upright again. Despite Solomon's instructions, James instinctively clung on to the knapsack. And then he was falling.

He threw an arm out and caught hold of the stump of a branch. Somehow his grip held, leaving his legs dangling over the plume of raging waters below.

Aghast at this turn of events, the dwarves grabbed their weapons and rushed to help James. Solomon called to him above the din of the river: 'James, lad, you've been attacked by a giant spider and he's attached his thread to you!'

'You must cut it before the spider pulls you off that branch and into the river.' James heard the dwarf's bullhorn voice and nodded his understanding. He let go of the knapsack, which fell into the river below. James managed to pull himself up between the branch stump and the trunk, his legs still swinging free. Next he reached down and unsheathed his dagger, careful not to drop it. He slashed at the thick strand. Over on the far bank Solomon and Tempus ran off into the forest to hunt down the attacker.

'Be quick about it, James,' Bartholomew urged. 'There's no time to lose.'

James felt desperation take hold. A few strands broke but the spider thread still held. A sudden jolt reminded James of his peril. The silken thread pulled on his coat, tightening it around his shoulder like a tourniquet. The pressure became unbearable. His shoulder strained at the socket. Driven by fear he hacked and hacked, with Bartholomew yelling for him to hurry. Suddenly the spider strand gave way with the crack of a whip. He hung, exhausted and on the verge of tears, so great had been the fear. But he clung on to the dagger.

By the time Solomon and Tempus returned, Bartholomew had carried James the rest of the way and was examining his bruised body. 'No broken bones,' he informed James. 'Well done, lad, well done.' James rose unsteadily to his feet. His coat was badly torn. He looked at it dejectedly.

'Not much use as a travelling cloak anyway,' said Bartholomew as he handed a spare to the boy. 'This'll serve you better.'

James struggled into it. He picked up his dagger and sheathed it, now truly grateful for the gift.

They continued on their way, James unaware of the slower pace now set by Bartholomew.

'Who attacked us?' James asked.

'Not so much of a *who* as a *what*,' replied Bartholomew. 'The culprit was one of the dragonspiders that live under these mountains. It was a fair-sized one; you can tell by the thickness of the thread it cast.'

James looked startled. 'A dragonspider!' he exclaimed. 'What are they?'

'They're the work of evil intent, a mongrel breed of two species that were never meant to be joined, part spider and part dragonfly,' explained Solomon.

'But it would have to be enormous to spin a thread like that,' James replied.

'Aye, it was,' Solomon said. 'But fortunately the dragonspider that attacked you wasn't as big as it might have been. They come a great deal bigger.'

'And that's why we are here, to lead you safely through the forest.' Solomon emphasised this with a cautious glance about them and a wave of his axe. 'Hard to believe the forest was once a safe haven for travellers.'

'The forest has been silent a long time. Listen, James,' Bartholomew instructed. 'Can you hear birdsong? Can you hear anything of nature in this place?' Only the trees moving and the sound of their own feet disturbed the eerie void. 'The forest has been invaded. We catch the occasional dragonspider but they're devilishly hard to kill. The small ones can fly, but if they get too big their wings can't support their weight.' Bartholomew's tone was full of contempt.

'But now there's some real hope,' said Solomon, his voice filled with purpose.

'What makes you say that?' James asked. The dwarves stopped mid-stride and turned to him in surprise.

'Why, you, of course!' they answered in unison.

'We haven't been keeping a beady eye on you for nothing,' said Solomon.

'All on the express orders of the Guild,' said Bartholomew. 'Now let's press on.'

Hidden deep within a stand of trees, a pair of yellow eyes observed the passing of the small party. For a brief instant the trees moved and afternoon sunlight spilled through the branches, momentarily revealing the creature. Shrouded in black, with enormous claw-like hands and long, cruel-curving talons, the creature flinched in the warmth of the sun. Its head was hooded, revealing only a cruel beak, yellowed and riven with tiny fissures like those on a skull. The creature stood on clawed feet similar to its hands, the talons biting into the solid ground beneath. The drezghul stood motionless long after the trio had vanished.

All afternoon they toiled across the valley. The path had petered out and they were obliged to force a way through the dense scrub and thorn bushes.

Solomon led the small party using his axe to force a path, annoyed at having to dull the blade on such a chore. He complained repeatedly.

'Never mind my brother, young James,' Bartholomew said, in a low voice. 'He's annoyed the path we used not a month ago has disappeared so quickly. It is a sure sign of the evil seeping into the forest.'

James understood Solomon's unhappiness. Long thorns stabbed and tore at their cloaks, impeding their progress. Tempus followed behind, picking his way carefully through the dense carpet of broken branches.

'Why did the dragonspider attack?' James asked. 'Was it hunting for food?'

'No,' Solomon answered. 'There are too many of us for the creature to dare attack if it was simply hunting for food. It was summoned to the task by our enemies.' He fell silent as he swung the axe. 'We can assume the enemy knows of your arrival. If you are as important as the Guild believes you to be, then the enemy will try to kill or capture you,' said Bartholomew. 'The enemy can call upon all manner of evil and base creatures to do their bidding.'

'They've lost the element of surprise,' continued Solomon as he swung his axe. 'But they'll be more determined next time. And as we draw nearer to safety, so the enemy will become increasingly anxious to strike us down. We can only hope that they have few allies in these parts or we face being outnumbered and hunted down in this entanglement.' He motioned at the dense thorn scrub still ahead of them.

'But if it slows us, it slows the enemy. And as long as we're in this stuff, we're hidden from view,' suggested James.

'True, lad ... as long as there is nothing hunting us that can fly or burrow,' replied Bartholomew.

James gulped and fell silent.

Solomon called, 'The way is thinning. We must not tarry.'

Once they got clear of the thorny forest they made better time.

Suddenly Tempus gave a warning bark. To their left a net of ropes hung amidst the pines, bending the trees under the tension of the web.

'More dragonspiders?' James asked.

'A particular one,' replied Bartholomew. 'Morbidren. Her name means "deadly in the dark".' The name carried more than a ring of menace. Bartholomew went on, 'She's a giant dragonspider, bigger than a horse, they say. We've never set eyes on her, though I'll vouch Tempus has. Morbidren's the only thing we've ever known Tempus to be frightened of, and I can't say that I blame him. By Creation! She must be a frightening thing to behold.' He let his breath whistle through his lips. 'She's too big to fly. She builds her webs between the pines, strung across the trails. Then, when she catches a meal, she drags it into the branches to dine in peace. Sometimes we find piles of bleached bones at the bottom of a tree.'

'What does Morbidren eat?'

'Eat? Well we've found the remains of bear and deer, wolves and forest-phant – a small, hairy relative of the elephant. I suppose she'll have a go at anything she can haul up to her lair,' answered Solomon from up ahead. 'Morbidren grew too large to hunt in the caves and fissures underground where dragonspiders prefer to hide.'

'Well, we're lucky we avoided her trap,' said James.

'I'm afraid it's a bit more serious than that,' said Solomon. 'Morbidren never comes this far down the valley. She's setting her webs to herd us, towards an ambush probably. The fact that she's been

## The Balance Between

summoned is serious. There can be only one reason – and that reason is you.'

James was finding it hard to believe what he was hearing. 'Why me?' he asked, his voice full of despair. 'I've never hurt anyone.'

Bartholomew came up beside him and placed a steadying hand on the young boy's shoulder. 'Know this, young lad. While we accompany you, there is plenty to hope for, not least our salvation. While it's not our place to boast, the Guild, in all its wisdom, has placed you in our care. Bartholomew and Solomon Bandamire are not about to fail their judgement. So chin up, a keen eye and we may yet avoid the enemy.'

They were now traversing fields of scree that lay tumbled from the rocky valley walls. The party stumbled and picked their way over the broken ground and slowly snaked up the mountainside. Above them the Col towered, a good thousand feet up. The going was hard, but finally they arrived at the summit, just as the shadows of the mountains stretched across the pass. A breeze sprang up behind them.

Solomon gave a nod of agreement to his brother and turned to James, 'Well, Master James. Our earlier adventure has delayed us significantly. As we descend into the land beyond we'll be overtaken by night. In the distance you can make out the Western Tower,' he pointed. 'But between here and the Tower is a desperate enemy. Things lie in ambush ahead that are as frightening as the creature behind. So we face a dilemma. Ahead is an unachievable goal, behind an impossible retreat, and in the dark they have the advantage.' Solomon let the portent of these words sink in.

James looked at the dwarves. They were talking as though failure was inevitable.

'Excuse me, sirs,' he said. 'Are you saying we haven't got a hope?'

The dwarves broke into guffaws that gave way to belly laughs and knee slapping. Bartholomew clasped James by his good shoulder. 'Not a chance of it, lad. It's a pleasure to have your wit and your company, though you're a stranger to the ways of dwarves such as we.' Wiping a tear from his eye he continued, 'My brother Solomon Brunel Bandamire and I, Bartholomew Shakespeare Bandamire, are sons of the dwarfish clan of Bandamire, fabled for noble deeds and heroic failures. Our grandfather, Borrowmason Goldenbeard Bandamire, fell in the titanic, but ultimately hopeless, struggle that became legend as the Battle of Highfall Heights. Our father, Splayfoot Teutonica Bandamire, languishes in the dungeons of the enemy, captured at the cataclysmic fall of Palalia.'

Bartholomew's chest visibly swelled with pride as he continued. 'We sir, are ennobled and uplifted to the challenge of a forlorn hope, a hopeless situation, a doomed venture, a catastrophe waiting to happen. In such circumstances we fighting dwarves draw upon our great heritage to ensure that, should no future await our bloodline, our blood shall be spilled in glorious great pools.' His voice boomed across the valley, reverberating back in a ghostly echo.

Solomon took up the battle cry. 'In glorious great pools. With wounds that carve our bodies, and gore to fill a barrel.' James was somewhat shocked as they began chanting battle cries of old.

> *Make a stand, heed the horn,*
> *Swing the axe, cleave the bone,*
> *Unsheathe the sword, knock the bow,*
> *Now we pray to fight a foe.*

Followed by,

> *Killing is a pleasure,*
> *When fighting over treasure,*

And,

> *Fighting dwarves, rally round,*
> *Let not the enemy steal this ground.*

And,

> *Dwwwwaaarrrvvvessss,*
> *Dwwwwaaarrrvvvessss,*
> *Makers-of-warrrrrrrrrrrrrrrrs.*

And finally,

> *Take our lives, take our arms,*
> *But leave us with our family charms!*

James was aghast to discover the dwarves were apparently looking forward to a bloody battle with the enemy. As white as a wisp of fog, he sank to his knees, trembling. Finally the dwarves stopped their tomfoolery and noticed poor James's evident fear. They quit their chanting and fell into an embarrassed silence. Bartholomew gave a polite cough and mumbled, 'Of course our mission is to save you, Master James, sir. That really is the most important part of our mission. Before we find ourselves in a pickle the sort of which –' he coughed again '– we were singing about a few moments ago, we would ensure your personal safety. We've no intention of providing you a terminal glory at such an early stage in your career.'

James looked from one dwarf to the other, both wringing their hands in despair at having upset their young charge.

'Sirs,' he began, collecting himself, 'I may not know the ways of dwarves. Nor do I understand your desire for battle and a tragic end, but I do appreciate your helping me.' This cheered the dwarves up, and soon all three had forgotten the earlier bout of nerves.

'If you don't mind a suggestion,' James ventured, 'I would quite like to keep going. Whatever lies in front can't be any more frightening than what's behind, and I'm sure Tempus would agree.' The dog came over and nuzzled James's hand. 'In any event, little good will come of turning back.'

'Sound words, sound words,' replied Solomon, who nodded sagely at Bartholomew.

'We'll light the torches and be off then,' declared Bartholomew.

In the gathering darkness they made their way down, guided by the flickering torchlight. Each held aloft a stout wicker torch bound with rags and soaked in tar. The flames guttered off into a star-encrusted night sky. James recognised Taurus and the Centaur, but he had little time to stargaze. Beneath their feet the ground slid away in fields of shale and flint. Tempus padded noiselessly out in front, his keen eyes and nose alert to the enemy. Only the scrabble of their boots on the rock and the whistle of the wind filled the night air.

High above, other eyes followed their progress into the night.

## ∽ 3 ∾

# A Wicked and Cruel Night Out

Despite the thick cloak that James wore, the night air cut into him like a scythe through standing corn, a blade of freezing cold. Shepherded by Tempus, the companions descended the Col quickly, their legs weary with fatigue. First James, then Solomon stumbled.

'Careful now,' Bartholomew warned. 'If someone falls it's likely to be painful and delay us further.'

'We're near the tree line,' said Solomon. 'It'll be even more dangerous once we're in the trees.' It was only moments later that the first stunted trees materialised out of the darkness.

'The enemy will know of our whereabouts. They will use the cover of darkness to attack. Now we are at our greatest peril.' Solomon unstrapped the axe from his back. He led them in a zigzag through the smattering of trees and laurel bushes that clung to the slope, avoiding potential ambush sites. At one stage they retreated back up the slope to bypass a dense stand of trees that blocked their path. The dwarves used their skill and instinct to evade potential hazards, but eventually, they ran into the enemy.

Tempus gave the first warning with a single bark and bounded over to stand beside Solomon. James was so tired, he barely stopped himself stumbling into the back of Solomon. The dwarf whispered something to the hound, but James couldn't hear what was said. Solomon turned and laid a hand on James's shoulder. 'Up ahead,' he whispered in James's ear, 'Tempus scented something but he's not sure what. Draw your dagger and be ready.' As James stared intently into the darkness he could hear something moving over the rough ground, coming towards them. Tempus's hackles rose.

James crouched with his dagger in hand. Silhouetted against the night sky he could see what looked to be a pale upright column moving towards them with something trailing in its wake. As it entered the pool of torchlight James recognised it. A reptile? No, a colossal snake!

'It's the great slitherer Alabaster,' hissed Bartholomew.

A mixture of excitement and dread charged through James. He'd never seen anything so enormous or frightening, much less fought it. Only the presence of the dwarves and hound stopped him from running away.

'Stay behind me at a safe distance James, so I may swing my axe without striking you,' Solomon commanded.

Bartholomew stood next to James, sword drawn.

Then the slitherer was upon them, like an express train hurtling out of the dark. The white head feigned towards Bartholomew, but changed direction and struck with lightening speed at Solomon. Its fangs were like spear tips, slashing down at the dwarf's shoulder and driving into bone. James heard the sickening crunch of flesh and bone mashed in the creature's jaws. Bartholomew reacted instantly, raising his sword high and rushing forward to bring the long blade slicing down onto the reptile's head. Keenly sharp steel split the scaly skin and sank deep into flesh. The slitherer convulsed, loosened its grip on Solomon and flailed its long tail from out of the darkness, sweeping Bartholomew off his feet. Tempus barked again and again. James stared in frozen disbelief at Solomon as he lay slumped on the ground. The great axe slipped from his grasp. Bartholomew struggled to get up, but a massive coil roiled out of the dark and pinned him to the ground. His sword flailed at the serpent's body. Galvanised by fear, James rushed to the serpent's flank and hacked at it with all his might.

Bartholomew cried to the boy, 'The head. THE HEAD! Strike at the head!'

Another coil came running up its body and hit James, sending him sprawling to the ground and his torch flying. To his left he heard the high-pitched hiss of the enemy. James rolled to one side and crouched. The torch lay in the distance, its flickering light catching the slitherer as it advanced towards him. A quick look at the brothers and James realised that it was up to him to save them all.

Without a second's hesitation, he leapt to attack. In a single bound he covered a huge distance, landing in front of the slitherer. Driven by the adrenaline of battle, he lunged at its face with a powerful stab, his blade sinking to the hilt. The slitherer sprang its jaws closed and James just avoided being caught by its fangs. The serpent roiled in angry pain, and Bartholomew seized the chance to roll out from under the coiled body. In a flash he was on his feet, attacking with single-minded rage.

James stabbed again. His blade punctured the slitherer's eye and embedding the dagger tip in the creature's skull. It convulsed in writhing agony, ripping the dagger from James's grasp and catapulting him backwards. He landed badly, the breath knocked out of him. Clutching his already bruised left side, he watched the enraged slitherer rear up, hunting for its attacker. Bartholomew hacked remorselessly at the long body, but the serpent swung its tail and batted him away, as a horse's tail flicks an irritant fly. Turning from side to side, the slitherer cast about in the dark, searching for James. Although blinded in one eye, its remaining good eye was the size of a dinner plate. Any second now it would find James as surely as if it were broad daylight.

At that moment something distracted the serpent. James instinctively rolled away into the dark, ignoring the pain of his injuries that raked through him. He rolled right over Solomon's fallen axe. Without thinking he grabbed it and continued to roll, praying that he wouldn't cut off his own head in the process.

Bartholomew called his name but he dared not answer. Instead he rose to his feet, leaning on the axe for support. Tempus barked, distracting the enemy, as a bearhound was trained to do. James took a moment to study the body of the slitherer stretched across the ground, as thick as a pine tree and covered in scaly armour. The serpent's body narrowed into something like a neck just behind its head. This was where he would strike. Lifting the axe to his shoulder, he staggered forward under its weight. Tempus spotted him preparing to attack and renewed his own efforts to distract the enemy, darting beneath the serpent's head and sinking his teeth into its jowls, holding it for a matter of seconds. But seconds were all that was needed. James swung the axe high overhead. Then the axe was arcing forward and downwards, carried by its own momentum.

The blade bit cleanly, slicing through the softer neck scales. The weight of the blow carried it deeper, severing the spinal cord. Mortally wounded, the serpent's head jerked wildly in shocked spasms. Tempus was hurled, yelping, into the night. Still holding the axe shaft, James was shaken violently by the thrashing agony of the monster, but the blade's work was done.

Yet the creature was not quite dead. James saw the serpent's head swinging round towards him. It hit him like a steam-hammer and he collapsed to the ground, stunned. Even in the final moments of its own death, the creature's head reared one last time to strike.

Bartholomew stepped over the fallen boy and rammed his sword into the slitherer's remaining good eye. The point of the blade exploded out of the back of its skull. The slitherer fell back, dead.

'There's no time to lose,' warned the dwarf. 'Grab your sword and a torch and stand guard over Solomon.'

James rose shakily to his feet and did as he was told, his hand scrambling over the rocky ground to retrieve his dagger. Bartholomew swept up a discarded torch and raced into the night. When he returned he was carrying the pitifully broken body of Tempus. As he lay the hound down next to his unconscious brother, Tempus licked Bartholomew's hand in gratitude.

'We make a stand here,' Bartholomew decided. 'There is nowhere else for it. We can't move these two and defend ourselves at the same time.' He looked at the lad and smiled. 'We've done well. The enemy is dead and you've fought like a true warrior.' Then he sighed and sank down next to James. 'Not quite the way I envisaged it,' he said absently. 'What a pity we're not in full battle armour, helm, shield and all. Then it would be a real fight. But we bested the creature nonetheless.' His eyes scanned the perimeter of torchlight. 'Sit back to back with me James, that we may guard every direction,' he said, and they prepared for the long night ahead.

The night crawled slowly and vigilance waned with the moon as tiredness overtook both of them. They talked to keep each other awake as Solomon and Tempus lay in fitful sleep.

'The great slitherer Alabaster is dead,' Bartholomew generously announced. 'Vanquished by the hand of a young warrior.' James knew he'd played a part in the desperate fight but he was nonetheless embarrassed by the dwarf's kind words. Bartholomew smiled at him over his shoulder, cheering the lad. 'I mean that, lad, but there's still Morbidren to contend with. If we're lucky she may decide not to attack after seeing us kill the slitherer, but I doubt it. She cannot refuse her masters any more than we could abandon you, James. No, Morbidren will make her move, before sunrise.'

## 1895

'I've seen a case like this before,' Harrington informed Corrick and, for the first time, the man's calm exterior showed a hint of concern. A less observant person would have missed this, but Corrick spotted the subtle change in manner.

'I see,' the policeman said.

Harrington considered him for a while and then went on. 'The victims have all been left in this hideous fashion,' he indicated the mutilated corpse.

'Yes,' replied Corrick. 'But then you already knew what to expect before you got here. You wanted confirmation.' It made perfect sense, of course. This chap Harrington would never travel up to Purbeck on the off-chance that the murder might be similar. If he did then he'd be running all over the country to inspect every murder scene. Corrick went on, 'So what can you tell me about the others? How many have there been?'

'This is the fourth,' Harrington replied.

'Four? Are there any other similarities between the four cases?' he asked. Harrington thought about this for a moment before answering.

'The victims were all female and approximately the same age. They were all murdered in remote locations and they died in a similarly distressing condition. Other than that, I cannot tell you.'

Corrick nodded his head in acceptance, wondering whether the last sentence was an admission or a refusal.

Outside, the Chief Inspector looked up at the sky. The long day was almost spent. Light shone at every window of the mansion. He'd ordered the house be secured and the forensic evidence sent to Cambridge for examination. The body needed identifying, and there was that other thing. What was it? He couldn't quite remember; it kept slipping away from him. An important detail? Perhaps. It would come back to him later.

He turned to Sergeant Smith. 'Get the shutters closed. We can do without the publicity.'

'Very good, sir.'

## 1910

James's torch spluttered and guttered before finally going out. They only had one remaining torch and sunrise was still at least an hour away.

'She'll have to attack soon,' said Bartholomew. 'Dragonspiders hate daylight even more than they hate fire.' They peered into the dark but the torchlight revealed nothing except stony ground. James noticed Venus cresting the horizon to the east, dawn's faint herald.

'Over here,' called a voice from down the hill. James looked round in surprise, the voice sounding familiar. He turned to Bartholomew, who was grinning.

'A useful trick, being able to throw one's voice,' whispered a voice up the hill. 'But a lot of good it'll do us now. Still, the enemy might think there are more of us.'

Bartholomew spotted the planet as well. The remaining torch burnt low and died. Darkness closed in. Slowly their eyes grew accustomed to the night until the whole valley was infused with the powdery light from Venus and the stars.

'*A maiden of the night to ease our plight,*' Bartholomew recalled a line of dwarfish poetry.

With this celestial canopy of stars, it would be difficult for an attacker to gain the element of surprise.

Although very tired, James caught a flash of movement and whispered, 'I see something. Over there, to your left by that spinney.' Now they both spotted the enemy as it loomed out of the night. Even across a distance of thirty yards or more the dragonspider Morbidren looked immense, easily as big as a grand piano.

Morbidren sat low on her eight legs as if sagging under the weight of her immensely bloated body. She edged closer, until she was only ten yards away. Bartholomew and James crouched side by side, shielding their companions, and faced the giant arachnid. A filament of web shot out and arced over the huddled group. Bartholomew used the axe to ward off the falling line. The axe stuck fast. He let go and the weapon was dragged off into the dark.

'Go for her legs or eyes. Forget the abdomen. It'll be too tough to inflict much damage. But, above all, avoid her jaws. One bite and you're done for.' And with those words, Bartholomew raised his sword to meet the onrush of their foe.

The dragonspider covered the distance faster than a galloping horse. She sprang at them, attempting to isolate and crowd James beneath her body as if catching a fly. James slashed at a leg but to no effect. Something wet ran down his neck and he looked up to see the gaping jaws scissoring open and closed. Above the jagged, claw-like mouthparts, eight gleaming black-button eyes stared soullessly down at him. Time slowed. James could see every tiny hair that sprouted over the horrible face. The mouth pulled back and a slime-coated, needle-thin proboscis slid down between her jaws, ready to stab down at him and inject her poison.

Bartholomew bellowed as his sword crashed into the creature's legs and was rewarded as two of them sliced clean at the joint. Morbidren lost her balance and retreated a few paces, her useless stumps leaking trails of blood. James, driven by an overwhelming fear, struggled to save himself. His cloak ripped free from her pincers and he squirmed away. Angry at the loss of her prey, Morbidren danced on her remaining legs, feinting to left and right as she sought an opportunity to strike. Her ineffective wings buzzed furiously on her back as her spinner shot out a thick streak of webbing across the ground like a fire hose sprays water. But this spray was deadly in its entrapment and the ground glistened with filaments. Dwarf and boy edged backwards as the trail of material threatened to snare them.

'Wait a moment for it to dry,' Bartholomew ordered. 'Then use your sword to cut it to pieces. I'll keep her off us.' He advanced a pace, placing his foot firmly in the mesh and stabbed his sword at

## The Balance Between

the enemy's face. Now there could be no retreat. One side would prevail; the other would perish. James slashed at the webbing but it was a hopeless struggle. Web glued Bartholomew, and then James, to where they stood. Morbidren grew bolder, and shot a jet straight at Bartholomew, the filament hitting him in the chest and arms and seizing him in a mess of stickiness. Another jet caught him in the face and his roaring battle chant was smothered. James looked up and the dead, empty gaze of Morbidren was upon him. In that moment he fell under the hunter's spell, his sword slipping from his hand. James stood mesmerised, helpless, like a fly that knows there is no escape. All was lost.

But a strange thing happened. Morbidren froze. Then, with what sounded like two charging bulls colliding, the monstrous dragonspider collapsed in slow motion, her long, angled legs splaying in all directions. Something equally large and dreadful reared up over her back. An enormous mound of shaggy black hair growled from on top of the hapless Morbidren. Teeth and claws flashed, black blood spilled into a wide pool and the dragonspider was dead.

James looked on in amazement. On top of the dragonspider carcass sat a big black bear. Bartholomew's mouth hung open. The bear looked at him and James, and then said: 'That's an old score settled.'

The band of travellers huddled together on the bleak hillside for warmth and protection. James watched the sky lighten and darkness fade to the west. Tempus lay stretched out asleep next to him. Solomon had woken a short while earlier with a groan of pain and his brother tended to his wounds before lighting a fire to brew coffee. James looked at Solomon's exposed shoulder but quickly turned away, sickened by the sight of white bones sticking out from the bloody, mangled flesh. He sat up, and gazed over at the lifeless form of the spider, listing on the ground like a boat left by

*The Balance Between*

the receding tide, its black blood congealed like a tidal pool around it.

Further off he could see the motionless carcass of the slitherer. The bear was nowhere to be seen. James laid his head back. Daylight would bring safety. He shut his eyes.

But danger is most acute to the unwary. Having got the fire going Bartholomew dragged himself to his feet. His gaze took in the sweep of hillside all around; it was empty but it didn't feel safe. Something was out there.

'Get up, James,' he commanded. 'It isn't finished, not yet.' Exhausted though he was, James slowly got up. Dawn beckoned. James groaned.

'Surely the enemy ...' but the words froze on his lips. In that fraction of time the hillside was plunged once more into inky blackness, the sun's first light blotted out completely. James let out a cry of fear as the fire was snuffed out. Then with a thump of heavy leather wings, the enemy was among them.

The Drezghul crashed down from a great height, its coal-black outline invisible against the darkness it cloaked itself in. Tempus howled in fear and cowered. Terror clutched at their hearts and their souls quaked. Clawed feet knocked Bartholomew over and raked the ground, then missed him, instead tearing at the rocky hillside as if it were a feather cushion, for the Drezghul's attention had shifted to the boy. Facing the hideous, spectral creature as it reared on its hind legs, membranous wings held pinioned back behind its body, James was utterly doomed. The yellow slits of the Drezghul's eyes locked on to his. He was transfixed by its spell. A clawed limb stretched out towards him, but he didn't see the skeletal, mummified body; he was held by the lidless eyes, set behind a savage and ragged beak. Its black mouth gaped and the reek of vile filth, of pestilence and disease, of death, escaped it.

It gazed into his soul to work its deadly magic.

But instead, something unexpected happened. Doubt flickered

in the yellow slits. The drezghul stumbled backwards, away from the small lad, and its forearms clawed the air between them. A small shard of intense light suddenly appeared before its fearful eyes and exploded into a ball of incandescence, blasting the creature back. A shrill screech rent the sky and tore the false night away.

Metal streaked across James's vision. A broad axe blade sliced into the Drezghul's upper arm, severing it in a cloud of smoke. The Drezghul screamed, its wings thrashing the air wildly as it took to the sky. Bartholomew crouched next to James, axe in hand. They searched the retreating darkness above them, but the bitter cry of the drezghul was already far away.

In the Western Tower a cloaked figure sank slowly into a chair, exhaustion sweeping over him, drained from his efforts moments before. He'd felt the overwhelming threat of evil that had hung over the small embattled party and had only just managed to intervene in time. The enemy's strength had surprised him. It proved the boy was the key!

'Luck again, by Odin! Twice in a night!' exclaimed Bartholomew. James lay on his back completely spent from his encounter with the drezghul. The dwarf had restarted the fire and was brewing coffee, glancing at James from time to time. 'I would never have believed it. Not for all the gold in the City of Oloris would I willingly stand up to one of those demons. That was the bravest thing I've ever witnessed, fighting off a drezghul. Truly, you're the stuff of legend. And sorcery!'

'Thank you but it wasn't bravery, or magic on my part,' James said, despite his state of exhaustion. 'It scared me senseless. I couldn't move.'

'Be that as it may, what I saw was this: the Drezghul's spell was upon you and its powers failed it,' declared Bartholomew.

'Something in you, James, countered the enemy's black sorcery. I swung the axe at it, but it was already defeated.' But James was fast asleep.

Solomon spoke quietly to his brother as they prepared coffee over the camp fire. A spoon clanked quietly around in a tin mug. The aroma of coffee overcame the repugnant smell of death that lingered on the hillside. James, waking briefly, reached over and wrapped an arm around the neck of the big dog, hugging Tempus and burying his face in his friend's fur as he fell back into a dreamless sleep.

## ~ 4 ~

# Clues, Now and Then

### 1895

In Cambridge, Corrick sat at his desk lost in thought. He was trying to picture the scene he'd witnessed at Purbeck Hall. He recalled images of the dead woman. This was a violent murder with no obvious motive. He felt the pull of long-buried emotions and memories from deep inside, and he pushed them away. That part of his private life was in the past.

It was a week since he'd made the trip to Purbeck on the Norfolk coast. He'd dealt with the witnesses and assessed the crime scene. His superiors expected him to solve the case quickly but he had no answers to the many questions. The scene had provided no clues. A crime such as this would require detailed science to solve it, and the police didn't possess the knowledge or the necessary skills.

It appeared to Corrick that Scotland Yard was being difficult about the case. Although they'd sent a Foreign Office official to assist, he'd also discovered the forensic evidence had been sent to London behind his back. His investigation was losing momentum. He was expected to finish writing the report and close the case promptly. Something at the back of his mind was telling him not to bother . . .

Corrick sat bolt upright.

What had he been thinking? This was his job, his profession! He got a grip on his thoughts, shaking off his mental lethargy.

Searching through the Purbeck file on his desk, he found there was no autopsy report on the victim. Methodically he re-read the witness statements and the coroner's report. They were both inconclusive. They recorded a dead body being found on the first floor and the general circumstances leading up to the death of a vagrant, but . . .

'Nothing says that she was a murder victim,' Corrick said aloud. This fact had been overlooked. That in itself was an uncharacteristic oversight for such an unusual case. Or had it been deliberately left out . . . ?

Just then a short, sharp pain stabbed behind his eyes and he winced at the hurt, rubbing his temples with his fingertips. The pain eased.

Where was I? he thought to himself. Yes, the Purbeck case.

He recalled he'd written some notes down when he'd first arrived and he fished out his notebook. There, scrawled in pencil, were the words:

BODY – 1st floor
2nd BODY? – Hall, ground floor, victim/culprit?
FO – Harrington to call.

He looked at the words he'd written, but he had no recollection of a second body. Come to think of it, he wasn't sure if the body that he did remember had been formally identified. And if a second body was found in the hall, it wasn't mentioned in the witness statement or police reports. For a moment Corrick doubted his own notes. Had there been a second body? He wasn't sure now.

The pain in his head returned and he screwed his face up in

agony. He'd have to see a doctor if it continued. The moment passed and when he'd recovered sufficiently he realised he'd forgotten what he'd been thinking. He glanced down at his notebook. A thought struck him, one born of instinct, connecting two apparently unrelated events. The last entry he'd written down concerned Harrington. The pain came back again but Corrick gritted his teeth and ignored it.

If his notes were correct and there was a second body, somehow it had been overlooked by everyone. It didn't make sense to the policeman. It was as if someone wanted the second body to be forgotten. He wondered if that had been the reason for Harrington's visit. And if Harrington was in any way connected to the disappearance of evidence and the omissions in the case report, then he already knew something about the case. Now the pain in Corrick's head grew intense, but he concentrated on holding his thoughts in focus, talking aloud as he went. 'Whatever is going on goes further and deeper than Scotland Yard, or Harrington.' Abruptly the pain left him and he slowly slumped back in the chair exhausted.

The telephone rang. He reached over and lifted the handset. The exchange operator put through a call.

'Hello. Hello. Can you hear me? Is that Chief Inspector Corrick of Cambridge?' called a voice.

'Yes. This is Chief Inspector Corrick speaking,' he replied, raising his voice over the crackle of interference on the line.

'Hello, Chief Inspector. This is Harrington. Foreign Office, illegal aliens department. You remember?'

Something triggered in Corrick's mind. It was odd that Harrington called only moments after he'd made a connection between the Foreign Office official and the events at Purbeck. Anyone would think Harrington was reading Corrick's mind. The policeman dismissed the notion as quickly as it arrived.

'Yes, Harrington. Strange that I should hear from you,' Corrick answered. 'And yet not unexpected.' Intuition now convinced Corrick that the man was directly connected with the incident itself.

'Quite.' Harrington's reply was short and clipped as he wanted to dispense with small talk. 'Listen, Chief Inspector, I don't suppose you've had much luck with your investigations.' Harrington seemed to know Corrick was struggling, with both his memory and the case. In all probability Harrington knew quite a bit that he didn't. The policeman remained silent in the hope that Harrington would spill the beans. 'I have a proposition for you.' Harrington cleared this throat. 'It appears that the Belgians have a similar case to your Purbeck affair. Word has reached me via our embassy in Bruges. Suffice to say the Belgians are not really up to the task. Now, I need to get over there but I don't have any official capacity that would allow me to review their evidence.'

'So you would like me to get us both invited,' Corrick finished the supposition.

'Well put, Chief Inspector. I am sure we will benefit from a trip to the Continent. Can I take it that you will meet me tomorrow morning, ten sharp at St Katherine's Dock?'

'By Tower Bridge? Yes, I'll be there.'

'Good day to you, Chief Inspector.'

'Good day.'

Corrick arrived at Euston on the early-morning express, waved down a hansom cab and was driven across the city. St Katherine's Dock was a hive of industry; lighters and small river boats crowding the wharves, cranes and gantries swinging overhead in a feverish race to unload and stow the cargoes from a dozen merchantmen moored in the main channel. Hundreds of porters and stevedores scurried like ants over the dock and boats. Boatmen's calls, the chugging of steam winches and the cry of gulls added to the cacophony of the scene.

## The Balance Between

Corrick strode down a rocking gangway. The waters beneath were oily and turgid, floating scum and rubbish slopping against stone walls. A dead rat bobbed upside down. Ignoring the filth he continued along the wharf past a line of small sailing craft. A docker dodged out of his way, his back bent beneath a heavy sack of grain. The riverside of London, the mightiest port in the world, was a microcosm of the largest empire ever known. Men slaved to keep its industrial engine turning. The jet-black men from the Niger Delta rubbed shoulders with the lighter-coloured men from the Empire's East Africa territories, who in turn toiled alongside Egyptians, Arabs, Chinese, Hindus, Muslims, and men from every city and town throughout the length and breadth of the kingdom. The stench of humanity was almost overpowering, yet the air also carried the smell of exotic spices, lumber, burning coal and wet rope.

Harrington stood talking to another man, and as Corrick approached he waved a hand in acknowledgement. The other man stepped briskly away, as if avoiding the policeman.

'Good morning, Chief Inspector. You will have had an early start from Cambridge, I'm afraid, but it will be worth it.'

'Let's wait and see, shall we?' Corrick replied. A small cutter was arrowing towards them, and beyond lay a naval gunboat. Corrick noted the name at the bow, HMS *Obedience*, with mild surprise.

'Our little venture has the blessing of some important people.' Harrington answered the look on Corrick's face. 'I've decided to let you in on rather more information than my superiors have authorised, but I have a feeling that you and I will be forced to work together sooner or later.'

The launch burbled in the tidal waters as it manoeuvred to come alongside. They clambered down a short iron ladder and sat in the waist of the launch as it retreated back across the River Thames to the gunboat.

Once ensconced in the captain's cabin, Harrington found a decanter of sherry and poured two glasses, handing one to Corrick.

'I know it's early, but it's going to be a long day.' He took a sip and went on, settling in the captain's chair. 'The Belgians mustn't know my official status since it may complicate diplomatic relationships so I would be grateful if you would refer to me as your assistant.'

'Then I ask the questions.'

'Quite,' accepted Harrington.

'All right then,' Corrick agreed to go along with the ruse.

Harrington smiled at this and continued.

'Now, my people have already sent word to the Belgians that you've a similar case in hand, and explained it as voodoo mumbo-jumbo, witchcraft from the farthest, darkest corner of the Empire.'

Above them a donkey winch began its mechanical braying as it hauled up the anchor. 'They've agreed to let me and you,' Corrick emphasised the *me*, 'examine the crime scene. Apparently nothing has been touched. It was discovered yesterday afternoon. A bridge arch near to the docks. Woman's body, horrible mutilations.'

'They'll try to pump us for information,' said Harrington. 'Which we, of course, won't have. No leads as yet.' His eyes glinted with cunning.

Corrick perched on the corner of the desk and leaned forward. 'And what information, precisely, don't we have?'

## 1910

'James! James!' The words were lost in the rising wind. Up and down the coast, dozens of police and locals were conducting a search for James.

When Sir Philip and Lady Kinghorn returned from their trip to observe the naval gunnery exercise off Banburgh, they were not initially concerned by his absence. He was a resourceful, adventurous lad with enough common sense to avoid any real danger. It was only when he failed to return by nightfall that his father alerted the constabulary. Ten o'clock that night a policeman interviewed Sir Philip and Lady Jennifer, as well as taking statements from duty hotel staff. The police arranged a search at first light. James's parents had slept little that night.

Before dawn Sir Philip was on the telephone to his office, instructing his private secretary to call in a few favours. Soon a detachment from the local army garrison at Alnwick in Northumberland was en route to join the search. In addition, a warship at Tynemouth would cruise along the coast for the next forty-eight hours.

James's mother was desperate to join the search, but Sir Philip requested that she remain at the hotel in case James might make his own way back. Thus, unencumbered by his near-distraught wife, Sir Philip motored down the coast to join the search among the sand dunes.

❧

James picked up one end of the makeshift stretcher on which Tempus lay wounded. Bartholomew carried the other end, together with their weapons. The brothers refused to abandon Tempus or put him out of his misery. He would be carried. Solomon was on his feet, a sling cradling his right arm and a mound of bandages swathing his shoulder. Groggy with pain, he stumbled along behind the stretcher. His backpack was hidden among the rocks, to be retrieved later.

They made slow progress, stopping frequently, but eventually they passed through the valley and out of the pine forests into more open wooded country. Here oak and ash softened the landscape. The air was warmer and the meadows buzzed with bees while birdsong filled the air.

Ahead, in the distance, James could see the tower Solomon and

Bartholomew had talked of. They eventually arrived after nightfall.

⁓⊶⊷⊶⁓

Sir Philip stood on the sand dune looking out over the line of soldiers and civilians that necklaced across the countryside. They were conducting a sweep south behind Embleton Bay, towards the castle on the headland. The young officer standing next to him raised his binoculars and scanned the grassy hillocks, watching as a policeman tripped and fell in the long grass. Away to the west, the bank of dark clouds over the moors heralded a turn in the weather. Standing solemn and majestic, no more than twenty paces from the two men, the Sea Arch loomed above them. The subaltern was oblivious to its presence, cloaked in its own magical invisibility. But Sir Philip could see it plainly.

'See here, Jeffries,' Sir Philip addressed the young officer. 'Don't you think it would be prudent to get the transport moved down the coast to rendezvous with the searchers at the castle? The wagons are not much use stuck back there.' He indicated a distant farmstead behind them.

'Oh!' exclaimed the inexperienced junior officer, embarrassed by his lack of foresight. 'Of course, Sir Philip.' He went off at once to give orders to the drivers.

Now that he was alone, Sir Philip clambered down the dune, his black leather shoes filling with sand. He came to a standstill before the padlocked gates.

It wasn't the first time Sir Philip had seen the arch, but the last occasion had been many years ago. He'd often wondered if he'd ever see it again. The Sea Arch was a law unto itself as to whom it chose to reveal itself to. There was no randomness to the selection. Sir Philip and his father, Sir Neville, had seen it together, and yet Sir Philip's brother, Joshua, who'd been with them, had been blind to it. It was, in every way, an enigma.

## The Balance Between

Sir Philip walked around the arch until he came to the brass plaque on the seaward side. He gasped as he read the inscription.

> A son you gave this world has gone
> And journeyed from this crossing place
> Seek not what's lost when lost it's not
> But mind the comings of this way
> For his return will be anon
> A gun to start a desperate race
> His motive with ancestry forgot
> To silence the killing of a day
>
> Steady now your hand must act
> And recall silence in your past
> Your father's eyes you too may see
> That which empire may not spy
> Seek out the other in this pact
> Who sifts for one in numbers vast
> And chase the wates in ministry
> Or heralds forth a time to die

Sir Philip stood transfixed. Digging into his coat pocket he drew out a small black notebook and pencil stub and carefully wrote down the words of the inscription. This gave Sir Philip a great deal to ponder as he returned to his motorcar. The chauffeur was pulling up the canvas roof at the first smattering of rain.

## 1895

The gunboat bumped against the fenders on the quayside. While Harrington popped up to the bridge to have a few words with the captain, Corrick stood thinking of what he'd learned on the trip over to Zeebrugge. He was also worried about his loss of memory, something he became acutely aware of when relying on Harrington to describe the recent scene at Purbeck Hall.

According to Harrington, Purbeck was the fourth such similar incident. The first was originally thought to be the work of an escaped madman, but enquiries turned up no likely culprits. The next victim was thought to have been attacked by a large predatory fish but, on finding a third victim with similar wounds in a barn, this theory was also discounted.

All had died by extreme violence, as if a series of murders was taking place, possibly by the same person.

This last point was the most troubling to Corrick. In twenty-three years as a serving policeman, he'd never investigated anything so chilling. He'd learned to listen to his intuition and it was telling him there was more to link these cases than just the murders of four women. Whatever it was that bothered him, only time would tell.

Harrington also revealed that the Purbeck victim had been transferred to the Natural History Museum for investigation by experts. The choice of this museum to conduct scientific examination surprised Corrick, but there was little he could do about it now. However, Corrick made a note to visit the museum on his return. He began to sense he was deliberately being kept from the evidence. As he thought about the Purbeck victim something triggered in his memory, but he still couldn't put his finger on it.

Sorting the clues in his head, the Chief Inspector summarised what he knew so far. Four reports. The first report from Burnham. Second report, and the first that Harrington attended, was in London, at the outflow of the River Roding into the Thames, where the body had been in water for some time. The third report, from Southend. Fourth, Purbeck. So the only common factors so far linking all the murders were the age and gender of the victims and the horrible manner of their deaths: mutilation.

Where is the motive? Corrick asked himself. Something grabbed at the edges of Corrick's memory...

## 1910

Sir Philip sat next to his wife, cradling her delicate hands in his. She'd been in despair since the disappearance of their son and despite the brave show she put on for the police, had cried a great deal during the day. Only now was she regaining some of her composure. It was Sir Philip's incredible revelation about the Sea Arch that gave her new hope.

Sir Philip's notebook lay open on the coffee table in front of them. He told his wife all that he knew about the Sea Arch and the inscription.

When he was a boy, Philip Kinghorn often visited the Northumberland coast with his family, Sir Neville and Lady Julia, his mother, his brother Joshua and their three sisters. The family took to renting a comfortable property near Beadnell Bay for the duration of the summer. Often the boys would go hiking with their father. Their favourite destination was the Sea Arch.

The arch resembled a monument to some forgotten battle or triumphant victory. But the most perplexing thing about the Sea Arch was that, while Philip and his father, Sir Neville, could see it as plain as a nose on a face, Joshua was unable to. No amount of pointing or deriding could make Joshua see it. Sir Neville later explained to Philip that for many years he had often visited the Sea Arch in the company of others, but Philip was the only other person who'd been able to see it. Sir Neville was secretly relieved that Philip shared the vision, since he had begun to doubt his own sanity. But other than acknowledge its existence, Sir Neville would say no more on the matter. And then this morning, while searching for James, Sir Philip had returned to the Sea Arch and read the inscription.

Lady Jennifer sat back to ponder this story. She too had walked the beach many times but she had never seen any such arch. For a fleeting instant she considered the state of her husband's mind, but Sir Philip had one of the clearest heads in government. She accepted his story and began to study the text that he'd transcribed from the inscription.

'Well, it would appear to be both a message and a riddle,' concluded Lady Jennifer, 'and it is telling us that James is alive.' She pointed to one line that stood out. 'Look here.'

*Seek not what's lost when lost it's not*

'It may help get our son back.' She smiled at this and found her heart lifting. She turned to her husband. 'This should focus our attention and take my mind off worrying for a while,' she said, brightening noticeably. She scrutinised her husband's notes. 'I do love puzzles and I know you, darling,' she patted his knee affectionately, 'have no idea I've been completing the crossword in that stuffy old paper of yours every day for the past three years.' She smiled at her own revelation, and Sir Philip could see her inner strength returning.

'What a beautiful woman you are,' he said in adoration.

'Thank you, Philip. Now let's look at this verse and see if we can unravel its meaning.' She read the first two lines.

*A son you gave this world has gone*
*And journeyed from this crossing place*

'Well, that seems perfectly clear, if a bit strange. It would appear that the inscription is meant for you, if we interpret these words logically.' She looked up at Sir Philip.

'That would fit if the gates hadn't been locked, but they were.'

'Perhaps they were closed after James passed through,' Lady

# The Balance Between

Jennifer suggested. She saw the look of scepticism on her husband's face. 'Now Philip. You asked me to believe in an arch I cannot see so please humour me. If this archway is visible to some but not others then it must be magical.' At this, Sir Philip raised his eyebrows in disbelief but Lady Jennifer stopped him before he could go on. 'Philip. Either you accept this or you must seriously consider that you're losing your own senses.' Sir Philip reluctantly accepted her reasoning. 'Good. Let's press on and see where it takes us.' Sir Philip nodded assent.

> *Seek not what's lost when lost it's not*
> *But mind the comings of this way*

'In which case this line's telling me, *us*,' Sir Philip corrected, 'James isn't lost, but knows where he's going, presumably somewhere beyond the arch.'

'And that we must keep an eye on the arch in case there are further comings and goings,' chipped in Lady Jennifer. Now they were making progress she was even more convinced.

> *For his return will be anon*
> *A gun to start a desperate race*

'This line gives the clearest sign he'll be coming back,' Sir Philip decided.

'If "*he*" means our son. And what about this word "gun"!' Some of the anxiety that had left James's mother returned as she spoke.

'But a starter's gun . . .' Sir Philip's voice trailed off. 'It could be metaphorical, do you think? James might be some sort of catalyst for events?'

'Well, anyone disappearing through a magical archway must surely provoke some sort of event, even if only by reappearing,' she said with incredulity. They looked at each other, both secretly praying the event would be James's return.

*The Balance Between*

The next two lines were much more difficult to understand.

*His motive with ancestry forgot
To silence the killing of a day*

After a few moment's contemplation Lady Jennifer spoke. 'Let's leave those lines for now. I always find that's the best way to approach a tricky clue.'

Sir Philip couldn't help but chuckle at his wife. 'Perhaps one day you'll have a letter published in *The Times*.'

'But I have, dear,' Jennifer replied calmly. '*The Times* knows me as The Very Reverend Maurice Todpole.' Sir Philip was speechless.

James's parents worked late before finally going to bed. But by then they were both convinced that James wasn't in harms way and that cracking the clues would somehow help him.

The next morning they reviewed their plans over breakfast. Sir Philip was to return to London. Lady Jennifer would stay on renting a farmhouse near to the Sea Arch where she would keep an eye on the immediate vicinity, as instructed by the inscription. Sir Philip showed her the exact location after breakfast. He also arranged for the War Office to install a telephone line to the house so they'd be in direct contact with one another. Sir Philip thought it best if the Sea Arch and its inscription continued to remain a secret. Finally Lady Jennifer asked him to contact her brother and invite their niece Amanda to come north and keep her company while she kept her vigil over the coming days.

# 1895

A Belgian gendarme led the Englishmen along the muddy canal path. Above them the sky was slate grey and it was raining,

## The Balance Between

steadily. Puddles formed a mirroring mosaic over the ground. Corrick followed in the gendarme's footsteps as they tried to avoid the worst of the potholes, with Harrington splashing in their wake. They ducked and passed beneath a low railway bridge. Other gendarmes waited in the bridge's shadow. Portable arc lights focused attention on a crumpled figure on the ground.

A senior officer saluted the newcomers. 'Good afternoon, messieurs.' He held out his hand. 'I am Inspector La Forge with the Criminal Department in Ghent. I am to assist you with your enquiries.' He spoke with a Walloon accent, a people with close ancestral ties with East Anglia.

Corrick gave a smile, 'I hope we may work together to solve both investigations.'

La Forge nodded in agreement and stepped aside to let them examine the body.

It was not a pretty sight. The lower portion of the body had been torn to shreds and bones lay smashed, protruding white against the red pulp. There wasn't much blood. The sightless eyes stared down in startled horror. Inspector La Forge clicked his fingers at a gendarme.

The gendarme opened a pocket notebook and read aloud in good English. 'Victim unknown. Aged approximately twenty-three years old. Occupation . . . uncertain.' He looked up to his superior, who added, 'He means that she was probably a "lady of the night".'

The gendarme gave a shrug and continued. 'Of no fixed abode.'

'Merci, monsieur,' thanked Corrick. He squatted on his haunches to study the corpse more closely, despite the horrific smell. 'This attack is just like Purbeck,' he said to Harrington. 'There is a link, something we are missing. Perhaps the perpetrators are religious maniacs, anarchists, possibly a secret society. Who knows?'

'Yes, well, if there is nothing more, Inspector? No, then thank you once again.' Harrington extended his hand to the bemused

Belgian, and signalled Corrick to follow as he rushed away. Corrick ran a few steps to catch up.

'What the hell was that?' he asked angrily.

'We saw everything there was to see. A corpse mutilated like Purbeck and Burnham and the others, nothing more.' Harrington was off-hand, evasive. Corrick grabbed his arm and span him around.

'Yes?' Harrington said testily.

'We didn't come here just for a cursory visit.' Corrick kept his voice low. The gendarmes were only just up the path.

'Like the inspector said, "that is all".' Harrington met the policeman's anger with a calm but challenging silence.

Very cool, thought Corrick, seeing a hint of something behind the other man's gaze. Harrington turned away and splashed off down the path. Corrick followed.

## 1910

Sir Philip was back in London. He'd made arrangements for a motor vehicle to be at his wife's disposal. He'd also sent Polly the maid to keep house for her. His private secretary Theodore cleared his diary for him and raised the necessary requisition order for the laying of the telephone line for Lady Jennifer (which caused a bit of a stir since in the entire War Office, with a staff of over twelve hundred, there were only thirty-seven lines). Then Sir Philip went to visit a man called Rawlings in Fleet Street.

Rawlings was an unusual contact of Sir Philip's. Over the years Sir Philip had dealt with a number of rather delicate matters. Some concerned affairs of state, while others were of a more private nature. In both, Sir Philip had come to regard Rawlings as exceptionally talented with a rare combination of skills and discretion. He was a spy, and he came with a colourful but rebellious past.

## The Balance Between

Sir Philip had first learned of him years ago. Two army officers, worse for drink, were discussing a recently cashiered fellow officer. 'Quite brilliant' was how one described the man in question. 'Brilliant, but maverick.' 'Didn't fit in,' agreed the other.

Curious, Sir Philip checked the regimental lists and tracked down the individual. Needless to say the young man was feeling bitter towards the army after recent events, but he proved to be resourceful, and had already found employment. Sir Philip approached him and, despite his initial wariness, was soon in Sir Philip's employ. He retained his industrial representative's job as cover and set about making himself indispensable to Sir Philip.

'This is an unusual matter Rawlings,' began Sir Philip, but Rawlings interrupted him, 'Aren't they all, Phil?'

'Yes, yes indeed,' Sir Philip agreed with him. 'But this time it's much more so'.

Contact between them was kept deliberately low key. Sir Philip was cautious to avoid any association with Rawlings lest the man be exposed as a spy. But the spy's casual attitude and change in demeanour did not go unnoticed by his employer.

Sir Philip looked at the man sitting opposite. Ten years of sleuthing and skulduggery had taken their toll on Rawlings. He was prematurely balding and appeared overweight. Sir Philip knew the picture belied an energy and stamina that had pulled Rawlings through many a tight spot, and would no doubt do the same in the future.

❦

James had been confined to bed with his injuries since the bedraggled, weary companions finally reached the Tower. On the morning of the second day Bartholomew visited him with news about Solomon. The fearful wound Solomon received from the slitherer had not poisoned him and he was making a rapid recovery. News of Tempus was less encouraging. Bartholomew struggled to keep the tears from his eyes as he explained, 'Tempus is in that place between here and there. They don't know if he'll make it.'

'I said that you'd grown attached to the hound and that you'd be sorely hurt were he to die.'

James leaned forward and grabbed the dwarf's hand. 'Thank you for that, Bartholomew. Tempus is a great hound. The best I've ever known.'

Bartholomew was ushered out by a tall, elegant woman, who said to James, 'Now sleep, young man, for it is rest you need.' And James was asleep in an instant.

# 1895

Corrick climbed the marble steps beneath the imposing frontage and slipped into an echoing entrance hall. A sign with 'Enquiries' painted on it hung from long chains above a desk at which stood a clerk.

'Yes, sir?' the clerk asked as Corrick approached.

'My name is Chief Inspector Corrick. I'd like to talk with someone concerning a specimen recently delivered for examination.'

'Yes, sir.'

The clerk directed him to the second floor, east wing, down the central corridor to the third door on the left. There, someone would be able to help him.

The Natural History Museum in South Kensington was one of the most magnificent recent buildings in London. Opened just fourteen years previously to replace a motley collection of disparate institutions, it was an architectural gem. As Corrick made his way through the building he marvelled at the intricate Romanesque interior, enormous fossil creatures on display and the endless ranks of glass cabinets housing stuffed creatures.

The room he'd been directed to turned out to be the head

secretary's office. Corrick repeated his request and the head secretary personally led him back through the building to the west wing where the man knocked at another door. A muffled voice answered and his guide slipped through the door leaving Corrick standing in the corridor.

Moments later the door swung open, and the head secretary invited him to enter. Corrick walked in.

'Good day, Chief Inspector.' The man behind the desk rose and signalled Corrick to take a seat. 'My name is Sir Roland Crozier. I am the Museum's Chief Curator and Chairman of the Board of Governors. How may I help you?' Corrick made a note of the man's over-egged attitude and apparent vanity.

'I'm enquiring about a specimen recently sent to your . . . institution.' Corrick chose his words carefully. 'It was found at a crime scene I am handling.'

'And you had it sent to us?' the curator asked, bemused that police evidence should be sent to a museum.

'No, not exactly. It was first taken up to Scotland Yard, before being sent here.'

Sir Roland sat back, his elbows resting on the leather armrests and his hands forming a delicate lattice, fingertips to fingertips.

'How odd to send a crime specimen to the Natural History Museum. I can't imagine any reason for it.' Sir Roland's voice rang with sanctimony.

'Yes, it is rather strange,' Corrick was forced to agree. 'That's why I'm here, to retrieve it and have it examined.'

'Yeees,' said the curator, his superior attitude hastily diminishing.

Corrick waited but the curator seemed reluctant to elaborate. 'So, Sir Roland, if you would be so kind to have someone furnish me with the specimen, I'll be on my way.'

'Yeees,' came the same reply. Another stretch of silence passed between the two men. Corrick got the feeling something wasn't quite right.

*The Balance Between*

'Sir Roland. Is there a problem?'

'Weeell,' Sir Roland dragged the word out while he contemplated the chandelier above his head. 'There is a slight problem.'

Corrick leaned forward to give the man the full glare of his attention.

'You see,' Crozier began in a reedy voice, 'with such a new and large institution, and so many wonderful exhibits to catalogue – we have brought five separate museums under one roof, you do realise – well . . .' He tried a worldly sigh on Corrick to extract sympathy. 'We are unable to say precisely what we have in storage at this time.'

The Chief Inspector sat back in disbelief.

'Of course,' Sir Roland blurted, 'the likelihood is that we haven't got it. Even under present circumstances I am fairly confident that any inappropriate material would have been returned to the sender with an apology. Yes, that is what will have happened.'

Corrick stood, disgusted at the obvious bureaucratic pretentiousness of the man.

'You have been a great assistance with the enquiry,' he said, his voice hardened with anger. Sir Roland's prominent Adam's apple in his skinny neck bobbed like a duck in a storm. The Chief Inspector turned to leave.

'You might wish to check with the Natural History Museum in Oxford. They do get our mail from time to time,' the curator called as the door swung on its hinges.

Outside, Corrick let his anger settle. He thought about the implications of his visit. If Harrington had told him the truth then the specimen was as good as lost in the museum. This only served to reinforce Corrick's feeling that the evidence was deliberately being kept from him. Nothing made him more determined than difficulties of this sort. If necessary he'd obtain a search warrant and forcibly drag the evidence out of the museum. *If* it was there . . .

But Crozier had mentioned Oxford. Corrick couldn't afford to ignore any possibility, no matter how remote. So that left Oxford. He checked his timepiece, then hailed a hansom cab.

# ∽ 5 ∽

# The Western Tower

### 1910

James woke and rubbed the sleep from his eyes. He vaguely recalled being carried into the room and a visit by one of the dwarves, but little else. He sat up in bed and looked around. The room looked like a hospital ward with immaculately made beds and whitewashed walls. His heart leapt! He was home...? The sudden burst of joy faded as swiftly as it arrived. James knew he was still far from home and that the events of that night on the hillside were not a dream. Tears welled in his eyes and, for a while, it felt like his first day at boarding school, alone and cut off from the ones he loved.

His clothes had been folded and placed on a chair by the bed. His belt and dagger hung from the back rest. Wiping away the tears he took more notice of his surroundings in an effort to stop himself thinking of home. Narrow, slit-like windows cut through a thick stone wall that ran in a graceful curve from one side to the other. James realised he must be in the tower the dwarves had spoken of.

His thoughts were interrupted by a woman at the door who smiled at him.

'Good, you're awake,' she said in a warm, friendly voice. 'You've got a visitor or two.'

## The Balance Between

Tempus trotted into the room, followed by the dwarf brothers, Solomon looking well on the road to recovery from his wounds. There were greetings all around and handshakes and hugs, and the three of them recalled events over the past few days.

'We've been the talk of the tower since we arrived. With you two in bed I've had to recount the tale so often my head's begun to spin,' joked Bartholomew.

'Or is it the tale that's spun?' quipped Solomon, winking at James.

'Where exactly are we?' asked James.

'Why, this is the Western Tower,' replied Solomon, 'that sits at the heart of Lauderley Forest.'

'Lauderley Forest is an ancient forest,' he began to explain. 'It spans a hundred leagues from east to west, and marks the edge of the world where the sun sets. The Western Tower was built many millennia ago by the Guild as the regional seat of power, and is famed as a centre of learning.

'But with the passing of centuries the power of the Guild has declined. Where once a dozen wizards worked in the tower now we have but one.' Solomon's voice had fallen to a near-whisper. 'Though he is of greater importance than any wizard before him.'

'To be sure,' agreed Bartholomew.

'A wizard!' exclaimed James at hearing this revelation for the first time.

'Ssshh, young sir,' warned the brothers, furtively looking about to see if they had been overheard.

'Yes, a wizard. That is what the Guild is all about. It's an organisation of the wisest and most brilliant minds in the world,' said Solomon. 'Once their ranks were counted in the thousands but now they are few in number, two hundred at most. Many wizard towers have been abandoned and fallen into disrepair, but the Western Tower still has its wizard.'

'Oh,' replied James. 'Then why are you speaking in hushed voices and being so secretive?'

'Because our wizard lives upstairs,' answered Bartholomew, pointing with his finger directly up.

'Oh yes,' a fair voice interrupted, 'he's right upstairs. But don't worry, he's far too busy to eavesdrop. You can tell him everything at your meeting with him tomorrow.' And with that the tall graceful lady shooed the brothers from the room to let the boy rest a while longer. Tempus hid beneath the bed until Solomon and Bartholomew were shepherded out. Then he jumped up and lay down next to James. James reached forward and gave the hound a scratch behind the ears.

'Up a bit. Aaaah yes, that's it.'

James's hand froze. He stared at Tempus in disbelief. 'You can talk?'

'Yes,' replied the hound matter-of-factly, 'though I'd prefer it if you didn't make it public knowledge.'

James stared at him a moment longer and then laughed out loud. 'I heard the bear talking that night he killed the dragon-spider, but I thought I'd just imagined it.' He gave Tempus a quizzical look. 'Do all animals talk in this place?'

'No, only those that haven't forgotten the ancient lore.' The dog's voice sounded guttural, as if he were giving a low, husky whine.

'Wow!' exclaimed James. 'A land of talking dogs and wizards! So magic really does exist?'

The hound raised his head to reply. 'Of course, though animal speech is not magic as such. We call animals that still have the gift of speech "parls": parlanimals. I prefer to think of myself as a hound. So I am a parlhound, but hound will do.'

'Well it's nice to make your acquaintance, Tempus parlhound,' said James.

'And an honour to make yours. Now, if you'll just continue

scratching behind my ears, I'll be happy to answer more of your questions.'

'How did animals learn to speak?' asked James.

'The Lore of the Animals is the history of parlanimals from the beginning of our time. The Creator bestowed gifts to all living things. To animals he gave speech, to the fish he gave silence, to the crawling creatures he gave society,' Tempus explained.

'You said animals that still have the gift. Why have some animals lost the power of speech?' James asked.

'In the beginning animals cherished their independence and used their gifts wisely. But with time most fell under the influence of man, accepting his domination over all others. Some animals became domesticated and no longer had the need of speech. Those who would not accept subjugation took to living in the forests and the mountains and so became wild. In the depths of the forest they had more need of skills in order to survive and escape man, who took to hunting all things wild.

'Over time we parlanimals have become few, and dumb animals many. Nowadays most humans consider talking animals as servants of the enemy. So we rarely speak and then only to those we know and trust. Because of this we too are slowly losing the gift.'

James shook his head in disbelief. 'I'm sorry to hear that. This is the most amazing place,' he said reverently. 'Do Solomon and Bartholomew know you're a parlanimal?'

'The brothers are dwarves, entirely different to man. I am safe in their company but we keep my parl a secret amongst ourselves. It has proved useful on occasions. Men of your world would probably react badly to talking animals too.' Tempus sighed. 'Please excuse me, but talking makes me very tired. I need to rest now.' And with that Tempus laid his head down and was soon fast asleep.

With these amazing revelations the last thing James wanted to do was sleep so, without disturbing Tempus, he climbed off the bed to explore.

Tiptoeing barefoot out of the room, James found himself in a large circular hallway at the centre of the tower. In the middle a spiral stone staircase corkscrewed from below and passed up through the vaulted ceiling to the floor above. There were three other doors leading off from the hall at opposite points of the compass. He heard singing coming from behind one of the doors and he lifted the latch to investigate. Looking round the doorway he found the lady busy at her needlework.

She looked up and smile. 'James! I'm pleased to see you up and about. Now that you are, how about getting dressed, and we shall go for a gentle stroll?'

James ran back to the ward and dressed himself in new clothes laid out for him. As he started back across the hall to rejoin the lady, Tempus fell in beside him, no doubt keen for a walk.

'Mind yourself,' the hound cautioned. 'She has a way that will turn your insides to marrow jelly.'

'Thanks, Tempus, I'll bear that in mind.' As they descended the central stairwell James noticed how the steps appeared to glow, and he commented on it.

'Yes, the stone used in its construction has a quality about it that makes it trap light at the top and channel it down the spiral to light the tower interior,' the lady explained.

They passed down through many floors, most of which were silent and empty, a measure of how the population had diminished. Turning off the stairs they crossed to a wooden door set in the exterior stone wall. The door swung open effortlessly and in front of them a narrow wooden causeway stretched away into the distance, the far end resting on a grassy knoll.

'This is the Rose Door, leading into the rose gardens and the parkland beyond,' the lady explained.

James gazed into the distance. Parkland spread out before them like a beautiful tablecloth with splashes of colour lovingly sewn on. It reminded James of Richmond Park in London, only more peaceful.

## The Balance Between

The lady guided him into the rose gardens where she pointed out some of the many different types of flower. Her words were like the taste of honeysuckle, and she entranced James with her warm, willowy voice.

James had no idea how long they walked together but eventually he found they'd returned to the causeway. James stopped and looked up at the tower for the first time. It took his breath away. The graceful line of the tower ascended five-hundred feet or more, dominating the countryside. Its white granite shone clean and fresh in the daylight. James had never seen a building like it.

'It impresses you, young man? Do you not have such buildings in your own world?' the lady enquired.

James shook his head in awe.

'The Western Tower is but one of many in our land. It was built in a time when miracles such as this were possible, and the necessary skills were still to hand.' She contemplated the majesty of the structure. 'This world will never again build something as wondrous as Faldamare.'

James turned to her and asked, 'Faldamare, my lady?'

'The name given to this tower by the elves who built it,' she answered.

That night when James climbed into bed, he realised he'd been too awe-struck to ask the lady her name.

'Tempus?'

'Yes, James.'

'Who is that lady?'

'She is Lady Orlania.'

'Oh.'

After breakfast, James and the dwarves set off up the staircase, ascending to their appointment with the wizard.

They climbed and climbed, passing endless floors, for the most part accompanied by nothing more than the echo of their footsteps. After a dozen floors the spiral of the stairwell would reverse in a tricky feat of engineering that perplexed the eye in its subtlety.

'It's a defensive measure,' explained Solomon.

At last they reached the top. To James it was like arriving inside a rainbow. Everywhere he looked there were no walls or windows, simply bands of colour and light arcing high above their heads and twisting into a spinning top of loops and curves. It was like riding a roller coaster at night, only far better. He looked down to find himself standing on a pool of aquamarine water, with vividly coloured fish gliding beneath him. When he lifted his eyes again the rainbow was fading, replaced by a blue-black sky powdered with light. It was many more minutes before the spectacle faded to be finally replaced by nothing more than a stone vaulted ceiling.

James saw the room was a library, its walls covered in oak bookcases. Shelves were filled with books of every size, mounds of manuscripts, bundles of scrolls and haphazard stacks of charts. There were books as big as James, others embossed in gold, while a few actually glistened with encrusted gemstones. The smell of old leather filled the air. A stillness seemed to permeate every corner of the room. To James the place seemed to shimmer with latent magical power.

Bartholomew turned to his brother and clapped him on his shoulder, unable to contain his excitement. 'Did you see it, brother? The Seat of Elder Mosenor and all the slain! What a pyrrhic victory that was. What splendour! What a way to cross to the far side.' Bartholomew hopped from foot to foot as he shook his brother in happiness.

Solomon was equally excited but for a different reason. 'No, no, brother. It was the most amazing battle banquet I have ever witnessed. They were up there,' he gesticulated. 'Old Axer Tollominos sat beside Borofeare the Enslaver. They were toasting the death of their enemies. There must have been a hundred dwarves celebrating.' He threw back his head and roared a dwarfish battle chant.

James stood watching them. He realised that each of them had seen their own personal vision.

'Come up, come in,' called a voice from above.

The brothers stopped in mid-embrace, remembering where they were. They shuffled apart and looked up the final flight of stairs.

'Come up, come in,' the voice repeated.

James followed Solomon and Bartholomew up until they were standing beneath a glass dome enclosing the entire tower roof. The room resembled an observatory, filled with strange apparatus and shelves of bottles, boxes and jars. Chests and cauldrons lay on the floor. Plants with giant fronds arched overhead beneath the glass. Several climbing plants grew their way up the inside of the structure. An enormous telescopic contraption on casters pointed a black accusatory finger skyward while other, lesser machines and devices crowded around it.

James glanced out of the dome window where the sky was a brilliant azure blue. It was as if the room was perched far above the world.

'Welcome to you. Welcome, James Kinghorn.' An old man walked forwards and placed a fatherly hand on the lad's shoulder before turning to the two dwarves. 'Welcome, Solomon Brunel Bandamire and Bartholomew Shakespeare Bandamire, offspring of Splayfoot Teutonica Bandamire, warrior and prisoner-not-at-large, and grandspring of Borrowmason Goldenbeard Bandamire whose fall at Highfall be remembered in lore.'

The brothers beamed in satisfaction at these words.

The old man whispered out of the corner of his mouth to James, 'Dwarves love this sort of stuff, as you probably know.'

James nodded agreement, although in truth he knew very little about dwarfish likes or dislikes.

'Now, my good dwarves, what shall we be about? A cup of tea

and then I think we really ought to explain a thing or two to our young friend here, who has been kept in the dark long enough. Let's sit together and I'll make amends for this delay.' And with this they sat down to tea and biscuits that the wizard had already prepared.

The dwarves sat on two low-slung seats that were just the right height for their short legs to touch the ground. James sat next to the old man and watched while the teapot poured itself. 'They like this sort of magic too,' whispered the wizard to his young visitor.

'Allow me to introduce myself,' the old man said, turning to James. 'I am Sibelius, Keeper of the Western Tower and representative of the Guild.' James looked at him as Sibelius took up his cup of tea. His face was at once young and old, alive with energy yet steeped in wisdom. The man's eyes glimmered and told of a thousand lifetimes, were a man to have lived as long. It struck James how familiar Sibelius appeared to him, and yet they'd never met.

'You entered the ancient world of Eldaterra by way of the Sea Arch,' Sibelius continued, 'and you've arrived safely by the guiding hand of the Guild and, in no small part, by the brave and loyal actions of these two gentle dwarves.' This set the brothers grinning again.

'Your family has been of service to Eldaterra in the past, and for this we are grateful.' The wizard's tone grew serious. 'But now our land has need to call on your services, if you will oblige?'

This news took James completely by surprise. When at last he managed to find his voice he politely corrected the wizard.

'I'm afraid, sir, that you have made a terrible mistake. My father works for His Majesty's Government and he'd never work for a foreign power,' James said in a hurt voice, determined to defend his father's reputation.

Sibelius smiled. 'Indeed that is the case, James, and I do not seek to impugn your father. It was in fact your grandfather, Sir

*The Balance Between*

Neville, who aided us in our time of need. You may be assured that Sir Neville never betrayed his own country.'

'I never knew my grandfather,' James said with regret. The wizard placed a fatherly hand on his shoulder.

'You can be very proud of him. Though we know little of his deeds he has been influential in events between our two worlds.'

'Why are there two worlds?' James asked, still unsure of what he'd been told by the dwarves.

Sibelius nodded. He knew the enormity of the truth was a lot to accept when confronted with it for the first time. 'This is quite an experience for you, I know, my boy,' Sibelius acknowledged. 'Eldaterra doesn't appear on any map you've ever seen and it never will. It's a different place altogether, a place set apart from the world of the British Empire. Eldaterra is a secret world. One that exists alongside your world, but one that is hidden from it.'

James thought about this for a moment. 'Do you mean that Eldaterra is a subversive political organisation planning to overthrow governments?' he asked earnestly.

Sibelius chuckled to himself. 'No, James, I do not, though I see your father's taught you about politics. Eldaterra is hidden by magic, powerful magic. Thousands of years ago, wizards created the deepest magic to divide earth in two. They hid Eldaterra from the new world in the hope that the influences of change in the new world wouldn't affect the old world, the one we call Eldaterra.'

James listened closely as the wizard continued. 'Earth is a gift to the stars. That is the most ancient of beliefs in Eldaterra. It was Creation that first gave form to Eldaterra. When Creation placed life on earth, its work was a most resplendent achievement, as beautiful and intricate as anything that existed in the universe. The world was filled with marvels and astonishing diversity. All manner of living things were gifted to the world, and it was to be a world of goodness.' Sibelius's eyes twinkled as he spoke. 'But the act of creation can only take place when there is harmony; stasis; equilibrium. For Creation to bring forth the firstborn there needed to be balance in the world. And for something to be in balance implies that there are exact opposites for everything.'

The old wizard picked up a measuring rule to demonstrate. 'James, by balancing this ruler in the middle there are equal lengths on either side. There are also extremes at either end of the point of balance but together they balance each other out. Take one away, and the other will make the ruler fall. Taken in their most potent form these extremes represent forces that we may determine to be beneficial or not. Thus Creation invokes what we know as good and evil. And because we have balance, one does not exist without the other.' The old wizard laid down the ruler and sipped his tea before resuming.

'When Creation placed life in the world with all its inherent goodness, it also created an imbalance. Creation sought to make the world with nothing but goodness and keep it separate from all else, but in doing so forfeited any equilibrium and balance for the world. And though the world exists in the vacuum of the stars, evil seeped in, seeking to return the world to a natural state of equilibrium. Because of this good things that started pure are corrupted. The balance begins to shift from purity to equality, good and evil in equal measure.'

The old man took another sip of tea. James thought Creation sounded a bit like religion. Sibelius had described the Garden of Eden in a way, but he hadn't called it that.

'And among those gifts that were bequeathed to the world was *Knowledge*, an understanding of Creation. *Knowledge* is the greatest of all gifts and is marked by the possession of a soul. Many creatures in the world possessed such a soul, and with it came other gifts: love, loyalty, compassion and all things we know to be good. Yet as evil seeped into the world many souls were converted. True perfection in the world was lost forever.

## The Balance Between

'Thus life in the world divides into good and evil. The possession of souls gives direction to the living; the good strive to be ever more pure in their goodness, while evil seeks to distil into its most corrupting form. Everything that has a soul turns to one or other of these opposites.'

The dwarves and the boy sat gripped by the story.

'Oldest among all the forms of Knowledge is what we call magic, though it was once deeper and more complex than what we know today. At the beginning of time when Creation first invoked the world, all peoples knew this magic. Much has since been lost, forgotten. Of all the magic that ever existed the very first was that which divined life. But no one was ever allowed to know of this first magic, for to know it would be to make a son the father to his father.'

The room was perfectly still, the listeners awed by the wizard's story.

'Understand this. Those who were given the lore of magic are the offspring of Creation. And with our souls we have freedom to think and to be individuals. There are also many, the majority now, who have forgotten the gifts of magic and the *Knowledge*. They still possess souls but no longer understand their place in the ordering of the world. They are not outcast from Creation, simply lost.

The wizard set down his teacup and looked at all three of them in turn.

'I tell you this, James, because you need to understand that when the world began, magic was a great gift for those who possessed a soul, the oldest gift after life itself. Creatures used it to shape the world to their requirements, and ultimately those who possess it use it for good or evil.' Sibelius's voice dropped at this point. 'And ever since, good and evil have waged war on one another. Over the millennia countless lives have been lost in the struggle. And over time we have also lost *Knowledge*. Eventually parts of the world were left with no magic, no *Knowledge*, no ancient lore. These places contained living creatures Creation never intended. They possessed souls, but without *Knowledge* they were base. In their baseness they created false gods and worshipped craven idols. They could not understand their place in the world so they had to create a meaning for their existence. They had to begin again.

'It was at this point when the peoples of the world who still wielded sufficiently potent magic decided to act. They determined to create two separate worlds; one where magic would be protected; the other where magic was all but gone forever. Eldaterra remained hidden, while the world you know as your own, James, has grown and developed without magic. In your world – the New World – nearly everything of what was gifted by Creation has been lost. Mankind has risen to dominate all else. Man set forth to learn, first through the process called religion and then through the process of science. Mankind stumbles down this path of learning where the distinction between good and evil is blurred and ill-defined.

'Eldaterra is a world of ancient knowledge and magic, where one is *either* good or evil. There is no in-between. Our struggle is straightforward, a physical one, a battle between two intractable opposites. In your world, all mankind is part good and part evil and each individual faces a personal struggle inside between these two opposites. It is a struggle within the individual's soul. It is "spiritual", as your world calls it. Mankind is caught in the greyness that exists between the light and dark, good and evil.'

Sibelius stopped and gathered his thoughts for a moment.

'Your grandfather, James, was a rare person, someone who was an imbalance in himself, with such a depth of goodness in him that he was able to see our world, even though he belonged to the other one. Sir Neville came into our world, and now you have followed.'

## The Balance Between

The eyes of the dwarves upon him, James sat there, considering the implications. Did that make him 'good'? Sibelius appeared to read his mind.

'We do not know, James, whether you represent *goodness*. You may represent the opposite. But it is the possession of one of these in the extreme that allows you to pass between the two worlds. We do not know which yet. It was only through the actions of your grandfather that we understood him to be on the side of good. In Eldaterra –' he spread his arms about him '– there is a design woven more closely to life. Life is pre-ordained, set out in a plan we may not fully understand, but one that allows us some insight. We call this design *fate*. In your world mankind lives more by its actions than by a plan.'

'But sir, if I am here then presumably there is a reason?' asked James.

'Yes,' Sibelius answered as he produced a map and spread it before them. 'This is a map of the Lauderley Forest and the country that borders this region. To the west is the very edge of Eldaterra, and it was here that you crossed into our world. To the north, beyond the range of mountains indicated, there lies a desolate land. To the east lies a fertile region more populated than Lauderley. Farther east lie realms of strange races and beings that we have little contact with. To the south is where the Guild sits in Eldaterra's principal cities. Beyond there,' he said pointing to the very foot of the map, 'the source of our troubles lies.'

As the wizard spoke these last words, the room noticeably darkened. James looked up at the sky outside but it remained as bright blue as before. Sibelius scowled.

'By this darkness you see a hint of the powers that assail us,' said Sibelius in a grave tone. 'James, as the Guild's representative, I am a wizard of some considerable standing. This tower is my domain.' His eyes flashed in anger. 'For evil to dare intrude into my stronghold, let alone the Forest of Lauderley, is evidence enough there is an imbalance in this world. I believe you have been sent to resolve this imbalance.'

'But how, sir?'

'Call it fate, or chance, if you like. The powers of darkness seek to overcome goodness. Somehow they have created an imbalance, and you have been chosen to decide whether equilibrium shall be returned, or whether evil will breach the deep magic that separates our two worlds. Were the magic to fail, then Eldaterra will cease to exist. The ignorance and science of your world will crash into the last of the true *Knowledge* like an overwhelming enemy, and it will be lost forever.'

'If fate wanted me to be here, why did we have to fight for our lives, and why didn't magic come to assist us?' James wanted to know.

'Ah, fate is but the inevitability of events, not the course of them. So your survival was foreseen by the fates, but only if you were determined to survive, which, happily for us all, you were.' The wizard laughed. 'As to why magic did not come to your aid, well, that is my department, and I apologise for a lack of it during your journey here.' He made a short bow of his head to James. 'You see, James, when one uses magic one leaves tracks behind, an ethereal footprint that may be read by a skilled hunter. When you came through the Sea Arch a ripple of change in the magic and balance of this world took place. I sensed your arrival, and others will have done the same. They will have limited knowledge of who you are and what potential you represent. For my part, I had the brothers Bandamire watch over you and spies inform me of your progress. But to use magic to assist you would have been to show our enemy how important you are. The most I dared was the little courtesy with the fireflies, until, that is, you encountered something of a magnitude of evil that I had not anticipated, the drezghul. Its presence tells me that the enemy already know how important you are to us all.'

## 6

# More Questions than Answers

### 1895

Chief Inspector Corrick was busy with seemingly endless paperwork when a duty officer tapped on the door and stuck his head into the room.

'Excuse me, sir. There's a telephone call and the caller is asking for you, we think, sir.' The officer looked uncertain.

'Thank you, sergeant.' Corrick knew many of his colleagues were uneasy with this new technology. Some of the senior officers in the station questioned the need for having a telephone installed, which allowed divisional HQ to stick their oar in far too easily. Corrick gave a wry smile. Some people didn't like change, himself included.

'Hello, hello. I wish to speak with Chief Inspector Corrick, please.' The voice at the other end of the line was disjointed and interference on the line cut into the words.

'Speaking.'

'Chief Inspector Corrick?'

'Yes.'

'Bon. This is Inspector La Forge. We met only a few days ago? You visited our country on a police matter?'

'Yes,' Corrick replied.

'Mais oui. I am calling from the telephone of Monsieur Barras, a very upstanding citizen of Zeebrugge. He is the only citizen who has a telephonic instrument installed. Because of the importance of the matter under police investigation he has allowed me to contact Scotland Yard who then connected my telephone call to you.' La Forge's delivery was slow and precise.

'Yes, Yes.' *Let there be a development,* Corrick prayed. 'Please, go on,' he urged.

'We have new evidence linked to the murder. It was only discovered after your departure. You may wish to see it for yourself. It is, how you say, very strange.' La Forge sounded cautious, as if letting Corrick into a secret.

'Yes. That would be good.' He thought quickly. 'I will catch a ferry tonight from Felixstowe. I will have somebody send a cable with the ship's arrival time.'

'Bon. I shall await your cable, monsieur. Au revoir.'

'Merci, Inspector. Au revoir. Au revoir.'

Corrick boarded the *Claudilia* at Felixstowe that evening. The boat, a small steam packet carrying a mixed cargo and a handful of passengers, was struggling with the weather conditions, pitching badly in the swell as she headed across the grey waters to the Lowlands.

'She's the wrong length when the swell is this deep,' explained her captain. 'Must be coming down from Arctic waters. Unusual,' he added. He'd invited Corrick to join him on the bridge. The cable to La Forge had been sent and a long night's passage lay before them. 'I'd be happier if we were to tack across it, as would the passengers and crew no doubt,' the captain said, hoping to persuade Corrick to rescind the official police request to steam directly to Zeebrugge.

'Thank you, Captain, but I am on the most urgent police business and I would be much obliged if we could reach Zeebrugge at the earliest opportunity.' Corrick's answer ended any question of a slower, more comfortable crossing. He gazed up at the black smoke curling away to the west, the steam engine thumping reassuringly through the deck.

'I suppose cookie will be happy,' the Captain sighed. 'There won't be much call for catering on this trip then.' He smiled at Corrick and winked. 'But there's no reason why we shouldn't enjoy a snuftie,' and he pulled out a bottle from below the map table.

## 1910

Rawlings sat opposite the clerk in a booth at the back of the coffee shop just off Whitehall. Rawlings slid the envelope containing the crisp five-pound note across the table. The clerk drew out a small piece of folded paper and surreptitiously exchanged it for the money, his eyes darting left and right in fear of being discovered selling government information. Rawlings' unfolded the note and checked it briefly. The clerk got up to leave, sweat beading his brow below the scruffy bowler hat he plonked on his head. Rawlings nodded farewell. They hadn't exchanged a single word.

Lady Jennifer was joined by her niece, Lady Amanda Brightmere, at the end of the week. Amanda was a tall, elegant eighteen-year-old possessing grace and poise and a happy demeanour. She was also intelligent and blessed with an inordinate sense of purpose, making her confident and outgoing. She was the ideal companion for Lady Jennifer during this time. Although the request by her aunt had come out of the blue and clashed horribly with some of the most important events of the social season, Amanda was happy to come to her aunt's aid. If Aunt Jennifer had need of Amanda, there would be a good reason, and Amanda, who was close to her aunt, could be counted on for support.

They greeted each other warmly. Amanda could tell her aunt was not in her usual spirits and soon learned of James's disappearance. Jennifer explained that Sir Philip had so far managed to keep it out of the newspapers to enable discreet enquiries, lest the matter be connected in some way to affairs of state. She had stayed up in Northumberland in the hope that James might still be in the area. Despite what she was told by her aunt, Amanda had an uncanny feeling that there was more going on.

The ladies took to walking along the shoreline twice a day. They ventured out in whatever the weather. Amanda soon noticed that her aunt always walked the same stretch of beach. It was evident that Lady Jennifer attached particular importance to the location. It was as if she were conducting a vigil.

---

Sir Philip studied the pages before him. Rawlings had done his work well. Each page contained a short list of names, and each list was in a different handwriting. Opening a desk drawer he took out a fifth page and an envelope. He passed the envelope to Rawlings and placed the new list with the others.

'Thank you,' he said. 'This looks most promising. Now I need you to do one more task for me,' he told the spy.

It would be an important job. Sir Philip would never suggest meeting at his London residence unless it was important. Important enough to be worth a hefty fee, Rawlings reflected. He smiled at the thought.

Sir Philip noted his employee's expression, watching as the man gave up trying to conceal his satisfaction.

'Some years ago, I was a junior officer in the Excise Department. An incident occurred which I'd like you to investigate.'

Rawlings' interest was now more than financial. Sir Philip had never mentioned anything in his past about an 'incident', and perhaps his investigations would provide something of value for his own purposes.

Sir Philip handed a second, larger, buff envelope across the desk. This one contained the documentation for this new task. 'And if you wouldn't mind going out the way you came,' he added, concluding their meeting.

Rawlings stood up, tucking the envelope into the recesses of his coat, and took his leave. Ascending the stairs to the third floor, he climbed into the roof space and passed along the adjoining terrace mansions that lined the street before exiting via a discreet side street.

Sir Philip looked through the lists. Each contained between four and thirteen names of individuals working in various government departments. The information covered four ministries: Customs and Excise (known as Excise prior to its merger with the Customs Department), the Inland Revenue, the Foreign Office and the Lord Chancellor's Office, while he had compiled a fifth list from his own department, the War Office. Sir Philip was certain the person he was seeking was a careerist, perhaps someone with ambition. Such a person would naturally gravitate to one of the more influential departments and Sir Philip had targeted these.

He recalled the night he'd revealed the story of the search to his wife. They'd sat together deciphering the inscription, unlocking clues that may help explain James's whereabouts.

> *Steady now your hand must act*
> *And recall silence in your past*

Sir Philip had despatched Rawlings on a mission that would address the silence in his own past.

> *Your father's eyes you too may see*
> *That which empire may not spy*

## The Balance Between

The next two lines were remarkably telling, and related to events in Sir Philip's own childhood. When he was a boy, he and his father had shared a vision. It transpired that no one else shared the vision. It had remained a secret, until now.

> *Seek out the other in this pact*
> *Who sifts for one in numbers vast*

Jennifer made sense of the next lines, as far as anyone could. Sir Philip must look for another person who shared knowledge of these events, who may know of James's disappearance. And whoever it was would be hard to find.

'Mmm, where,' Lady Jennifer asked, 'would you hide so you couldn't be found but still had access to information to continue secretive activities?' He replied that when he wanted to get some work done he went to the office and told his private secretary to tell everyone he was out.

'Exactly!' she declared in triumph. 'And that links perfectly with the end of the next line, "ministry".'

Sir Philip had agreed it did sound feasible and a logical conclusion to draw.

> *And chase the wates in ministry*
> *Or heralds forth a time to die*

These final two lines required more word play. Since he'd discovered his wife was an avid crossword puzzler and player of the fiendishly tricky game of Double Acrostics, he wasn't too surprised when Jennifer drew out a travelling Thesaurus. Together they'd listed reams and reams of words. Again it was Jennifer who made the connection – after ten minutes of silent work she presented him with two columns of words. Down one column she had written every alternative for the word 'chase'. Down the second column she had written down every alternative word for the derivatives of 'waits' and 'weights', since the word 'wates' was medieval English and had fallen out of use years ago. With a degree of remarkable prescience, Jennifer had seen the final lines as revealing a name, a very old name, or a very old individual.

So, with two long lists of words, they played at lexicographers, compiling a final list of all the names that could be made up with paired words, one from each column. They narrowed the field further by striking out any unusual name since whoever they were looking for would, according to the inscription, be hiding and therefore be unlikely to draw attention to themselves. On this last point Jennifer had also discounted the possibility of the person being a woman. Although many women were employed in the ministries, none had significant roles in the chauvinistic Civil Service. Sir Philip had reluctantly agreed with her.

From the final list of names that satisfied the inscription clues, Sir Philip had sourced employees in each ministry whose names matched those on the list. Finally, his private secretary Theodore had 'borrowed' employee files on the candidates from the respective ministries. Now Sir Philip studied each candidate in fine detail.

# 1895

Inspector La Forge greeted Corrick at the quay as he disembarked. 'Bonjour monsieur, we meet in more favourable circumstances.'

'Good morning, Inspector,' replied Corrick, looking skyward at the pleasant day that promised. 'The weather is definitely better.'

'Oui, Chief Inspector, but I am referring to the absence of your associate. How did you describe him? Your assistant?' The Belgian policeman was watching Corrick closely.

'So you weren't impressed?' Corrick answered, neither confirming nor denying anything.

'Pah! You do not believe that yourself. That man was not your subordinate any more than he was a police officer. Do not take me for a fool, Chief Inspector. I had just decided to like you.' La Forge said with genuine warmth in his voice.

Corrick laughed and apologised for the crude ruse, which he was pleased to say wasn't his doing. Together they climbed into a police carriage and headed for the city morgue.

'You see, Chief Inspector. It is most unusual, n'est-ce pas?'

'Very,' Corrick replied. The two men stood at a marble morgue table in the centre of a brightly-lit, cold room. The city coroner stood waiting, ready to answer any questions.

Stretched out in a battered metal specimen tray lay a mass of convoluted, meaty flesh. It was discoloured, with patches of brown and yellow, but in the main it was off-white, like it was bleached, washed out. A thick cord was attached to it, perhaps two feet in length, and frayed at the end.

'Please repeat your description, Doctor,' requested Corrick, who wanted to check the notes he was making.

The doctor shrugged. 'It is a placenta, but I do not think it is human. External examination shows severe lacerations to the posterior section, consistent in depth and pattern to the actions of a propeller from a motor vessel. The umbilical cord is damaged in a manner as to suggest the propeller caught it. The foetus or newborn infant, if it were human, would have died in the trauma. Based on the placental weight and dimensions one may say with almost absolute certainty that it was from a full-term foetus. But it is not normal . . .' The doctor shrugged his shoulders again. 'In my experience I have never seen one like this, one with so many anatomical aberrations. It is not my field of expertise, but to find this has . . . a heart within it . . . this is impossible!'

An awkward silence followed as each of them considered this impossibility. La Forge thanked the doctor and the latter took his

*The Balance Between*

leave. Corrick turned to La Forge, but the Belgian had anticipated the question.

'There will be no further investigation. The city Prefecture would not agree to the use of taxpayers' money for such activity. This is unnatural, ungodly. It will benefit no one. She is mort.' As they left the morgue La Forge continued, 'We checked the waterway thoroughly. We have not recovered the infant's body.'

La Forge drew out a pipe and began to fill it with tobacco. He seemed to be weighing something up in his mind.

'Chief Inspector,' the Belgian pulled on the pipe, 'we have interviewed many people. No one knew her. We don't even know her name. It was only when we found that "thing" – the placenta – that the coroner examined the body a second time. It was then that we learned the victim had been pregnant at the time of the murder. The mutilation of the body disguised much of it, but sufficient evidence remained for the coroner to be certain.' La Forge took another draw on the pipe. 'Yet the placenta, he says, is not of human origin. How do we explain this?'

'Are you are saying that thing in there –' Corrick gestured back to the mortuary '– is not connected with this case?'

'Oh, undoubtedly it is. It was found near the scene of the crime. We do not find such things very often, you know.'

Corrick sat in a deckchair as he re-crossed the North Sea by boat, this time heading to Dover. Before leaving Zeebrugge, Inspector La Forge had advised him not to mention this trip to his 'assistant', Harrington. La Forge had information of his own concerning this man and he urged Corrick to cut him out of any investigation if it were possible.

'The less he knows the better,' were La Forge's final parting words.

Corrick considered the evidence. A pregnant woman killed in a

85

frenzied attack in an isolated location. No offspring had been recovered but they'd found an abnormal placenta. Corrick wondered if this last find was some sort of joke or hoax on the part of the killer? Could the evidence be planted, or the coroner wrong? Perhaps the witnesses were wrong? None of the questions appeared to have answers. Corrick couldn't reach any conclusion. He'd have to get access to the other reported cases. That meant a trip to London, polluted, dirty London. At least his headaches appeared to have cleared up. Thank the Lord for small mercies.

# 1910

The day after his visit to Sibelius, James sat with Lady Orlania taking tea in the rose garden where they enjoyed the warm, sunny views. He reflected on the previous evening when he and the dwarves had stayed with Sibelius late into the night. The wizard had spoken of the rich and evocative history of Eldaterra, his words painting a graphic image of a world slowly torn apart by a war between good and evil. Yet now, as James sat and contemplated the peaceful parkland and gardens around him, he had found it hard to believe that anyone would wish to destroy such a place.

'With so few living in the Western Tower I am grateful for your company, young sir,' Lady Orlania said and expressed a wish to learn of James's world. For the first time, he forgot the pangs of homesickness and enjoyed telling her of England and the world. She was interested in everything and, by the end of their day, James was glad he'd paid attention at school. Somehow, being with Lady Orlania made everything seem better, hopeful, calmer.

After a while, the lady leaned forward and, taking his hand in hers, asked, 'James, are there any questions you would ask of me?'

In truth there were many, many questions but James felt flustered by the intimacy and felt his cheeks burning.

## The Balance Between

'You wish to know more about Sibelius, and then, perhaps, myself,' she answered for him.

James nodded slowly. It was as if Lady Orlania could read his mind. His hand tingled with her touch.

'Where does one start when talking of Sibelius, Principal Wizard of the Western Tower, Keeper of the Sword of Lind and Master of the Shadows? Sibelius has been a wizard for as long as I can recall, and I am ancient by your reckoning. He ascended to the position of Principal only after proving himself to be a great wizard. There are some who say he is the greatest wizard alive today, although there are many claims to that title. But Sibelius holds the Western Tower, and with it the surrounding lands. It is only by his power that the lands hereabouts are kept safe. The war has sent hundreds of thousands of our people south and there is but a smattering left to work the forests and tend the land. It is as if this war is slowly consuming us until there will be no one left to fight evil. Within the Western Tower there can be no more than three hundred, four hundred dwelling here, at most. We couldn't defend ourselves for long if it should ever come to battle. Our wizard is our only defence for now.'

She sighed. 'And he is hard pressed, though you would not guess it by his manner. The demands of war draw ever more upon his resources, and the time he gives to watching our borders grows less with every month.

'James.' She leaned forward and again placed her hand upon his. James's hand tingled with electricity. 'You are a new dimension to the worries that Sibelius faces. It has fallen upon him to guide and assist you in whatever it is you are here for. Had you entered our world by another portal, then it would have been a different wizard in a different tower with this responsibility. But it is fate that has brought you to the Western Tower, and to Sibelius. Do not fail him . . .' she hesitated for a moment, 'or yourself.' These last words were ominous, and she squeezed James's hand beneath hers.

'As to myself,' the lady went on, lightening the mood again, 'I am the daughter of Handrial, Once King of the Lauderley Elvenfolk, who now lies in rest forever on our borders to the south.'

James looked aghast.

'Fear not, child, for he fell in battle over five thousand years ago and the hurting has passed. I now remember him with joy and pride.'

James was astonished at this last piece of information. The Lady Orlania hardly looked thirty years old and she didn't look anything like the elves he'd read about in fairy stories.

'Do elves *really* exist, Lady Orlania?' he asked in amazement before realising that he may have sounded rude.

She laughed in return. 'Do I not sit before you? But I forget that in your land these things are but myths and legend. My, hasn't the truth been lost in your world!' she exclaimed, and James found he agreed with this sentiment. The world he knew as home was sorely lacking without the wonderment of magic.

They walked through the parkland until they came to a stockade and gate. The gate swung silently open for them and they entered a farm enclosure. Looking around, James could see all manner of well-tended animals, but no evidence of people.

'In this farm and many score like it we are growing the foodstuffs and gathering the crops to feed our armies in the south. But there is no one to watch over the place, only the animals,' she told him.

James looked at the lady in surprise, and then it dawned on him. 'Is this is your work, my Lady?'

'Yes, James, even a lady must help in whatever way she can,' she replied.

'And do these animals have any . . . magic?' he asked.

'No, James, these are dumb animals now. They have long lost their magic and any other gifts. We accept that when magic is lost, the animals remain beasts for our purposes. These animals here can no longer speak, and few remain who can. Those that still have the gift must be careful, for there are many who would harm them.' She was sharing a secret that few men knew of. Even in this world parlanimals were not safe, but James already knew this from his parlanimal friend.

Returning to the tower, she thanked James for his company and was about to bid him goodnight when she stopped and drew his hands into hers once more.

'Eldaterra is in mortal danger, James. I feel it.'

And then he realised the purpose of their time together. The Lady wanted James to help her, to help Eldaterra!

And that was precisely what Lady Orlania sought. However, she was also worried. Worried that this boy from another world was too young to carry the burden that would decide the fate of two worlds, his own and Eldaterra.

## ∾ 7 ∾

# The Warkrin

'James, thank you for coming to see me again.'

Sibelius stood at the top of the spiral staircase to greet him. This time James's jaw dropped open as he found himself in an open park, standing near a bandstand. A military band played 'Jerusalem' as light streamed through the trees. King George V stood on the podium taking the salute of marching soldiers, James's father standing close by. Flags waved, people cheered and James felt the electricity of excitement. War! He came out of his dream to find Sibelius humming the tune.

'You were there too?' asked James incredulously.

'Yes. Occasionally I find it a pleasant distraction to look in on other's dreams, particularly if they are entertaining. This room is a dream generator. Its purposes are numerous, but when visitors come they always enjoy some entertainment. What you see is your subconscious, picked up and amplified in a way to make them appear real.'

He stroked his beard and gazed intensely at the boy. 'It does also have another, more meaningful, purpose. Everyone who enters produces a dream that reflects his or her inherent nature. This is of course pleasing to anyone who is on the side of goodness, if you can bear such a description. But for those who have fallen into the darkness, the dream generator is a very deadly weapon, for they are

## The Balance Between

assailed by dreams as dark as the soul they possess. It is an ancient type of magic, and one that is rare nowadays.'

'My dream was of war. Does that mean I am on the side of evil?' James asked.

'Your dream was more complex than that, James. And since you come from the other world, it could be a combination of many aspects of your life we don't yet understand, the influences of religion, science and others. Sadly, we don't know enough about your world to interpret them. Dreams are easy to observe but difficult to deduce. But the music was good.' He ushered the boy onwards.

'Now, on to more pressing things.'

They ascended into the glass-domed observatory. James was as enthralled as he had been on his previous visit. He walked around the room, studying objects and reading the spines of books in the bookcases scattered about. Most of them were in strange languages with symbols and squiggles James couldn't understand.

'James, we must talk about the reasons for you being in Eldaterra. When we last met I spoke briefly of the history that separates our two worlds but I felt it best to wait until we were alone to talk about the issues in more detail. They will weigh heavily on you in the future. This is a very serious matter.'

The wizard sat at the desk and James found a stool.

'I have given much thought to this subject. You will recall I explained how the wizards of old divided the world using arcane magic. When the wizards separated them, they left doorways to enable passage between the worlds, doorways that were guarded and secured. These are the portals. The Sea Arch is one of them, made from very deep magic, a type that only our forefathers could wield, in the time when magic was the way of the world.

'These portals were given their own magic, and they became as living creatures. Almost, but not quite living, for it has never been and never shall be within our grasp to create true life other than as nature intended.

'The portals received powers greater than any single wizard would ever possess. The portals can show themselves at their choosing or remain invisible as they please. They choose who shall pass through and who shall not, and they can even communicate with whoever they choose to.'

'Yes, the Sea Arch wrote a message to me on a brass plaque,' interrupted James.

Sibelius nodded in approval. 'It is as I guessed. I hope you will share this information with me so that we may learn more of your reasons for being here.'

James scratched behind his ear as he thought for a moment. Something had flickered into his mind and then out again. 'I'm afraid I can't recall the inscription. I didn't think it was important, sir.'

'Not to worry,' the wizard assured him. 'I can give you a mild memory potion to restore your thoughts on the matter if you wish. I should hope to learn something from the words, James.'

The wizard continued, 'Last night I was in communication with a colleague in the south. What I learned has disturbing implications for us and, more importantly, for you. We may need to act sooner than I had anticipated.' A worried look passed over the wizard's face. 'We have captured a spy. He is being taken to the Tower of Cruxantire, some three-hundred leagues to the south. Once there, the Wizard Ptarmagus and I will use our powers to facilitate the prisoner's onward journey to here.' The wizard's eyes held James's.

'What we have learned so far is this man is not from our world, but from yours.'

James didn't comprehend the significance and seconds of silence passed.

'James, this tells us two things. First, that the enemy has discovered the means to pass through the portals, something we have long feared. Second, they would appear to be in alliance with

## The Balance Between

someone from your world. And from this we may conclude that your passage through the portal is a counterbalance.' James didn't quite understand. The wizard patted his arm as he explained, 'The passage of the enemy's spy upset the balance in this world between good and evil.' The wizard's eyes shone. 'You are the counterbalance, you are here to help the good!' James was very glad to hear this piece of news.

'It also means that the enemy will have noted your arrival.' Sibelius's voice was again sombre. 'They will try to stop you.'

James felt the sensation of fear creep up his spine. Sibelius laid a reassuring hand on his shoulder and the fear subsided.

'Do not be afraid, James. The Guild will do whatever it can to protect you and we are not without considerable powers of our own. But first you must decide.'

'Decide what?' James asked.

'Whether you wish to help those on the side of Good.'

James didn't hesitate. 'Yes, yes I do. But how?'

'That we do not know. Only time will tell what is to be your fate. Until then many possibilities lie before you,' answered the wizard, 'many paths to choose.'

James looked quizzically at the old wizard. 'Paths? Possibilities?'

'Yes. There are many to choose from, and with each choice you make new paths open before you. Call them opportunities, opportunities to decide what you do next. Thus you can influence your fate James. With every decision you make, every direction you choose. Every path you take.' The wizard looked wistful.

'That is one of the freedoms that you enjoy in the New World. The freedom to choose your fate. In this world, our lives are already written, our fate and destiny sealed. Your fate is written as you live it. Ours is pre-ordained. But such an inevitable fate as ours is not without benefits too. By studying ourselves we may know something of the future.'

'Does that mean you can see what will happen in this world if I decide to accept the fate Eldaterra has for me?' asked James.

'A good question, James. Yes, we can see something of the future, but we cannot see the whole path down which fate travels, only glimpses of it, and I see hope where others may not.' The wizard's gaze burrowed into James's eyes. 'You are that hope, James.'

'Can you influence fate, Sibelius?' James asked.

'Yes, and no,' he replied. 'Yes, if I seek to influence you and your choices. And no since, by the very argument that my fate and destiny are pre-ordained, any influence I have over you is already taken into account. So you see, James, it is really you who has the power.'

James looked perplexed. 'So it is my choices that decide my fate, but I can be influenced.' Sibelius nodded. 'And do I choose my destiny?' James asked.

'Fate and destiny are two separate things. You may choose your fate, but you *fulfil* your destiny, whatever it may be.'

James thought he understood. The wizard rose from the chair.

'Now, James, there is work to be done.'

Half-an-hour later the two of them were poring over the words of the inscription, remembered with the aid of the memory potion.

> *The roaring seas are silent now*
> *And secrets are themselves once more*
> *Complete the earth and fill the void*
> *To mark the time when earth was whole*
> *Locked are these gates to keep the vow*
> *To end a world on barren shore*
> *Protect a place to be destroyed*
> *By man's belief, a lack of soul*

*Yet stand a vigil and wait a time*
*When stranger from the stranger land*
*Before the gates, behind the sun*
*Gives passage to the unsouled son*
*To pass to wild and pass to grime*
*The places split by sea and sand*
*Where one is slaved beneath the gun*
*The other stalked and evil begun*

Sibelius looked disappointed.

'It tells us little now, although it would have been quite useful at the time, James.'

James agreed. The words did indeed describe everything that he'd learned since entering Eldaterra.

'One other thing. We touched on your encounter with the *mortalator*, the drezghul. Bartholomew told me of it while you were recovering. He said something strange happened between you and the creature at the crucial moment in battle, something that stopped the *mortalator* in its tracks. Can you tell me more?'

James thought for a bit.

'I don't recall much about the attack, except that it looked at me, and its eyes were strange. I think I was in a dream. In it there were three princes and each had a large hole in their chest. There was also a boy who stood in shadows watching as hundreds of faceless people walked past him, and there was fire, lots of it . . .' The boy fell silent for a moment. 'When the drezghul looked at me it felt like I was looking into a very deep hole, a pit. Then I thought it said something to me, but I don't remember. . . .'

'James, by looking into that pit as you describe it, you have already faced what few could and yet survived. That creature, the drezghul, is a black myth, something from legend. It is one of the undead, a *mortalator*. The enemy have expended great time and power on creating this entity. Until now they were rumoured to exist, but yours is the first sighting.' The wizard considered this for a moment. 'The powers and intent of *mortalators* is unknown. I fear that they are among the most dangerous of the enemy's servants, and yet I see hope. If a young boy can stop such a demon, then there is indeed hope.' The old man smiled at James. 'I will consider your dream but you should not concern yourself with it. The meaning will not be quickly forthcoming. In fact we may never know, but let us wait and see. Now, James, thank you for coming. I have pressing business to attend to. Please return at sunset when we must decide a course of action.' And with that James departed.

---

They sat on their haunches beneath the low-hanging pine branches deep in a stand of trees. All were exhausted from a hard night's marching. The light was strengthening from the east. They would make no more progress today, not until the sun fell beneath the horizon again.

The leader swivelled on his flat, splayed feet and looked at the company. They numbered perhaps forty. Each hand-picked; the fittest, most aggressive and most skilled fighters in all the eastern army. They wore the armour of their kind, heavy jerkins of leather bound with plates of a fibrous material pummelled into a smooth hard shell and attached to a coat of coarse chain mail sown on to the jerkin. They wore helms of black iron with lethal spike and blade embellishments. Each carried a short halberd consisting of a cruel sickle-like cutter and reverse spike. Equipped thus, they were experts of war. They were olorcs.

'We rest here till dusk. Get your heads down and no talking. The enemy will be watching for us.'

---

In the tower chamber, Sibelius stood silently. He held a long, worn staff of ebony in his outstretched left hand facing south-east, in the direction of Cruxantire, with the sun almost behind him. His head was lowered as he wordlessly spoke an incantation of summoning. Across the great distance the wizard of the Tower of Cruxantire repeated the same words and together they formed an unseen bridge of powerful magic. With this invisible bridge established, the wizards anchored it to a font-like stone structure called a vallmaria, one being in each tower. The vallmaria would hold and maintain the spell until such time as it was released from this task, or the spell broken.

Freed from the necessity to hold the spell himself, Sibelius stepped back and waited. At the other end of the bridge Wizard Ptarmagus would be preparing to send the prisoner. He would be rendered unconscious to make the journey swifter and easier.

In only a few short minutes a crumpled figure lay on the stone floor, successfully transported to the Western Tower. Sibelius sent silent thanks to his friend Ptarmagus and broke the summoning spell.

The wretched figure on the floor was that of a man dressed in dirty, worn clothes. He looked like a corpse, but Sibelius knew that it was simply the effect of the summoning spell over such extreme distances. Sibelius prodded the inert body with a wooden staff and the man startled out of his condition, sat up and looked around.

'Where am I?' he cried in a thin voice full of indignation but mixed with fear. He spoke in German.

'You are here,' replied Sibelius, his voice authoritative.

'Well that's not telling me much.' He got to his feet and glanced about, surprised to discover he was alone with the old grey-bearded man. The visitor straightened his dishevelled clothes and addressed Sibelius.

'Old man, tell me where I am.' His voice was bullying, his confidence returning.

'I think it best if we begin with me asking the questions, and you providing the correct answers,' said Sibelius. The man said nothing, less sure of himself again.

'What is your name?' Sibelius asked.

Silence.

'You are already familiar with the means by which we can extract information,' Sibelius said, watching the man flinch at these words. 'Although I dislike the practice, I am very effective at interrogation.' The prisoner's efforts at resistance failed him and he blurted out a hasty reply.

'My name is Otto Freislung.' The man spoke with an accent. They were conversing in a dialect closely related to ancient Germanic, a language long fallen out of usage in Eldaterra.

'You are Prussian?'

'Nein. I am Swiss, but my family is originally from East Prussia.'

The wizard nodded, picturing in his mind a workable map of the New World. Swiss would place him far to the south, corresponding to enemy-held territory in Eldaterra.

'And how did you get into this world?' After a moment to consider his answer Freislung replied.

'I came through a tunnel in the alpine district of Bern Oberland, near the base of the Wildstrubel.'

Sibelius knew little of the geography of the region. 'Who are you in the employ of, and what is your mission?' he asked.

Freislung shook his head and his mouth clamped shut. The wizard could see and feel the man's state of anxiety. He was very frightened.

'Come now, you are safe from your fears, and you know we will discover everything,' Sibelius said calmly but purposefully.

Freislung swallowed nervously. 'Please. You must understand. They will kill me if I tell you anything . . .'

'And they will kill you even if you don't,' Sibelius answered. He could see the man's nerve was near breaking point.

Freislung broke suddenly, the spirit to resist dying inside him as if a blow had flattened his willpower. Stifling sobs of despair he pleaded, 'You must help me, protect me from them. They will never let me go. I can never go back.'

Gently Sibelius coaxed the information he required from his prisoner. He comforted and promised to help him, but added, 'You have nothing to fear if you are truly prepared to change and make amends. But be warned, Freislung, turn again to the darkness and you will be lost forever.'

❦

'Make ready.'

The troop roused themselves in the dying light of day, anticipating another night of hard marching. The last of their provisions of dried flesh were stowed away and their drinking skins slung on their backs. The leader, Kagaminoc, berated one of their number for tardiness.

Kagaminoc was a large, powerfully built olorc who'd risen to lead by mercilessly killing off all would-be rivals. Only the strongest, most evil and most cunning could command, and there was nothing stronger, more evil or more cunning than Kagaminoc.

The olorcs had come from the empty lands far to the south. They lived in a place where the sun beat down and dried the earth until it cracked and screamed in silent torture, where the land turned to dust and sand, where the only thing that flowed was the thick black ooze from deep within the earth. The olorcs made their lair underground, living beyond the reach of daylight. They dug deep in search of the black ooze that nurtured and fed them. It gave them strength and filled their bellies, the ooze they called Shol.

Kagaminoc swung a halberd over his shoulder and the troop set off in single extended file, running at a pace that would have quickly exhausted a human. But for olorcs it was a pace they could sustain all day and all night, and one that ate up the leagues. As they left the temporary camp, two olorcs stayed on briefly to

*The Balance Between*

destroy any evidence of their stay. They would catch up with the rest of the raiding party.

The troop headed due north, towards the Forest of Lauderley.

ᘝᘞᘝᘞᘝ

James met the wizard at the appointed hour. Sibelius related some of what he'd learned from the prisoner.

'My name is Otto Freislung and I am a Swiss national; my family originally came from East Prussia. I have worked all my life at the Kulbinz Bank in Zurich, that is to say for the last twenty years, where I was a clerk, nothing more. My employers worked me continuously on slave wages. I spent my entire career in a little office counting their money and stamping bits of paper with their official seals, making them rich while I remained impoverished. Then one day I was plucked from obscurity and escorted to the boardroom where I met a director of the bank and was introduced to an important client. The client's name was Herr Dorpmuller.

'Herr Dorpmuller described himself as representing a group of individuals working for a better world. Herr Dorpmuller learned of me through a recommendation and requested an opportunity to interview me. Naturally the directors obliged such an important client. Before the interview the directors made it abundantly clear to me, that I, as an employee, was to agree to any request from the client.

'As a result of the interview I was taken on as an employee of Herr Dorpmuller.

'My new job was to convey letters and other communications to a third party on behalf of my new employer on the infrequent occasions as required. For my first assignment I was ordered to meet Herr Dorpmuller at his mansion in Bern.

'When I arrived there was a dinner party in progress. I rang the doorbell and asked for Herr Dorpmuller. The butler took me to an alcove off the main entrance hall and there I was to remain until I was summoned. I could hear the party in the dining room as the doors were opened and closed. Two people walked to the foot of the stairs. One of the voices I recognised as that of my employer, Herr Dorpmuller. I didn't recognise the other voice.

'I overheard him say, "He is waiting for me in my study, Frau Colbetz. I will give him his orders. Tomorrow I am travelling to China for three months, four at the most. Should I instruct him to contact you?" The unseen woman replied in the negative, and I got the impression that the woman did not want me to know of her involvement. I was convinced that Herr Dorpmuller acted as a go-between and nothing more.

'After that the butler, who knew nothing of the incident, retrieved me and took me to the study where I was instructed to wait. Presently Herr Dorpmuller came in. I was given a small portfolio and a set of instructions on where I must go. Herr Dorpmuller was quite specific in saying that I had to act without question.

'By this time I was more than compliant with my employer, since I was now on a salary five-times greater than I'd earned at the bank. I was also able to enjoy a lot more leisure time to pursue my hobby of taxidermy.

'As per my instructions I travelled into the mountains to a village called Lenk. There I proceeded up the southern valley that led to the lower part of Wildstrubel.

'That part of the mountain is privately owned, and I was surprised to find a gate and fence at the far end of the valley, just below the summer snowline in fact. With a key Herr Dorpmuller had given me I gained entry. Further up there was a tunnel entrance. I walked as far as I could down the tunnel and after that found myself in some other place, a most strange place, which I thought must be on the other side of the mountain.

'There I came upon strange, repulsive creatures, troll-like, straight from hell. Before I could escape they fell upon me and put me in chains.

'Held prisoner and tortured by these horrific beings, there was no doubt in my mind that I had stumbled upon a network of anarchists preparing to overthrow the Swiss government.

'Somehow I survived. Once they had their fill of kicking and beating me they examined the letters I was carrying.

'After that it was only a question of surviving the barbaric conditions and occasional kicks that came my way until I was released and told to await orders. Eventually I was hauled before their leader, General Balerust, handed a letter and told to return whence I came.'

Thus Freislung completed his first trip to and from Eldaterra. He returned twice more in the course of three years, each time to be subjected to the most inhumane treatment but rewarded with increasing quantities of money back in Bern.

On his fourth and final trip there was no return message, so he was thrown out and left to wander in the desolate lands thereabouts. With no way of finding his own way back to the tunnel, he stumbled about the barren countryside, starving and crazed, until captured in the marshes of Turmalor by soldiers of the Guild.

'Why did they just abandon him, Sibelius?' James asked.

'Presumably his usefulness had come to an end. That he was not killed by the enemy is an unusual act of mercy . . .' Sibelius seemed to calculate something. 'But it may also indicate something. We know the enemy has been in communication with the New World for the past three years, perhaps longer. Maybe other couriers have preceded Freislung. Maybe he is simply the first to be released rather than executed . . .' Sibelius appeared lost in his thoughts.

'Sibelius,' enquired James after a while, 'why did they choose this man and not another?'

'It would appear that this Frau Colbetz is the one who first knew of the Old World, and Herr Dorpmuller is her minion. She must have recruited Herr Dorpmuller and then Freislung. As to the choice of Freislung, that is straightforward. Freislung's soul is given over to darkness. He is unimportant in your world, although he has almost certainly acquired a past that would not bear too much scrutiny by the authorities. But this woman was able to see his potential for evil and has used him accordingly. *She* is the real worry.' Sibelius tapped his lip with his forefinger as he contemplated this point.

'I shall make what enquiries I can on this matter, but in the meantime we must assume that Frau Colbetz is the prime concern in your world. Mmmm. This is an unexpected reversal.'

While the wizard and the boy were in conversation, Lady Orlania entered the room. She wore a look of concern as the wizard and James rose to greet her.

'Dear Sibelius, James. I am sorry to intrude on you at this time but news has just arrived.' She turned to Sibelius. 'The forest is whispering. The trees speak of an enemy that has entered our domain. They approach from the south.'

Sibelius threw a look at James. 'This is worrying news indeed. Please continue, my Lady.'

'It is but a small force of olorcs that entered soon after sunset last night. I fear the message has waited until this morning when I walked in the parkland and heard it in the gentle motion of the leaves,' the Lady Orlania apologised.

'What does it mean?' asked James.

Sibelius turned to James. 'James, as you will have gathered, the forests act as watchers on our borders and tell us when the enemy is abroad in the land. The enemy has come searching for you. They fear that you will upset their plans. Now we know those plans reach across the portals, it is certain they will not let you cross back.

'I am afraid, my boy, that they force our hand. This moment has come far sooner than I had anticipated. You must choose now.' Sibelius's voice had grown full of power and strength and James felt the weight of the wizard's words upon him. 'You must decide.

Will you accept a fate from this world and embark upon an undertaking for which you have been chosen? Or will you decline it and return to your own world and leave us to ours?' The wizard watched James closely, adding, 'Only you can make this choice.'

'But Sibelius, you said their plans cross the portals, so I can't escape whatever it is they plan, regardless of which world I'm in,' James argued.

'That is true. But your choice is whether to raise your hand against the enemy, or stand aside and let them do as they will,' Sibelius explained.

But you could make the choice for me,' James pleaded. But the wizard shook his head.

'No, James. Whatever I decide is already writ. Nothing will change. Only decisions by you may change the fate we face – you must decide.'

James looked into the eyes of the wizard. Sibelius stood before him, his hands on the boy's shoulders, like a father.

James thought of the Bandamire brothers and their battle together against the enemy. He remembered the terror and excitement and the elation of victory. James had felt more alive in that moment of success than at any other moment in his life. His loyal friends, Solomon and Bartholomew and Tempus, and now the wizard, and Lady Orlania, they'd all become important to him.

'I should like to do what I can to assist you, Sibelius,' James said in a serious voice. 'I want to help.'

***

Kagaminoc halted the troop and motioned to one of the olorcs. The olorc was skilled as a *sensii*, able to read and interpret the surroundings through the ground, a very rare but useful quality. The olorc fell to his knees and placed his face to the ground. His large squashed nose with its wrinkles and excessive skin now became a tool to assist him. Breathing deeply, vast quantities of dust and foetid air from the tiny pockets of space in the soil flowed into the *sensii*. He exhaled slowly and repeated this again. Sitting up on his haunches, his hands gesticulating in numerous directions as he spoke the crude and base language of the olorc, he reported to Kagaminoc.

Kagaminoc barked out orders. He split the raiding party into two groups. One group he placed under the command of his subordinate, Kreesang, a suitably unimaginative, vicious and ruthless deputy. Kreesang would to cross into the next valley and close on the enemy fortification, set up the transmitter device and protect it until its task was completed. Kagaminoc would lead the other group further north to their second objective.

Noiselessly, the groups parted.

⌘

High up in the tower Sibelius spoke with James as the final arrangements for his departure were being completed.

'James, I don't know what awaits you on the other side of the portal, but I'm sure that it is where you must go. I believe it is somehow connected to this Frau Colbetz.'

James nodded agreement and Sibelius continued,

'The enemy has entered the forest, something that they have not attempted for many years. They are intent on stopping you. You must leave at once if you are to evade them. Return to the Sea Arch and your own world. I'm sending the brothers back through the arch with you. Troops are being sent to find and intercept the enemy, but I must remain here to ensure the safety of the Tower lest they attack here.'

The look on James's face told of his disappointment.

'Understand, James. You must reach the Sea Arch. This is the last opportunity the enemy has to seal your fate in this world, and they will try with all their might to kill you.'

James was shaken at these words.

Sibelius held out his hand, in which lay a small bundle. 'There hasn't been time to tell you everything you should know, but know this. A portal may not let living magic pass between the two worlds. That is why the enemy sought out Freislung to pass through the gates. Therefore we must expect Frau Colbetz to be a witch, or worse, and unable to pass through herself.' The wizard saw the concern on the young boy's face. 'Do not be alarmed, James. In your world magic is scarce and long diminished. Few wielders of power from the past will remain, and what power they have will be limited. Do you not recall your own stories of Merlin? He was a minor wizard who at the time of the separation elected to pass through to the New World. There will be only sorcerers of limited powers, the remnants of the past. That much we know.

'Take this.' He handed the bundle to James. 'It will be useful to you. Inside I have placed two items. The first is an Antargo stone for seeing the enemy, and the second is a pocket edition of *Talmaride's Answers to Questions*. It is a very knowledgeable book. You will find them helpful, I am sure.'

Sibelius guided the boy to the stairs. 'I think we shall take the fast route.'

With that the whole staircase spiral began to corkscrew, whisking them downwards to where the cavalry and soldiers were marshalling.

'Make haste, make haste,' Solomon cried. In the four days since they'd arrived at the Western Tower, Solomon's shoulder had healed and he was preparing the party to depart once again.

The inner courtyard was full of bustle. A troop of horsemen were saddling up, their lances and pendants pointing to the vaulted roof high overhead. A group of elves had already left to track and shadow the enemy. Solomon and Bartholomew were to accompany James back to the portal.

The captain of the guard, a tall, handsome warrior with an imposing jet-black moustache and bedecked in a shining chain-mail shirt and uniform, spotted Sibelius's arrival and cried out: 'Company, present arms!' The soldiers came to attention.

Sibelius waved his hand above his head and then spoke. 'Good people, brave soldiers. The hour of battle draws near. Though we are far distant from the war in the south, so the enemy seeks us out, here in Lauderley Forest. They seek out this boy.' The wizard pushed James gently forward so that everyone could see him.

'They wish to end his life before he can do service to our cause. We must not let them. This boy has placed his life in our hands and we will not fail him as he will not fail Eldaterra.' Sibelius's voice thundered into the chamber and the people of the Western Tower responded in one voice.

'We may not meet for a while, James,' the wizard said through the cheering. He embraced the boy. 'But we will meet again. I know,' he added with a wink.

---

'The tower!' The olorc gestured toward the stone edifice.

Kreesang struck the back of the creature's head with a sharp crack of his halberd. 'Fool! As if I don't know where the tower is. Don't think, just act, or I'll beat your snot-brain until it pores out your ears.' Kreesang was on edge. He didn't like sneaking around on secret missions. 'Give me a massacre any day,' he said to himself. 'None of this skulking and tip-toeing in the shadows.'

He turned to the olorc carrying the transmitter device. 'Place it in the open ground. Be careful that it's set firmly upright and away from trees or overhanging branches, or it will be the end of us all,' he snarled in warning. 'The rest of you, form a defensive ring.'

The transmitter was made of heavy iron standing almost three yards in height with a spike for driving into the ground. A large copper dome was fixed at the top attached to the main rod by alchemic magic. Around the dome ran a crown of short copper spikes. Two olorcs were detailed to stand guard over it.

※

Crouched in the corner of the room, Freislung hugged his knees to his chest and slowly rocked, his eyes squeezed shut. His nerves had got the better of him since he'd been left alone in a room.

'I wish I was back home. I wish I'd never got into any of this,' he said to himself in a wretched, sad voice. What Freislung didn't realise was that these thoughts were keeping him alive. As he sat there with his regrets and his remorse, he held the darkness at bay. Eventually, however, thoughts of a different nature returned. He wished himself at home, not to forget or to make amends. No, to escape back to his own vices. And despite Sibelius's warning, he let the darkness creep back.

'I'll quit my job with Herr Dorpmuller and retire on what I have earned,' he told himself. 'Get on with my hobbies.'

Yes, he could settle somewhere quiet, somewhere where he could go about his nasty habits: the slaughter and dissection of animals; stuffing and mounting of creatures. He found them so irresistible. Yes, he'd find somewhere he could be himself.

But in that moment of self-pitying and mental gratification Freislung allowed darkness to bleed back into his heart. And it became like a conducting rod.

※

Far to the south, where evil lay in its deepest lair feeding on the fear and despair of the world, black storm clouds of fury boiled into the sky. The volcano Vomigragna spewed into the eye of the storm, a giant mushroom of filth blasted straight into the atmosphere. Roiling banks of darkness plummeted from the sky, heavy and laden with choking poison. Deep within the storm a spell was shaped and cast, and the storm magnified the spell. It rippled and spun within the eye, gaining power and intensity before it cannoned outward.

It took form as a bolt of lightning, blasting out horizontally, stabbing forward with blinding energy to connect to the first transmitter. Instantly the bolt arced onwards to the next transmitter placed on the distant horizon, and then the next, and the next, all placed by the olorcs as they'd marched northwards.

※

Freislung stood and crossed to the window. Something was calling to him, something . . .

※

A flash of energy blazed in the clearing for a fraction of a second and then it was gone. When the flash-blindness faded and their sight returned, the olorcs found the remains of their companions who'd been standing guard. They were nothing more than black, frizzled piles of dust and twisted armour.

※

The bolt of lightning sheared through the atmosphere, crackling with surplus energy, the tip of it searching with unimaginable speed for the point of earthing. Striking through the window and blasting into Freisling's face, it catapulted him across the room. At the same time his head and upper body exploded in a spray of flaming crimson gore.

※

The tower was rocked to its foundations. The courtyard was thrown into turmoil, women screaming and horses whinnying, riders struggling to calm their mounts.

Sibelius spoke above the clamour. 'It has happened. They have struck out and dealt with the traitor. They have murdered their own.' The wizard waved his wooden staff above his head. 'Be gone,' he cried. 'Ride out and find the enemy. Go.' He turned to James. 'Can you ride, James?'

'Yes, sir, quite well.'

'Good. Then up on your mount, quickly. You must be away, for I fear the enemy is already at the gates.' He helped the young lad with his stirrup and then reached up and clasped his arm. 'James, now you must be a man. Remember to hold true to that which you love, and you will not go wrong. Go! Be off!'

And with that the gates swung open and the cavalry thundered out, streaming away to the south. James, the two dwarves and an escort of lancers headed off to the west with Tempus running behind.

## 8

# A Surprise in the Dark

**1895**

Upon his return from Zeebrugge, Corrick headed for Scotland Yard where he made enquiries about the Roding case Harrington had mentioned. After some delay, the clerk returned with a worn manila folder with the words 'Metropolitan Police' printed in large black capitals across the front.

The folder was empty. Corrick studied the scribbled notes on the exterior. Duty clerks recorded details of each file's movements and usage. Officer DC Pallbrook had last accessed the folder, and it was he, Corrick assumed, who'd forgotten to return the contents to the folder.

Corrick spotted two more case numbers scribbled down in pencil on a corner of the file. The policeman's intuition pricked. Could DC Pallbrook have requested several files at the same time? Did the clerk make a casual note to remind him of those numbers? Was this a trail, a stroke of luck? Corrick played the hunch, asked for the two file numbers, and the clerk went off to hunt for them.

This time he was away longer. On his return he only carried one file. 'Sorry, Chief Inspector. We only have the file on the Southend murder. The other file never arrived from Essex.' He raised his eyebrows in despair. 'You know how it is with these things,' he added. Corrick had to agree.

'Look here,' Corrick pointed out. The clerk feigned surprise to find both folders empty.

'Good lord, sir. I'll make a note of this immediately and we'll chase up the culprits for the return of the paperwork.' The clerk checked the records. 'Now isn't that odd?' he said. 'DC Pallbrook's mislaid both sets of papers. What is the world coming to?' The clerk began recording the details. 'Now, sir, if I could have your name for the records.'

Corrick leaned over the desk and brought his face close to the clerk's. 'Under the circumstances, I don't think you need to record my details. I didn't, as it happens, get to see the records.' He brandished an empty case file below the clerk's nose. 'So let's just forget my enquiry for the time being and concentrate on getting the paperwork in order.'

The clerk gulped down his sudden nerves. 'Yes, sir. I shall see to it at once.'

Outside, Corrick was oblivious to the light rain beginning to fall. Something the clerk had said bothered him. Essex? But he'd seen the Southend file. What did the clerk mean? And then it struck him. He headed off for Oxford Circus, using the walk to sort out his thoughts.

Half an hour later he stood outside the premises of Holbeck & Newton, Cartographers to the Empire. Corrick entered the premises and an elderly gentleman approached, asking if he required assistance. Corrick said he was trying to locate Burnham.

'Would that be Burnham on its own or with an addendum?' enquired the shop assistant.

'I'm afraid I'm not too sure. What are the options?' Corrick asked.

The assistant proceeded to name them from memory. 'Well,

there's Burnham in Buckinghamshire, of course. And then there's Burnham Deepdale in Norfolk, Burnham Green in Hertfordshire, Burnham Market, Burnham Overy and Burnham Overy Staithe in Norfolk.' He counted them off on his fingers as he recalled them to mind. 'And then there's Burnham-on-Sea in Somerset and ... oh, I forgot, Burnham Thorpe, that's in Norfolk as well. And there's one more ...' He screwed his eyes up, squinted at the electric light bulb and clenched his hands together in professional anguish as he struggled to complete his mental map.

'Ah, yes. Burnham-on-Crouch, in Essex,' he declared in self-congratulation. He looked back at his customer, but the man had already gone.

## 1910

Sir Philip had gone through the employment records of every name on each of the lists that he and Rawlings had gathered. The names were all assembled from clues within the last riddle of the inscription. Lady Jennifer had translated the hidden meaning of the line as a riddling clue, and it was from her list of possible solutions that the two words were recorded:

*And chase the wates in ministry*

Chase =   harry
          hunt
          track
          go after
          hound
wate =    weight(?)      ounce
                         pound
                         hundredweight
                         ton
                         deadweigh

The records themselves were quite dull, just the usual sorts of things employers collect on employees. It was all pretty bland and revealed little. Except for one file. The one whose name fitted the riddle best. They had found their man. Harrington.

The file showed Harrington enjoyed a long career in various departments. He was to all intents and purposes a gifted employee who'd made steady progress up the career ladder but had never quite shone or stood out as an individual.

What made Sir Philip uneasy was that Harrington had the hallmarks of outstanding ability and yet his career was too uniform, too dull. After years of vetting his own staff for security purposes, Sir Philip could spot a potential mole. He was sure Harrington was working to his own agenda, or someone else's.

Sir Philip stood and crossed over to the tall windows that looked out onto Whitehall. His intuition told him this was the man the inscription referred to, the person who might know where his son James had gone.

Sir Philip called his private secretary in the next room to arrange a meeting with Harrington's boss, the Foreign Secretary, Lord Grey. He'd have to move carefully to avoid arousing the Harrington's suspicions.

☙❦❧

It took little over an hour for the cavalry troop to run down the band of olorcs who'd placed the transmitter.

They struck hard and fast, charging down the enemy, lances finding olorc flesh and dealing death.

Kreesang watched helplessly as his command disintegrated under the onslaught. Half his force were dead before the battle had begun! He gave a roar and raced into the fray, bellowing at the survivors to regroup. Olorcs leapt up and sprinted back to join him. Together they formed a new defensive line, halberds at the ready. When a horseman came within striking distance the olorcs spit and gutted the charger in seconds. But outnumbered as they were, they stood no chance.

'Fall back to the treeline,' Kreesang yelled. In front of their position a dozen lancers were circling two olorcs who'd been separated from the main group. 'They are too far away to help,' Kreesang told the remnants of his command. The half dozen olorcs with him kept up a fighting retreat, warding off riders with pikes and halberds. In the distance, the two isolated olorcs fell to the lancers, who then turned to pursue Kreesang's dwindling command. One rider came too close and suffered the consequences. In an instant the horse's head was lopped off and his rider cut out of his saddle.

The sight of one of their number being struck down infuriated the lancers. They wheeled away, turned into line and charged at the beleagured orlocs. The orlocs looked on in dread.

'Into the trees. We have served our masters. Scatter!' Kreesang screamed, and promptly turned and ran.

His warriors were slower to respond. One or two followed Kreesang, but he had a good head start. They were running through the woods as fast as their fear could carry them. Behind them, hooves beat into the ground. The lancers were gaining.

Kreesang fell to the ground, his chest heaving as he struggled to catch his breath. He rolled under a thorn bush, his armour and tough hide impervious to the long thorns. He'd run for three straight leagues without stopping. The sounds of the enemy and dying olorcs were far behind. Kreesang felt sure he was safe. He crawled further into the bush and hid in the lee of an oak tree. He pulled his helmet off and listened, but heard nothing. Cramming his face into the ground he attempted the *sensii*, drawing in odours from the earth to interpret them. There were no horses or men nearby, just as he had thought. Only the scent of dead olorc had leached into the ground, and that at least half a league back. No, it smelled clear. Except for a trace of something, something too remote, too faint to discern. Kreesang thought for a moment longer. He'd smelled it before, but couldn't identify it now. What was it? Where had he smelled it?

He rolled over on to his back to rest and think. His eyes adjusted to the light and shadow of greenery above him. What was it he smelled? His eyes came to rest on a branch. His eyes dilated as his brain strove to recognise and sort the two bits of information, visual and olfactory. The speed of his thinking reduced proportionally. The image above him swam into focus. It wasn't a branch. It was a longbow. Kreesang finally identified what he saw, as two arrows slammed into his chest. An elf!

## 1895

Corrick caught the train to Chelmsford, the nearest town of any size to Burnham-on-Crouch, which lay on the north bank of the River Crouch. It was likely that any investigation would be staged from here.

He arrived within the hour, and made his way to the police station where an efficient duty officer corrected Corrick's assumption. The case in question was being handled by the Maldon police station, where Essex constabulary supported both the excise and customs operations. Corrick thanked the officer and asked the quickest way to reach Maldon. With no direct trains, Corrick borrowed a horse from the police stables.

The ride was a good six miles over rutted, unpaved roads. Corrick was grateful that the horse was docile. It was a long time since he'd ridden.

Apart from a traction engine clanking from one farm to the next, the countryside was empty.

He reached Maldon in due course and dismounted, tethering the horse in the station's stable.

*The Balance Between*

The station was rather large, but it transpired it doubled as the excise house due to the building's close proximity to the river. Though Maldon was not a port of any significance, this stretch of the Essex coast was a frequent haunt of smugglers trading across the channel, and the station held jurisdiction over most of the River Blackwater.

It took only a moment for the duty sergeant to locate the case file. It consisted of nothing more sophisticated than a bundle of unsorted papers tied up in string, undoubtedly making it easier to lose or mislay, and yet here they were to hand. Corrick enquired why it hadn't been sent to New Scotland Yard. The answer was refreshingly straightforward.

'Our governor transferred out of the Met. Came down here for a quieter life, and that he's found,' replied the officer in a strong Essex accent. 'He knows what they're like in London. Send them something and that's the last you'll see of it. And seeing as we'll be the ones who have to close the case, we'll be needing the papers, not some clerk up in the Smoke,' replied the officer. Corrick had to laugh at his frankness.

'If I promise to sit in the canteen and not leave the premises with the file, may I read it?'

'Since you've obliged us with a visit to this beautiful part of the world, it is the least we could allow, sir.' The sergeant smiled. 'Would you like a cup of tea?'

## 1910

They'd been riding steadily for six hours, stopping only to lead the horses over the steep Col. From there they'd ridden hard to make it to the upper valley lodge.

The front door was smashed from its hinges and Bartholomew's mantraps sprung. Oily blood trailed from the dwelling along the path and off into the trees. Solomon dismounted and cautiously entered the lodge. A moment later he called out the all-clear. He emerged carrying a bloodied olorc foot in each hand while kicking a third before him.

'Bloody clumsy creatures,' he said and threw the two appendages over the wall. A well-aimed boot carried the third in the same direction. He winked at James. 'Turnbull, Manchester United, FA Cup final, ninety-four.' James smiled, surprised to discover the dwarf was a fan of the same football club he supported.

'So we know there were at least two of them. You got two left feet and one right,' joked Bartholomew, pointing at the severed feet lying in the grass.

'As like as not they've been killed by their own kind. That's the way of these vermin. They'll not be far off,' the captain of the guard declared. James noticed him for the first time since their mad gallop from the tower. He was oldish, his face weather-beaten while his manner and confidence marked him as a veteran. James felt reassured by this, knowing they would soon be facing the enemy.

Solomon took a few moments to rub his saddle-sore backside before remounting, using the low wall as a mounting block to scramble back into the saddle.

'We ride on. Our orders are to get the boy to the Sea Arch. We'll light our torches at dusk. Move off,' the captain ordered.

They had barely gone a hundred yards when they were set upon. The first of the lancers had just trotted through a narrowing of the path when a halberd lunged from behind a tree, gashing the flank of the mare as it passed. The rider tumbled to the ground as the horse skittered and sank to its knees, neighing in fright. The next rider immediately kicked on to meet the threat, dropping his lance tip and aiming for the enemy. The lance caught the olorc as it stumbled from behind the tree, its progress impeded by the lack of a foot. The point took the olorc in the shoulder and pinned it to a tree behind. Screaming and lashing out with its weapon, the olorc was finished off by a second lance.

The horse was lost, and so the lancer doubled up with James, the lightest rider of the party.

They rode on, more vigilant than ever. Solomon spurred his pony and caught up with the captain.

'The wounded haven't been despatched by their own kind, as is their practice.' Solomon lowered his voice. 'That can only mean one thing. They intend to kill the boy with everything at their disposal, including their wounded.'

'Agreed,' said the captain. 'And that makes them all the more dangerous. They'll use their wounded to delay us while the rest prepare an ambush.'

'In which case the other wounded olorcs are probably just around the next corner,' Solomon reflected.

'Yes, I've sent two riders ahead to flush them out. They will not catch us unawares a second time. And I thank you and your brother for your foresight. Your traps have lost the enemy the element of surprise. They would have planned an ambush for us at the lodge if your traps hadn't put paid to that plan. Take my arm in friendship. I am Dolmir, of the city of Narima.'

'Well-met, friend,' the dwarf replied.

## 1895

The last train to London had left Maldon hours ago and Corrick was obliged to book into a commercial hotel for the night. The next morning, as the carriage swayed from side to side and smoke from the engine passed down the length of the train, filling compartments and eyes with soot from the cheap coal, Corrick mulled over what he'd learned.

Firstly, he'd tracked down the Burnham case to the proper location. So all the murders had occurred with close proximity to the sea.

Next, the Burnham victim was found in similar circumstances

to the others. No newborn infant or foetus was mentioned in the report. No autopsy had been carried out on the grounds of the deceased being of questionable moral character. Instead the mortician had been paid to conduct an appraisal of the body. For this he charged two shillings and so saved the public purse the expense of a visit by a pathologist. But because Corrick kept getting the feeling that information was being deliberately withheld or falsified, yesterday he'd interviewed the mortician.

Corrick had walked to the funeral parlour and stood outside the front window, the company name painted in gold on the glass. Why is it, he thought, that they always have appropriate names? He pushed open the door. A bell rang, and a sombre man in black mourning attire glided between the heavy black-velvet curtains.

'May I help you, sir?'

'Perhaps one day. But for the moment I am here to interview Mr Grimend about a mortician's report of a recent corpse.'

'Deceased.'

'Yes, the body was dead,' Corrick replied dryly.

'No, sir, we refer to a customer of ours as the deceased. It conveys more respect, in keeping with the Alun Grimend & Family ethos,' the man explained.

'If you will wait a moment, sir, I will see if Mr Grimend is available.' And with that the funereal man glided back behind the curtains. Corrick studied the craftsmanship on a display coffin sporting rather fine interior coachwork.

'Good day to you, sir.' A deep voice said from behind the coffin lid. Moments later Mr Alun Grimend stepped around the display and gave a slow bow.

'Good morning. My name is Chief Inspector Corrick. I am investigating the murder of a young woman. I'd like to ask you some questions concerning the mortician's report you provided.'

'Ah yes.' Grimend was a short man with a face like wax, set in permanent sobriety. He possessed a mouth that was disinclined to move when he spoke and eyes that were half open, or perhaps half closed. It was, Corrick observed, like speaking with the dead.

'I recall the work, though it grieves me to hear it called a mortician's report. In truth my autopsy work is perfection, and I doubt if anyone takes greater care of the deceased than Alun Grimend & Family.' He encompassed the room with his arms. 'We seek only absolutes in the determination and preparations for the final laying of a loved one to rest.' After a moment of respectful silence the funeral director continued,

'The young lady died of a number of simultaneous causes. These included massive haemorrhaging of the lower body organs including the liver, kidney, spleen and pancreas, the severing of every major artery and vein below the diaphragm, the rupturing of large sections of the large and small intestine, evisceration of the kidneys, bladder, the reproductive organs and of course the removal of the unborn infant.'

Corrick stood thinking for a few moments. Grimend's delivery had been surgically clinical in its detail and chillingly forceful. Although Corrick had spent many years investigating murders the science of examining dead bodies was quite a recent advance of investigative practices and proved both complicated and exacting. Somehow the mortician's description sounded less like a crime and more like a butcher's list. Did the murderer see it in the same way, he wondered?

'Your report didn't go into such detail,' said Corrick.

'Chief Inspector, in my experience the average policeman is incapable of distinguishing a retina from a rectum. Furthermore, the reports I provide reflect a modest two-shilling service. Were the powers-that-be prepared to purchase a better grade of service then a better grade of report would be resultant. Needless to say,' he went on, 'we provide our services for the benefit of the deceased, not the living.'

Corrick shook his head in disbelief.

'Mr Grimend, can you recall any further detail? This may prove useful.'

'Not for us. We are in the business of death, so to speak,' he replied. But the mortician gave a number of further observations before adding, 'It was a sad end. We conducted the funeral for the deceased. She was never identified by the police and she went into the ground without a single mourner present. So sad, especially considering it was a double tragedy.'

'What do you mean?'

'The woman was gravid,' the mortician replied.

'What does that mean?'

'The woman was with child. Full term. The evidence was pretty much obliterated by the attack, but without question she was carrying an offspring at the time of the murder.'

# 1910

The horses stood blowing noisily, their flanks lathered with sweat. They'd ridden hard since the last footless olorc had been beaten from the bushes and put to death.

Pine trees hemmed them in ever closer. Captain Dolmir called a halt and they lit torches, the new moon being thin and veiled.

'By night the enemy has the advantage,' Dolmir explained for the benefit of his lancers, many of whom were newly commissioned. 'Their eyes are best suited to the dark, for they live mainly underground. With torches we will see what assails us when close to, but the light also marks us out. Keep together. Do not become separated.' Dolmir then turned to Solomon. 'How far now, Solomon Bandamire?'

''Tis no more than three furlongs up this trail. It is as you said. They will seek to ambush us before we reach the Sea Arch,' the dwarf replied. 'We draw near to battle.'

## The Balance Between

Dolmir rubbed his stubbled chin in thought. The last stretch would be the killing ground. He needed a plan.

'Bartholomew, you and James have half-an-hour to make your way around to the north,' he said. 'I'll provide a couple of riders as escort, but stealth will be your best protection. After that I will lead the remainder of the troop forward. Once we engage the enemy we'll make a slow fighting withdrawal and act as the decoy. The olorcs will be intent on killing the boy, so if they see him they'll follow in pursuit. Solomon will act as the double. In the dark they are unlikely to spot the difference. Let's pray the deception works, for there is little else we can attempt,' admitted Dolmir.

Half an hour later the main body of riders set off at a steady walk up the trail. Dolmir ordered the troop to the trot, and then to the canter. With luck, the enemy would concentrate their forces for the ambush and leave the flanks unguarded.

Further up the valley James could hear the troop riding the last furlong to the Sea Arch as, no doubt, so could the enemy. The lancers rode bravely into the ambush.

A cry went up as the enemy rushed the horsemen in the darkness. Horses whinnied in fright, men called out and metal crashed. Sparks flew. The captain barked orders above the yells and screams of the attacking olorcs. Torches flared and flailed the dark, one falling to the ground, then another.

The commotion began its slow retreat back down the valley as Dolmir had planned. The captain intended maintaining contact with the enemy to encourage pursuit by the olorcs.

'An olorc with his blood up can be trusted to run down the length of a lance,' Dolmir had promised his men who were, in the main, yet to be blooded in battle.

As the noise of battle retreated, Tempus led the riders through the trees towards the dark outline of the Sea Arch.

'Wait until they're close, real close,' commanded Kagaminoc in a low growl that carried to every olorc. This was going to be beautiful slaughter, he told himself. They could hear the riders from the other side of the valley.

'The stupid humans are carrying torches.' The olorc leader couldn't keep the sneer of contempt for the enemy from his voice. 'Must be scared of shadows, especially if the lads did a good job further back. Pity to lose them, but a footless olorc is a near useless olorc.' At least he'd given them the chance to taste blood one last time, and not their own. He'd have sooner split their gizzards for stepping in the traps in the first place but he needed to buy time to reach the portal ahead of the enemy and set the ambush. Now the set-up was perfect.

Kagaminoc checked to left and right. The line was bunching a bit. He knew it was nerves; excitement really. They could see the riders coming up the hill now. There would be plenty of human and horsemeat for dinner.

'You!' He elbowed the olorc next to him. 'What did I tell you about bunching in the line? I told you *extended line*. Now get back and guard the portal. Make sure no one breaks through and reaches it.'

The olorc began to protest, not wanting to miss the ambush. Kagaminoc bashed its face with his fist. 'Get going,' he snarled. The olorc, growling in pain and anger, slunk away into the dark.

~~~~~

Tempus gave a howl and leapt at the shadowy figure. The olorc whirled around and aimed a clawed foot at the hound, catching Tempus in the side and knocking him away. Then the creature turned and faced the two horsemen carrying James and Bartholomew. Slashing at a horse with its halberd, the beast went down, tumbling its rider and Bartholomew over its bowed head. The olorc reversed the sweep of the weapon to bring it down on the prostrate dwarf when a lance caught the creature in the throat and tore its head from the still standing body.

'Bartholomew, are you all right?' James called from behind his rider, who was struggling to retrieve his lance from the dead olorc. Bartholomew moaned, stunned by the fall. Ahead, no more than twenty yards, James could see the grey outline of the Sea Arch, picked out by the starlit sky.

'I must help Bartholomew,' he said to his rider, and slipped off the horse, calling back to the man, 'Don't worry. I'll get Bartholomew and we'll head for the Sea Arch.'

⁂

Dispersed in the darkness around him, the olorcs were whooping and hollering as they fought with the cavalry. Despite the clamour of combat, Kagaminoc heard the brief fight behind, near the portal. He stopped in his tracks, wondering what it could be. Why weren't the horsemen disengaging and retreating quickly, or driving through to reach the portal, he wondered? Realisation dawned in his ugly features. He'd been fooled! The horsemen to his front were merely a diversion, and he'd fallen for it. Anger burned in him like red-hot coals, breathing rage into him. For a second he lost control, slashing at everything that moved. 'Back! Back!' he screamed, but his orders went unheeded in the storm of combat. He grabbed the nearest olorc, hit it squarely in the face to break the bloodlust that ran through its veins, and screamed, 'We must secure the arch! The enemy is at the portal!'

The dazed olorc nodded understanding and the two of them ran back at full pelt. In the shadowy distance Kagaminoc could see two figures on the ground and a third in the saddle. He leapt forward, halberd at the ready but his accomplice let out battle cry and gave away the advantage of surprise. Two lances cut the olorc down but Kagaminoc immediately avenged his fallen comrade with a swift chop that beheaded one of the lancers. The second, still in the saddle, spun his horse around and drove it forward to shield the boy from the olorc. Kagaminoc brought his halberd up and the horse died on its feet. The reverse sweep clove the rider from his saddle before the horse had fallen.

James turned to see the last rider fall. Kagaminoc rounded on the boy as James knelt over the stunned dwarf. James looked into the olorc's glinting, wickedly murderous eyes. His hand scrambled to draw the dagger from its sheath. He was too slow. He saw the cruel blade swing up high over the olorc's head, the edge already notched and blunted in places from recent use.

Suddenly the darkness behind the olorc exploded and his halberd went spinning into the black night. An enormous clawed hand raked the side of Kagaminoc's head, tearing off his helmet and an ear, and slicing skin away like a butcher's knife. The olorc let out a spine-wrenching shriek cut short as its head disappeared into a pair of enormous jaws. James was numb with shock.

'Get up, get up, James,' a voice called. He felt a wet slap in the face and woke from the trance to find Tempus licking his cheek. 'The arch, make for the arch. Come on.' Tempus grabbed James's sleeve in his teeth and began pulling, but James's couldn't move.

'Please, James, please,' pleaded Tempus. 'They're coming back.' James somehow staggered to his feet and stumbled forward. Behind them the noise of the olorcs was growing louder. Tempus kept pulling at him. James knew he wasn't going to make it.

Suddenly an enormous arm swept round James and lifted him off the ground. He was being carried. The angry howling of the olorcs came in waves. The enemy was right behind. The distance closed, and then they were through.

## 9

# Footprints and Claw Prints

James felt the slap of wet sand on the side of his face as he dropped to the ground. His ears rang with the roar of the surf pounding on the beach. The darkness hid clumps of marram grass through which the wind whistled. He rolled over, pushing an arm under him to lever himself up. Behind him stood the dark mass of the Sea Arch, looming like a leviathan, the gates chained shut.

He sat up, brushing sand from his face and arms. A large mound sat a short way off. Thank goodness Bartholomew is here, he thought.

Getting to his feet, he stumbled forward towards Bartholomew, spotting Tempus sitting nearby.

He collapsed next to the hound, wrapping an arm about the dog's neck in welcome, and turned to thank Bartholomew for rescuing him. But it wasn't the dwarf. James's eyes widened in surprise.

'So you've decided you can walk after all,' said a big black bear.

James could only gasp in disbelief.

Tempus spoke. 'This is Baranor. He's the one who rescued you.'

The bear looked down his long snout at the boy. He had beady, black, intelligent eyes. He sat as tall as James stood, three times as tall if he were to stand fully upright.

'So this was what all the fuss and bother was about.' Rows of sharp, yellowing teeth flashed in the dark as the bear spoke.

James was unsure how to address the bear. 'How many others came through, sir, Mr Bear?' he asked as politely as possible.

The bear stared at him for a time and then burst into a low rumble of a laugh that made his body quake. 'Others? There were no others, only the foul-tasting creatures – olorcs you call them – but none of them made it through the gates. And you so very nearly didn't make it either. If I hadn't been within a bear-leap of you there would be no cheer in the wizard Sibelius's cup tonight. And to think that old charlatan sent you into this.' The bear rocked back and forth.

Tempus put his head close to James's and whispered, 'He seems friendly enough but be careful. Bears can be awkward and ill-humoured. They don't generally have much to laugh at.'

'What's that, dog? Nothing to laugh at?' The bear's hearing was more acute than Tempus had expected.

'My name is Tempus, and I have heard tell of the sorrow of bears.'

'Mmmm. So you say, dog. But tell me, how do you know this? Do you go hunting bear?' The bear leaned forward, sniffing threateningly.

'My bloodline is bearhound, as you so rightly have concluded. But I've never hunted your species, so I speak only of legend,' Tempus replied in a calm and sure voice.

'What legend is this that you speak of, dog?' the bear Baranor challenged.

'I think,' the young lad started to speak, not wishing the two animals to become antagonists by name and nature, 'that we should get away from the Sea Arch as soon as possible. We've returned to my world and we will need to hide before the sun comes up.' He cast a furtive eye to the east. Fortunately dawn was still some way off.

## The Balance Between

'Why, boy?' asked Baranor who seemed quite a pleasant bear to James. 'I do not fear the little black creatures that taste of the ground, and as to this land, what dangers will we face that a bear cannot overcome?' The bear was chuckling at the thought.

James looked at the giant lump of a fur coat. Baranor was indeed an impressive animal but James couldn't help but note the incongruous sight of a great big bear shaking with laughter. Survival would be no laughing matter for him.

'Mr Bear, sir. In this world bears do not exist. Well, not here any more.'

'How is that?' the bear enquired. 'Did Creation never make them? Did they never come camping?' The bear looked about him at the quiet, darkened coast. 'It seems the ideal place for a bear to dwell. Mmmm, probably Kodiak. They love the water.' The bear looked at James for an answer.

James gulped. 'No, sir, Mr Bear. It's just that, well … a long time ago bears ceased to live in these parts.'

'So they left? Where did they go?' he mussed. 'It must be quite the perfect place wherever they went. It takes a lot to persuade a bear to move house.'

'No, sir. They were hunted.' James looked pale.

'Hunted. Yes. Hunting is good,' declared the bear. 'We all love hunting. But hunting is about winning some and losing some. *The-doe-may-be-gone-so-far-lately-but-we'll-bag-a-roe,*' Baranor sang.

James felt faint at the thought of the bear's response when he heard what James was about to tell him. 'No, sir. They were hunted, all of them … to extinction!'

The bear stopped his humming. His beady eyes got even beadier. 'Are you telling me,' he said in a very low growl, 'that every last single bear in this world is a trophy?'

'No, sir … not all of them. Only in this place. It's an island, a quite small one actually.' James's mind leapt ahead. 'And there are some bears still. They live in zoos.'

'Zoos? Where is Zoos?'

'It's not a place, sir, Mr Bear. They are like … like … homes where bears can live safely.'

'Oh,' said the bear. 'That sounds sensible. Especially if everyone is hunting and the bears are outnumbered.' The bear scratched an ear. James saw the claws flash. 'Nice that they can have a place to rest and catch their breath. Hunts should be fair, evenly matched. Mmmm, yes.'

James wondered how on earth he would correct the misunderstanding. He decided not to try for the present. 'So we'll need to find somewhere to hide during the day.'

'And we'll need to have something to eat,' said the bear.

James and Tempus looked at the bear, anxiously.

'Oh, you two are safe with me,' he said, 'but I do have to keep my strength up. Winter is always just around the corner. Mmmm. I smell mutton. And lamb. Mmmm.'

'But Baranor, we can't go eating sheep from the farm,' said Tempus. 'It will alert the hunters to our presence here.'

'So we must eat and be away from here before they can catch us,' replied the bear, sniffing the night sky expectantly.

The hound turned to James, 'How far must we travel to where we are going?'

'I'm not sure where we're going yet, Tempus. I need to think.' James frowned as he thought of the options.

'Then we need to be as far away as possible when the sun rises,' answered Tempus.

The bear agreed. This was sound reasoning. The two animals looked at James and his two legs. The boy was not built for speed.

'I suggest that you, Baranor, carry James upon your back. That will allow us to go at your pace!' Tempus said this with a cunning look about him.

The bear growled. 'You think yourself faster than me, dog? I could outrun you and outlast you, even with a human on my back.

Even with a human on my back and a belly full of mutton. So watch your every canine step.'

'Well then, Baranor, the blackest of black bears. What say you to a fine leg of lamb, and then a sporting race?' Tempus had persuaded the bear into a plan of action.

'Sounds good to me. Do you really think me slow?' Then, in anticipation of dinner, the bear sang in a tune James vaguely recognised, '*Do-a-ram-for-my-tea-but-cook-it-rea-lly-slow,*' and ambled off into the night.

'They like to hum and sing when they are contented,' whispered the hound to the boy. 'And our Mr Baranor will be quite contented with some mutton in him. His dander was up with the fighting, and he needs to let off steam.'

'But Tempus, why do you call a wild bear "our Mr Baranor"?' asked James as he unpacked his rations from his only-slightly squashed knapsack, which had somehow stayed on his back. He shared them with the hound.

'Because Sibelius sent him.'

## 1895

Corrick had changed his mind and changed his ticket, returning to Cambridge after his visit to Maldon. He checked through his messages at his office and then went home where he lived alone and got into bed. It was midnight.

He was still awake at three o'clock in the morning, considering the rest of Mr Grimend's review of the post-mortem. The man had revealed two other remarkable points of observation; namely, that the victim's lower body cavity was striated with what looked to be multiple blade slashes, and that there had been remarkably little blood inside, as if it had been bled off.

Corrick was more intrigued, however, with a throwaway comment that the mortician had made.

'One could tell a great deal more if the deceased's organs could be recovered.' Corrick vaguely remembered the tattered human entrails sprayed across the bed at Purbeck Hall, but the start of another headache distracted his thoughts. For the moment the Purbeck victim's body was missing in transit to the Natural History Museum, but there were still the remains of the Zeebrugge cadaver available for examination.

The next day Corrick reconsidered the conclusions he had drawn as a result of his most recent enquiries. He listed them.

1  The murders were now strongly linked by the fact that they all took place near a river or coastline. (Query: a sea-going suspect?).
2  All the murder victims died as a result of massive injuries as described by the mortician. (Query: evaluation of organ remains – Zeebrugge).
3  All victims pregnant (?) New-born missing. (Query: second sample from Purbeck – query: Natural History Museum, Oxford).
4  Evidence of attacker using a sharp implement. (Query: marking on body – Zeebrugge, Burnham).
5  Victim's blood drained prior to death? (Query: blood content – Zeebrugge).
6  Evidence missing. (Query: DC Pallbrook, Met).

An hour later Corrick had despatched a note to his divisional commander to request sight of the personnel file for DC Pallbrook of the Metropolitan Police, station unknown. He'd also reached Inspector La Forge on the telephone after a lot of difficulty. La Forge agreed to have the body re-examined by a suitable specialist, the expense to be reimbursed by Cambridge police, specifically for details concerning the internal organs and causation of the wounds. Until he got this report from La Forge, he couldn't follow those lines of enquiry. That left Oxford.

*The Balance Between*

# 1910

'Here. I knew you'd be hungry,' said the bear as he threw down the bloody hind leg of a sheep to Tempus. Tempus thanked him and licked the joint.

'Now. Where to, boy?' The bear swung his head at James.

'Well, sir, Mr Bear. I suggest we head for a quiet place further west, to the moors. But I also think I should head south, to the city of Newcastle, if we're to find out what I'm supposed to be doing,' James explained.

'Good reasons for both directions, boy. But where is your home? Can't we go to your dwelling to rest and consider the options in comfort?' Baranor quizzed him.

'I'm afraid, Mr Bear, sir, that I live far to the south, in Oxford, many hundreds of miles away.'

'Well then, why is the Sea Arch here? If we were hunting I'd suggest we take the shortest route from the den to the quarry and back again. It seems that we are on a hunt of sorts. So we have left the den and come here, not Oxford or Newcastle. And if we're here it is because we're meant to be here. So let us lie up somewhere and see what we can unearth.'

And with that Baranor decided the issue. He waved a shovel-sized paw at Tempus and instructed James how to climb aboard. 'I once gave a lift to a fair forest elf, a beauty she was. She knew how to ride bearback, but I don't suppose you do, boy. Let your legs and feet hang loose around my shoulders. Don't hold them, for I need my shoulders and sides free to work hard. Grab tufts of my hair and twist your hands in them. Go on, tighter. That's how you ride. Now off to the west we go.' Baranor let out a mighty roar of exhilaration and bounded into the night, Tempus racing beside him with the fresh joint of meat clamped in his jaws.

'What was that?' whispered Amanda to her aunt. They'd awoken to the sound of a wild beast, and Amanda had rushed to her aunt's room. Polly the maid crowded in after her. All three were very frightened.

'Whatever it was, we'll investigate in the morning,' said Lady Jennifer, her voice quavering .

※

'Good day, Sir Philip, good day. How is the War Office without Richard Haldane? Is the new man fitting in well?'

'The New Secretary of State for War is "fitting in" well, Lord Grey, busy with his ambitious reforms of the Army and the War Office,' replied Sir Philip.

It was almost four months since the Liberal government of Herbert Asquith had taken power but Lord Grey, as Foreign Secretary, seemed to be a permanent fixture of government.

He nodded sagely. 'And now, Sir Philip, humph, you have enquired about one of my staff – a mid-ranker called Harrington. I have his file here on my desk and have had a quick look at it.' He twisted the end of his beard, mimicking the most recent and irritating habit of the King. 'The man is a solid careerist. Your interest has brought him to *my* attention, Sir Philip.'

Sir Philip knew the minister was only interested because Sir Philip had shown an interest in Harrington.

'I consider Harrington the ideal candidate to liaise between departments at the Foreign Office and the War Office, in the interest of inter-departmental co-operation.' Sir Philip's reply sounded like typical bureaucratic claptrap, the sort that governmental departments thrive on.

'Humph. Well, yes, a good idea. Please feel free to interview my man,' Lord Grey said graciously. 'Let me know when committee selection is at hand. Good day to you, Sir Philip.'

'Good day to you, Foreign Secretary.'

※

'This will do nicely,' said Baranor as he pushed aside the dense hedge and allowed James and Tempus to crawl in beside him. They were high up in the fells of Northumberland beyond the road to Wooler, north-west of Alnwick, where the farms gave way to open moors and occasional stands of wind-bent trees. The bear lay down and his head sank to the ground. With one eye already shut he said to James, 'Now we rest. We will talk later.'

---

Lady Jennifer looked to the clearing sky and gave a silent 'thank you!' The barometer in the farm had risen overnight, and the weather promised to be better.

'I'm ready now,' her niece called from the top of the stairs.

'Good. Let's see if we can discover the cause of that ghastly howling last night.' Lady Jennifer set a quick pace and Amanda had to run to catch up.

They walked down to the beach and then turned south, with the sea to their left. They reached the location where her husband had indicated the invisible arch stood. The two women stopped and stared, amazed at what they saw. An enormous set of animal footprints appeared out of nowhere and made a line across the wet sand before vanishing among the dunes. A set of human footprints ran parallel to these, and what could only be a large dog-like creature had left a third set. The two women followed the tracks back down to the flat expanse of sand where the footprints began. 'It's as if they materialised out of thin air!' Amanda exclaimed in a hushed voice. Despite the air of expectation, they found nothing else on the beach.

Returning by way of the inland road they heard raised voices across the fields. Struggling over a sty and through muddy fields, the ladies made their way towards the commotion. Standing a respectful distance away, they watched a farmer cussing and flaying the long grass with his walking stick. Two farm labourers joined him and they stood examining something upon the ground. One of the men then ran off towards the distant farm returning after ten minutes with a heavy bundle. They unfolded a tarpaulin and covered whatever lay upon the ground.

The women returned to the rented farmhouse in silence. Lady Jennifer was concerned by these latest events, in particular the question of what lay beneath the canvas. Over morning tea, Amanda decided to confront her aunt.

'What is going on, Jennifer?' Amanda asked as she poured the tea.

Lady Jennifer was on the verge of sidestepping the question when she stopped and looked at her niece. Amanda had a very keen mind, one that could handle the facts as well as any grown-up.

'Amanda, dear, I've heard that the farmer lost a ewe during the night. They found the remains this morning.' Jennifer grasped the girl's hands in her own. 'Polly spoke with the womenfolk. Nothing like this has happened in a hundred years. Apparently the poor beast was savagely ripped apart. The farmer is so angry, he's demanding the army be called out to search the countryside for the culprits. They say it's a pack of wild dogs.' Lady Jennifer held back a sob and reached in her skirt pocket for a handkerchief.

'But surely this has nothing to do with James,' said Amanda, leading her aunt to a couch where they sat close together. She studied her aunt closely.

'Amanda,' Lady Jennifer began. 'The footprints we found are connected with James's disappearance. I cannot explain them but I know they are connected. If the farmers or the army find the tracks it may make things more difficult. You must believe me.' The words came out slowly and calmly.

The younger woman comforted her aunt. 'But what are we to do about them?'

'We must erase them,' Lady Jennifer replied.

## The Balance Between

'Darling, what is it?' Sir Philip asked down the telephone. The line was very poor, the call probably routed through half a dozen switchboards up the length of the country.

'Philip, something has happened,' replied his wife, her voice ghostly and hollow. 'We found tracks in the sand. A man's footprints and a dog's. And there was a third set.' Her voice quavered over the hundreds of miles.

'Footprints? What sort?'

'They looked to be those of a wild animal, a large wild animal.' There was a short pause and then her voice returned. 'Amanda thinks they may have been made by a bear.'

A bear! Sir Philip sat forward in his chair, thinking quickly. 'Listen, darling. I know for a fact that bears were hunted to extinction in this country long ago. There are no more wild bears. It was probably a large dog. Please do not get upset. The local constabulary will deal with it. Just keep the door locked at night, and don't go wandering too far from the farmhouse.' He wanted to reassure his wife, but the telephone apparatus was so impersonal that he baulked at telling Jennifer he loved her.

'But Philip, the footprints came out of nowhere, in the middle of the beach. I think they led from the Sea Arch.'

---

The sun was lowering into the west when the three companions roused themselves. They'd covered over ten miles the previous night and James felt sure the local farmers would be unaware of events at the coast.

Tempus sat on his haunches and spoke. 'James, I've been giving thought to what Baranor said earlier. I believe he is correct. Fate has decided this is where we must be. That is why the Sea Arch was revealed to you in the first place.'

James thought about this for a moment. He had no idea where

to go and travelling through the English countryside with a big bear meant they were highly likely to be shot at.

'Listen, Tempus, Mr Bear . . .' James began. 'You need to know some things about this world. Things that will keep you alive here.' Baranor gave an inquisitive smile. 'In this world, the New World, we have no magic, or none that you would recognise as such. As Sibelius described it to me, this world has replaced magic with science.

'In this world there is such a thing as a gun. It can shoot bullets – small pieces of metal – faster and further than an arrow. It is a very powerful weapon that will hurt and maybe even kill you.' The dog and bear exchanged bewildered looks but remained silent. 'This is what they used to kill all the bears, so you must accept that it is dangerous.' He looked very seriously at Baranor.

The black bear looked back at the boy. 'I understand that it is a terrible weapon, if it could kill all the bears. But what must we do to avoid this gun?'

'There is not one gun, there are many. And any human we meet could be carrying one. So we must be very careful. It is best if you, Mr Bear, stay hidden during the day. This world considers dogs to be man's best friend, so you are not at risk, Tempus. Oh, and remember, animal don't talk in this world, so be cautious.'

'As for what to do,' he went on, 'I have these gifts from Sibelius. They might help.' James pulled the velvet pouch from inside his travelling cloak. The pouch's lining had protected the contents. Inside, the book and jewel were undamaged. 'This –' he held out the crystal '– Sibelius called an Antargo stone. He said I could see my enemies with it though I'm not sure how it works exactly. And this book is *Talmaride's Answers to Questions*. Sibelius promised it would be useful.' James opened the pages, only to find them all blank.

'What . . .?' he started but Baranor interrupted him.

'Answers to questions, is it? Well then, boy, why not ask it a question?' said the wise old bear.

## The Balance Between

James looked from the bear to the hound and back again.

'Go on, James. You have nothing to lose,' Tempus agreed.

James shrugged his shoulders. He didn't have the heart to embarrass Tempus or anger Baranor by explaining how encyclopedias should really work. This copy was just a printing error.

'If you say so,' he replied and then half-heartedly asked, 'What should we do?' The page before him remained blank as James knew it would. And then, faintly, four words appeared on the page. They read:

*Use the Antargo stone.*

## ∽ 10 ∽

## Abroad in the Land

### 1895

Chief Inspector Corrick left word with his office that he'd be in contact shortly, and then departed for Oxford, carrying a fresh change of clothes in his portmanteau. He'd lived alone for several years and only the routine of a housekeeper kept the place in any sort of order while ensuring Corrick a steady supply of laundered clothes.

The next morning he was on the steps of the Natural History Museum when it opened, and headed directly to the enquiry desk.

'My name is Chief Inspector Corrick,' he began. 'I wish to enquire after a specimen that may have been delivered to the museum for investigation.'

'Very good, sir,' the man behind the desk said as he opened a large, cumbersome ledger and leafed through the pages. 'Would you have a date of delivery, sir?'

Corrick did a quick calculation. 'It would have been the beginning of the third week in February of this year,' he answered.

'February, I see. Let me have a look. Any idea on the nature of the delivery, sir?' the clerk asked hopefully.

'I'm afraid not. You see, the specimen was supposedly being sent to the Natural History Museum in London but got diverted here instead.'

## The Balance Between

'Ahh, I quite understand, sir,' said the clerk knowingly. Corrick expression showed that he didn't understand so the clerk explained. 'You see, sir, we are quite often confused with our colleagues in London. There would appear to be quite a muddle since the reorganisation of museums in London and it is not unusual for us to be receiving their mail, as it were.' His finger raced down the left-hand column of the open ledger. 'Here we are. The seventeenth of February. Anatomical specimen to NHM, attention of curator. It was delivered to the storeroom pending examination, a large sealed specimen jar.' The clerk continued reading. 'It arrived at the same time as a second consignment for the Pitt Rivers Museum.'

'The Pitt Rivers Museum?'

'Yes, sir, it is one of the foremost museums of anthropological study in the world, located to the rear of the building,' the clerk replied. 'Sir, which constabulary did you say you were from?'

'I'm with the Cambridge Constabulary, sir,' Corrick replied.

'Ah, well that explains a great deal. As I was saying, Chief Inspector, the Pitt Rivers Museum had a delivery at the same time. It was entered as being a "Human anthropological" specimen. To PRM labs. It would appear that it is earmarked for dissection or teaching purposes, since it was delivered in a large chest containing nothing more than a pine coffin. A specimen won't keep for long under such conditions.'

Corrick thought for a moment. He knew he was trying to track down a body. That would be in the coffin. But what was in the specimen jar? Something in the far reaches of his mind was trying to come back to him. What? The note he'd written down? The one about ... the second body? That must be it ...

He asked if it would be possible to inspect the large specimen jar first. A clerk and an administrator were soon found to assist. He was taken into a musty but brightly lit laboratory with tall windows down one wall and work benches set out in ranks across the room.

'Hello,' a bespectacled man in a white laboratory coat greeted him. 'I am Professor Pollen, senior research fellow with the University Museum.' He held out a hand and Corrick shook it. 'I understand you wish to examine a recent acquisition. Fine. They're just bringing it in now.' And he turned as a brown-coated porter staggering into the room, his arms wrapped around a large, thick-walled, glass specimen jar. The top of the jar comprised an enormous glass dome and the lid was sealed with a wax rim.

The porter placed the jar carefully on a workbench and wiped his brow. Corrick gazed at the contents that rocked backwards and forwards in the briny solution.

Professor Pollen referred to the packing notes. 'I see that the contents are described as "large rodent creature". Mmmm. Not much of an attempt at cataloguing or identification. Very shoddy work.' He shook his head in professional displeasure as he read on. 'And there doesn't seem to be anything to say who's responsible for the labelling and preservation work. Mmmm, careless of them. Very careless indeed.' He looked at Corrick. 'Shall we see what we can make of it then, Chief Inspector?' and he turned to examine the specimen jar.

Floating behind the uneven, distorting glass was a large creature the likes of which the policeman had never seen. Evidently Professor Pollen also found it to be a revelation, as he wore a look of consternation.

'I am afraid to say this is not a rodent of any sort, Chief Inspector. Superficially one might think it a member of the order *Rhinophidae*, but it is much too large and the bone structure is not correct. No, this is something quite different,' Professor Pollen stated.

'Could you tell me exactly what it is then, Professor?'

'Well, we will need to examine it more closely. I'll have to stop what I am doing. That'll take a good fifteen minutes to put in order. After that I suppose that we –' he looked at the porter to recruit him into the task '– can get cracking at once. Should have an answer for you within the hour, Chief Inspector,' he said obligingly.

Corrick thanked the man and then took his leave to make enquiries at the Pitt Rivers Museum. There too he found an academic happy to assist him with his enquiries. Corrick was led to a low-roofed vault under the main exhibition hall where yet another brown-coated porter searched through a large array of boxes and cases stashed in long piles along the floor and on shelves running the length of the back wall.

'No, sir. It must be in the preservation room. If you'd like to follow me.'

They walked through a narrow whitewashed tunnel and into what looked to be a workshop of some description. It contained giant copper kettles and heavy-looking tin baths. Marble workbenches were covered with brown and green glass bottles and metal utensils lay to one side fresh from an autoclave.

'This is where we do the preservation and embalming work, sir, and through there –' his arm waved to a flight of steps leading up to a sort of greenhouse '– is where we do taxidermy and fine detail work. Because of the lighting, of course,' he added.

The porter again rummaged through various crates on the floor and peered into several of the covered baths. At last he gestured to a metal container, perhaps six feet in length, placed on a low bench to the rear of the workshop. The clerk read a label silently and then straightened up. 'This is the one, sir. No notes were received with it. I believe one of the staff may well have decided to use it for practical work with the students.'

Corrick thought about this for a moment. 'Is there any way we can get a detailed examination of this corpse?' Corrick leaned over the metal container and lifted the wooden lid. Inside the corpse lay stretched out, the body glistening from the effects of preservative fluids. The stench rose to sear the men's nostrils. Corrick gagged and stepped away. The porter quickly replaced the lid.

'I can make enquiries, sir, but it may be best if you were to speak to the curator directly. He can make the arrangements. Let me take you back to his offices.'

'Hello. Hello. This is Chief Inspector Corrick speaking. Are there any messages for me? La Forge did you say? Right ho. Thank you.' He replaced the telephone receiver and looked up at the duty officer. After making the necessary arrangements to have the corpse examined, Corrick had taken a cab to the main police station on Oxpens Road, to use the station telephone.

'I need to place another call, sergeant, to Belgium,' he requested.

'Very good, Chief Inspector. It may take a while. Shall we bill it to Cambridge?' the officer asked cheekily.

He got a message through for La Forge to call him and then waited twenty minutes for the return call.

'Chief Inspector, bonjour. I have the findings of the examination you requested. It is indeed interesting. The pathologist expressed the opinion that the tissues were torn with a sharp instrument, or instruments. The markings are consistent with a pattern best described as being claw-shaped rather like the marks of a wild beast, or perhaps a trident spear or something similar.

'These same markings were found on the organ remains, as if the body and its contents had been slashed from within. Finally, the pathologist did note there to be very little settling of blood. This would suggest an abnormally high blood loss at the time of death.' La Forge's voice went quieter. 'You may recall, Chief Inspector, that at the scene in Zeebrugge there was a lot of gore, but much less blood. I believe you have a theory concerning this, yes?' asked the Belgian.

'I have a lot of theories, Inspector La Forge, but very little yet to substantiate them.'

# 1910

Jennifer had felt compelled to disclose more about the circumstances surrounding James's disappearance to her niece. Amanda accompanied her back to the beach and they had carefully erased all evidence of the footprints, all the while Lady Jennifer revealing the full story to her.

༄༅

'I should like to see the place. I am told it resembles Bavaria but without the mountains,' said Frau Colbetz to the fawning Julius Dorpmuller. She gazed out the window of the private railway carriage heading north through the drab grey of the Ruhr valley, the industrial centre of Europe. 'Oh, to escape this little human world.' Her accent was as heavy as her perfume, both reeking of money and privilege, something Dorpmuller found very alluring.

'Yes, Fraulein. Beautiful, if not quite as beautiful as your homeland.' He held her hand in his and lightly stroked it.

'Don't try to worm your way any further into my affections, Julius, or you may regret it,' she warned, flashing her perfect teeth at the obsequious man.

Frau Colbetz was a most unusual woman. She could trace her ancestry right back to the times of the High Court of Chivalry, when Minnesanger in Germany rivalled King Arthur in Britain. The Colbetz family was reputed to be descended from Charlemagne, perhaps even Attila. To Herr Dorpmuller, this woman was a goddess.

'I shall need to meet with Frau Feder. We shall of course travel together.' She fixed an icy stare on Dorpmuller. 'Julius, dear, you will make all the necessary arrangements. This meeting must go off without a single mishap, you understand. There can be no mistakes.'

Dorpmuller felt his blood run to ice. He shivered in delight. How he loved the fear that rose up inside him and the nauseous waves that made him feel faint. 'Yes Frau Colbetz. Everything will be as you desire,' he panted.

༺༻

James and Tempus made their way down to the road and sat on the verge. They had left Baranor sleeping in the hide.

James pulled the Antargo stone from the pouch and held it to his eye, squinting through the clear, blue-tinted jewel. Through it he could see pale blue fields and pale blue trees. Presently a cart drove past and James and Tempus begged a lift from the driver, who was heading to the small town of Whittingham, a few miles to the south. James studied the back of the driver through the jewel, but he just turned pale blue.

When they arrived at the market square, James climbed down and thanked the driver, Tempus at his heels.

'Remember, Tempus, in this world animals can't talk,' James reminded his friend.

They found a place at the top of the town hall steps overlooking the busy market and James proceeded to spy on every person through the jewel. They all remained a shade of pale blue. After a time James moved to a new location between the railway station and the town hall. Here they sat and ate their remaining provisions, all the while checking every passerby.

A passenger train arrived at the station, big billows of white jetting up above the station roof to signal the train was stopping. Passengers disembarked on the southbound platform and rail porters in blue and gold uniforms marshalled luggage and hatboxes for the first-class customers. A motor car rolled up to the front of the station, its driver calling, 'Guests for Cragside. Guests for

## The Balance Between

Cragside.' A stream of men pushing trolleys laden with baggage navigated against the tide of people to the waiting car. James watched as an elegantly-dressed woman was helped into the rear of the motor, her baggage piled high about her. The car's hood was down and the chauffeur turned to talk with the lady. James couldn't hear what was said but saw the man nod in agreement and replace his driving gauntlets. The car was cranked over by a porter and, with a wave of thanks, the driver slowly edged the car through the crowds and set off southwards. James raised the jewel to his eye, wondering if the burgundy-painted car would be better suited in pale blue.

James was shocked to find himself staring at a tall dragon, sitting erect and imperious in the back of the motor car, its tail making lazy coils in the passing breeze.

'You must get back to Baranor, quickly,' James stammered to Tempus. 'I'll stay and try to find out more. Meet me on the road south. We must get to Cragside and find out what's going on.' Tempus gave a wag of his tail and sped off.

James sat a while longer and watched the station. Another train pulled in, this time heading north. Passengers boarded and left the train, but none of them changed shape when James held the Antargo stone to his eye. Finally he set off to rendezvous with his friends.

Tempus came bounding up to James with his tail wagging. 'I've got him,' the dog said. 'Follow me.'

The two of them raced away, James eventually short of breath and calling for Tempus to slow down. They rounded a hill where a tumbled-down stone building sat by the side of a stream. Two gnarled, stunted trees grew in the lee of a wall.

Beneath the trees they found Baranor, together with the carcass of a recently-killed sheep.

The bear looked up. 'I brought dinner with me. Thought it

wouldn't be missed for a while, on account of there being so many sheep up in these hills.' Baranor looked wistful. 'This country is ideal bear country. I reckon it's so long since a bear roamed these parts that the sheep have forgotten to be afraid.' He prodded the dead animal with an outstretched claw. 'This one just watched me amble right up to it. A very dumb animal.'

James looked at the sheep with a mixture of revulsion and hunger. 'I'll make the fire if you like,' he offered.

The bear looked closely at him and said, 'I am partial to cooked meat it must be said. The smell of roast mutton makes my mouth water like a rain cloud. But I'm less taken with fire, boy. Mind how you manage it.'

In the waning light of evening they sat around the fire, picking at the last of the meat. Baranor had a leg bone between his teeth, cracking it and sucking on the marrow. James felt contented as he leaned on the big bear and felt the warmth of his shaggy fur coat. Tempus lay with his paws before him, alert to the noises out on the moors.

'Don't worry, dog,' said the bear. 'All's quiet.'

'Yes,' replied Tempus, 'and it's time we were going.'

## 1895

'Chief Inspector, we have a most unusual situation here,' the curator of the Pitt Rivers Museum began. Corrick had returned to the museum and was ushered into the Department for Human Anatomy where a small group of men were waiting for him. 'This body, according to my colleagues, is that of a young female who died in quite unusual circumstances. I will ask them to explain.'

'My name is Doctor Pearson, head of the department,' one of the gentlemen began. 'With me are Professor Kingston, head of Biological Anthropology, and Professor Rees of the medical school. Together we have conducted a thorough examination of the corpse.' Dr Pearson looked over his half-moon spectacles and absent-mindedly pulled at his earlobe. He was a short, frail, bookish sort of man with a slight list to one side and a left hand that remained in his coat pocket. 'I was asked by the curator to examine the body and in light of the circumstances agreed. Upon my preliminary findings, I called in my esteemed fellows.' He turned to the man introduced as Professor Rees.

Professor Rees cleared his throat. 'My findings are that this woman suffered death by gross destruction of the lower anatomy, probably the result of an attack by a wild creature. Together with Doctor Pearson –' he politely acknowledged his peer with a deferential bow of his head '– we conclude that the creature sought the removal or destruction of the unborn infant.' Corrick secretly cursed under his breath. This was the one thing he hoped they wouldn't discover.

'Furthermore,' continued Dr Pearson, 'the attack resulted in the blood being drained from the victim by means unknown.'

'And therein lies a dichotomy,' Professor Rees added. 'A wild creature would not be capable of draining blood from a victim, except of course some sort of giant bat.'

'And there aren't any of them . . .' stated Dr Pearson.

'So you see, Chief Inspector. The material evidence all points towards an attack by a wild beast: striated claw marks, systematic shredding of the abdomen in a similar fashion and so on. Yet disproportionately low levels of oedema post rigor mortis suggests the forced removal of blood prior to death, an indication of premeditation.'

'And then there are Professor Kingston's findings,' continued Dr Pearson.

'Chief Inspector Corrick,' began the third academic. 'I was only asked to consider the biology of the victim in case there were any anthropological issues that may give the police clues as to the origin of the dead female. I am able to conclude with a very high degree of scientific confidence, but absolutely no logical assurance, that this female is not from any racial grouping known to science. Although she appears to be, she is in fact, not even human.'

'Chief Inspector, you're back so soon.' Professor Pollen was clearly unprepared for the policeman's return, despite it being at the agreed time of three o'clock. 'I am so sorry to ask you this, Chief Inspector, but could you give us a few more hours? What we are looking at is something quite unusual. I wouldn't want to rush into giving you incorrect information a second time,' he pleaded sincerely. Corrick agreed and went off to sit in a nearby coffee house.

When he returned to the Natural History Museum it was closed. Corrick knocked on the large wooden entrance doors to be let in. Professor Pollen had been joined by a large group of fellow scientists. There was a buzz of excited voices around the laboratory workbench as he approached. Professor Pollen spotted him and the crowd of academics made way for Corrick who joined the professor in the centre of the gathering. Without formalities the professor began.

'What you see here, Chief Inspector, is quite the most bizarre specimen the University Museums have ever received.' Laid out upon the marble table was what looked like an enormous bat. Its wingspan was fully four feet and its tail hung over the end of the bench, dripping preservative fluid on the ground. Similarly the neck hung over the far side, out of sight.

Professor Pollen addressed the audience at large. 'Gentlemen. You will see that it's possible to make out the bone structuring in the wings. Please note that there are six finger bones making up each wing. In zoological classification terms this means the creature is not a member of the bat family, since bats have five finger bones in their wings. Furthermore, the creature is not a bird, since it lacks any feathers whatsoever.' The professor looked over his reading spectacles at the gathered faces, as if he were conducting a lecture, and continued, 'Therefore, one may presume the specimen to be of a more ancient order, perhaps newly discovered from deepest Africa. Perhaps it is related to marsupials? However, three aspects should be considered. Firstly, the tail is a skeletal feature one would associate with mammals, with a high degree of muscle and bone to enable it to act as a limb rather than a simple vestigial balance. Secondly –' and here the professor used a small wooden rod to lift the head into view '– one may see that the head consists of a bird-like cranial structure, but without a conventional bill. Instead this creature has a soft palate and a prehensile tongue as one finds in certain specialist or higher orders of mammalia, the dromedary for example. Please also note the complex and highly-developed dentition, marking it out clearly as the teeth of a predator, perhaps that of a crocodile or similar creature.

'Finally, and most conclusively, the evidence of the upper body.' The professor nodded to a technician who stepped forward and, with heavy gauntlets on his hands, proceeded to manoeuvre the preserved creature's body around the table.

'Please note that below the upper-wing limbs we find a pair of highly-developed articulated legs, capable of grasping and, almost – but not quite – uniquely, the possession of an opposable fifth claw, similar to that in primates and man.' An audible gasp went around the room. Corrick, too, was stunned at the information, although he had no real idea of its implications. 'Gentlemen, we have a creature that is not of the group Insecta, yet has six working limbs.'

Professor Pollen paused while the room filled with chatter. He tapped his stick on the marble surface for silence, and continued. 'There are a number of other observations that are of interest, but these are of less importance.' He waved the stick over the specimen.

'Therefore, in summary, we have a specimen before us that is mammal-like and yet not mammal-like, bat-like and yet unlike any bat – or any flying creature for that matter – that science knows of, bird-like but without feathers, predatory in nature with dentition that is both complex and yet closest in type to the ancient order of Reptilia, possessed of six working limbs in a similar arrangement to certain groups of Insecta but sharing no other similarities with that Order, and finally the creature has an opposable fifth claw – finger, if you like.'

The room burst into uproar at these findings. Corrick stood quietly alone in the midst of all this, an outsider within a closed community. The wooden stick beat down upon the bench.

'Gentlemen, please,' called Professor Pollen above the noise. Slowly the noise subsided. 'Thank you. To conclude this informal seminar I would like to thank Chief Inspector Corrick of . . .'

'Cambridgeshire Constabulary,' Corrick was obliged to speak.

'Chief Inspector Corrick of the Cambridgeshire Constabulary for bringing this magnificent example of a *Hydra* to our attention.' The words rang out clearly and slowly, as the professor deliberately enunciated every single word. 'I am of course speaking of a mythical creature. Here today we may all learn the importance of sound scientific research, for this, gentlemen, is nothing more than a hoax!' His words rang with portentous supremacy as Corrick turned scarlet and elbowed his way from the room.

# 1910

Later that night James and his two animal companions passed into Rothbury Forest, to the east of Cragside. They found a suitable place to lie low, under an overhanging escarpment where a cave ran a good way into the cliff face. The entrance to the cave was well hidden by bushes and small trees that grew nearby. Baranor had brought provisions, though James was less than pleased to sit astride the bear sharing the ride with yet another dead sheep. The forest was remote and quiet, allowing James to light a small fire.

That night the three of them snuggled together and slept as soundly as bears.

❦

Sir Philip called his private secretary to arrange a formal interview with Harrington, on the pretext of a new inter-departmental co-ordination initiative. To avoid spooking the man Sir Philip had the meeting booked in the name of one of his junior staff. He didn't want Harrington to suspect anything until the meeting...

# 1895

Corrick knew there was nothing more for it but to confront Harrington with the information he had and somehow extract the final pieces of the jigsaw from the civil servant. He was definitely holding something back.

Corrick stopped briefly at the local police station to place a call to Harrington and was surprised when he came straight on the line. It was as if the man had been expecting his call. Corrick gave him a cursory greeting and demanded they should meet at New Scotland Yard tomorrow.

'Of course, Chief Inspector. But would you oblige me by joining me on one more trip? It will help a great deal to explain everything. Can we say eight o'clock tomorrow morning sharp? At the Pools of London? Very good then. Goodbye, Chief Inspector.'

## 11

# The *Parsimony* Paradigm

Corrick was at the Pool of London at eight o'clock sharp. The waterway was never busier than at this time, with ships and vessels of every size and nature moored or in the process of moving up and down stream. He watched the forest of black timbers that rose above the docks, like trees burned by forest fire. The china clippers, the coal barques and down-at-heel East Indiamen of a previous century crowded the water. These were the last huzzah for a fragile and dying breed. Amidst the sailing vessels there were also the harbingers of change, steam and paddle. The noise and grim filth of this newer breed of vessel already clung over the docklands like the smog of war: industrial power versus nature and the elements.

Harrington was waiting for him in the Excise building. Despite himself, Corrick smiled and shook the man's hand as they passed through the warehouse to the quay.

'I have arranged for the use of a different vessel on this occasion, something of a treat, really,' said the civil servant. They passed down a gangway and reached the gently rocking deck of a long, sleek vessel. 'She's His Majesty's Excise Vessel *Parsimony*, and a more aptly-named ship you will never find.'

It was clean and brand new, still in the process of being fitted out, but there was nothing particularly special to see.

## The Balance Between

Harrington guessed what Corrick was thinking. 'It's all below decks, Chief Inspector, in the engine room. This vessel is the first of her kind, running a twin screw set-up from a syncromated gearbox. Only one engine, of course, not enough room on a ship this size for two, but the arrangement gives excellent manoeuvring. It's particularly useful when chasing smugglers close inshore.'

Harrington waved up to the captain on the open bridge, who called orders to the crew. 'Let go aft. Bring the helm around. Let go fo'rard. Push away. *Put your back into it, man!* Helm to midship.' And so it continued as the crew worked the vessel into the midstream and eased her nose towards the open sea.

Harrington and Corrick were offered steaming cups of tea and they stood sipping from enamel mugs as the commercial world of the docks slipped past.

'I know you're keen to question me, old chap.' Harrington smiled over the lip of the mug. 'But for reasons that will become clear soon, can we wait until we've reached our destination?' Corrick nodded agreement as he took a gulp of tea. He'd bide his time a little while longer. Besides, he was enjoying the view for the moment. Corrick watched as the cityscape fell behind and the riverbanks emptied to reveal a gentle green horizon of farmland and wilderness on either shore. To the north a dark smudge on the horizon looked to be gas works. To the south a string of little fishing harbours dotted the shore, with Chatham just off in the distance.

Corrick made out the towering thunderhead of a Channel storm to the south east.

Harrington acknowledged it. 'We should be there and back before we're obliged to pull on sou'westers.'

By eleven they stood off the Essex coast, to the east of Shoeburyness. Captain Gilchrist had invited the men to share his bridge for

*The Balance Between*

the duration of the voyage. They'd just passed through a line of buoys stretching north-easterly.

'They're artillery range buoys,' the captain explained. 'The navy use Foulness Island for gunnery practice. It makes for an ideal, if risky, smugglers' coast, and the wildfowl is quite exceptional to boot.'

Behind them the southern horizon darkened. Mindful of this, the captain turned to Harrington. 'If I may point out, we're on a rising tide. With the wind backing a few degrees we may be placed at a disadvantage. Should the storm break we will be in harm's way.'

Harrington patted the officer's arm in a reassuring fashion. 'And with this vessel's seakeeping abilities that is precisely why we are aboard the *Parsimony* today, Captain.' He turned to Corrick. 'Now, Chief Inspector, we're going to make landfall just along here, once the men have cleared a boat for us. We shall row in together. The tide seems to be agreeable with this proposal, if you are.'

Corrick agreed and presently they were seated in a small wooden rowboat in the lee of the larger ship.

The captain called down to them. 'Be sharp about your business, if you please, gentlemen.'

Harrington looked up and ordered, 'You will stay on station until you recover us, Captain.' Corrick noted that for some reason Harrington exerted overwhelming authority over the captain. The captain's face was nonetheless red with indignation.

'Right, Chief Inspector. I'll row while you ask your questions.'

Corrick considered for a moment where to begin. 'The crimes,' he said, 'in chronological order, were Burnham, Roding, Southend, Purbeck and Zeebrugge, all situated on or near the coast. Each of the victims may be linked in some way to the sea. You tried to hide these facts. Why?' he started.

Harrington gave a pull on the oars. 'In actual fact I didn't hide anything from you, I merely failed to correct the mistakes of others. And of course, I didn't mention this to you.'

'Why?'

'Well you see, Chief Inspector, it's important that you investigated each of the cases as thoroughly as possible rather than simply reading reports and listening to the opinions of others. I needed your investigative mind to tease out the clues and facts. In learning the facts first-hand you would come to *see* the truth.' Harrington thought for a moment longer. 'In any event I do believe you were able to ascertain more from the evidence than I.' The little boat rode up and over a wave like a cork, and spray caught in Corrick's face.

'And yet the evidence was not always available,' Corrick challenged. 'When I went after the corpses taken from Purbeck they had disappeared – or almost disappeared, I should say.'

'Yes, Chief Inspector. The corpses were the most contentious aspects of the whole investigation. They would have thrown up too many unbelievable questions had you examined them early on in your investigations. They may well have dissuaded you from continuing with the case. So I had them spirited away. I had intended you to find them once you had run to ground all other avenues of enquiry.'

Their eyes met in understanding.

'Yes, Chief Inspector, I am aware of your second trip to see the Belgian, La Forge. It was clear he wasn't prepared to talk while I was with you. You policemen do seem to stick together, and he saw through my charade immediately. But I also knew he'd eventually talk with you. That's one of the reasons I didn't want to waste any time on the first trip.' He leaned on the oars. 'What did he tell you?'

'He showed me a portion of anatomical evidence that was found only later.' The policeman went on. 'You knew the victims were all pregnant women. But did you know it was because they were pregnant that they were attacked?'

Harrington nodded as he pulled on the oars. 'Yes,' he replied. 'You discovered enough to learn the truth.' He sounded enigmatic, as if he was an outsider. 'Your investigations provided you with sufficient insight before your final trip to Oxford, Chief Inspector. Despite the scientific opinions to the contrary, you saw what you saw, not what the scientists wanted you to see. You believe the unbelievable!'

Corrick yelled his reply above the crash of the surf as the boat approached the beach. 'The victims weren't like normal women. The scientists said they weren't even human. They'd never seen a being like them before. That's why you had the bodies disappear.' Again Harrington nodded. 'So without a human victim it wasn't really a murder case. But that still leaves a lot of unanswered questions,' the policeman said, as the boat grounded in the surf.

## 1910

Rawlings waited inconspicuously in a doorway. In his pocket was the list of names supplied by Sir Philip. The list consisted of just two names. Rawlings was tailing the first individual, and he'd led him a merry chase that ended at the Houses of Parliament. Rawlings would need a pass to enter the Palace of Westminster but Sir Philip could provide that. In the meantime, Rawlings would investigate number two on his list.

'Guten morgen, Frau Colbetz.' The officer gave a rigid, formal bow as his guest stepped aboard the warship. 'His Imperial Excellency Kaiser Wilhelm II extends his most gracious welcome and, on his behalf, has requested that I place myself and my ship at your disposal.'

'Why thank you, Captain,' Frau Colbetz purred as she looked around her. 'My! Isn't it a wonderful ship. What do you call it?'

*The Balance Between*

She took his arm and led him away for a personal guided tour of the vessel. Captain Raeder melted in the heat of her brilliance and delighted in granting her request.

An hour later they were on the ship's bridge and Captain Raeder gave orders for their departure.

'As I understand it, Frau Colbetz, the light cruiser *Ausburg* is to convey you and your small party to Britain for a conference of some international standing,' the captain surmised.

Frau Colbetz gave a naughty grin and flicked an imagined piece of thread from the officer's arm, brushing against him sensuously. 'Captain, you are almost perfectly correct. We are on something of a "mission" for Kaiser and country. If you could deliver us safely to where we need to be, and wait for us, we won't be very long.' She ended with a little pout, to which the captain responded, 'Your wish is the wish of my Kaiser, Fraulein.'

'In that case, Captain, could you arrange for those lovely men in uniform to embark with us? I do so like to make a grand arrival.' She pointed to the Bremenhaven dockside where a company of naval marines were marching.

Once at sea, the cruiser *Ausburg* made for the coast of northern England under full steam, her bows cutting through the unusually calm North Sea waters. Below decks Frau Colbetz held court in the captain's wardroom.

'Well done, Julius. You have exceeded yourself today.' She gave praise lavishly, watching her lackey lick it up. She turned to her travelling companion, Frau Feder. 'Now, Eva, we are expecting . . .?' she enquired.

'There have been two hundred and eighteen replies to the two hundred and twenty invitations sent out. Frau Schwerin is expected to attend although she is arriving directly from Egypt. And we have no knowledge of Mrs Sedger of Hartford, Connecticut.'

'Good. That will be a near complete turnout.' Frau Colbetz looked down the list in front of her. 'I see that we can all be accommodated in the grounds of the estate.'

'Yes, Helga.' Frau Feder addressed her informally, hesitantly. One could never tell with Frau Colbetz, so much depended on her mood. 'I've arranged to have the entire estate and surrounding countryside cleared of occupants the week before and after our conference, with the added inducement of a quantity of English pound notes, of course.'

'Good. It will be much more convenient. Now, I have asked, no, demanded, that our nice young captain sail us directly to the coast near Cragside. We shall disembark the Benz and motor up to the house. The boat and her crew will wait for us to return, and then we'll scoot back home to a hero's welcome, I should imagine.' Her words were full of confidence as she helped herself to the contents of the captain's drinks cabinet.

## 1895

They dragged the dinghy up the beach, out of the crashing surf, their shoes and trousers getting soaked in the process.

Harrington yelled across the booming surf: 'See anything?'

The policeman looked up and down the beach and across the low rugged tundra that backed onto it. He shook his head.

'Tell me then, Chief Inspector, what are the unanswered questions?'

Corrick looked at him. He replied, 'That creature, the other thing found at Purbeck. It disappeared with the victim. When I eventually found it and had it examined, it was declared a hoax. But it isn't, is it? It's genuine.' Harrington nodded and Corrick continued, 'At the time there seemed no rational explanation for what happened the night of the Purbeck murder. All the evidence was there, but I couldn't put it together. It was too fantastical, impossible. And then, afterwards, I started having headaches and forgot the details. But now I see,' realisation at last dawning on him. 'It was the creature, that abomination, that killed the woman. It was growing inside her. It literally clawed its way out. *It* was the offspring!'

Rain began to fall.

'Chief Inspector, look around you,' Harrington commanded.

Corrick turned and looked down the beach. An enormous gateway stood a short distance away, complete with open portcullis, shrouded in the rain.

Corrick could have sworn it wasn't there a moment ago. He looked back to Harrington incredulously.

'It was there all the time, only you couldn't see it,' Harrington explained, holding on to the boat gunnel to steady himself in the rising wind. 'To know the truth you first had to learn about it. Your investigations have led you to the discovery of a great secret, one that only you and I know. You are the man to unravel the mystery of the slayings and discover the truth.' The wind and rain heralded the onset of the storm. 'Chief Inspector, I asked you here for a reason. Behind that gateway are the perpetrators of the murders. I know it sounds fantastic and unreal, but listen to me.' The wind picked up still further. 'The creature at Purbeck, it wasn't of this world. None of the victims were. That is why your scientists refused to believe it was real.' He paused as Corrick nodded to show his understanding. 'I know all about your past, Corrick. I know you were once married, and that your wife died in childbirth, and you lost your son too.' He was shouting to be heard over the breaking storm. 'I know of the pain you've suffered at every step of this investigation, *I know*. And I know you've bottled up your anger and are determined to find the perpetrators of these crimes. That's why you've gone to the lengths you have.'

Harrington lost his footing. He glanced around and saw the excise ship disgorging black puffs of smoke against the inky bluegrey of the storm clouds beyond. The ship was struggling against wind and sea, dropping sea anchors to hold herself against the rising storm. Harrington turned back.

'I know what you're thinking, Chief Inspector,' he continued. 'Listen to me. The victims came from through that gate. There may be other gates, other victims, but they all come from one place, and it's on the other side of the portals. If you want to avenge those dead women you'll have to go through the gate.'

'Why are you telling me this? Why me? Why didn't *you* try to stop it?' yelled the policeman.

'I can't. I cannot pass through the gateway. I possess *powers* that prevent me from passing through it. Remember those blinding headaches, Chief Inspector? How they came on suddenly? That was my doing. In this manner I was able to steer your investigations and ensure that you weren't overwhelmed by the "science" of what you found.' Something in Harrington's words made a connection.

It was true! Immediately Corrick had left the crime scene he'd forgotten most of the details. He'd even had difficulty understanding the notes he'd made that night. He'd even managed to forget the specimen found at Purbeck. It was only when he saw it in the laboratory in Oxford that he remembered. 'What are you implying?' he asked.

'My kind, Corrick, we cannot pass through the gateway. I would die. To catch the culprits you have to go, alone,' Harrington replied.

Corrick looked back at the gate. It was too fantastic. The gateway led nowhere. He could see the beach on the other side.

'Trust me on this, Chief Inspector. What do you have to lose if I am wrong?'

Corrick turned to face the open gateway, at once menacing and yet strangely forlorn. It didn't make sense, yet he felt compelled to do as Harrington requested. That vague feeling of being under another's influence returned, but it wasn't important any more.

'All right. I've come this far. I'll walk through the gate. Then we go back and you'll tell me everything or I'll pin the murders on you!' he shouted but his threat was lost in the storm-driven rain.

Harrington leaned into the dinghy and pulled out two bundles. He handed them to Corrick. 'You'll need these.' One of them was a bandoleer, the other a heavy rucksack.

Corrick shouldered the items and trudged along the wet beach, leaning into the wind with his shoulders hunkered against the rain. He reached the gateway. Through the arch he saw the seas surging over the sandbanks that made this coastline so notorious. Then he walked beneath the arch and was gone.

# 1910

The *Ausburg* stood a mile offshore in the night. The moon had risen early and travelled to the west where it now lay against the horizon, making it unlikely the ship would be seen from the shore. Captain Raeder was with his passengers.

'Ladies and gentleman. My crew is currently preparing for your departure. You will disembark by boat, together with your automobile. I am assigning two of my crew to act as shore party. They will remain on the beach to facilitate communications between this ship and your party during your visit. For the purposes of this *unofficial* visit my ship will retire to international waters until the signal for the pick up is made. That will be in three days' time. I don't anticipate any difficulties during your stay and trust you will find the brief crossing invigorating and refreshing.' He looked at his watch and then Frau Colbetz, who made eyes back at him.

At the ship's stern the crew was stripping off the tarpaulin covering the Benz motor vehicle. It was lashed to the deck under the aft turrets-raised gun. The long barrel was then used as a makeshift crane to lift the automobile over the ships side and lower it onto the steam-driven pinnace. The vehicle was lashed in place, the wheels hanging over the gunwales threatening to sink the little vessel. The passengers embarked in a second boat. Captain Raeder bade farewell to his guests, kissing Frau Colbetz's hand as she stepped down the gantry to the waiting boat. 'Until we meet again, Fraulein.'

The journey to the beach went without mishap. The pinnace ran through the gentle surf until its keel stuck fast in the sand. Then the vehicle was cut free and pushed along special wooden stirrups the ship's carpenter had made, up over the bow and onto the wet sand. The second boat followed and the ladies were carried safely through the surf.

Frau Colbetz climbed into the driver's seat as Herr Dorpmuller cranked over the engine. It fired on the second attempt and the party were soon on their way, motoring through the dunes and off into the dark.

'Funny that,' observed a naval rating, 'they drove off without any lights.'

'Yes, very dangerous,' replied the chief petty officer.

※

Unbeknown to their enemy, a second much larger band of olorcs had set out the day after Kagaminoc's troop. Led by Goramanshie, an experienced fighter and thoroughly unsavoury character, they numbered four hundred. Striking further west and then north, Goramanshie's orders were to use a circuitous route to ensure they arrived at the portal undetected. And when they could no longer conceal their movement Goramanshie drove the olorcs underground, crawling through a crack in the rock, deep into the bowels of the earth. In the dark they found tunnels and crevasses through which they could crawl. Slowly, deviously, they drew nearer to the portal. And when they were beneath it they dug their way out and slipped unseen through the open gates.

※

'James. James, wake up.' Tempus was licking the boy's face.

'Yeeuck,' exclaimed James. He sat up, wiped his face with his sleeve and rubbed his eyes. Dawn glimmered in the sky overhead.

'If we're going to investigate Cragside House we need to go now, before it's too light,' said the hound.

Baranor was already awake, scratching himself and no doubt thinking about breakfast.

'Are we going to take him?' James asked Tempus.

'Who is "him", boy?' asked the bear.

James, still grouchy at being woken up, turned to Baranor and asked, 'And who is "boy", or "dog", for that matter?'

Tempus looked on in amazement. He'd never heard anyone use that tone of voice with a bear, especially a big one.

Baranor sat a moment longer. Then his body began to shake with laughter, his chest emitting a deep and joyous sound. 'Yes indeed. I have been a bore of a bear to you both. Please forgive me, James, Tempus. I have been in the forest on my own for far too long and have forgotten my manners.' He sat with his legs before him, his forepaws resting on his wrists in the manner which bears have. To his companions he looked just like an oversized teddy bear! It was easy to accept his apology.

Baranor lumbered onto his hind legs and stretched with a tremendous yawn. 'Right you are, Tempus dog. Shall we be off then?'

They found a rocky outcrop with sufficient cover where they could observe the main house at a safe distance without being seen themselves.

'Cragside. Mmmm. The name's appropriate,' said Baranor.

'Yes. Imagine if we'd had to spy on a house called Swampside,' replied James, making a joke to prove he was in a better humour. They laughed at the thought and settled down to watch.

With the help of the Antargo stone, James identified the woman they'd seen the day before while she chivvied the last of the housekeeping staff. They took it in turns to watch the big fat dragon squeeze in and out of the front door, all the while her human form harassing the departing servants. The house was evidently being vacated, or perhaps prepared for new arrivals.

After the three friends shared a meagre lunch, the remains of the mutton, things became busier at the house. A fleet of cars and charabancs started to arrive. James gasped as he watched them through the Antargo stone.

All the passengers were ladies, and all the ladies were dragons!

## 1895

Harrington watched the policeman disappear, then turned to look out to sea. In the grey rain-swept distance the excise vessel was just visible, plunging and rearing in the erratic North Sea swell, held bow-on to the wind and the waves by a solitary sea anchor. Sheets of rain drifted down, obscuring the scene one moment, only to part and reveal the ship in the next. The horizon was black in every direction, bringing night to the day, and jagged lightning lit the sky like the arc lights of Crystal Palace.

He leaned against the boat and gave it a push but the keel was stuck fast. He was stranded for the duration of the storm. Just as well, Harrington thought.

Five-hundred yards out, the *Parsimony* lurched drunkenly in the heavy tidal surge. North Sea storms are some of the worst on the planet, setting up contrary winds and seas that can change in the blink of an eye. Captain Gilchrist was extremely worried. Any ship close inshore with wind and currents against it was in a serious situation. He'd left it too late to order the ship further out to sea. They'd had to drop the sea anchor where they were, paying off as little cable as they dared, to ride out the storm. Now the ship was battling wind and sea with barely enough water beneath her keel.

## The Balance Between

'By the mark, a quarter fathom,' cried the deck hand from the bow. The sands were shifting in the tides. Either that or the boat was dragging its anchor. Captain Gilchrist looked around but there were no lights visible to gauge their movement; the Maplin, Middle and Nore lights were all lost in the storm.

'Prepare to winch on the sea anchor,' he called. 'Make full steam, bearing one-twenty degrees,' he ordered. Despite the evident danger Captain Gilchrist had to do something. He'd attempt to pull his ship along the sea anchor cable, away from the threatening shore. Damn the beaurocrats, he thought bitterly. The ship was designed to carry no less than three sea anchors for just such a situation as this but the powers-that-be had ordered him to sea today, despite the *Parsimony* not being fully equipped. Damn them, damn them to hell!

'Make haste!' He'd waited too long and now his ship was in danger. 'Make haste, man. Make haste!'

Harrington sat in the lee of the dinghy with his knees drawn up, watching the *Parsimony* struggle into the teeth of the storm. The storm had blown up so quickly. Was it because of Corrick going through the gateway? Did there still exist that much power in this world, or was it the gateway itself, he wondered? The little chugs of black smoke from the ships funnel changed to grey then white before stopping altogether. Harrington watched in horror.

'Captain!' roared the voice pipe. 'She's gone out, sir! The boiler fire's gone out!' screamed the metallic voice from the voicepipe. Captain Gilchrist stared at the mounting seas, transfixed. These were the words no ship's captain wanted to hear. Without power they'd be wrecked if the anchor dragged or was lost.

'What's happened?' he yelled back down the pipe, his voice choked as he fought his own fear.

'Water coming over the stern, sir. The bilge pumps can't cope.

It put the fires out. We'll need to clear and re-set the furnace. It'll take a few minutes, sir.'

The lumpy, storm-tossed waves were breaking over the ship's side from every direction and the shallow draught of the *Parsimony* made it worse. Minutes without engine power could spell disaster. The pumps were electrically driven, fed by the turbine. Without them the ship would literally fill up with water and sink, if she weren't already battered to pieces.

'Bridge to crew. Everyone man the pumps except the engineers and stokers.'

Perhaps a few minutes might have saved them, but the minutes never came. As the men below-decks struggled to re-light the boilers, the anchor cable parted, throwing the vessel broadside to wind and tide, signalling the doom of the *Parsimony* and her crew.

The surf pounded the sides of the little vessel. Captain Gilchrist snatched himself up and looked over the side in horror. His ship began to break up.

From the beach, Harrington realised the *Parsimony* was lost. Beam on, it would only be a short while before the ship was destroyed by the angry seas.

The crew won't stand a chance, he thought to himself. But as he watched the final moments another thought came to mind: perhaps it's for the best.

# 1910

Rawlings had found his man, the second name on the list.

First he'd had to trawl the dockside bars and dives where, over pints of watered ale, he'd listened to bar-room gossip and other people's conversations. Eventually he found a landlord who could help, one who knew all the rumours and dirt on almost every seafarer that'd passed through the port of London in the last twenty years.

## The Balance Between

'If memory serves me correct he took to being a recluse. 'E were never the same again,' the landlord recounted. 'Took to being a lighthouse keeper. Loved the sea, but never went back.'

Rawlings visited Trinity House and, with the help of a small back-hander, was able to check the records. Among the names was one in particular, a long-serving employee. Almost fifteen years. A long time, a lonely time, Rawlings thought. Maybe the man was escaping something. Maybe he had something to hide, something to fear.

## ∽ 12 ∽

# Breaking and Entering

### 1910

'Good day, sir. I am here to see Mr Weatherburn.'

'Ah yes, Mr Harrington, is it? You are expected. Unfortunately Mr Weatherburn is no longer available,' the secretary explained, 'but Sir Philip, his superior, as you probably know, has kindly agreed to chair the meeting.' Harrington nodded and took a seat in the outer office while the secretary announced his arrival.

A few minutes later Harrington was ushered into a formal room. Heavy ornamental silverware gleamed from the table centre. Imposing oil paintings of long-dead men stared down impassively from the walls.

The doors at the far end of the room opened and Sir Philip strode in. He was taller than Harrington, and many years younger.

'Good day to you, Mr Harrington. Sorry to keep you waiting. I'm to sit in on behalf of the absent Mr Weatherburn.' He ushered Harrington into his private office and directed him to a leather chair. 'I think we shall be more comfortable in here,' he said. Sir Philip pulled up a chair and sat opposite. Harrington looked slightly perturbed at the informality of the meeting.

'I understood, Sir Philip, that this was a meeting to determine

## The Balance Between

committee selection ...' Harrington began, but Sir Philip waved this aside.

'Please forgive me ... Harrington.' Sir Philip looked down at the file in his lap to acquaint himself with the man's first name, but it had been omitted. 'There seems to be a detail missing from your file, Mr Harrington.' A cold sensation came over Harrington as he realised he'd been duped.

'Your file omits to give your first name,' Sir Philip stated, but his eyes were watching Harrington the whole time. Already the meeting felt more like an interrogation than an interview.

Harrington recovered quickly. 'Not so much an omission as a preference, Sir Philip,' Harrington explained. 'I chose many years ago to forgo a first name. Our department still insists on formality, and it helped simplify matters, sir.'

Sir Philip considered the reply to be a textbook civil servant answer ... and a smokescreen. But what was he hiding? 'Very well. The thing is, Harrington, I've been studying your file for some time and I think you're the man I've been looking for.' Sir Philip chose his words carefully.

'I am much gratified to know I am in demand, Minister. But pray, what do you find in my file that is so interesting?'

The two men were sparring, each seeking to gain information without giving any away.

We could be at this all day, Sir Philip realised. He closed the file and placed it on a nearby table. The wily old man opposite had spent a lifetime hiding from inquisitive superiors.

'What sort of person prefers to shun the bright light of achievement and advancement?' Sir Philip challenged. 'The only reason I can think of is if one needs to keep a low profile. A need for secrecy.'

Harrington didn't answer. Instead he cleared his throat and said nothing, the favoured fall-back position of beaurocrats the world over.

'Harrington, do you know my role in the War Office?' Sir Philip asked with a deviousness of his own.

'Yes, Minister, you are a senior minister for the government handling appropriation and financial administration for the army and senior service.'

'Come, Harrington. Surely you've been in governmental service long enough to see behind the veneer. If not, then . . . you must be deaf to the rumours that circulate in Whitehall.'

'Yes, Minister. I have heard that you run the War Office intelligence service,' the older man confirmed, bowing his head in respect of Sir Philip's true authority.

'Good. And I've a feeling that you are in the same business in a civil capacity.'

Harrington didn't answer.

'Now that we know who you are, or otherwise, perhaps it's time for Sir Grey to pension you off?' The threat was delivered with alacrity, but the older man did not react.

'If Sir Philip thinks that appropriate,' was all the man would say.

'And the file is correct in stating that you are sixty-two, Harrington?' Now that Sir Philip thought of it, Harrington could have passed for fifteen years younger.

'Yes, Sir Philip, and young with it.' Harrington knew he had to be very careful. The minister sitting opposite him could deal with Harrington officially or otherwise and, as head of the Intelligence Services, Sir Philip would have a wide range of methods for his disposal.

Sir Philip pondered a while. 'Do I take it that you refuse to answer questions that I deem pertinent to this nation's security? You are aware of the powers I have to deal with any threat, real or perceived, and that I can impose the extreme sanction.' By this he meant summary execution.

'Sir Philip, you are, you must concede, something of an iron fist inside a velvet glove. I'm quite aware that this interview could terminate my career permanently.'

'Then let's talk of our real professions and not waste time,' proposed Sir Philip. But it was clear that Harrington had no intention of being cowed or bullied by authority. He wouldn't get this man to talk against his will and Sir Philip always preferred to avoid physical techniques to extract information. He wondered if an inducement would work.

'Tell me, Harrington, would you like to come to work for me?'

Harrington gave a visible start to Sir Philip's offer, unexpected as it was. It was also extremely tempting. Military Intelligence was much more influential than his department at the Foreign Office and Harrington's secret work would be much easier to perform if he were to be on the inside, as it were.

'So, you're interested?' said Sir Philip. Does that make him on our side or theirs? he wondered to himself.

Harrington licked his lips. He was tempted, very tempted. He would be able to work from within, accessing sensitive material and with greater resources at his disposal.

'Might I know the reason for such an offer, Sir Philip?' Harrington asked cautiously.

'Let me just say that I have identified the career civil servant as being the mainstay to long-term continuity,' Sir Philip replied slyly.

'I would be most interested, Sir Philip,' Harrington acknowledged.

'Good. Then we have a task to perform, together. I am clearing my diary and will be speaking to your minister, Lord Grey, this evening. On the understanding that you will be seconded to the War Office, I would like you to be ready to travel the day after tomorrow.' Sir Philip would have to keep a very sharp eye on the man to discover his true motives.

'Very good, Sir Philip. Very good.'

After brief niceties, Harrington departed.

Sir Philip thought to himself, Whatever possessed me to enrol him in Military Intelligence? Whatever indeed. He found it quite amusing.

༄༅༅༅༄

Frau Colbetz was the last visitor to arrive. Although she possessed excellent night vision, she and Herr Dorpmuller proved incapable of reading a map. Consequently they got lost many times on minor country roads before they reached Cragside.

All day James counted the number of arrivals, reckoning there to be at least one hundred dragons at the house but it was impossible to keep track of them as they shuttled back and forth between the main house and the various estate lodges being used for accommodation. By late afternoon all the estate staff had left. James couldn't see a single person through the Antargo stone who remained pale blue and normal. When the last automobile drew up at the entrance, a limousine carrying two distinguished-looking lady dragons, James gave a gasp. The man sitting at the steering wheel was as brightly coloured as any of the dragons, but he remained the figure of a man.

James, Tempus and Baranor discussed the meaning of this new development until Tempus came up with an answer.

'Perhaps the stone is telling you that the man is an enemy, but that he is not a dragon,' he suggested.

'Or perhaps he is the enemy, but he is of this world,' said James.

They all agreed this made sense and, if it were so, then these last arrivals were particularly important.

'But what are they here for?' asked James as he placed the Antargo stone back into the pouch and tucked it inside his cloak.

Baranor made a suggestion. 'When a bear is hunting, he searches for spore, clues about the quarry. I think tonight we may be in for a spot of hunting.'

\*

Darkness fell across the valley. Light exploded from every window at Cragside as the guests were entertained to a welcoming dinner dance in the sumptuous ballroom. Music and chatter drifted up the hillside to where the three companions lay in wait. While the guests were occupied it proved a good time to make their way down to the house. Tempus led the others cautiously down into the formal parkland with Baranor bringing up the rear.

At the back of the house a multitude of buildings and garages were built into the cliff face. Tempus went off to inconspicuously investigate the main building while James checked the sheds and glasshouses. Baranor snuffled round the ground to learn the lie of the land. They met up again a little while later.

'Over here,' whispered Tempus in a growl. The others joined him.

The big wooden doors to a coach house stood open and several automobiles had been herded into the dark interior. At the rear a wooden staircase rose into the gloom. Tempus and James climbed the tread warily, leaving Baranor among the silent automobiles. They found themselves in a cobwebbed roof space from which a tiny window looked out on to the rear courtyard below. The attic appeared to be used for storing canvases and vehicle covers, the sort of which you finds in posh car showrooms. They heard a grunt from below and went back down. Baranor had his head crammed under a vehicle, which rocked noisily on its suspension.

'What is it, Baranor?' James hissed.

The bear looked up and spoke. 'The thing with noses is that you can learn a lot from them. There's a draught coming from under this,' he said, slapping his paw on the bonnet of the car.

Tempus crawled under and called back. 'Yes, there appears to be a space underneath. It's covered with wooden beams, but there's more than meets the nose down here.'

'Well, we'd better find out where it comes from, or leads to.' James jumped into the automobile and released the handbrake.

Then he directed Baranor to push the vehicle backwards and they pulled up the wooden floorboards. Beneath the boards they found a flight of stone steps descending into the darkness. Tempus didn't hesitate. He darted down the steps and was gone.

The bear and boy waited five minutes, then ten. Fifteen minutes later, Tempus came running back up the stairs with his tail wagging. 'This tunnel leads to several places. In one direction it runs towards the house and into the cellars, and in the other direction it runs in a wide semi-circle with lots of doors leading from it. The end is down by the ornamental lake. There's a metal-railed gate that's locked, but a big fellow could bust right through it,' he added, looking at Baranor.

'Right,' said James. 'I'll nip back to cover our tracks and then head to the cellars while you and Baranor see to that gate. We may need to have an escape route prepared.'

James slipped back up the stairs and replaced the wooden boards, leaving a gap big enough for him and Tempus to slip through, and pushed the automobile into position so that it partially covered the underground entrance, in case anyone should glance in while passing the garage doors. James squeezed back down the stairs and into the darkened tunnel where Baranor and Tempus were waiting for him. They said their 'good lucks' and went in different directions.

James stumbled forward in the dark, edging along crumbling walls, until he felt his way barred by a door. It was bolted shut from this side and he had a devil of a problem freeing the rusty bolt.

The low-roofed cellars were extensive, made up of a series of brick-vaulted rooms with arch spans between the building's foundational columns. The cellars were full of discarded objects and possessions. Family heirlooms lay piled everywhere, cloaked in shrouds of cobwebs. Dust matted every surface. James was soon covered in a grey veil of the stuff, but he ignored it as he crept

## The Balance Between

carefully through the labyrinthine dark. Then, sensing rather than seeing something looming over him in the darkness, he involuntarily cowered. An image sprang to mind and for an instant he was sure he saw the shiny, beady eyes of Morbidren staring at him. A minute passed, then another. James fought down his fear and inched forward. A thin band of light set high up shone in the distance. It was just sufficient for James to make out the tangle of lamps and hat-stands leaning crazily across the aisle. Banishing thoughts of the spider from his mind he forged on, making his way towards the light. It proved to come from the jam of a wooden door at the top of a flight of stone stairs. He made his way carefully up the uneven steps until he stood facing the cellar door. James pressed his ear to the rusty keyhole.

Somewhere in the interior of the great country house, voices were raised. James listened for quite a while, but the noises never came closer or moved further away. Plucking up his courage he lifted the heavy latch and pushed the door ajar. It opened into a pokey scullery that led off from the ante-kitchen at the back of the house. James guessed this was the service quarters where servants would work. Having studied the house all day, he felt sure no staff remained in the building tonight. Perhaps the dragon-ladies didn't want nosy humans in the house during their stay. It seemed likely. Slipping noiselessly round the door, he pushed it to and made his way further into the building.

The house had obviously been designed to accommodate a large domestic staff within the household. It was arranged with a good many staff rooms and offices to the rear. An estate as large as Cragside would have a fair population living within the house and grounds, and it was suitably provided for. As well as the main function rooms and hallways, there were ancillary rooms such as boot rooms, gun rooms, a sewing room, multiple pantries and many others, as well as what seemed miles of connecting corridors running behind and between the walls. This warren of servants' corridors and through-doors were designed to facilitate the speedy and discreet movement of staff to meet the demands of the residents. They also proved perfect for spying on the household.

To the front of the house the formal rooms were set around the main hallway, with an enormous staircase as the very centrepiece of the building. James discovered he could, if he was careful, walk through the servant areas without meeting the houseguests, who preferred the luxurious front-of-house. Once he had to dive into a cupboard to avoid a guest who'd evidently taken a wrong turning into the domestic apartments and got lost. But the sterile servants' offices held no interest to her and she quickly returned to more sumptuous surroundings.

Having gained a sound knowledge of the layout – every formal room was connected to the service quarters by means of discreet doors and hatchways – the young lad made his way to a doorway leading from the back-of-house to the drawing room. A lot of noise carried through the door and James placed his eye to the keyhole to see what lay beyond. His field of vision, though extremely limited by the narrow aperture, made him gasp. If there hadn't been so much noise coming from the room itself, he would surely have been heard and discovered.

The colours of a painter's pallet paraded before him: silvers and golds vied for dominance over vivid blues and emerald greens. Tiny delicate scales of pink and shiny broad scales of sunshine yellow crowded his vision. James rocked back on his heels. A room full of dragons! They'd transformed out of their human forms and into the most spectacular display of rainbow-coloured leather. What lay beyond the door was an utterly amazing scene, but James needed more than just a glimpse. He'd have to find a better vantage point to spy on the dragons.

James found the servants' doorway to the dining room. Peeking through the keyhole he could see the dining table prepared for a banquet. The table was enormous, stretching all the way down the room before doglegging and disappearing off to one side. It literally groaned with food and drink. This would be the perfect spot to spy on the enemy.

Baranor and Tempus made rapid progress, both having better night vision than James. The tunnel led down a slight incline past the first of a number of doors leading off to siderooms.

'Lean on it,' suggested Tempus. The bear did so and was rewarded with the splinter of wood and the hinges ripping from the frame. Tempus darted in, only to reappear seconds later. 'Paint store,' he said and they moved along.

The next door received the same treatment. This time the room contained a mass of metalwork and instruments with dials and funny workings that neither could understand. They went on. After several more disappointing discoveries, which included a room containing a giant red contraption with ladders and hoses attached to it, they came to the end of the tunnel. Here Baranor dealt with the metal gate in a similar fashion to the wooden doors. They stepped outside to find themselves in a small enclosure, hemmed in on three sides by rough stone walls. The fourth opened out on to the lakeside. Cut into one of the walls was a flight of steps leading to the top of the rockface.

'Should we go on?' asked Baranor, whose curiosity was getting the better of his wariness.

'We need to know where it leads. Let's go.' The dog raced up the long flight of steps that switched back on itself, the bear following behind.

James settled down by the keyhole to watch and await developments. His patience was duly rewarded when a gong sounded in the main hallway and dragons began filing into the banquet room.

'Ladies, ladies,' a voice cried above the cacophony of female dragon chatter. 'Please study the seating plan before finding your seat in the dining room. There are rather a lot of us and we must respect social rank!'

James had a good view of the far end of the room where a scrum of tails and wings formed around the seating plan pinned to the wall. Eventually, after a lot of delays and manoeuvring, and a good few grumbles from individuals unhappy with the pecking order, the dragon horde took their seats and James found he was looking over the shoulder of a garish orange and pink dragon. Everywhere he looked, long muzzles of teeth flashed, bejewelled claws waved and scaly tails curled. The dragons came in all shapes and sizes. Some had tails that ended in a diamond, others had two tails with spikes, others were shaped like armoured cudgels. A green and yellow patterned dragon even had two sets of wings. James counted more than sixty dragons and there seemed many more out of sight.

There was a rapping noise from the far end of the room. One of the dragons was knocking a long slender claw against a porcelain bust on a plinth to get everyone's attention. The head fell off the bust in a shower of plaster but no one minded.

'Ladies, lady-dragons,' called the voice. James recognised the man who'd driven the motorcar that afternoon. As master of ceremony he stood at the head of the table in James's line of sight. Next to him sat a very important looking lady-dragon, one of the two James had spotted in the limousine. 'Welcome to the seven-hundredth meeting of the Exile Club of Dragons,' said the man. 'On behalf of the committee may I say how pleased I am that we have a full turnout.' He turned from side-to-side and smiled at his audience. James saw that dragons don't smile back. 'To start the evening I would like to ask you to welcome our own entertainment manager, Frau Feder.'

A medium-sized dragon bedecked with white and red scales and matching wings stood up. 'Thank you. Welcome to you all.

## The Balance Between

I am pleased to say that we expect this meeting to be the most successful ever. We have the run of the lovely Cragside estate for the next three days and I hope you will all enjoy your time here.' The dragons clapped politely. 'Over the coming days we will partake in some excellent fun and games designed to bring us together as one big happy ... family. And we will be presenting to you our plans for the coming century, as well as a range of seminars on topics such as –' Frau Feder glanced down at a list she held in her claw '– "Cooking with humanity", "Fashion tips from the guru we all love, Christian Gore", "The monster diet programme", and lastly, "How to have a holiday in hell". Enrolment is in the reception hall afterwards.

'We also have an exciting lecture by our honorary dragon, Herr Dorpmuller, on the future prospects of breeding.' A gust of applause greeted this announcement. The honorary dragon bowed his head in gratitude of the audience enthusiasm. 'Might I say that Herr Dorpmuller is working with a team of quite brilliant members of a soon-to-be-revealed secret society. They are seeking to perfect a technique that will allow all us ladies to enjoy again the thrill of motherhood in the not-too-distant future.' There was rapturous applause. 'Finally, I know you will all enjoy the announcement to be made tomorrow by our host.' Frau Feder had worked the crowd admirably. 'Now, without further ado, I would like to introduce our chairdragon and principal host, Frau Colbetz.'

The room once more filled with applause as a very tall and slinky dragon, covered entirely in flashing scales of gold, blue and silver, rose at the head of the table, directly opposite where James sat with his eye pressed to the keyhole.

'Ladies, ladies. Thank you.' Frau Colbetz flashed a jaw full of spiky, sparkly white teeth in every direction, tossing her head back to accentuate the long muscles running up her scaly neck. 'I know all you ladies are looking forward to a weekend of fun and thrills, and no doubt Frau Feder will provide this. And I'm sure we all

## The Balance Between

have very old friends we want to catch up with. But there is an important side to our centenary "Dragons in Exile" Conference. One must remember that back in our home towns where we live, a decade of our time is like a day to humanity, and time stands still for no one, except we dragons of course. Change is all around us. Humanity is on the move. And so should we dragons be. Therefore I will be revealing the most exciting plans for the Exile Club of Dragons in millennia.' Frau Colbetz stopped and looked slowly round the room. Her eyes came to rest directly at where James sat crouched behind the servants' door, still glued to the keyhole. It was as if their eyes met. The dragon's steely gaze seemed to lance through the keyhole like a needle, piercing James's head with withering pain. He fell back into the dust and darkness of the service corridor, clasping his head in his hands to relieve the ache. As it eased he heard the words of Frau Colbetz continue from beyond the door.

'Let me tell you, ladies, that I have a plan to free us all from the ceaseless grind that is our lot. No longer will we be forced to live in the shadow of humanity. No more the secretive world of disguises and denial. We will be *liberated.*' There was thunderous applause to this announcement and several dragons rose to their hind feet. 'So now, let us have a toast.'

At this, every dragon threw back her head and jets of flame flew up to the ceiling.

James sat nursing his head, reflecting on the scene he'd just witnessed. It was clear to him that his fate, as Sibelius had referred to it, must be linked in some way to these dragons. It couldn't be coincidence that he was here at Cragside with the Antargo stone and one hundred or so dragons. James and Tempus would have to eavesdrop on the big announcement.

He listened a while longer to the branches and associations represented in the Exile Club. Each speaker in turn stood and gave their name and a brief summary of the most recent happenings or activities of that particular association. Most consisted of boring summaries; lists of sheep killed, cattle rustled, petty theft and occasional grand larceny. But some were more memorable.

There was Rianasorine Pettyplunder who had a tendency to rob pensioners in Birmingham. Everyone agreed she was supremely spiteful, since everyone knows pensioners don't have much gold or jewels. Then there was Garanolaura Savagespitter who professed to never kicking the habit of eating forty stray dogs a day. She was badly received which pleased her enormously. James was particularly repulsed by a most hideously fat dragon with an unfamiliar accent called Ballasifimor Crazychainsaw, who still rode over the prairies burning up the buffalo and Indians on the reservations, and had the slide show to prove it!

James was about to set off through the empty servant quarters to find his companions when the voice of Frau Feder carried over the chatter and general party hubbub.

'Ladies. Please be ready in ten minutes for the midnight hunt. Everyone has been given a number and you will be paired with a partner, one hundred and ten teams in total. We'll be flying according to the revised Lambton rules. The objective will be to capture the sheep that corresponds to your number. They have all been prepared. It's one sheep per dragon only, please. And remember to keep clear of the local town for the sake of good relations with our neighbours. Ten minutes to take-off, ladies.'

James froze. Two hundred and twenty dragons! Hunting! The dragons were limited to sheep, practically the only animals to be found on the moors, and only one each. But there was no mention of other animals being off-limits, in particular dogs or bears. If Baranor and Tempus were caught in the open they'd be killed instantly just for sport. James had to find them.

He raced as fast as he dared back to the cellar, vaulted down the steps, and stumbled through the dark until he found the rear doorway and set off down the tunnel. He ran into the wall and banged his knees as he tried to hurry in the gloom, but he made it to the broken metal gate. Without hesitating he climbed the steps.

Tempus and Baranor were standing at the top of a wall, looking out over a reservoir. The man-made dam stretched between the sides of a ravine high up on a hill behind Cragside. At one end of the dam stood a small building, its door locked. Baranor flicked a paw and dealt with the hasp efficiently. Inside they found yet more dials and strange metal instruments that held no interest for the parlanimals.

Baranor looked out of the window and saw James puffing and panting as he staggered to the top of the flight of steps. 'Trouble,' he said and they ran to meet him.

'A hunt!' gasped James. 'They're having a hunt. We've got to get under cover.' As he spoke, the sound of the mass beating of leathery wings travelled to them. It sounded like a thousand rugs flailed by a thousand housewives in a thousand courtyards, the dull crack and thump reverberating in the valley. James spun around and looked over the roofline of the house below. The dragons were rising en masse from the front lawns. In the moonlight it was a spectacular and ominous sight to behold.

'Quick, back down,' cried James. 'We can't afford to get caught up here.' Tempus flashed past the boy and raced down the steps with ease, while behind him James and Baranor followed, both crashing recklessly down the stairwell in the rush. Above them dragons circled in the night sky. James was certain they'd be seen, but the stairway proved dark and protected, and the dragons were too excited to spot the three spies.

༄༅༄༅༄

Rawlings had a successful conclusion to his visit to Trinity House. For the modest fee of a guinea in the back pocket of a seedy clerk, he was allowed half an hour to peruse the files of the company's employees. From there he went by cab to Liverpool Street station and boarded a train bound for Lowestoft. He'd found the second man named on the list.

The seaside town of Lowestoft is set on the very eastern edge of England, where the flat fenlands of East Anglia jut out into the grey North Sea. This desolate and remote part of the country has a starkness about it that can be breathtaking. In mid-May the unreadable sea and changeable sky make for the seascapes that fascinate artists. To Rawlings, however, it was a windy extremity of land that no one in their right mind would bother to visit, let alone live.

He detrained at Woodbridge and then travelled by cart through a string of villages until he came it to the seaside town of Orford. No rain or wind threatened today, but he couldn't find it in his heart to say the place was attractive. Wind-stunted trees and miles of drainage ditches, arrow-straight roads and small cottages did not endear the Suffolk coast to him.

Rawlings trudged out of the town, past the Jolly Sailor pub to the quay and took a ferry across the River Alde to the far bank. The boatman was unwilling to take him any further so Rawlings was obliged to walk across the marshes until he reached Orford Ness.

Orford Ness is a tongue of shingle that runs parallel with the Suffolk coast and forms a protective spit for the outflow of the River Alde into Hollesley Bay. Flocks of seabirds thronged the barren beach, their angry cries marking Rawlings's passing. Ahead the lighthouse waited, its white walls the only vertical object for miles.

Rawlings gave a cursory knock on the door before pushing it open and stepping inside. The lighthouse's ground-floor room was used as a storeroom, filled with equipment and materials, upended barrels and coils of rope. Around the inner wall, a spiral staircase wound up to the next floor.

'Hello?' he called into the cool, peaceful interior. Above him he heard footsteps. A man appeared at the top of the stairs. He wore a full beard, thick woollen jumper of indiscernible colour, canvas work trousers and boots. In his hand he carried a paintbrush, the kind used by artists rather than decorators.

'Come up,' said the keeper. 'I don't often have visitors. Come up and I'll put the kettle on. Then we will see what you've come for.' He winked as Rawlings tried to decline the invitation. The lighthouse keeper would have none of it. 'All in good time. Mind, I knew you were coming. I saw you miles away.'

It was much later by the time Rawlings said his goodbyes. The keeper had been an affable host and Rawlings had admired the keeper's seascapes before he headed back to Orford. The pictures had inspired him even less than the real thing, but he didn't say. As he trudged back over the shingle, disturbing nesting birds as he went, he reviewed what he'd learnt. Was it an eye witness account of murder, or the excuses of a broken man? He wasn't sure. It wasn't much to go on, the word of a broken man, the word of Captain Gilchrist.

⸙

Goramanshie led his troop to the foot of the arch. Scattered amidst the undergrowth were the decaying bodies of the first party. They found Kagaminoc next to a dead horse. Wild animals had eaten the horse's body, but none had preferred the bitter taste of olorc flesh. They performed the ritual debasement of a hated commander's body, and chopped it into pieces. The olorcs ate heartily that night as they camped near to the arch, feasting on the flesh of their fallen brethren and sucking on the bones.

⸙

'We've got to go back to see if we can discover their plans,' explained James. The three of them were safely inside the underground tunnel. Baranor was left to guard the tunnel at the cellar door while Tempus and James set off for the house. They slipped through the domestic quarters, up the back stairs and onto the main landing. The house appeared deserted; the dragons gone to ravage sheep in the dead of night.

James tried a door that looked promising. It opened into a suite of rooms that he realised was the master bedroom. Dresses and clothing lay everywhere in the room. Frau Colbetz's clothes! He crossed over to the desk at the window, but found nothing. Then he looked in the cupboards. They were filled with more clothes and dresses of all descriptions, feather boas and furs. Dozens of shoes littered the floor. Everywhere he looked he found the woman's accoutrements. The room reminded him of his mother's dressing room – although his mother had far fewer clothes than Frau Colbetz – and for a moment he recalled the pain of separation.

Suddenly the door opened. James dived to the ground and rolled noiselessly under the bed. He watched as a pair of men's feet crossed the room to the bedside table.

That was close, James sighed, relieved as the feet turned and left, closing the door behind them.

James waited a moment before pulling himself out from under the bed and going to the bedside table. There was a map on the top. It looked similar to one of the maps he'd seen in Sibelius's library. The map showed part of Northern England and part of Eldaterra where the two worlds met at the Sea Gate. He studied it for a while longer, listening for anyone coming. Then he refolded the map and replaced it where it had been. Crossing to the door, he listened and heard a scratching. It was Tempus signalling the coast was clear.

## ～ 13 ～

# In the Land of the Marked

'Stop!' The voice carried across the hallway and, as if by some unseen force, every muscle in James's body obeyed the command. He was halfway to the servants' door under the stairs, following Tempus's tail, when, behind him, the front door swung open and Frau Colbetz entered. She stood on the threshold with the carcass of a dead sheep hanging from her mouth. Crimson blood splashed down and pooled on the black and white marble floor, curling around the creature's clawed feet. With his back to her, James didn't see Frau Colbetz in dragon form.

James turned slowly towards the direction of the unseen voice, his body controlled by the dragon's magic. His eyes swivelled round to find Frau Colbetz standing in front of him in the hallway. She appeared slightly dishevelled but otherwise quite normal. The dead sheep had gone and the front door was closed behind her.

'What are you doing in this house?' she demanded, her voice rising as she fought to control her temper.

Out of the corner of his eye, James caught sight of his own reflection in the mirror. An idea sprang to mind. 'Excuse me, ma'am. I'm looking for the butler. I've chores to do and I must find him.' James tried to make his voice sound as small as possible.

The woman took a step closer, glowering even more fiercely.

'Chores, you say? But the staff have all been released for the week. What chores are there to be done? Answer me this instant.'

James cowered in genuine fear of the woman that loomed over him. 'I'm the chimney-boy, ma'am. I go up the chimneys and clean out all the soot from the stacks.'

Frau Colbetz studied the boy for a moment before saying, 'You're a bit big to be a chimney-boy, aren't you?'

'Oh no, ma'am. Not here, on account of the chimneys being so very large. I've worked here the last five years.' James certainly looked the part, covered in the filth and grime of the cellars.

'Well, your services aren't required at the moment,' she replied. Frau Colbetz was considering what to do when the main door opened again and Herr Dorpmuller entered.

'Herr Frau. The dra ...' His words petered out when he saw James.

Frau Colbetz turned to him. 'Herr Dorpmuller, this is the chimney-boy. He's come to clean the soot away.' Her voice sounded dangerously sarcastic. 'Perhaps we may find employment for this young soul elsewhere?'

Something passed between the two of them. Herr Dorpmuller smiled. 'Yes, we can use a healthy lad for a weekend. Come,' and he signalled James to follow him through the house. James looked first to the woman and then the man. He caught sight of a trail of bloody footprints behind Frau Colbetz. James ducked his head to hide his face from scrutiny and obediently darted after Herr Dorpmuller, escaping any further investigation by the woman.

They reached a small study at the end of a hall where Herr Dorpmuller indicated James was to sit on a hard leather chair. 'My boy. Your timely appearance here may be fortunate for the entertainment of the lady guests. I will make arrangements concerning that shortly, and I believe you will find them –' he searched for a word '– amazing. But first, please explain how you came to be in this house. All the doors are locked and tonight the house has been very busy. How did you get in unnoticed?'

James knew this was a trick question. If he pretended that he'd asked one of the ladies to let him in they'd know he was lying, since the ladies had transformed into dragons the whole night.

'I didn't, sir. I live in the cellar,' said James innocently.

In the hallway Frau Colbetz moved slowly to the servants' door under the stairs. Putting her face to the half-open door jamb she breathed in a lung full of air. Slowly she released it. Something called to her in the back of her mind. She couldn't remember. It was like a long forgotten memory struggling to be found again. She shut the door.

James was left in the study while Herr Dorpmuller went to consult with Frau Feder. He heard the rasp of the key in the lock. When he was sure the man had walked off, James stole over to the wooden panelling next to the fireplace. He fumbled about for a bit before finding the hidden handle and pulling the servants' door open.

Tempus sat waiting. 'I followed you.'

James patted the hound's head and said, 'They don't know about the servants' passageways and let's hope they don't go looking. I had to tell them I live in the cellar. The man, Herr Dorpmuller, was suspicious about how I'd got into the house and I couldn't think of anything else to say.' The words poured out of him in excitement. 'It's important that you and Baranor stay out of sight for the moment. They may check the cellar to confirm my story so you'll have to drag some blankets down there. Quick, I hear someone coming.' And with that Tempus turned and padded back down the corridor. James closed the secret door and returned to his seat.

Herr Dorpmuller returned with Frau Feder and another woman

who was dressed in pink. The ladies tidied their hair as the three of them talked. James could hear snippets of the conversation. 'Yes, we could do that. No, no one will notice. Not immediately. An exciting climax, definitely.' The ladies stared over at James. Mrs Pink-dress dabbed her eyes as she said, 'Such a sweet boy. How lovely! Just the right age. Strong, yet tender.' The women whispered among themselves and then left.

Herr Dorpmuller lit a cigar and puffed on it a while. 'You're going to have a wild time tomorrow, my boy, a wild time.'

It was almost sunrise before Herr Dorpmuller had finished making a cursory inspection of the cellars and left James to sleep until he was called for. The man also gave him some leftovers from the banquet. As expected, the doorway at the back of the cellar had not been discovered, the piles of junk and paraphernalia having discouraged a more rigorous investigation. James heard a key turn in the lock as Herr Dorpmuller closed the cellar door at the top of the stone steps. Soon James was down the secret passage with his friends.

'They want me to be involved in the entertainment tomorrow,' James told Tempus and Baranor.

Tempus growled and put his head between his forepaws. 'I don't like the sound of it. There isn't any sort of entertainment that dragons indulge in except the killing sort.'

Baranor agreed. 'I've never met with a dragon, but what I know of them is not to their credit. As I recall, the dragons were exiled from Eldaterra a long, long time ago, back when the worlds were first divided. Leastways, nothing good will come of this entertainment.'

James had to agree with them. 'But,' he resolved, 'if they don't find me in the cellar when they come to look, they'll be worse than suspicious and then we won't stand a chance of discovering their plan.'

'What about that book of yours? Maybe it's time to ask it a question or two,' suggested the bear.

'Good idea,' said James and reached for the pouch.

## 1895

Corrick stepped out from under the arch just as the portcullis crashed down behind him. He spun around, surprised by the sudden loud noise. The storm-swept beach was visible through the bars of the portcullis but on this side it was a different scene altogether. The gate stood at the bottom of a flight of worn stone steps lit by torches guttering in the stale, dank air. The walls were black and covered in centuries-old grime, cobwebs and decay hanging everywhere.

Somewhere in the distance came a low wail of desolation. Corrick felt the low frequency reverberations through the floor and with it came a feeling of abject failure. His whole body washed with a sense of loss and inevitability. His knees began to sag and the pack on his back dragged him down, suddenly a weight too great to carry.

The noise faded and, as it did, Corrick recovered his morale. It was as if the very sound had sapped him of his willpower. Everything about this trip was unreal, a nightmare. He leaned against the wall and gathered his wits about him.

'I've got to stay alert and focused,' he said to himself.

Corrick investigated his baggage. Harrington had thoughtfully provided provisions and a selection of spare clothes. There was also a handgun, the type with a big magazine to hold plenty of bullets. 'That explains the bandoleer,' Corrick thought.

Setting the bandoleer across his shoulder and the rucksack on his back, he studied the archway looking for clues. With the portcullis down and no means of raising it, he would have to find another way back, but then something that Harrington had said

*The Balance Between*

just before he'd stepped through the gate came back to him. '*If you want to avenge those dead women you'll have to go through the gate.*' Harrington had known what was driving Corrick. He wouldn't go back until he had justice for the victims.

Looking closely at the gateway he found a modest, black metal plaque set into the stonework, bearing an inscription, which Corrick read.

> Let us speak of evil deeds
> That at present nurture here
> Its scaly curse to plant the seeds
> In divided worlds for those to fear
>
> Seek out the canker of these crimes
> Before this place forever falls
> To those all counted in the nines
> Turned up and on by deathly calls
>
> Know that you stand alone as first
> And last to follow is the younger
> Together seek those whose a'cursed
> Knowledge drives this wicked hunger
>
> Find them in their darkest dream
> Before the alchemy is finished
> The horror of this crime wiped clean
> Or stand mankind to be diminished
>
> Look to blackest heart of granite
> Ancient in its most secret magic
> Science end this rainbowed birthpit
> A weakened world the coin for logic

Corrick couldn't discern a meaning to these words. He moved on, mounting the steps carefully, his gun at the ready. More torches flickered at the top of the flight, where a roughly-hewn tunnel led away into the dark. Gazing along it, he could see the distant glow of yet more torches. At its end he came to a crossways leading left and right. Slipping down the left-hand passage it ended at a closed door. Carefully lifting the latch he pushed against it and stepped onto an empty balcony looking down into a cavernous space.

The cavern, so wide that Corrick couldn't make out the other side, was busy with creatures moving about on the floor far below. The distance was so great that he couldn't make out any details of the creatures or the duties they performed. It reminded him of the view from the top of St Paul's Cathedral into the crowded, dirty streets of old London.

## 1910

'Sibelius, I believe we have made a terrible error.' The wizard Ptarmagus spoke with a grave expression. His image hung over the vallmaria at the top of the Western Tower. 'We have allowed the enemy to grow unchecked in the south for too long. Reports tell of the enemy gaining new numbers every day. They spawn new hordes while we are diminished by every inconsequential battle with the foe.'

'We can only raise our young as we have always done,' Sibelius replied to ease his friend's despair.

'I have spoken with other members of the Guild,' the apparition went on, 'and there is wide agreement that the Guild must seek the help of new allies.'

'What allies would there be? The elves? Except for a few, the elven nation no longer takes any interest in Eldaterra,' Sibelius replied. He knew of course that the Guild was tempted by the prospect of help from beyond the portals.

'There is much debate about help coming from our descendants in the New World,' replied Ptarmagus cautiously.

'By that I take it to mean the Guild has no means to coerce the other races in Eldaterra?' Sibelius asked. These days the Guild was made up of more politicians than wizards, such was the decline in the pre-eminence of magic. The Guild relied ever more frequently on politics rather than magic to undertake its bidding. Ptarmagus, Keeper of Cruxantire and therefore a wizard of greatness, was close to the central cities of Eldaterra where the main body of the Guild gravitated. Political machinations and intrigue threatened at every turn, even threatening to stifle the practice and study of magic, the true power of Eldaterra. Ptarmagus was not immune to this pressure.

'Sibelius. I know how you feel on the matter. Every single member of the Guild respects your opinion –'

'The portals exist to separate two incompatible worlds, Ptarmagus, not to bring them together,' cut in Sibelius. 'The Guild is panicked and would seek to open Pandora's box and bridge the gap between the two worlds. Do they still not fathom the depths of lore that they plan to tinker with? The wizards of old were much more than we understand them to be. They were sorcerers in the truest sense. Some were divined without body, so magical were they. Mages of their stature worked to create the great divide, and we who remain should never be compared to them, not even spoken of in the same breath.' He shook his head in disappointment but his voice was charged with suppressed anger. How often had he argued with the Guild for them to drop contemplation of such action? Too often to recount. For these last hundred years Sibelius had fought and won every debate. But for his refusal to sanction such action, Eldaterra would already be a dying world rather than a wounded one. Eventually, when the temptation was too great and the need too urgent, he would lose the argument.

## The Balance Between

Ptarmagus looked helplessly at his old friend. 'Dear brother wizard, I tell you this because I know they will bring up the debate again at the High Council. I will help your cause as much as I am able but I cannot undermine my own position. Such a consequence would hurt your situation even more.'

Sibelius affirmed the loyalty of his friend and thanked him. Privately Ptarmagus did much to help Sibelius keep the protagonists at bay and the portal closed. Yet the politicians wielded such power in the administration of the Guild that they could threaten to unseat even a senior wizard, and Sibelius knew that Ptarmagus would be obliged to follow the majority and vote for the opening of a portal if it came to such a thing.

'We will rue the day the Guild was opened to non-magi. They will be the undoing of this world,' added Sibelius wryly. He considered the options. 'Ptarmagus, there are things afoot that the Guild is not aware of. Things that concern only me and the Shadows. They will transpire soon enough and show good reason why the portals must remain closed.

'But I need more time, Ptarmagus,' he explained. 'Will you grant me it and delay the calls for a meeting of the High Council?' Sibelius knew he could ask this much of his fellow wizard. To delay the meeting was to delay the moment when Ptarmagus would face Sibelius in public and be forced to vote against him. Ptarmagus would delay as long as he could.

'Very well, my brother. Your Shadows have their time. Make good use of it.'

'May your wisdom guide you, Ptarmagus,' Sibelius said, bidding his friend farewell.

'And your wisdom save us, Sibelius.'

☙❧

Tempus asked the first question: 'What is the history of the dragons?'

## The Balance Between

The reply was:

*The dragons are of the Origin (Old World) and were amongst the first to be created. They were given the gifts of flame and rainbow (the ability to change coloration at will) over all other creatures. With the corruption of Creation the dragons were found to be most susceptible to the corrupting influence and the effects thereof, in part due to the negative aspects of the rainbow, that is to say, vanity, greed, envy and avarice. This resulted in their exile from Origin when the Great Divide took place. Dragons have remained in exile in the unmagic world since that time. Current status, unknown. Further reading:* Origin of Species *by I. Land,* Creatures Extinct and Exiled *by M. Thatcher.*

Next, Baranor asked: 'What do dragons do for entertainment?' The book replied:

*Dragons are difficult social creatures at the best of times (for reasons, refer to Deadly Sins: Vanity, Greed, Envy and Avarice), and occasions for social interaction are few. No official holidays or celebrations are recognised by their kind and social family structure usually lasts for two minutes after birth of offspring. History shows several recorded occurrences of formal entertainment,*

1. *The brief collective hunt of 11,256 BC (local time).*

'That's the entertainment they enjoyed tonight,' said James.

2. *The tournament Talon Grab of 11,247 BC (local time).*

'That might be what they plan for tomorrow,' gulped James.

3. *The Raffle of 11,232 BC, 11,011 BC and 10,996 BC (local time).*

*The Balance Between*

'That one sounds fine,' sighed James. 'What is the Raffle of 11,232 BC?' he asked the book. It replied:

> *On the rare occasion of a dragon social function, a raffle for all participating dragons was arranged (absentia applications were rejected). The prize-winner, Desmoraktor of Macedonia, won the privilege of single-hunt status.*
>
> *The prize-winner chose to hunt a large under-mountain warrior. Hunt duration, 7 minutes. Time to kill, 2 minutes, thirty seconds.*
>
> *Postscript: The final hunt of 10,996 BC led directly to the exile of the dragons when the choice of hunt was a wizard representative of the Guild.*

This didn't look good from James's point of view so he asked, 'What is the Tournament of Talon Grab?' The book replied:

> *Talon Grab is one of three recorded social activities that have ever occurred between socialising dragons. The game consists of combat between two dragons. It is lethal.*

'I suppose that rules you out of that one,' said Baranor with relief. James looked sick. 'That leaves the world's fastest hunt as the likely entertainment, and I'm going to be the hunted!'

Tempus gave this some thought and then asked the book, 'How can you stop a dragon?' The book replied:

> *There are seven theoretical means to stop a dragon. All require the death of the dragon in question. Of these, three have proven fatal to the party attempting to stop a dragon, one has proved near fatal to the party attempting to stop a dragon and two have proved that the theories do not work.*
>
> *One has provided a suitable means of stopping a dragon, once.*

## The Balance Between

> The successful proof of the theory led to it becoming known as The Promalski Principle, named after the party that successfully stopped a dragon.
>
> The Promalski Principle requires the party seeking to stop a dragon to be attired in 100% flame-retardant armour. The party is then required to enter the oesophageal passage via either the nasopharynx or mouth cavity and then assault the soft inner tissues. Persistent assault will enhance the stopping.
>
> No theory on exiting a stopped dragon has ever been proven.

Tempus quickly asked another question before James had time to finish digesting the implications of the last one. 'How can one survive a dragon that is hunting you?' The book replied:

> Dragons are magical creatures. They use magic to hunt (as well as flight, fright, scent and sight. Instinct and the auditory sense play less significant roles when a dragon is at leisure – for reasons refer to vanity). Dragons do not use reason.

This didn't answer the question, so Tempus asked it again. 'How can one survive a dragon that is hunting you?' The book replied:

> Dragons do not use reason.

They all scratched their heads trying to work this out. Finally James piped up. 'If the book says dragons don't use reason to hunt, then maybe that is precisely what the hunted must do.' This sounded sensible enough to the others. So James asked the next question: 'How can one use reason to survive a dragon hunt?' The book replied:

> Reason will enable the hunted to satisfy the hunter's requirements without the actual conversion of hunted to victim.

*Example:*

*Hunter – Purpose to hunt: hunger, revenge, boredom, satisfaction of blood lust.*

*Hunted – Purpose for being hunted: food source, revenge, stupidity, naturally selected victim.*

*Reason will seek to satisfy all the relevant hunter purposes listed above while seeking to avoid satisfying any of the hunted purposes.*

*In addition, extra reason will seek to satisfy all irrelevant purposes that may also exist.*

This gave the friends a lot to think about.

James returned to his bed in the cellar, there to await dawn and the 'entertainment of the dragons'. He was exhausted, not having slept in the last twenty-four hours, but he could not rest. Instead his mind churned away, thinking about what they'd learned.

## 1895

From his vantage point, Corrick came to realise that he was watching a crude production line in the vast cavern. What at first looked like just an incoherent set of actions performed by the figures below had slowly formed into a discernable pattern of repetition. Corrick had once visited a shipbuilding yard on Tyneside to interview a suspect and had ended up chasing the man up a lifting crane. Looking down now reminded him of the scene he'd witnessed in the yard, the systematic approach to building the ships and the scale of activity. The noise was deafening in both cases.

Down in the cavern the creatures, which looked like something from a Brothers' Grimm fairytale, rolled barrels into the cavern and stacked them in a holding area. Others were opening each barrel in turn and draining off the fluid in them, leaving a solid material lying in the lower portion of the barrel. Then another group took the drained barrels and upended them; the large shining black lump that fell out was stretched out and placed on a large belt affair that moved slowly over rollers. The belt reminded Corrick of a giant slow-running flywheel belt, ran under a series of rudimentary sprinklers that cleaned the residual fluid off the inert mass before it was placed on a trolley-type device and wheeled out of the room by yet more of the labouring creatures.

Corrick couldn't make out any form of security or guards. There wasn't anything else to learn from where he stood on the balcony so he retraced his steps back to the crossways and proceeded along the other passageway. Moving down a seemingly endless stairway that twisted this way and that through the rock, he eventually found himself at the cavern floor. He made his way stealthily around the side of the cavern, keeping close to the rock face to avoid being seen by the workers. They seemed not to notice his presence. Growing more confident he stole closer to one of the workers as it was stacking empty barrels. He angled to one side, intending to slip between two stacks and pass by unnoticed. But as he started to move one of the barrels slipped from the stack and crashed to the ground. Corrick was half way across the gap when the creature turned towards him. He stared straight back at it, transfixed.

Its eyes had been cut out!

Corrick was horrified at this discovery. Where the creature's eyes should have been, two gaping cavities gouged deep into its skull. It was also immediately evident that, judging from the state of the wounds, the poor creature had been blinded deliberately. Inspecting several other workers nearby he saw that they too were sightless. The scale of the barbarity left him numb.

That's why they took no notice of me, he thought to himself.

With the ceaseless din of work and the stink from the barrel contents, it was unlikely that the creatures would be able to detect him by other means. He was safe as long as he kept out of their way. He left the cavern following the loaded trolleys. Presently the passage down which the trolleys passed gave way to a second, brightly lit cavern. Here the systemised approach to work was again evident. Corrick hugged the wall to stay out the way.

A different creature, one with large, limpid, pool-like eyes walked past the parked trolleys, inspecting each of them in turn as part of a selection process. Occasionally it would tap the shoulder of the blind worker responsible for a particular trolley, signalling the worker to move the trolley to leave the queue. The rest of the trolleys remained in a long, silent line waiting to be hooked to a heavy chain that dragged endlessly along the ground. The attached trolleys were pulled from the cavern by the clanking chain off down a smaller tunnel where sparks and blasts of powerful light emanated sporadically.

When the inspector's back was turned, Corrick slipped past and around a shoulder of rock where the selected trolleys had disappeared from view. Rounding the corner he walked slap bang into one of the workers, bumping into its thin, meagre body and sending it stumbling backwards against the wall. As Corrick pulled the gun from his coat pocket the creature flinched and immediately cringed, its arms jerking up to protect its head. Mouth stretched wide in terror, it began to scream but no noise came forth. It tongue had been cut out, and probably its vocal cords too. Corrick watched with pity as the creature cowered for several minutes, shuffling this way and that to escape its unseen tormentor before eventually backing into a corner where it curled up and sat quivering in fear.

It's waiting to be beaten, Corrick realised.

Meanwhile, oblivious to the incident, others of its kind continued with their own work. They could not hear or see events going on around them. Corrick tucked his gun in his waistband and resumed his exploration with more caution. Somewhere far behind, a loud bang echoed off the walls and through the tunnels.

The next room resembled an abattoir. Corrick studied the inert

## The Balance Between

mass on a trolley nearby. It was a creature of indeterminate form; lifeless. He crossed over to the trolley and looked more closely at the body. It was a greyish-black figure with two long arms that ended in wide lumpy hands with six fingers. The body was lean and featureless at the front. Corrick noticed it had two protruding shoulder bones at the back. The legs resembled the arms, only longer. But it was the head and face of the creature that held Corrick's attention. The face was broad, with wide-set eyes at the top of a nose that resembled a foreshortened lizard snout. The skull was streamlined with tiny aural passages towards the top of each side of the head. The eyes were closed and the creature was not breathing. Ahead of Corrick another of the inspector-type creatures was at work on one of the bodies. It took no notice of him as he made his way carefully along the row of trolleys. It was as if they were only interested in their work.

Spread out in front of him, under the glare of a hundred torches fitted with polished metal reflectors, was an enormous operating theatre. A dozen trolleys were positioned in a line along the centre of the room, each with a small team of creatures clustered about it. They were performing some form of medical examination. No, operation. As he watched, Corrick recognised what each team was doing. They were caesarean operations.

Corrick stumbled backwards in total revulsion. He had to bite his lip to stop himself from gagging as the stench hit him. He watched with tears in his eyes as the team nearest him worked in sequence, first cutting open the victim and preparing the gaping wound. Next, a large jar was fetched and the lid removed. Then the truth dawned on him. They weren't removing a baby from the mother, they were implanting one! Now, instead of the disgust he'd felt only seconds before, Corrick was astounded at this amazing medical feat. The implications were fantastic. As he watched in disbelief, he got a better look at the foetal implant they were putting into the mother. Corrick gasped. The foetus was the same as the one examined and found to be a hoax at the Natural History Museum in Oxford!

## 1910

James was roused from his bed by a foot gently rocking his shoulder.

'Get up, lad. Get up,' a voice ordered.

'Yes, father.' James mistook it for Sir Philip's voice.

'Not your father, boy. Your new employer,' said Herr Dorpmuller, who wore a thin smile that couldn't be described as friendly.

James was led upstairs into the servants' quarters where he was told to wash and make himself presentable. Next he was taken to the dining room where a frugal meal awaited him.

'Stay here, boy, until I call you,' ordered Herr Dorpmuller, far less affable than the night before.

James turned to see the servants' door swing open and Tempus was beside him, hidden beneath the table.

'Any bright ideas on ways to stop a dragon?' James enquired miserably.

Tempus laid his muzzle on James's knee. 'We were awake all night after you fell asleep trying to think of something. Baranor suggested using a sheep as a substitute but the book never mentioned anything about dragons being gullible,' Tempus offered.

James sat with his head propped up in his hands, dejected, gnawing at his lower lip in worry. There was no way out of this conundrum. 'This will be the fastest ever dragon-kill in entertainment history,' he reflected. Then his misery fled. He had an idea!

'Ladies, please. I hope you've had a lovely morning at the various seminars on offer today,' called Herr Dorpmuller from the dais on which he stood. The whole of the assembled room turned to him in anticipation. 'I will now ask Frau Feder to introduce the

## The Balance Between

lunchtime entertainment.' Herr Dorpmuller stood down and Frau Feder took his place.

'Ladies, thank you,' she said in response to the brief but excited clapping. 'For your lunchtime entertainment we have an additional feature to the programme. We have been lucky enough to gain the services of a young huma– *boy*,' she corrected herself. 'As a result of which we are running another exciting and hopefully successful social event, a raffle.' At this there was an audible gasp of delight from many in the crowd. 'You will each be given a book of raffle tickets. Please put your name or guest number on the tickets and then pop them into the tombola barrel at the rear of the drawing room, next to the fireplace. We shall conduct the prize draw in one hour so there is plenty of time to get your entries in.'

Tempus heard the announcement from behind the servants' door but decided not to tell James the gist of it. He went back down below to help Baranor.

James was locked in the study, wondering how his friends were getting on. Time crawled by like a wounded slug. Even the clouds in the sky outside seemed to stop drifting. The hubbub of chattering ladies and occasional dragon screeches drifted through the mansion house. His nerves began to fray and his stomach turned like a steam engine's wheel.

Elsewhere, Tempus and Baranor carried out James's instructions as best they could. The plan required some nifty handiwork, but between them the two animals made do with paws, teeth and claws. At the last moment Baranor raced off over the hills searching for the final ingredient.

'Right, boy. Up on the dais you go. That's right, stand there.' Herr Dorpmuller kept a light but firm arm resting on the boy's shoulder to deter any attempt at escape. The excitement in the room was palpable. It thronged with guests, all in their human form.

Frau Feder called out over the room of craning heads. 'Ladies. The hour is upon us. It is time for the prize draw. I should like to call upon our host and President of the Exile Club, Frau Colbetz, to make the draw.' A loud burst of applause signalled the enthusiasm of the audience.

Frau Colbetz joined Frau Feder next to the wooden tombola drum as it was set slowly spinning. When it came to rest the hatch was opened and Frau Colbetz put her hand in. She pulled out a green ticket and read it aloud. 'Number 10032. Frau– Why, it's me,' she said in false surprise.

All around the room there was an instant murmuring of disgruntled voices. 'Fix!' someone called from the back. Frau Colbetz shot a withering look of pure evil across the room, vainly seeking out the barracker.

The crowd was not to be bullied out of the prize draw. The hubbub rose an octave and Frau Feder began to look flustered at the mutinous reaction.

Herr Dorpmuller leaned over to Frau Colbetz and whispered urgently in her ear. A look of pure demonic detestation crossed the woman's face. Herr Dorpmuller whispered again, even more urgently. Then Frau Colbetz grew still, her mouth becoming very small and her eyes dark slits, the skin around them like crazed glass. 'Ladies,' she began with pure venom. 'I find myself unable to take full advantage of this prize.' Every word came out as though dragged from between her clenched jaws. 'Therefore I am *forced* to decline the prize and make a new draw.' The discontent eased somewhat, although the barracker risked another anonymous retort.

'One should think so.' Frau Colbetz missed identifying the person a second time.

The next number to be read out was 19897, belonging to Mrs Mable Ardlibuckle, who gave a growl of pleasure and one-upmanship.

## ～ 14 ～

## Doctored in So Many Ways

Armed with the pass that Sir Philip had provided him, Rawlings was able to gain entry to the Palace of Westminster to continue tracking the first name on the list. Once inside, Rawlings made himself look busy. Ever since the assassination of a former Prime Minister, security had been tightened. He found a bench in the main entrance lobby where he could study the crowd over the top of his newspaper as they entered. He'd no interest in the splendid architecture, and any sense of occasion at being in the mother of all parliaments eluded him. To Rawlings parliament was just a place where the establishment met to do business. It was a place that epitomised everything that he'd secretly come to hate, a system where insiders greased the wheels of power. And ever since Rawlings had been thrown out of army, he'd been an outsider.

As he looked about him he knew many of them by sight. He knew them because he was a spy.

Each morning the man who Rawlings was currently awaiting followed a route that took in a number of security checkpoints. This was evidently a procedure designed to lose anyone attempting to follow the gentleman in question. In order to find out where the man went once he was in the Palace, Rawlings had to already be inside, otherwise he'd lose him at the security barrier.

In due course the man came through the police checkpoint.

*The Balance Between*

The man strode down the main thoroughfare. Rawlings stood up casually, folded his paper and followed him. The target walked to the end and into the commons lobby. That was one place Rawlings couldn't go. He'd have to sit and wait some more.

☙❦❧

'Ladies, now that we've announced the winner of the raffle, I would like to welcome our young guest to the party. His name is –' Herr Dorpmuller bent down and hissed to James, 'What is your name, boy?'

'Smith, sir,' James replied, snapping out of his thoughts just in time to give a false name.

The man nodded and said aloud, 'Please welcome Master Smith.' And with that he pushed James to the front of the dais and raised the boy's arm with his own. James was feeling dizzy with worry as he looked out over the sea of expectant faces. If his plan didn't work, or if it was discovered, he'd be lunch for this lot.

'Right. Now I will explain the rules of the entertainment so that Master Smith and all the guests understand.' He grinned at James with a new coldness, his eyes battleship grey and his top hat like a furnace chimney. 'Our prize winner, Mrs Mable Ardlibuckle, has won herself a little game of hide and seek with you, young Smith.' Herr Dorpmuller used the most choice and inoffensive words to explain the otherwise simple principles of 'Hunt and Kill'. James was to be the bunny to Mrs Ardlibuckle's shotgun. James looked at his adversary. She was quite a bit smaller than him though somewhat rounder, with delicate little hands, small feet and a nice, granny-like face. Mrs Ardlibuckle was so inconspicuous that she could be anyone's neighbour and never be suspected of living a double life. James looked at her modest dress and dark blue court shoes. She certainly didn't stand out in this crowd. Perhaps he was in for a lucky break, a nice petite dragon to chase him. Her smile suggested otherwise.

'Master Smith, you will have ten minutes, no, we'll be generous to make it more fun, fifteen minutes for you to run off and hide somewhere. Then when the time is up, we'll relea– send dear Mrs Ardlibuckle after you. If she finds you within one hour, she's the winner. And if you stay hidden for one whole hour, then you'll be the winner and you will receive two shillings for your trouble. Now isn't that going to be fun?' He smiled a ruthless smile at James. 'This will be very rewarding, won't it?'

James had to stop himself swaying with giddiness. Let's just pray Baranor and Tempus have got everything ready, he thought to himself.

# 1895

Corrick found a place to be sick. He'd never felt so overcome with helplessness in his entire life. Behind his back, twelve operating tables were occupied as twelve implantations took place. It was like a charnel house, something out of a William Blake picture, but much worse. Corrick felt despair sap his strength.

Something caught his eye, a figure walking between the rows of operating tables, inspecting the work of those performing the operations. Not certain of this creature's intent, Corrick ducked down between two trolleys and watched as the figure came closer. It was a human, a man. He marched purposefully along, stopping once to say, 'Was ist dass?' He threw his hands up in despair at the docile operating staff, spending a few minutes instructing them on some technical point and correcting their procedure before turning back down another row and walking away. Corrick followed, keeping low, behind a line of empty trolleys.

At the end of the inspection the man walked out the operating theatre, up a short flight of steps and disappeared into a room. Corrick pulled the gun from his waistband and soundlessly followed up the stairs to the doorway. It was only partially closed. He looked through the gap into the room.

There were four men in the room. All wore white laboratory coats over stiff collars and ties. Two were talking together while a third sat in a comfy chair reading. The man that Corrick had followed stood talking with a fifth figure in the room. Corrick had never laid eyes on such a grotesquely fascinating creature, standing a foot taller than the men. It looked a fearsome and savage warrior, with ragged teeth, claw-like hands and enormous booted feet, swathed in black and red armour. A wicked blade hung from its side.

## 1910

Rawlings had seen enough to know he should report back to Sir Philip, so he set about arranging an early meeting using the dead drop at Sir Philip's place of work. He left an envelope marked in red ink for the attention of Sir Philip but with an additional identification message on the reverse, 'receipt for flowers'. He dropped it into his employer's postal box at the rear of the building.

An hour later Sir Philip opened his office window and placed a potted plant in front of the fifth panel of glass counting from the left. The meeting was set.

Sir Philip waited for Rawlings in his family's London residence. Rawlings was again obliged to arrive by way of the connecting roof spaces, entering from the modest end property further down the street that Sir Philip had bought years ago. He looked tired and out of breath. His employer greeted him and offered a whisky, which Rawlings accepted as he slumped into a chair.

After a few hasty gulps, Rawlings cussed, caught himself, and smiled sardonically at Sir Philip. 'I'll never get used to the tradesmen's entrance,' he said. Sir Philip weighed the words of resentment carefully, but said nothing.

Rawlings shrugged, tossed the rest of the fierce drink down his throat and struggled forward in his chair. 'I've been to hell and back to crack this one for you, Sir Philip. Well, Orford in Suffolk actually, but compared to London it's hell.'

Sir Philip didn't share the same opinion. His father had loved that part of the coast and he'd passed his appreciation on to his son.

'It's where Gilchrist lives, as keeper at the Orford Ness lighthouse. I had to trek all the way out to that ruddy tower in the middle of nowhere just for a chat. Never heard of telephones, have they!' Rawlings saw Sir Philip wasn't interested in small talk and continued. 'In any event Gilchrist was able to tell me a few things that were never put into any official report and he never volunteered the information, until now, that is. It seems that there was a number of passengers on the *Parsimony* on the day she went down.' Rawlings didn't elaborate. 'He talked of two men, one a policeman and another a civil servant, who left the vessel before it sank. He said he could recall only one name. But perhaps he didn't want to give the other. Anyway, he'd never met them before and he never saw them again. His orders were to expedite their every requirement. The orders came from someone senior at the Excise Department, high up.'

He leaned out of his seat conspiratorially and lowered his voice. 'He reckoned the orders came from the Head of the Excise Department, a Mr Thomas Audrey.'

'And,' went on Rawlings, 'that's who your old boss is now working for. He's a parliamentary lobbyist for Mr Audrey.'

This was indeed news to Sir Philip, but he didn't show his surprise.

Rawlings went on. 'As to the identity of the third unlisted passenger, well, Gilchrist wasn't too sure ...' Rawlings left the statement unfinished.

Sir Philip saw Rawlings's motive. He was fishing for a financial inducement to reveal the name. Sir Philip had already guessed the name some time ago, but he needed it confirming. At last, the nature of the beast, he thought.

Rawlings's black piggy eyes gleamed and his face looked wet. The man involuntarily licked his lips. 'The thing is, Phil, Sir Philip –' he corrected himself just enough to suggest it wasn't blackmail '– The thing is I could use a bit more in the way of a pay rise. Or a bonus.'

Sir Philip waved a hand to signal that he would agree to the demands but did not wish to negotiate the sordid details.

Rawlings pressed his luck. 'Five hundred pounds.'

Sir Philip didn't bat an eyelid. It was a considerable sum of money, but both men knew it would be appropriated from the Treasury by way of the War Office.

'It was your father, Sir Neville, on the *Parsimony* that day.'

―――

James felt the restraining hand on his shoulder ease its pressure. Herr Dorpmuller mentioned a few final rules. Buildings were out of bounds; all the ladies were to remain in the drawing room for the full fifteen minutes to ensure a fair game. The winner was to return to Cragside at the end to collect their prize.

James and Herr Dorpmuller stood by the large wooden doorway leading to the hall. Herr Dorpmuller coughed loudly to attract everyone's attention. He made a final announcement.

'Ladies, before I set young Master Smith on his way, I think there should be one last inducement for the boy to ensure that he's full of competitive spirit.' A few titters broke out from the crowd of women who now pressed forward in anticipation. Mrs Ardlibuckle, standing on the other side of Herr Dorpmuller, leaned close and leered at James. 'Would you lovely ladies kindly reveal yourselves to this young man?'

*

## The Balance Between

James was off as fast as his legs would carry him. He tore around the back of the house, catching the eager looks of dragon faces straining at windows before he ducked out of sight. He ran to the coach house and dived inside, slipped into the gap left in the wooden planking between the automobiles and down the steps. Groping around in the dark his hand caught the line that Tempus had managed to string along the length of the tunnel to guide James in the dark.

James set off at a fair trot, scared that he might run into a wall, but every yard told him Tempus had done a good job. Twice he grazed his knuckles where the rope looped around a wooden post or jutting rock, but that was a small price to pay. He ran on, faster still. Three minutes after starting his run, he was at the broken gate and mounting the stairs to the top. Here he met with Baranor and Tempus in the lee of the pumping station, away from prying eyes. James quickly climbed aboard the bear and they were off.

A bear can outrun a horse over a reasonable distance, such is their strength and stamina. After ten minutes they were almost three miles from Cragside at the base of Shirlah Pike where they'd found the cave two nights ago. This meant the dragon would have a potential search area of over twenty square miles to cover. And because James had used the underground tunnel she wouldn't be able to follow his trail.

Baranor climbed to the top of the cliff and James slid off the bear's back. Below them Tempus kept a sharp lookout towards Cragside.

The dragons were hysterical with the excitement of the hunt. It was a marvellous bit of impromptu organising on the part of Herr Dorpmuller. It had been priceless to witness the look on the human's face as every lady had transformed into her true dragon identity. Mrs Mable Ardlibuckle was now Friedeswine Mountainscorcher, a splendidly large, fierce, red and green dragon with satisfyingly cruel claws, an exquisite example of formidable dentition and a bloodlust to match. She had to be physically restrained, such was her desire to start the chase, but Herr Dorpmuller kept the drawing room doors shut the full fifteen minutes in the interests of fair play. Being a Prussian, Herr Dorpmuller always stuck precisely to the rules, and this would be a record-breaking attempt as well. At the stroke of fifteen minutes, the doors burst open and Friedeswine Mountainscorcher took to the air in a rush of wings and fire. Once aloft the dragon circled several times, her sharp eyes searching for movement nearby. Next she scented, attempting to locate the trail of the boy. She soared down to the coach house and smashed in the garage doors, wrecking a number of the vehicles inside. Scrambling over the automobiles she did yet more damage but failed to find the boy. He had gone to ground.

Enraged, she flew skywards again and spotted her fellow dragons crowded on to the front lawn of the house, all eager to watch the spectacle unfold. Friedeswine Mountainscorcher grew angrier by the second. She would have to hunt by sight, and she must catch the little vermin soon, or be humiliated in front of the others.

'I see her,' called Tempus from below.

James looked at Baranor.

'Right, where do you want it?' Baranor asked the boy, and James indicated his left cheek. A paw flashed out and James only just had time to see a yellow claw whistle past his face before the warm stickiness of blood ran freely down his chin and onto his clothes.

'Make sure you spread it about a lot, James,' advised Baranor as James wiped the wound with both sleeves.

'Now she's stopped,' Tempus called in a howl. 'I think she's seen you. Yes. Yes, she has. Get ready!'

\*

## The Balance Between

Mountainscorcher turned about, her wings working like oars turning a rowing boat on its axis. That boy had managed to evade her long enough! Then she smelled blood, human blood. There! She saw him, high up on a cliff a good way off. Her eyes narrowed as she watched. It was her turn to be amazed. The boy was battling a large furry animal. 'By all the black magic!' she exclaimed. A bear! She hadn't seen or heard of one in these parts for quite a few years, and it was a magnificent creature. What a trophy! The dragon watched a few moments longer, unperturbed by the jeering from the crowd below. This would make an even better hunt, one that would go down in history! In the distance the bear felled the boy with a giant swing of its paw. Then it too disappeared over the cliff. Quick as a blast of dragon flame, Mountainscorcher arrowed at the cliff face.

'There's no time to lose. Off with those clothes,' Tempus said. James stripped off his outer garments and threw them to the floor. They were covered in his blood. He ran further into the cavern where they'd hidden the carcass of a sheep Baranor had killed in the early hours of the morning. The head, coat and hooves had been removed and left out on the moors. It was now just a giant, bloody hunk of meat. James grabbed the heavy rug they'd stolen from the house and dragged it into position over a fragile wooden lean-to arrangement set against the wall, with the carcass beneath. Tempus and Baranor retreated to the very back of the cave. James followed and together they hid beneath a tarpaulin taken from the garage store and waited.

Mountainscorcher beat her wings as she hovered at the cliff face. A trail of blood led down from the top of the cliff to a clump of bushes at the base.

That's where that bear took the dead boy, she thought. She let a jet of fire fall on the bushes below. 'A little wake up call for Mr Bear,' she laughed.

*The Balance Between*

Far off, the spectators 'oohed' at the sight of flames. The hunt was hotting up.

The dragon landed, pushed her way through the burning bushes and stopped at the cave mouth. She gave a dragon roar and was satisfied to hear the bear's defiant reply. She stepped into the entrance of the cave, but the walls narrowed too quickly for her to make much progress. Her wings struck the sides, preventing her from entering the cave any further. Frustrated, she let out another bellow and the bear answered with an equally ferocious response.

Mountainscorcher strained her eyes. She could just make out the figure of the bear. She smelled the blood of the dead boy, his bloody clothes scattered at her feet. And the bear stank, a smell she'd not smelled for hundreds of years. She let out a blast of red-hot flame. It seared right to the back of the cave, catching the bear full on. She saw it burst into flames and collapse on the floor. Another blast for good luck and it would be toast.

The dragon craned her neck as far as she could and managed to nip a tuft of scorched fur between her teeth. She dragged out her trophy. All that remained was a bear paw and a strip of skin. A lump of charred meat rolled out from underneath it and she gulped it down without thought, satisfied and smug with victory.

Friedeswine Mountainscorcher rose up in the air and triumphantly carried the meagre trophy back to the roaring assembly. With a satisfactory time of four minutes sixteen seconds for the Time to Kill, Mrs Mable Ardlibuckle gained additional status for having successfully hunted the hunter. A bearkill was many times superior to a young human.

James, Tempus and Baranor looked over the top of the heavy tarpaulin. The surface was scorched black and still smouldered. All three had crinkly hair from the blast of heat. They looked at each other, and then burst out laughing. Never try to reason with a dragon.

*The Balance Between*

## 1895

Corrick stepped into the room with his gun levelled. The occupants were surprised by his unexpected arrival and stood in bewilderment. All, that is, except for the warrior creature. It made a grab for the long jagged blade that hung by its side. Corrick didn't hesitate. Two shots crashed around the confines of the room. The creature staggered, but kept coming, the knife now in its hand. Corrick aimed one more shot and blew the monster's head from its shoulders. The body fell, lifeless, to the ground. Everyone's attention was fixed on the gun.

'We'll have no more sudden movement,' Corrick commanded. The four men remained motionless. Corrick edged round to cover the door as well as the men. 'Are there any more of these things lurking about?' He nudged the dead creature with the toe of his shoe.

The men shook their heads. 'Nein,' said one of them.

Corrick looked down at the figure. 'What was it?' he asked the man who'd replied.

The man checked with his colleagues before shrugging and answering, 'An olorc. That was General Balerust, chief of the olorcish armies in the south.' The man had a heavy European accent, German, Corrick guessed.

'An olorc?'

'Ja. They are cruel and terrible creatures, but make for excellent slave labour, und are fierce warriors.'

Corrick made the men empty their pockets on a table and then herded them into a corner. He sat in a chair, the gun trained on them as they stood with their backs to the wall, hands on their heads. 'Now then. You gentlemen are going to tell me exactly what is going on here.'

*The Balance Between*

# 1910

The friends slipped cautiously from the cave after Tempus had checked the coast was clear. They couldn't afford to be caught if the dragons came hunting for more trophies. They made their way by a circuitous route to the head of the dam, down the staircase and back into the tunnel. Once inside, they fell into discussing the recent events.

'What made you think of that ruse?' Tempus asked James.

'Well, when I went into Frau Colbetz's room looking for clues I hid under the bed to avoid being caught. I saw the bear rug in front of the fire. I reckoned she wouldn't notice its absence, especially with the way that dragon sticks her nose in the air.' He turned to Baranor. 'I'm sorry we had to resort to such a ploy, my friend. It was disrespectful to have used that bear's skin so cruelly,' he said.

Baranor looked at the lad and replied, 'It was a fine way for that bear to be laid to rest, helping us all survive. And now that his hide has been given a dragon-flame cremation there is nothing but dignity for the old bear.' Baranor's eyes glistened with gratitude. He placed a paw on James's shoulder and continued, 'I am proud to call you my friend, James Kinghorn. You took that wound like a warrior. You played the hunt like a true hunter and you have the cunning of –' he thought a moment '– the cunning of a human. A good human.' James and the bear gave each other a great big hug.

It was Tempus who now set off to eavesdrop on the dragons from inside the servants' quarters. The hound had warned that the smell of James's wound might arouse the dragons. Baranor went off to forage on the other side of the hill and James lay down for some sleep. It seemed like only a few moments later that James awoke from his slumber and they were all back together. They retreated to the outdoor stairwell, and, under cover of the darkening evening, enjoyed roast mutton, again.

'That dragon Frau Colbetz has shown her hand at last,' began the hound. 'She intends to use the blackest of magic to conquer this world. Somehow she's found a way to communicate with the other side of the portals. Her allies in Eldaterra are planning to send assistance to this world and help the dragons in their conquest.' Tempus gnawed briefly on a bone before starting up again. 'There are a number of portals that they've used. For years the enemy have sought to cross these portals. Apparently magic creatures may not pass through. And they know that, without magic, the science of this world will cruelly slaughter them.' Again there was a pause for a spot of bone gnawing. 'They have found a way around the portals.'

Frau Colbetz sat in the study with Herr Dorpmuller. 'Julius, my lover. It is time. You must make your way back to the coast. The time has come when we must set our plan in motion.' Her hooded eyes watched as a tiny nervous tic pulled at the side of Herr Dorpmuller's mouth. It was as she expected. This little Prussian had proved big on words, but when it came to the crunch, he was showing a distinct lack of spine. She pressed him further. 'You must set off soon. Take my car, it will be more comfortable. But –' she slid her hand to his knee and the hand transformed into a claw that grabbed him with just enough pain to make him whimper '– do not fail me.'

Herr Dorpmuller dragged the wreckage of the car from the coach house, kicking the board back into place over the mechanic's pit. The car was in a sorry state. 'That dragon,' he thought. 'That putrid lump of reptilian –' He cursed under his breath as he cranked the car, got in and drove off.

Baranor stuck his head up over the top of the stairwell and saw the headlamps of the car making their goggly way along the drive, the motor vehicle lost behind the brilliance of the lights. 'One of them is leaving,' he called.

'We need to know who it is,' said James with the sound of increasing authority in his voice.

'Hang on, then. This looks fun.' Tempus ran off into the dark to chase his first ever motorcar.

When he returned, panting and exhausted, all he could gasp out was 'man'. That was all that was necessary.

## 1895

Corrick sat back and took a while to take on board what he had just heard. Of the four men in the room, three of them were surgeons. The fourth, Victor Brack, was the man responsible for the organisation. The policeman looked at his captives. 'What you are doing is an abomination to God and humanity,' he said in revulsion.

The young surgeon named Mrugowsky shrugged his shoulders in a dismissive fashion. 'They are not human, nein?'

Corrick stared at the man in anger. 'And what of the women, the ones you placed those "things" in?' He spat the word out.

'Ach, only the first few experiments were conducted on human guinea pigs, the women captives. But they were not satisfactory carriers. Zo, we switch to these creatures. They are a much slower gestation, yes, but a more effective female carrier. They are of this world. Strange beings. The dead one –' he pointed at the corpse '– Balerust, he despised them. He called them the *marked*. He provided us with "volunteers" for our research. We could not refuse.'

Another doctor, whose name was Sievers, joined in. 'Ja. The work we have done here. It represents a great step forward in medical and scientific discovery. Think how this knowledge may be put to use in our world.' His young face lit up with a strange fanatical glow.

Corrick hated the single-minded, amoral zeal with which they justified their work. 'And how exactly would this work benefit "our world"? Isn't it enough that there are too many mouths to feed across Europe? For God's sake, can you not see our world doesn't need this and neither does theirs?' Corrick read their blank faces. These men of science lacked any shred of humanity.

'But we give these *mischlinge* the chance of a future,' Mrugowsky justified. 'You see how they treat their own kind. This way they become *kindersegen*, blessed with children.' Mrugowsky squared his shoulders in defiance.

Corrick cocked the pistol and pointed it at his chest. 'Don't try to justify your horrific butchering, you psychotic filth.' He breathed deeply, calming the rage that threatened to overwhelm his own morality.

He rounded them up, drove them down the steps and through the halls to the gateway. He had no idea what he was doing, but he had reckoned on one of his prisoners knowing how to raise the portcullis. When they got there, it was open.

'Now, I don't make a habit of killing people in cold blood so I'm going to turn you out of that gate and you're going to get the hell out of England because, when I'm through here, I'll search high and low for you. If I find you, I'll kill you,' he snarled.

The doctors cowered at his threat and Corrick had to push and goad them through the gateway. When the last one shuffled fearfully beyond the threshold, the portcullis fell with a resounding crash, and they were gone.

Corrick turned back. He knew his work was not yet done. The fall of the portcullis had told him as much. And now the words of the inscription were beginning to make sense. It would get harder, much harder.

He returned to the room where the olorc body lay. Checking to make sure he hadn't overlooked anything, he noticed the creature's knife had gone. Someone had been in the room. He turned left out of the doorway and continued through the tunnel complex, moving further away from the gate.

# 1910

Sir Philip sat in his office and contemplated his next move. It would be a very delicate one, one that could compromise whatever situation his son was in. He called his private secretary from the adjoining room.

'Get me a meeting with the Secretary of State for War, Theodore.' Sir Philip's tone ensured his private secretary took this to be a most important matter. Theodore went to speak with the Secretary of State for War's own private secretary personally. He was back in ten minutes.

'He will see you in forty minutes, Sir Philip.'

'I am much obliged, Theodore.'

Sir Philip was ushered into the palatial offices of his boss, the Secretary of State for War. The rooms were high up in one of the corner towers overlooking the River Thames and the Palace of Westminster. The secretary of State rose from behind the dreadnought-sized desk. On the walls, where oils of ships at sea had once been displayed, there now hung gaudishly graceless works by Romantic painters.

'Ah, Philip, glad I could fit you in.' The Secretary of State for War extended his hand and motioned Sir Philip to sit. 'How is it going with all that cloak-and-dagger stuff of yours?'

'We continue to turn up the truth occasionally, Minister.' Sir Philip returned the platitude adroitly.

The minister paused and looked at his subordinate. 'Jolly good. So what may I do for you?'

'It is a rather delicate situation, Minister, one that I am sure His Majesty's Government would wish to avoid at all costs.' Sir Philip

## The Balance Between

watched as the minister's ears pricked up. He'd only been installed in the War Office these past few months since the election, and with the prospect of a new election to break parliamentary stalemate, every Member of Parliament was keen to return to the hustings with a strong profile in government, however briefly.

'Well, something to rattle the opposition with, I hope,' the minister replied from behind the safety of his leviathan desk. Sir Philip knew him to be an ambitious man, a professional manipulator who had seen to it that his predecessor, Richard Haldane, had lost out in the post-election cabinet reshuffle.

'It may well do, if it were to leak out, Minister.'

'Oh, excellent. It would serve me, and the department of course, if we could get a quick success under our collective belts before the Prime Minister calls the next election.' Sir Philip was aware that this last bit of information was meant to be hush-hush, but the Secretary of State had spent his career bartering secrets for personal gain.

'Minister, I feel I should disarm you of your expectations of what I am about to tell you.' Sir Philip dropped his voice and the minister leaned over the desk in anticipation. 'Were you not at one time the junior minister at the Excise Department while it was still part of the Inland Revenue? Am I correct in believing that you were my minister while I was excise officer for the Pools of London division?'

The minister sat back, suspicious of Sir Philip's line of enquiry which had suddenly taken on a more threatening tone. 'Sir Philip, this is a matter of record. Where is your line of questioning going and to what do you refer?' The Secretary of State's Machiavellian mind was racing to remember and review details from his own past. Had this member of his own staff been prying into his history? He would put a stop to it. Instantly!

'Sir Philip. If you think it's your place to investigate the private affairs of your senior minister, then you are very much mistaken. I have been aware for some time of the potential conflict of interest that exists when a single member of government has control of the nation's intelligence service. I can only presume that you have been spying on me out of loyalty to my predecessor, Haldane.' The Secretary sat there, puffed up with his own self-importance. 'I shall be taking immediate steps to remove your authority prior to an official announcement that you will be retiring.' The minister had played his trump card and was gleeful in his victory.

Sir Philip remained totally calm as he dropped his voice an octave and left his adversary straining to hear. 'Mr Thomas Audrey, I have proof that your political manipulations led directly to the deaths of eleven seamen from the crew of the *Parsimony*.'

The minister was both enraged at the slight by Sir Philip in referring to him as a commoner and not as a minister, and dismissive of his accusation. 'Phah, Kinghorn. You know very well that the original testimony of the captain was proved to be worthless. That idiot drove the *Parsimony* onto a sandbar and paid the price. And you, as his immediate superior, paid the price too. You can't change the facts, and they've stood for fifteen years.'

'Yes, Minister. And after fifteen years I have a witness, an unimpeachable witness. Someone who was there that day.'

## ∽ 15 ∽

## A Line is Drawn

The automobile came to rest among the sand dunes as the early moon came up and began its journey across the northern firmament. The clear sky gave a ghostly feel to the night, washing away the colours of day and leaving long shadows trailing in the west as the sun lingered beyond the horizon.

Herr Dorpmuller climbed out of the car and staggered up a steep dune, the sands slipping away under his tread, making the going slow and awkward. At the top of the dune he looked around for the two German naval ratings that had made landfall two nights before. He couldn't see anyone.

He called out in a low voice. Nothing. He repeated his call, this time a little louder. Still nothing. As he finished hollering for a third time a voice piped up from the dark shadows of a sand dune. 'Shut up. We heard you the first time.'

The two uniformed men came marching out of the gloom. They were carrying their signals equipment. 'We were where you left us, further down the beach,' one of the ratings said by way of explanation.

Herr Dorpmuller didn't consider himself in the wrong, but he considered these sailor boys to be rude and discourteous.

'Signal the boat that I must be taken aboard immediately.'

The two ratings looked at each other and then humped the

*The Balance Between*

equipment they'd just dropped in the sand back onto their shoulders. They trudged off.

'Where are you going?' Herr Dorpmuller called, somewhat alarmed at their retreat.

'To set up the equipment in a suitable location for signalling the ship. We can't see it from here.' The other sailor added his own thoughts: 'Idiot.'

An hour later a boat landed from the *Ausburg* and Herr Dorpmuller was conveyed to the warship. Once aboard he was taken to Captain Raeder.

'And why, pray, have I the pleasure of your company and not that of the infinitely more interesting Frau Colbetz?' asked the captain. He was visibly disappointed to be denied the pleasure of the lady's company.

'Captain, Frau Colbetz requests that you escort me down the coast a short distance where I may deliver a message.'

Captain Raeder was nonplussed by this request. 'I may point out Herr Dorpmuller that my orders, from the Kaiser himself, were specifically intended for the benefit of Frau Colbetz. I do not intend to be a glorified taxi for any popinjay that attaches himself to her entourage. The answer is no.' With that the captain dismissed him.

Herr Dorpmuller gave a look of resignation. As he reached the door held open by the duty marine, he turned and said, 'In which case I believe Frau Colbetz will be here shortly.'

Herr Dorpmuller stood outside at the highest accessible point of the ship's superstructure and placed a small conical silver whistle to his lips. He gave one long, noiseless blast.

Far to the west in her suite at Cragside, Frau Colbetz was feeling slightly unsettled by something. 'What is it?' she thought. 'Something I've overlooked.' She was distracted by the blast of the ultrasonic whistle. The whistle worked like a dog whistle – inaudible to

## The Balance Between

most animals – except in this instance the sound was inaudible to dogs too. It also performed a pattern that only Frau Colbetz could recognise. She knew it was Dorpmuller.

She stood and went to the French windows, opening them to the deepening sky. Bathed in the copper-orange glow from the west she transformed from her human image into her dragon self, Komargoran Monarchmauler, self-proclaimed Queen-by-Violence of all Dragons in the New World and Deliverer of the Portal Lands. She spread her silver and blue wings and rode the evening breeze, her golden underbelly flashing in the last of the daylight.

'Captain, I am sooo sorry to intrude.'

Captain Raeder looked up from his papers and found to his surprise that Frau Colbetz stood at the open door to his sleeping cabin. His eyes caressed her lithe body. 'Liebe Fraulein. I did not hear you come in,' he began to apologise as he rose up from his desk and moved swiftly to lead the woman to a seat. Come to think of it I didn't hear her piped aboard, he thought to himself.

'Thank you, Captain. I believe you were too deep in your thoughts to have noticed little old me.'

'Never, my lady.' He spoke with a voice full of desire and hunger. Frau Colbetz could make every man act this way.

'I have come to plead the case of my extremely important assistant, Herr Dorpmuller. It was of course rude of me to assume you would graciously accept my request, and I so much understand the importance of your other commitments.' Frau Colbetz voice choked with syrupy femininity and guile. Captain Raeder found her hard to resist.

'Frau Colbetz, please accept my apologies. I did not mean to inconvenience you or your Herr Dorpmuller. It is, as you say, the pressures of command. I will arrange to have my ship raise anchor in the next few minutes. I must say how pleased I am that you have rejoined us, Frau Colbetz.'

## The Balance Between

'My dear Captain.' She fluttered her eyes at him and turned her face up to his, striking an alluring pose. 'I am afraid I cannot stay. I must fly.'

A short while later Captain Raeder watched the boat return from shore having disembarked Frau Colbetz. No one could explain how she had got on board in the first place.

---

James sat in the pale moonlight with the book Sibelius had given him. Baranor lay gently snoring, and Tempus stretched out next to him. James was worried, worried as no fourteen-year-old should ever be. Today he'd only just managed to escape from the dragon hunt, and earlier Tempus had overheard Frau Colbetz plot to 'drag evil from the darkest corner and overthrow the world of science'. Sibelius had warned of the struggle between good and evil in Eldaterra, but the wizard didn't know of events beyond the Sea Arch in the New World.

A groan of despair escaped James. 'What are we going to do?' he asked himself. He watched the stars above him slowly wheel. He thought of his mother and father. Sir Philip could help but he was too far away. And in any event he'd never believe James, and by the time he did it would be too late.

Something winked at him and he looked down.

*You must finish the entertainment.*

James looked at the answer on the page without understanding it. He asked, 'What is the entertainment?' The book replied:

*The dragon entertainment.*

'Why finish it?'

*To halt the spread of darkness.*

## The Balance Between

'Is this to do with the plot by Frau Colbetz and if so why exactly finish the entertainment?' The book replied:

*This will halt the plot of Komargoran Monarchmauler whom you call Frau Colbetz.*

*To finish the entertainment is to initiate the last activity, Talon Grab. This is the only proven means for a party to kill a dragon without the party being killed.*

*For the activity to successfully halt the plot of Komargoran Monarchmauler it is vital that each of the following criteria are satisfied during the activity.*
1. *That Komargoran Monarchmauler is one of the participants of the Talon Grab duel.*
2. *That Komargoran Monarchmauler is one of the participants killed in the Talon Grab duel.*

James looked at this new information. It was one thing to evade a dragon and quite another thing to come back from the dead to provoke a fight. 'How do I initiate a Talon Grab?'

*Use the weaknesses in all dragons. Please refer to specialist topics: Vanity, Greed, Envy and Avarice.*

'More information on the initiating, please.'

*You must provoke the enemy.*

The solution was too much for James, who was weary and worn out. His head slumped down on to his chin, just as he began to dream about Solomon and Bartholomew.

'We haven't got long. Shake a leg, sonny.'
James opened his eyes to find a big, hairy face close to his. Baranor was up early.

'Oh go away, you big bear. Leave me to sleep.' James tried to close his eyes but a mug of tea was pushed into his hands. 'Thanks, Baranor, but I am trying to sleep.'

'Since when do bears make tea?' said a voice remarkably like Solomon's.

'Or let young lads lie in after sunrise,' added a voice like Bartholomew's.

James sat up, rubbed his eyes and gave the dwarves a smile that showed how happy he was to see the them.

'Don't worry, James, my lad,' said Solomon. 'We've been up talking with your chums.'

Baranor and Tempus were lapping bowls of tea, something of a first for both of them. Bartholomew had recommended its revitalising qualities, but Baranor just drank the tea because it had sugar in it.

'We've heard all about your adventures from Tempus and Baranor,' Bartholomew told James.

'So we'll oblige you with our modest tale,' continued Solomon, who then told of how Captain Dolmir had rallied the remaining horsemen after the diversion. They'd all set off at the gallop, Solomon clinging to his pony with his arms about its neck, and raced round the hill and into the woods to meet the enemy from a new direction. Once their leader was dead, the enemy's courage failed and they scattered in the woods. The captain ordered the recovery of the fallen troopers and it was then that they found Bartholomew lying in the dark, sound asleep.

'I was not asleep,' Bartholomew interrupted in protest. 'I was knocked out. And I have the bear as a witness. He saw me fall.'

They all laughed and Solomon continued the story. After Bartholomew had recovered his wits, the brothers had decided to follow James through the Sea Arch the following night. Once in this world they'd tracked the three companions.

'There was something strange going on. Your footprints had

been erased, like someone wanted you hidden. So we made sure our tracks disappeared as well,' Solomon said, fixing a look at James as if expecting an answer. James couldn't think why this should have happened and said so.

'Anyway, all we had to do really was follow the dead sheep,' Bartholomew said. 'We eventually found you when we caught a glimpse of a dragon in the sky. We knew you'd be in the same place. Call it fate, if you like.'

James told the company about his questions to the book, and the answers. They all agreed it was a very grave situation. The two dwarves were quite excited about another opportunity for a pyrric dwarfish victory until Baranor pointed out they wouldn't be alone and not everyone else was quite so excited by the prospect. By now the morning promised a fine day. In fact, it was going to be a very hot day.

---

The *Ausburg* stood off the Thames estuary at just after one o'clock in the morning. Captain Raeder had raced his ship down the eastern coastline of England through the night. With each passing kilometre he wondered how Frau Colbetz had persuaded him into this mad dash. It was, he reasoned, her quite magnetic personality, and he swore never to fall for such a character again.

Herr Dorpmuller was put ashore on the Essex coast, but the captain informed him that the ship would be returning north immediately and that Herr Dorpmuller should in future consider civilian modes of transport. The *Ausburg* would be back on station in eight hours if luck had anything to do with it.

Tramping over the beach, Dorpmuller found the gateway and portcullis in the early morning haze. Walking up to it he hesitated a moment. Freislung had not yet returned from his last mission, and that worried Dorpmuller. Freislung should have brought word of final preparations being completed. His resolve tottered at the brink of quitting, but then he remembered the spell-binding beauty of Frau Colbetz, and her terrible wrath. He stepped through the gateway to deliver his message.

After the shock of changing from one world to another had worn off, Herr Dorpmuller pulled a map from his pocket, handed to him by Freislung on his last successful mission. He wondered whether Freislung was still alive and decided it was probably better if he was not.

And besides, Herr Dorpmuller thought, I have the details of his Swiss bank account.

Following the map he made his way quickly and directly through the corridors and caverns up to the room where Corrick had encountered the scientists all those years before. This was supposedly where the invasion army was to be assembled, ready to stream through the portals in a numberless multitude and conquer the whole of Europe. Then Frau Colbetz would be Queen and he would be her Consort, perhaps her King. But Herr Dorpmuller did not find what he expected. All the rooms and caverns were empty. A sense of apprehension crawled over his skin. He must find General Balerust and initiate the invasion.

## 1895

Corrick looked at the problem philosophically. He'd come through the gateway armed with a handgun seeking justice for the murders of four women, five if you included the Zeebrugge victim. He'd found the culprit, of sorts, and meted out rough justice to the dead olorc called Balerust, but the hideous practices of the creatures continued. So now he'd have to put a stop to that. Lord knows, I have good enough reason, he thought.

The complex of tunnels and caverns eventually led him to the lowermost floor deep underground. There, at the heart of the mountain, lay a dark secret: a volcano. It did not erupt and behave like most volcanoes, wild and unpredictable. Instead, dark powers had channelled its primal forces long ago and created a crime so original and yet so heinous that the energy of earth was utterly corrupted. What was once molten magma now distilled into a purity of evil unlike anything produced by the world in all its history. The volcano had been transformed into a huge engine capable of creating motherless life.

The scientists had revealed the secret to Corrick before he'd thrown them out. They'd pleaded with him to let them stay and continue with their work. They honestly believed that they could conjoin science and sorcery. The callow scientists spoke of rituals and magic as if they believed in it. Corrick only believed what he saw, but now, as he stood and beheld it, the most awe-inspiring revelation that one could witness, he understood its significance, and power. Distracted, Corrick was unaware of someone behind him.

'Now I understand,' a voice said.

Corrick was surprised by the voice but he couldn't tear his eyes off the spectacle before him. Slowly he turned around and saw the man, a short way off, holding the blade taken from the fallen olorc general. He too was captivated by the vision.

The man, tall, in his fifties and still remarkably fit-looking, ignored Corrick and gazed out across the enormous cavern. A radiance of such beauty and clarity filled the void like the sun. Every colour one could ever imagine shone forth, so rich they were like texture. The yellows were soft silk that caressed the eye. Reds were all the wine and fruits that nature provides distilled into an essence of colour that stained the retina. Blues were the delicacy of a million dragonfly wings all held in the curve of the iris. The room whirled with the vitality of it all. And at the very heart of the source of this pure colour they saw a small globe of light form and grow, capturing the colours and movements all around. Eventually the globe of light grew too large to hang in a cradle of rainbows and fell, slipping down a gentle incline and cooling as it rolled. Then another globe of light would form and grow in the same way, slowly repeating, again and again. At the bottom of the gently sloping conical hill the same creatures that worked throughout the complex stood patiently, waiting to pick up the cooling, coalescing globe and take it away. It struck Corrick that they wouldn't be able to see any of this.

'This is what the inscription talks about, in the poem,' the man said.

Corrick tried to recall the poem, but he couldn't. He turned to the other man. 'Do you remember it?' he asked.

'Yes. All of it.' And the man began to recite the inscription from memory.

As he spoke the poem, Corrick recalled it too. But where Corrick's message had run to five verses, the stranger's had a sixth and a seventh.

> *Let us speak of evil deeds*
> *That at present nurture here*
> *Its scaly curse to plant the seeds*
> *In divided worlds for those to fear*
>
> *Seek out the canker of these crimes*
> *Before this place forever falls*
> *To those all counted in the nines*
> *Turned up and on by deathly calls*
>
> *Know that you stand alone as first*
> *And last to follow is the younger*
> *Together seek those whose cursed*
> *Knowledge drives this wicked hunger*

## The Balance Between

*Find them in their darkest dream*
*Before the alchemy is finished*
*The horror of this crime wiped clean*
*Or stand mankind to be diminished*

*Look to blackest heart of granite*
*Ancient in its most secret magic*
*Science end this dragon birthpit*
*A weakened world the coin for logic*

*Accept a fate to wander wide*
*This bordered land in shadow*
*They seek you for the altered side*
*Hushed along this path must go*

*Or fall to that by choice makes free*
*To serve them by mere mortal sin*
*The snare is closed with subtlety*
*Then cast thy lot and serve Warkrin*

The other man spoke. 'I followed you in. Through the gate, I mean.' He could see Corrick's confusion. 'I was on the boat too. You might think of me as an unofficial passenger.'

Corrick nodded. The man didn't volunteer a name, and Corrick didn't feel like asking any more.

'Look, Chief Inspector … Sorry, I overheard your companion call you that. I don't admit to being very good at solving crimes, but I am fairly good at puzzles, and I think the verses contain clues as to why we are here. I'd say we've reached the deepest part of this mountain, and it might be described as a "heart of granite". The verse talks about magic and if that –' he pointed to the brilliant display '– isn't the most amazing display of magic ever, then we're not up to the task.'

'And I can see those globes forming in that cradle are dragons, or at least the embryos of dragons,' Corrick added. 'Which makes this the birthpit.'

'In which case we need to think how science can end it,' said the other man. They stood considering the position.

'Look, what do you have in your bag?' the man asked. Corrick swung it off his shoulder and emptied the contents on the ground. At the very bottom of the canvas rucksack, hidden beneath the clothes, two hand grenades rolled out. Corrick and the older man looked at each other, and at the grenades. It seemed a remote possibility, but the hand grenades were positively the only real science the two men could hope to employ.

Corrick stooped and picked them up, handing one to his new accomplice. 'You know how to use one of these?' he asked.

'Yes.' They checked the fuses on the grenades.

Corrick turned and judged the distance to be forty yards, a long throw for a trained person, let alone either of them.

'We'll throw together. That way the combined effect may do some damage. On the count of three.'

They destroyed the birthpit, a simple task as it turned out. When the grenades exploded it was like a sledgehammer taken to a shimmering chandelier. Instantly the colours and patterns splintered into shards and fell. Like a fountain turned off, the light faltered and failed, leaving only an after-image in Corrick's mind. The two men had cried after its destruction. Neither of them could help it. They knew they'd destroyed a most beautiful thing, which, despite its warped purpose, had somehow touched their souls.

They made their way back through the underground complex to the gateway. As they passed through the halls they saw the poor mutilated workers continuing at their mindless labour until the whole process ground to a halt. And then they just stood where they were, waiting for someone to come along and restart the work and their reason for being. The men cried again in despair at the wretchedness of the creatures known to be *marked*.

Now the gateway was closed, an inscription awaited them. It read,

> *Now Creation's fairest work destroyed*
> *Ended the mountain of black dreams*
> *Worlds step away this fate avoid*
> *Push back the issue of these schemes.*
>
> *One step forward if one step away*
> *The path lies here and there one goes*
> *But in this emptiness one must stay*
> *To work in silence and shadow.*

'I know the meaning of these words,' said the stranger, and in his heart Corrick knew them too. They parted as friends, having shared in that brief time together something they could never explain to anyone else. Corrick gave the rucksack and provisions to his companion, as well as the pistol and ammunition. They embraced and said farewell. The portcullis rose noiselessly and Corrick stepped through the gateway. His task, which the inscription had prophesied, was complete.

He stood with the wind ruffling his greying hair and the sea on his lips. The late February sky was clear, with high clouds streaming in the upper atmosphere, the only hint of the previous day's bad weather. Corrick was glad to be back. He marched along the beach. He wasn't sure how he was going to get off the island, but he'd figure that out. After everything else in the last thirty-six hours, it would be easy.

## 1910

Sir Philip met Harrington at the War Office very early that morning. They travelled in a ministerial motor car to King's Cross and caught a train north. Harrington was itching to know on what errand they were set, but Sir Philip was disinclined to reveal their destination. Harrington, for some strange reason unable to read this man, resigned himself to the situation and sat watching the countryside from their first-class compartment.

'You never did say why you were on the *Parsimony*.'

This hit Harrington out of the blue. He looked over at Sir Philip but his reaction had already revealed the truth.

Damn, he thought to himself. He'd dropped his guard. It was an obvious ploy now; lulled into a sense of false security. Harrington sat back and sighed.

'I wasn't sure until your reaction just now,' said Sir Philip, who didn't press the question again. Instead he turned to gaze out of the window, wondering what Harrington would make of his next surprise.

They alighted at Huntingdon and Sir Philip flagged down a hansom cab. Outside London the motor car hadn't yet replaced horse-drawn carriages. Sir Philip gave an address in Hemingford Grey, a small, quiet village near the old country town of St Ives. Eventually the cab halted outside a small cottage, 'Rainbow's End'.

Sir Philip knocked on the door and, presently, an elderly gentleman opened it. A young child peered timidly round from behind her father. 'Good day, sir. I am looking for Chief Inspector Corrick.'

~~~~~~

Goramanshie saw the sun's orb sink behind the ridge of trees on the escarpment. It was time to begin. He roused the troop of olorcs with well-aimed kicks and sharp insults. They responded with mutterings of rebellion but gathered themselves together and

## The Balance Between

made ready. It was a big command, with over four-hundred warriors, far larger than Kagaminoc's party.

The olorc captain gathered his troops to speak. 'Tonight we are the vanguard of a mighty invasion. We will pass through the portal and prepare the other side for our armies that follow. Beyond that portal await our allies, the dragons in exile.' Several voices called approvingly at this news. 'Our generals have planned this for many years and have worked relentlessly. Now our forces will crush the enemy. The darkness of our lives will swell and fill all earth. We have been sent to stop the enemy using this portal. We must not fail.' The olorcs stood silent. Words don't inspire them, Goramanshie thought, only the bloodlust.

Slowly they began filing through the Sea Arch.

---

Lady Jennifer was awoken by the sound of gunfire coming from the beach. Dressing quickly, she ran downstairs to find Polly the housekeeper in a state of anxiety, clutching her apron to her face to hide the tears. Amanda was up, too, but firmly in control of her own nerves.

'I have checked that the doors and windows are locked, Aunt, and I have stoked the fire,' Amanda informed her. Lady Jennifer thanked her and crossed to the telephone. Her call was put through to her London home, but she was informed that Sir Philip had set off for the office very early. The office informed her that he'd taken a train from King's Cross but it was not known where he was headed. Lady Jennifer rang off in annoyance.

'It could be farmers shooting,' ventured Amanda.

'No, dear. That is rifle fire, quite distinct from the sound of a farmer's shotgun. And it's coming from the beach.'

## ∽ 16 ∽

## The Talon Grab

The contingent of olorcs infested the beach area around the Sea Arch, spreading out among the dunes. Goramanshie gave strict instructions to stay hidden and there they waited. Goramanshie's orders were to hold this position until reinforcements arrived, either through the portal or from the exiled dragons.

It was only a matter of minutes after arriving that an olorc, moving through the dunes, stumbled upon the two naval ratings in their camouflaged position. As the marines stared in disbelief at the creature, the olorc reacted first. It raised the scimitar in its hand and brought it down on the nearest man, cleaving his arm off below the elbow. The sailor fell to the ground in a dead faint but his comrade scrambled at a holster, drew out his handgun and shot the creature dead, and the next one, and the next.

On this, the final day of operations, Captain Raeder had the *Ausburg* stand close in to shore after they'd steamed all night to arrive off the coast at first light. He ordered the Imperial Eagle not to be flown. In its place they ran up the White Ensign. Today would require subterfuge and guile if they were to avoid an international incident.

'Captain, lookouts report gunfire from the beach.'

Captain Raeder raised his binoculars and stared out over the two kilometres. He held back from uttering an oath. This was to be a simple exercise, but already they had trouble.

'All ahead one-third, rudder hard over to starboard.' He barked out the orders. 'We will close to five-hundred metres. Prepare to launch the marines in boats. We will hold the beach until our guests are recovered.' Around him officers and ratings moved swiftly into action. Raeder felt complete confidence in his ship and crew, the finest vessel in the Kaiserliche Marine.

Captain Raeder crossed to the map table. The nearest port facility where Royal Naval vessels were based was some fifty kilometres to the south. If they sent a ship to investigate, the *Ausburg* would be more than a match for any British warship, not that he wanted to get involved in an incident.

'Any message from the beach?' he asked.

'Not yet, sir,' replied the signals officer.

Goramanshie looked down at the body of the enemy. They'd been waiting in ambush. One of their number had killed five of his warriors with their magic, which left little holes in the dead from which blood trickled. It wasn't impressive, not like a sword slash, but it was effective, very effective. He cursed his superiors for sending him through the archway without at least some magic for protection. Why hadn't they come prepared? The olorc stooped down and picked up the metal rod that lay in the sand. It had wood bound to it, and complex workings on the top and underside. The metal was both smooth and rough, as if forged but not polished. Goramanshie could not understand its magic and let it fall to the sand.

Able seaman Holtz fell panting in the marram grass. He'd beaten off the attack but not before his petty officer had been cut down and hacked to pieces. Escaping by the skin of his teeth, Holtz had remembered to grab the signal lamp as he'd run. Now, amidst the dunes, he recognised the false sense of security they provided. The enemy could be just over the next dune, preparing to attack! His heart still beating madly, he grabbed the equipment and kept running.

'Five-hundred metres off the beach, Captain,' confirmed the quartermaster.
'Away boats.'
'Aye aye, Captain.'
Captain Raeder watched as the two larger cutters and the pair of smaller pinnaces made the journey across. He swept his binoculars along both directions of the empty beach. Things are getting out of control, he realised.

The officer of the watch diverted his attention. 'Captain, a figure is in the surf, waving. It's one of our men.'
'Yes, I see him. The boats are almost ashore. Lieutenant Reitsch will take control,' the ship's captain said confidently, but nothing could have been further from the truth.

Lieutenant Reitsch leapt from the boat at the first bite of her keel. Waving his arm he urged the thirty-eight marines onto the beach where they formed a skirmish line. Two marines ran to meet able seaman Holtz as he staggered the last ten metres. They took him under the arms and half carried him over to the lieutenant.

'What happened?' he asked the exhausted sailor. The man's eyes held a look of manic terror, as if he'd been chased by demons. It took several minutes to calm him down. Then he stumbled through a report of sorts. At the end of it Lieutenant Reitsch was reasonably sure the enemy was not some 'devil creature' but most likely a contingent of soldiers recruited from a remote part of the British Empire. He gathered his NCOs and, once briefed, they prepared to move inland and recover the body of the fallen sailor.

Goramanshie watched the humans from behind the scrub bushes, out of sight. He saw the enemy fan out and slowly march up the

## The Balance Between

beach in the grey, pre-dawn light. Turning, he hissed orders to his own subordinates. They would deal with these human vermin directly.

It took a minute for the line of marines to cautiously close with the dunes, covering the ground exposed by low tide. When they were almost into the first dunes, strange figures rose from cover and ran at them, brandishing swords and halberds. The marines, guns at the ready, made short work of the attackers. The first volley took twenty or more of them, the next a dozen. Away down the line the Lieutenant saw a marine fall. A second one followed, but these casualties were light compared to the slaughter of the enemy. He halted his troops at the line of dunes. Still the enemy swarmed at them. Lieutenant Reitsch doubted whether it was wise to attempt to clear the dunes, so numerous were the enemy. He blew his whistle to order his men to fall back on his position.

Goramanshie studied the humans. Over three score of his warriors lay dead, but only three of the enemy had died. This magic of theirs was accurate and powerful. The olorc had never seen anything like it. The dark sorcery of the Warkrin was strong, stronger than this, but if the soldiers of the enemy each had such magic, their army would be invincible. Goramanshie would advise his commander of this. He ordered his olorcs to stop attacking. After all, his orders were to defend the portal and await reinforcements.

'It appears that they have desisted from further attack,' declared Lieutenant Reitsch as he surveyed the beach. 'It is therefore necessary, gentlemen, to go in and deal with them if we are to secure this beach. I remind you that we are here to hold the beachhead until the ship's orders are complete, or until such time as the enemy makes our position untenable for Captain Raeder to maintain.

'The enemy would appear to be as able seaman Holtz described them. They are creatures unlike anything we have seen before.

They are cruel and ruthless and must be treated accordingly. It is no doubt the work of the British government and their colonial henchmen who've found these creatures and trained them so they may one day be used against Germany. I have ordered the removal of the seaman and one of the creature carcasses back to the *Ausburg*. Now we will deal with the others. Prepare to move forward.'

---

'I suppose we could just go in and ask them to arrange another entertainment activity. After all, they liked the last one,' said James sarcastically. They were all getting edgy. So far nobody had come up with a workable plan for provoking the enemy into a Talon Grab competition.

'Actually, that may be exactly what we should do,' said Tempus. And the hound outlined a plan that he'd been contemplating.

When he finished, the others readily agreed to it.

'You know, you can teach an old dog new tricks,' said Bartholomew respectfully.

'And I've never heard you talk so much, Tempus,' added Solomon.

'We must be ready by noon. That's when the dragons are having their final meeting,' decided James.

---

Things were not going well for Goramanshie. The enemy had pushed them back to the very portal itself. Olorcs lay dead or dying everywhere. The magic was powerful, seeming to strike his warriors even as they hid behind the archway for protection, and yet his olorcs could not get close enough to bring their swords and halberds to bear. One mass attack after another had left his troop worse than decimated. Perhaps a quarter of them remained. He now looked with loathing at the stone arch. Orders gave way to logic.

'Fall back into the portal. Let us flee this magic. Flee!' Goramanshie was the first through the arch.

'Cease fire.' The German marines stared in amazement, their weapons held limply in their hands. Seconds before, the strange, black and oily creatures had cowered helplessly in the open as if attempting to hide behind some invisible object, all the while succumbing to the marine's withering rifle fire. Now the survivors were running to the same spot where the bodies had piled up in the carnage and, literally, disappearing into thin air. Within a minute it was all over, leaving the German marines in possession of the beach.

Lieutenant Reitsch strode among the corpses. He kicked the sand at his feet but there was no hidden bunker where the escaping creatures might have hidden. He looked around, seeing the expressions of disbelief on the faces of his marines. 'Secure the area,' he called. 'Detail a squad to collect bodies for burial, Sergeant. No – cremation. It is better to rid the earth of this filth.' The lieutenant also sent out a patrol to reconnoitre the surrounding lands.

◦◦◦◦◦◦

It took a good hour for Corrick to recount the events that had occurred fifteen years earlier. He'd recognised Harrington the instant he saw him. He'd been too surprised to say anything, but Harrington had grinned and shaken his hand. Then Mrs Corrick had shooed the children from the parlour and the men sat and took morning tea. All the while Corrick remained flabbergasted at the sudden reunion.

'When I got back I learned of the loss of the *Parsimony*. The only survivor listed was that Captain . . .' Corrick searched for the name.

'Gilchrist,' Sir Philip offered.

'That's him. He was drummed out of the Excise Department after that disaster. I suppose he carried the can.'

'I shared in the blame,' said Sir Philip. 'As Excise Officer for the Pools of London it happened on my watch.' The two men looked at Sir Philip. While this was news to Corrick, he was sure Harrington had known about it. 'But it seems, gentlemen, your story dating back fifteen years is somehow linked to events now. And that is why we are here.'

Sir Philip turned to Harrington. 'I have learned more about you, Harrington, through the Chief Inspector's story than from you. I think it's time for you to give a full account of yourself. Otherwise . . .' and he left it unsaid.

Harrington nodded agreement.

'My true name,' he began, 'is not important since it is unlikely that you could ever pronounce it or do it justice in your own language. Suffice to say that I am descended from a race of people who dwell beyond the portals.

'I came into this world when it began, long before man or society, or history as you understand it. There is no record of my coming. I came not alone, but with a host of others. Since that time our numbers have declined until now, when I believe myself to be the last of my kind in this, the New World.

'I am old. Older than any living thing in this world. And I will continue to live until I am killed. I am Elven.' Harrington stopped for a moment, waiting for the incredible nature of his words to sink in. 'The notion of elves and other races are known to this world, and held to be simple folklore. But this is not the case. In a world beyond the portals magic exists as reality. It serves the purpose that science serves in this world. Great and wonderful things are made possible by magic, as great things are being achieved by science.

'My people came into this world freely, but left much behind.

We were cut off from the magic of our world and it has been a terrible loss. It was the price we paid when we were sent to follow the exiles.' Sir Philip and Corrick were engrossed by what they heard.

'The exiles are dragons. They are among the oldest of all living things made by Creation. The first dragons were born in the birth-pit that the Chief Inspector destroyed, in the other world we call "Eldaterra".' Harrington paused a moment and the sounds of children playing in the garden filtered into the room.

'My world, Eldaterra, the Old World, was the first world and it was created to be a perfect world. But nothing can ever be perfect; and imperfections arose, tainting the purity of the magic with a baseness that threatened to undermine and destroy Eldaterra. And so the portals were first proposed. They would be created to divide one world into two. One half would keep the magic and the other would be without.

And the corrupted magic turned to blackness and became evil. It was thought that this evil was born of the dragons, so when the world was split in two it was decided to purge the evil, and the dragons went into exile.

'My people came in secret to watch the dragons, to spy. Dragons possess powerful magic and it was feared they could use their power to break down the portals and seek vengeance on Eldaterra for their forced exile.

'But we and the dragons both discovered that magic is neither a birthright nor a skill one learns. It is a product of the world one inhabits. The Old World is infused with magic. It is strong and all respect it and know of it. In this New World there is no knowledge of magic, and no respect for it. The result is that magic doesn't exist, except where it leaks into this world from the other. Or if it is brought here. And the portals are meant to stop magic moving between the worlds.'

He looked at the two men with a sad, weary expression on his face. 'Do you ever wonder why mankind has such tales of magic and superstition? Why four-leaf clovers are lucky? Why any number of old wives' tales are still recounted? Your world cries out for magic. It is the cry of empty souls in a world that has lost belief, and that is why you have replaced it with science. This will never change. It is the way it will be for this world. In the Old World, my world, magic is the living proof of our reason for being. We live with it. But your world has only long-dead, half-forgotten prophets whose words have been twisted with time. We have our truth, you have your beliefs. We have certainty, you have philosophy.'

Sir Philip and Corrick sat in rapt silence.

'But now a new threat exists, one that threatens both worlds.' Harrington's eyes flicked from one man to the other and back. 'The Chief Inspector destroyed the dragon birthpit all those years ago. The portal inscription told him to.'

At this Corrick nodded.

'It is the portals that keep the balance between the two worlds. But enemies in the Old World believe they can breach the portals and by moving magic between the two worlds, gain an advantage over their adversaries. It was they who were behind the experiments fifteen years ago. They were trying to pass magical creatures through the portals. They experimented with implantation into living creatures from that world and passing them through to this. In your investigations, Chief Inspector, you uncovered the proof of these experiments.'

'But I came and went through the portal,' said Corrick.

'Yes. Only those who do not possess the magic arts may pass through. The portals stop the transfer of magic from one world to the next. Wizards and dragons and even elves, who are magical in their own way, cannot pass through. Those with magic in this world today came through in a time before the portals. Thus the female dragons, sent into exile without mates, have never reproduced again. That is why the enemy sought to implant dragon embryos into humans and other creatures, believing that the embryos would survive the passage. And as we witnessed, Inspector Corrick, they succeeded.'

'To a point,' said Corrick. 'You see, Harrington, when I went to Oxford I found the specimen that you hoped to hide from me. It was in the same shipment. I pressed the curator of the museum of anthropology, now what was its name –?'

'The Pitt Rivers Museum,' helped Sir Philip.

'That's it. Yes, thank you, Sir Philip. I persuaded them to conduct a detailed examination. They told me that the foetus could never have grown to full term due to the confines of the human anatomy.'

'That is correct, Chief Inspector. That is why they were implanting embryos into a different type of surrogate, those creatures that you described, the olorcs. They possess no magic, but apparently are more compatible with the implantation process. The enemy solved the problem of gestation.'

'So where does that leave us now?' asked Sir Philip.

'That, Sir Philip, is my worry. In the last fifteen years I have heard no reports of incidents that would lead me to any conclusions,' said Harrington.

'Then I'd better tell you about my boy.'

꼬꼬꼬

'Ladies and dragons. Today will be remembered as a most glorious day.' Komargoran Monarchmauler stood on her hind legs, wings outstretched, with her long neck weaving from side to side as she held the audience's attention. In front of her the throng of dragons packed the room, their revealed selves so much larger than their human form. The room was electric with the prospect of Komargoran Monarchmauler's words.

'For far too long we dragons have been forced to slither like common serpents and hide from this world.'

The crowded dragons gave a roar of agreement, singeing the wallpaper and ceiling.

'We have lived secret, miserable lives under mountains and in caves, away from the rest of the world, outnumbered and outcast, forced to conceal ourselves in pathetic human form lest they hunt us down.'

This brought a palpable wave of resentment from the restless dragons that were stirring with every word.

'We have been deprived of our rights as the eldest of all Creation. We have endured the ignominy and humiliation of exile. We have no power or position, no respect and no reward, no status, no satisfaction, no past and no future here in this world. None, unless we change it.'

The room vibrated to the cheers and stomping of claws on the polished wood ballroom floor. The jostling of the throng got worse as the dragons surged forward to be closer to Komargoran Monarchmauler.

'But we can end this miserable life we lead if we band together. Together we are stronger. We are Creation's chosen few,' she roared out, flames and boiling spittle shooting from her mouth. The audience bayed for more.

'As dragons we must decide to grab back what is ours, to demand a change in the order of this world. And today we can have it. Today, dear sisters, we will receive a new destiny. From beyond the portal we shall receive the gift of offspring. A new generation of dragons will come to us and aid us to overthrow this puny world of science.

'Today I have sent my loyal servant, Herr Dorpmuller, across to the Old World to give the order to begin the invasion. When the portals open and an army of darkness issues forth then we will gain another ally. My dear friend the Kaiser awaits proof of our army. Then he will commit his forces to the cause. We dragons will

## The Balance Between

subjugate all, and in time the Kaiser will come to realise that he too must be our servant.'

The dragons became ecstatic at this news.

'But first we must be united, fellow dragons, to change *this* world. Do you want to change it?' she asked her audience.

'Yes!' they roared back, and two-hundred dragons surged forward and smashed everything in their path.

'Do you *really* want to change it?'

'Yes!' they screamed, the windows shattering with their high-pitched screeching.

Komargoran Monarchmauler's eyes lit up with a power-tripping maniacal flash. Her silver and blue leathery wings beat the air and her taloned forelegs made wild slashing movements. Her breath tinged with blue flame, and her head writhed from side-to-side as she goaded them on. 'Do you *really, really, really?*'

'*Yes!*' Flames from the back of the room enveloped the dragons at the front.

And then one voice right at the back said, 'No, actually, I quite like things the way they are.'

A stunned silence fell over the gathering.

Komargoran Monarchmauler's eyes scalded the room, so intense was her glare. She ignored the voice and continued. 'Yes, you do, I know you do, don't you?' Komargoran Monarchmauler screamed.

And the crowd roared back its approval. All except the solitary voice. 'No, I don't, actually.'

An audible gasp went through the crowd. Dragons at the front now turned around to get a better look at the objector. Dragons at the back looked about, everyone trying to identify the culprit.

'Who is it that feels they aren't with the programme?' Komargoran Monarchmauler's voice was poison. She now looked particularly, cunningly dangerous.

Suddenly it was so quiet you could have heard a scale fall. No dragon breathed in case it was mistaken for an answer. Every dragon looked at her neighbours. A hiss from the mouth of Komargoran Monarchmauler was the only sound, until the voice felt brave enough to say,

'Well, I know that's what Desmogorra Slaughterhouse thinks. She told me.'

A ripple of menace passed through the crowd, to be replaced instantly by one of apprehension. Desmogorra Slaughterhouse was a particularly large dragon, widely disliked for her bossy and sneering ways. It was easy to see why she would disagree. A space opened up around her. Dragons on all sides bared their teeth and talons. It was as if the pack had turned on the bully, singling her out. But Desmogorra Slaughterhouse was not known by this name without good reason. She was fierce and proud and still preferred living in the Balkans, even with the problems humans cause. Slowly turning around and around, she confronted her would-be assailants. Even then, with eight dragons formed around her and many pressing behind, Desmogorra Slaughterhouse was reckoning her chances of winning a fight. She was so proud that she never once thought to repudiate the anonymous voice and deny the allegations. Desmogorra Slaughterhouse's spleen was engorged with spite for her antagonists, and she would be satisfied.

But before the adversaries could set to with tooth and talon, the voice said, 'And I know Ularinorra Slashmaster's been saying that Friedeswine Mountainscorcher never did catch that bear. It was just an old rug. She and Karliasa Stoneswallower rigged the whole thing.' More gasps circled the crowd.

'And who got to maul the maiden without it being part of the entertainment? Apparently the perpetrator promised Mrs Big-for-her-wings a weekend roasting bison on the plain, so we all know who that is.' This last remark hit home. They all knew that maiden-mauling was the single most sought-after nasty reward that a dragon could wish for. To show favouritism to one dragon insulted all the others.

## The Balance Between

With all the dragon-fever that swirled in their collective bloodstream it only took this final malicious rumour to get the forest to flash-burn. Instantly, dragon set upon dragon indiscriminately. In such a confined space, they fought eyeball to eyeball, tooth to tooth. Talons and teeth, tails and neck, all flashed and thrashed at anyone nearby. Soon dragon blood was being shed in large volumes, making the floor and walls sticky with a streaky mess of green and yellow slime. The smell of blood filled the nostrils, and the combatants fought with renewed frenzy. Injured dragons were collapsing to the floor where they were buried under the mass of dragons whose hind legs instinctively raked and clawed those on the ground. The noise was like that of steam trains continuously colliding. It was impossible to see who was fighting whom, and all about them the ballroom slowly began to disintegrate under the brutal hammering that the dragons meted out one to another, one and all.

James, Tempus and the two ventriloquist brothers had judiciously retreated through the servants' quarters and along the tunnel. Baranor joined them as they climbed the stairs to the top of the dam to enjoy a grandstand view of the Talon Grab.

Solomon slapped his brother's shoulder. 'Good one about Mrs Big-for-her-wings,' he congratulated his brother.

Bartholomew grinned back and said, 'Well you started so strongly with Desmogorra so I just had to have a go.' They watched for quite a while.

Below them the free-for-all fight was coming to an end. With the roof collapsed and the walls pushed outwards onto the lawn and drive, the dragons spread out, individuals duelling and debts paid back in full.

'Remember to stay very still,' said Solomon. 'Dragons can't see much when the bloodlust is on them. They can see movement, but not much else.'

The heat of the morning tired the surviving dragons. None were unscarred and many were sorely injured. Baranor counted forty-two dragons motionless on the ground.

'Look! There she is,' said James and pointed below. In the midst of the wreckage stood Komargoran Monarchmauler. She was bloodied but unbowed. A coating of plaster dust and dragon gore dulled her brilliant colours. She held her left foreclaw protectively to her body and limped on a hind leg. At her feet lay a green-grey dragon, no doubt killed for some minor insult, real or imagined.

The fight had broken up. Slowly, taking stock of their own wounds, individuals turned and headed for home. Some flew directly off, heedless to the dangers of dragon flight during daylight hours. Others crawled away to find somewhere to rest and use what magic they could summon to heal themselves. Several of the cooler heads transformed back into their female form, appearing like madames after a catfight, and beat a hasty exit. The dead and dying were ignored for the moment.

'That's as likely to stop their plans as anything,' said Tempus, and wagged his tail. James turned to the hound sitting next to him and gave him a pat.

Sixty feet below, in the shell of the ballroom, Komargoran Monarchmauler caught a movement out of the corner of her eye, and turned her head towards it.

'She's seen us,' whispered Tempus. 'Nobody move.'

The dragon continued to watch them. After a bit Tempus said in a very hushed voice, 'If she doesn't look away, or if we don't get out of here soon, she'll see us perfectly normally when the bloodlust clears.' Everyone greeted this news in silence. Komargoran Monarchmauler's eyes crawled over each of them, one by one, hunting for a movement that would give the quarry away.

'Over here,' a voice whispered in the ear of Komargoran Monarchmauler and she spun away, looking for the new tormentor.

*The Balance Between*

Quick as a flash the companions rolled over the lip of the dam and down the reverse slope out of sight.

A bellow of rage rose from the house.

'I will find you and tear your heart out, whoever you are!'

◦∽∾∽◦

Sir Philip caught the next train north, accompanied by Harrington and Corrick. Once Sir Philip began to talk of the Sea Arch, Harrington became anxious to be on the move, saying that they could talk some more when they were on the train.

While waiting at the station, Sir Philip had telephoned his wife.

'Philip!' Lady Jennifer exclaimed. 'I've been trying to reach you since dawn. Where are you?' She took a deep breath, regained her composure and gave a summary of events that morning.

'Are you sure it was rifle fire?' her husband asked, to make absolutely certain before he called out the local regiment, if they hadn't already been alerted. Lady Jennifer reassured him that she was quite sure of this fact, then said a silent prayer of thanks when Sir Philip explained that he was catching a train that instant and rang off.

'Well, it'll be for the good when Sir Philip gets here,' said Amanda, just as there was a knock on the door.

◦∽∾∽◦

James opened *Talmaride's Answers to Questions* at a fresh page. He hadn't noticed before that the questions and answers were all recorded on the pages. 'I wonder why that is?' he thought, but was glad to see the book couldn't read minds. He thought about the question he wanted to ask. It had been a long while since he'd seen his parents and, now the excitement was over, he missed them.

'Is my mother and father all right?' The answer was:

*No, your mother is not all right and yes, your father is.*

Then it added:

*'Is' is the singular possessive and incorrectly used. You should have used 'are'.*

James ignored the impromptu grammar lesson and asked, 'What is wrong with her?' The book replied:

*She has been taken by the enemy.*

'Where is she?' The book replied:

*In the house your father rented close to the Sea Arch.*

James slammed the book shut and ran to the others, who were sitting under the trees. With the threat issued by Komargoran Monarchmauler, everyone agreed they'd done all they could about the dragons for the moment at least, and that events at the Sea Arch should now be addressed.

Quickly he told them what the book had said. The dwarves looked especially concerned.

'After you'd gone through the Sea Arch, Dolmir returned to the Western Tower. The Warkrin must be sending troops through the unguarded portal to aid the dragons,' Solomon said with disappointment in his voice. 'What we did here today won't stop the invasion if they're already through the archway.'

'Now let's not get down about it yet,' said Bartholomew. 'We've seen off the dragons with a good hiding and now we have the chance to settle the Warkrin's hash, and perhaps –' he nudged Solomon in the ribs in a brotherly way '– perhaps we'll get that glorious grand finale.'

'What, you mean a pyrrhic victory?' asked a suddenly rejuvenated Solomon.

## The Balance Between

'Forget that,' yelled James in exasperation. 'My mother is in danger. We have to go after her now.' They agreed that the brothers should stay and watch the house while the dragons still represented a threat. James would set out at once with Baranor and Tempus for the Sea Arch, leaving the brothers to catch up when they could.

As the bear, hound and James disappeared, Bartholomew turned to his brother. 'Up on your Greek history, are you?'

✦

In the ruin of the ballroom, Komargoran Monarchmauler dined on the liver and juiciest parts of a dead dragon, rare cuisine indeed. She mulled over the day's events that had ended so disastrously. Now the bloodlust had passed she could take a more clinical, objective view. She recalled her disquiet last night. 'What eludes me?' she asked herself. Komargoran Monarchmauler was wise enough not to chase errant thoughts. She'd let her memories come to her. Her mind wandered back, to the times long ago when dragons were among the rulers of the Old World. A time when she had power, prestige and dominance over all, when only the Guild stood in the way of the dragons.

Komargoran Monarchmauler had amassed a personal fortune; stolen or won in battle, it made no difference. Ah, those were the years of plenty, years when no one, not even a wizard, dared stand before a dragon and question a dragon's rights over all others. And few dared to challenge a dragon, even if it were to save their own loved ones or valuables, whereas a dragon would fight to the death to protect a horde of possessions. 'Mmm, possessions.' And then it struck her. Now her old senses were flooding back. That scent from the cellar door. Now she knew. The bearskin!

## ∽ 17 ∽

# The Battle of Beadnell Bay

Amanda opened the door to find a military officer standing on the doorstep. Relief swept over the women as the man walked into the farmhouse followed by two soldiers. Polly the housekeeper broke into floods of tears and sank on to a kitchen stool, clutching her apron to dry her face. Amanda stepped forward to explain what had happened at the beach, but stopped short when she registered the look of shock in Jennifer's eyes.

The officer inspected the room's modest interior before his eyes alighted on the telephone. He signalled to one of the soldiers who disappeared outside, then returned shortly after and spoke to the officer in German. The officer then turned to Lady Kinghorn. 'Good day to you, Fraulein.' He clicked his heels with military precision, leaving little arcs of wet sand on the floor. 'My name is Lieutenant Reitsch of His Majesty's Imperial Kregmarine. We are currently conducting exercises with troops of Your Majesty King George's army,' he said, in the arrogant manner that came easily to him. He walked slowly round the room as if looking for something. 'Perhaps you heard the gunfire?' He didn't wait for an answer. 'But of course you did and, being three women alone in a farmhouse on a remote stretch of the coastline, you would have been frightened and called for help, yes?'

None of the women spoke, though Polly kept blubbing into her apron; her tears of relief replaced by hysterical sobbing at the arrival of the sinister foreign soldiers.

'Stop your whimpering, woman,' ordered the officer, irritated at her noise. He stopped pacing and looked at Lady Kinghorn. 'I would leave you in peace now, under normal circumstances. But these are not normal circumstances, are they? Why, I ask myself, would three women in a very ordinary farmhouse have a telephone when many wealthy people do not yet have such a device?'

The women remained silent, only the housekeeper's crying answering.

'Why, also, does this farmhouse merit a specially laid telephone line when it is the only dwelling in the area? And, most intriguing of all, who are you?' The question hung in the air.

'You see, Fraulein, my man here informs me this is British army field equipment. Very good equipment, not the sort your army leaves around or lends to anyone. So, if you are alone, and my men will search the property shortly, why do you merit this treatment? Is this a trap to provoke a political incident? I would like an answer!' he commanded. 'Now, if you please.'

---

'Corrick,' Harrington asked, 'when did you marry and have children?' He was curious to know of the intervening years since they'd last seen each other on that storm-swept beach.

The policeman turned from the window where the countryside raced by. 'Soon after I returned,' he replied. 'After everything I witnessed in that other place, it made me realise how important life is. Those slave creatures, the *marked*, had theirs taken away. The surrogates, the ones used for embryo implantation, had no choice. Even the dragon embryos were the products of evil forces. I suppose what I saw helped me get over mourning the death of my first wife.'

Harrington nodded in understanding, and a contemplative silence followed.

'Do you have any idea what the purpose of the Sea Arch is?' Sir Philip asked Harrington.

'Sir Philip, it could mean many things. I had no knowledge of its existence until you spoke of it. The few portals I have found or tracked down have all been in the south. In the beginning I believed the portals could not be opened, but my knowledge on the matter is extremely limited. If your son has passed through the portal it can only be for some very important reason, one that we may not fathom.'

'In which case,' decided Sir Philip, 'I'll go and see if I can get word to Lady Kinghorn and discover the latest news.'

'I'm sorry, sir,' said the guard, 'but there ain't no way to communicate when the train's moving except by droppin' a message at a passin' station. And were we to do that then it would still take hours before it reaches your good lady.'

Sir Philip clenched his fists in frustration. Every hour was vital. He hoped someone had raised the alarm.

*❦*

Siganatoris Bloodboiler eased her wings back gently. Her left-side wing was badly torn and she couldn't fly until it mended. Neither could she transfigure since it would leave her with a broken arm. She'd have to rest and work some magic to repair herself first.

Komargoran Monarchmauler walked up to her, the blue and silver dragon bloodied but magnificent, her demeanour as imperious as ever. As Frau Feder, Siganatoris Bloodboiler was a humble servant, but in her true dragon-self she was disinclined to do the bidding of others.

'Siganatoris Bloodboiler,' Komargoran Monarchmauler began. 'It was an excellent fight, superb entertainment. So very clever of you to have organised a Talon Grab for the final entertainment.' The words flattered and fuelled her vanity. 'It will go down in history, the final harvest of the weak before we stand victorious. Very clever.'

Siganatoris Bloodboiler basked in the compliments. In fact it was Komargoran Monarchmauler who was being clever, for she needed help if her plan was still to succeed.

'Siganatoris Bloodboiler, I must get to the portal and speak with our allies. By now Herr Dorpmuller will have been received and the army of the Old World will be pouring through the portals. Only when I confirm this to Kaiser Wilhelm will he make his move, and to do that I must first speak with Captain Raeder. I must ask you, as my very best friend,' her voice wheedled, 'and fellow liberator of this world, Siganatoris Bloodboiler, to help one more time.'

Siganatoris Bloodboiler was mollified and pleased with these platitudes and words of thanks, playing as they did on her ego. 'Very well, Komargoran Monarchmauler, I will assist. I will talk with those dragons that remain to see if an alliance can be retrieved from the situation. Perhaps they too found my surprise Talon Grab entertaining. Perhaps.'

At this, Komargoran Monarchmauler transformed back into her female form as Frau Colbetz and, with her dress in tatters and her hair in considerable disorder, she drove off to the coast in a motor-car taken from the coach house. As she drove away she called, 'Be careful Siganatoris Bloodboiler. We have enemies. The boy and that bear outsmarted that fool Friedeswine Mountainscorcher. They still live. Look out for them.'

---

Anyone who saw a bear walking in the countryside would report the matter in double-quick time, so when they had to cross the main London-to-Edinburgh road, James told Baranor to hide while Tempus and he made sure the coast was clear. Tempus ran off down the road to watch at the bend while James went north. A few minutes later Tempus pelted back, barking as he came.

'Quick James, out of sight. It's Frau Colbetz.' James had no sooner thrown himself down into the thickest spinney he could find, than Frau Colbetz drove around the corner going like a banshee from hell. Seconds later she'd disappeared in a wake of dust and exhaust fumes. James signalled to Baranor that the road was clear and, like a commando from the Boer War, he sprinted across and disappeared on the other side.

'We're almost there,' said James as the smell of the sea drifted towards them. Tempus ran ahead to scout the route to avoid bumping into unwelcome company. James climbed off Baranor's back and they hunkered down behind a stone wall to await Tempus's return.

The hound was gone twenty minutes, time enough to learn of the soldiers on the beach, dead olorcs and the arrival of Frau Colbetz.

---

'Lieutenant Reitsch, what has happened here?' Frau Colbetz's astonishment at the sight of dozens of the dead creatures being placed on a funeral pyre was genuine.

The lieutenant spun around to see Frau Colbetz struggling across the sand towards them. He moved forward, his arms outstretched. 'Come, Frau Colbetz, do not distress yourself with this. Such a scene is not for a woman of your delica–'

'Get your hands off me.' She pulled away and fixed him with a cold stare. 'I asked you a question. What has happened here?' Her voice matched the look she gave the officer and he hesitated. He was confused. Why would this woman behave so? he wondered. His eyes took in the tattered dress and her dishevelled hair. She must be in shock, he concluded.

'Frau Colbetz, has something happened? You look as if you have had trouble –'

## The Balance Between

Frau Colbetz took a deep breath, controlled her annoyance and spoke carefully to the officer.

'Lieutenant Reitsch, I am perfectly well, thank you. Though my appearance may be unsightly at this time, I do assure you that I am fine. Now, please, tell me what has been going on here.' Her request was a ringing demand.

'Madam, my men landed to give assistance to our shore party who were attacked by these strange creatures that you see. We killed many of them further along the beach before they disappeared, and we are disposing of the bodies while we awaited your return. Now that you are here we may return to the ship.' The lieutenant seemed relieved that the mission was coming to an end.

'No, Lieutenant, we are not going back to the ship,' Frau Colbetz said with a voice of iron will. 'You will wait here until I give the order to return.'

The lieutenant looked down his Prussian nose at her and said, 'Frau, I am an officer of His Majesty Kaiser Wilhelm's Imperial Navy and my orders are those issued by my commanding officer. If you disagree with these orders then I suggest you have words with Captain Raeder who you will find aboard the *Ausburg*.' And with that Lieutenant Reitsch turned and stalked off, angered by the presumption of the woman.

Further up the beach, James, Baranor and Tempus watched the boat as it made its way slowly through the surf towards the warship anchored in the bay. Something wasn't right. The white ensign flew at the ship's mast, but the marines on the beach were dressed in the wrong uniform.

James turned to the hound lying at his side. 'Tempus, you must search for the house that the book mentioned. Find it and see if my mother is still there. Then we'll decide what must be done.' Tempus sped off again.

*

## The Balance Between

The cutter bumped against the metal hull and Frau Colbetz was up the gangway before the boat was secured. On the bridge Captain Raeder had watched the woman through his binoculars as she sat in the stern of the cutter. 'Perhaps she is not the enigma she seems, but that woman has a power over men,' he thought.

'Captain, I demand that you keep your ship here until events transpire as expected.'

This woman makes bold demands of the Imperial Navy, thought Captain Raeder. His back stiffened in resolve as he replied. 'Frau Colbetz, I am not in a position to allow my ship to remain in these waters. This morning my lieutenant was obliged to defend himself against an enemy who made an unprovoked attack on us. These strange creatures necessitated a great deal of gunfire that will have been reported to the authorities. Even now I expect the British to appear in the sand dunes or over the horizon. My ship flies the British flag to confuse the enemy. We are illegally inside British territorial waters. My men have effectively invaded a foreign country. All these are sufficient reasons to create a political incident, perhaps even start a war. I have also learned that my lieutenant has been forced to temporarily detain the wife of a British government minister who coincidentally happens to be staying in a house nearby, something I find hard to believe.' He raised his eyes to emphasise the sheer unbelievability of it all.

'I am here at the direct request of the Kaiser to assist you in your venture. I am not here with orders to start a war.' His voice rose almost to a shout as he brought the full weight of his anger to bear upon this woman who'd caused him and his command to be in such compromising circumstances. His hands clenched into fists behind his back in an effort of supreme restraint.

'No, that is precisely what you *are* here for, Captain. War!'

\*

## The Balance Between

Tempus found the house and raced back to James and Baranor to report his findings. 'There are three women inside guarded by a soldier at the door, and one outside.'

'Baranor, could you deal with the soldiers?' James asked. 'One of us must stay here and keep an eye on events.'

'Picking a fight when there are only two of them will be an uneven contest. I'd be happier if there were more, but I suppose it's necessary under the circumstances,' the bear replied.

James warned his friends again about firearms so they wouldn't make the same fatal mistake as the olorcs.

※

The brothers reached the foot of the stairwell to the underground passage just as Siganatoris Bloodboiler stopped at the lake to bathe her wounds. Only a hundred yards separated the dwarves from the dragon, and it would have taken a fully fit dragon just a blink of an eye to cover the distance. But Siganatoris Bloodboiler's wounds slowed her, and the two dwarves scrambled to safety down the underground passage leading to the house.

'What have we here? Two dwarves out for a stroll? I think not.' The voice of Siganatoris Bloodboiler echoed off the walls. The dragon poked her head down the passage.

In the darkness Solomon and Bartholomew watched as her eyes, glowing a light blue with yellow elliptical pupils, sought them out. They'd ducked into a side room that contained all manner of equipment: buckets of sands, strange metal cylinders with hoses attached, ladders and long canvas pipes on reels. Bartholomew studied the equipment while Solomon kept watch.

'Solomon, I think we can use some of this stuff,' said his brother.

'Bartholomew,' he hissed back, 'we've got a dirty great dragon poking around at the end of the corridor, and you want to use some stuff! What for, exactly?'

'To kill the dragon, of course.'

~~~~~~

Tempus trotted round the corner of the house, his tail wagging, and made straight for the soldier as if they were already good friends. The soldier reached out to scratch the hound behind the ear and, in that moment of distraction, the giant black bear slipped up behind him and brought a massive paw crashing down on the soldier's head. The man crumpled to the ground in a noiseless heap.

'Get the window, quick,' whispered Baranor.

Tempus jumped up, his front paws resting on the window ledge, and looked in. 'The other soldier's coming to the door. He must have heard us. Careful, Baranor.'

Lady Jennifer glanced at Amanda. They'd all heard it, a sort of shuffling noise at the door. They watched as the soldier unshouldered his rifle and went to investigate. He was perhaps a yard from the door when Amanda spotted the face of a dog at the window and gave a gasp of astonishment. The soldier hesitated and looked to see what had surprised the young woman.

The door exploded inwards, the wood shattering into hundreds of splinters that cascaded over the soldier and across the room. An enormous black creature leapt into the room and, in a flash of claws and bared teeth, the soldier fell wounded to the ground. The women screamed, the housekeeper fainting on the spot, as the bear reared over the prostrate body.

Baranor roared once, looked around the room and said, 'Excuse me, are you James's mother?' Lady Jennifer and Amanda followed the example of Polly the housekeeper, and fainted.

'But they are all right?' James asked.

'No harm done,' replied Baranor. 'They didn't seem up to much in the way of conversation, but they came to no harm.'

'Well that takes care of that problem for the moment.' James pointed down at the beach. 'Frau Colbetz has returned from the ship and she's walking this way, to the Sea Arch, I expect.'

'The olorcs must be part of the invasion army set to come through the arch,' said Baranor.

'But the enemy would have to fight all the way through the forest,' disagreed Tempus. 'They would never make it.'

'Perhaps they were just a token force, a demonstration. And if I'm not mistaken, those men on the beach are the Kaiser's men. Father says trouble's been brewing on the Continent for quite a while. Maybe Frau Colbetz has persuaded the Kaiser to throw in his lot with her. That would certainly make sense of it all.'

'It seems, then, that the enemy have been fighting among themselves,' said Baranor.

'And that's why Frau Colbetz is so angry,' said James 'Her plan is coming unstuck. Without support from the Kaiser, the olorcs and all the monsters they can summon from the Old World won't be enough to beat a modern army.' James looked deep in thought. 'We must contact my father,' he said.

---

Sir Philip left the train briefly while it boarded passengers in York and placed a call to his wife, but was informed that the line was down. Placing a second call to his deputy, Weatherburn, he gave instructions to reach the commanding officer in Alnwick. Troops were to be mobilised.

Upon reboarding the train he fell back into conversation with his travelling companions. It was Corrick who asked how Sir Philip had come to make the connection between himself, Harrington and the *Parsimony*.

Sir Philip judged that the reasons for revealing his deductions outweighed the reasons for not doing so and told them. 'The inscription on the Sea Arch left me two perplexing clues that proved the hardest to unravel. The first led me to Harrington, and that was difficult enough. The second led me back to my past, when I was a junior officer in what was then the Excise department. At the time there was terrible inter-departmental rivalry and internecine combat between ministerial bodies seeking power and influence in government.

'My father was Head of the Board of Customs, within the Foreign Office. He was interested in restructuring the departments, but for purposes of efficiency rather than to increase his own influence.

'Then one day the Excise vessel *Parsimony* was lost. I was Excise Officer for the Pool of London. As you know, it transpired that my father had ordered the trip to sea that you gentlemen hitched a ride on. He wished to assess how closely Customs and Excise functions might integrate. At first he was blamed for the disaster, and some say his disappearance was to avoid the shame of being held to account. The loss of the *Parsimony* was then held to be my responsibility, and for many years my career suffered as a result.

'I, for my part, endeavoured to salvage what little I could from the situation. I kept my head down, accepted a transfer to the then out-of-favour War Office where I eventually landed the task of reorganising this nation's pitiably woeful intelligence service. Success in that department brought with it a different sort of power.' Sir Philip let the implications of this sink in before continuing.

'Under the excellent tutelage and support of the former Secretary of War, Robert Haldane, I have risen to discreet prominence, shall we say, within the civil service. In all these years I suppose I never really wished to revisit the question of the loss of the *Parsimony*. It was too close to home, one way or another, having accounted for my father and almost destroyed me as well.' Sir Philip looked out of the train window, oblivious to the rushing countryside as his thoughts wandered. After a few moments he resumed his narrative. 'But with James's disappearance and then the inscription on the arch, I was forced to rethink the incident. It was two particular lines that gave me direction.

> *Steady now your hand must act*
> *And recall silence in your past.*

'In so many ways this was a clue. *Steady now* I took as a nautical reference, and *your hand must act* was almost an instruction that was being conveyed to me. *The silence*, well, I took it to mean that part of my life I preferred not to revisit, which must be the sinking of the *Parsimony*. My wife, Lady Kinghorn, on the other hand, immediately assumed that it referred to the crashing silence of my superiors at the Excise department at the time of the sinking. With all the hostility between governmental departments it was unthinkable to believe a lowly officer in one department could be blamed for a failure they'd already tried to pin on a minister in a rival department, but no one in the Excise department came to my defence. I was not only a suitable scapegoat but also without allies.

'Recent events jolted me into action. With the resources at my disposal I had the Excise officers I worked with at that time tracked down. It transpired that my immediate superior left his post in ninety-six, within a year of the loss of the *Parsimony* and took up a position working for an up-and-coming politician.

'After a private meeting with the man I was able to exert sufficient – how shall I put it? – pressure on him to spill the truth. The *Parsimony* was deliberately sabotaged on the instructions of this politician. This politician stood to lose his ministerial position if there was a departmental reorganisation. He dared not risk a setback just as his career was taking off. In truth there could well have been collusion at the Foreign Office, but that may never be discovered. Nonetheless, when my father was unavailable as a scapegoat I was drafted in his place. My superior fed me to the lions.

'It was serendipity that my line of enquiries brought me to the one man who can testify to the incident. Both men were on the quayside the morning you joined the *Parsimony*. Had he not been present he would never have known of your unofficial trip.'

Harrington looked stunned as realisation dawned on him. He stammered as he revealed the last piece of the jigsaw. 'The vessel was without suitable sea anchors that day. I was aware of it but never understood the significance. The installation of them had been postponed for some reason. That means one of the persons you speak of is –'

But Corrick interrupted him saying, 'The man I saw you talking to on the dock that morning we first sailed to Zeebrugge. I recognised his face in the newspaper recently but couldn't recall where I'd seen him before. Now it comes back to me. It's the Minister for War, Thomas Audrey!'

---

'It's a good plan,' said Solomon.

'No, it's a great plan. It can't fail. Look at it this way. If we succeed and kill the dragon, we become heroes. If we succeed and kill the dragon but die in the attempt, we become legends. If we fail and die in the attempt, we become heroic failures,' said Bartholomew triumphantly.

'Yes,' agreed Solomon, pleased at the prospect of any of these outcomes.

'And since it's my plan, you get to hold the hose,' added Bartholomew.

Down the corridor, Siganatoris Bloodboiler was craning her neck into each of the storerooms opening off the corridor, searching for her quarry. Every now and then she'd send a blast of searing hot fire into a storeroom to make sure the dwarves weren't lurking in a corner or behind a pile of packing cases.

'We'd better get going then.' Bartholomew checked the dragon hadn't reached the doorway into the room where they were holed up, then he sprinted off into the darkness.

Solomon unwound the hose and laid it out in as straight a line as he could. Next he undid the stopcock fully, and watched a pressure ridge race along the canvas material of the hose. He grabbed the hose nozzle. 'Ready when you are, Bartholomew,' he yelled to his brother, throwing his voice into the other room.

Siganatoris Bloodboiler heard the voice and whipped her head into the corridor. 'It came from that doorway,' she said to herself, and sent a jet of flames up the corridor to cut off any retreat by the dwarves. Solomon shied away from the heat as it blistered the paint on the door. He'd left it open only slightly, but the intense heat sucked the air from the room, leaving him gasping.

Siganatoris Bloodboiler stretched out her neck as far as she could, jamming her shoulders in the gateway behind. Another roasting would do it, she decided, and opened her jaws to send a blast at the offending doorway. Her eye caught a movement at the door opposite and she hesitated, angling her head to redirect the blast. That fraction of delay allowed Solomon to swing the door wide, release the lever valve in the nozzle and send a powerful jet of water straight down the gullet of the dragon, extinguishing her igniter in the process.

The dragon choked and spluttered on the water that hammered into her throat. Clamping her jaws down sent the water blasting into her eyes, and her head writhed from side-to-side in the narrow corridor as she tried to avoid it. And then, just like any animal, Siganatoris Bloodboiler tried to bite the jet of water angering her.

Out of the darkness a figure loomed, dressed all in white, running as fast as his legs would carry him. It was Bartholomew, wearing a protective asbestos suit, the kind firemen wore. He ran straight at the dragon, his sword held in both hands in front of him. 'For the glory of the Bandamires!' His muffled cry could just be heard from behind the protective glass shield of the helmet, and with that he disappeared down the throat of Siganatoris Bloodboiler.

&c&c&c

While not a well-known fact, it is true that dragons, possessing frightful temperaments on account of their capricious nature, always reveal their true nature when they are angry. As Frau Colbetz stumbled along the beach she steadily became more and more furious. Her high heels sank straight into the sand and made it hard to walk, her dress was wet at the hem from the journey in the boat and now sand was getting into her stockings and shoes.

She arrived at the Sea Arch where a couple of marines were collecting the last olorc body when a new, strange scent filled her nostrils. Stopping dead in her tracks, she raised her nose and turned, tracing the smell borne over the wind. Bear!

Frau Colbetz could no longer control herself. Starting at her toes, an uncontrollable rage steadily grew in her, and as it took hold, her body revealed her true self. The shoes disappeared and were replaced by long scaly feet with white hooked talons at each toe. The dress changed into long silver-blue legs and a tail that uncoiled behind her. As her body rippled with the transfiguration, her arms folded back and into wings, and another pair of smaller clawed arms sprouted from her chest. Great spines burst through her skin and everywhere the shiny scales glinted in the sun. Next her neck grew longer, like a swan's but bigger, with a ridge of spines along the back, leaving only the head of Frau Colbetz on top of this coiling and snaking dragon neck.

The German marines on the beach nearby gave shouts of surprise and horror as they watched the woman's transformation.

Bang! A bullet flew past the dragon, only missing by inches. Frau Colbetz turned on the marine and, as her head stretched and formed into that of Komargoran Monarchmauler, she lunged forward across the sands and snapped her terrible, savage jaws down on the marine's head, removing it with one clean bite.

Further down the beach the rest of the soldiers momentarily froze in astonishment and then, under orders from the lieutenant, began to fire at the strange creature. Hidden in the dunes, James, Baranor and Tempus watched as the battle unfolded.

The dragon, infuriated further by the buzzing wasp-like stings that pricked her skin, turned on these new protagonists. In two beats of her enormous wings she covered the distance to the marines and set about them, her neck and tail flailing across the sand and tumbling soldiers like ninepins. She grabbed the arrogant officer in her foreclaws and tore at him. She pinned yet another soldier under her feet, pressing him deep into the sand until his struggling ceased. The remaining soldiers broke and ran for it, some to hide in the sand dunes, while others ran the boats into the surf and scrambled in.

'Gott in himmel!' gasped the duty officer on the ship's bridge.

Captain Raeder gaped in disbelief at what he saw. A dragon was attacking Reitsch's command! Could there be some truth in the story of Saint George and the dragon after all?

'Guns stand by for action!' he yelled down the voice pipe. 'Engine room, prepare to make full steam.' He turned to his fellow officers who were all mesmerised by events on the beach. 'Clear for action, gentlemen, if you please.'

From their vantage point, James and his companions saw the first gun fire. A puff of white smoke shot out of the end of the barrel and it was a fraction of a second later when the boom of the gun rolled over the water and reached them. A big gout of mud and sand sprayed up into a geyser only a few yards from where the dragon stood. Komargoran Monarchmauler let out a bellow of rage as her head snapped up and her gaze switched to the new enemy out in the bay. Leaving broken bodies about her, she rose into the air, her broad and powerful wings moving her gracefully across the water. It was a terrifyingly beautiful sight to see such a magnificent yet deadly creature wing its way effortlessly towards the long grey hull of the warship. James watched as the two adversaries closed. Guns roared from the deck of the cruiser, several striking the body of the beast. Tiny gaps of blue showed where the wings were torn. Then she was on the ship.

Clinging to the metal superstructure, the dragon crawled across the vessel, blasts of fire shooting from her mouth. Claws scrambled in doorways as her tail flailed the outer decks, tearing and twisting the railings and mounted equipment. Komargoran Monarchmauler hunted out sailors inside the ship, her head smashing through doorways and roasting those trapped inside.

Captain Raeder stood with his officers and men on the bridge. The armoured shutters had gone up at the call to action stations and the watertight doors had been sealed. For the moment they were safe, but they could hear the terrible cacophony of sounds and screams as the dragon attacked. Tearing metal and grinding steel mixed with the roar of the enraged beast and the erratic pop and blast of guns.

'That creature will tear this ship to pieces, Captain,' a panicked junior officer screamed, his eyes wide in terror. They could hear the dragon moving along the ship, getting closer.

'They aren't going to be able to stop her,' said James as the three of them looked on aghast. The grey warship was being battered mercilessly by Komargoran Monarchmauler. Tempus barked a warning and they spun around to see a long line of khaki figures climbing through the sand dunes.

'It's the British Army,' cried James in delight, only to bite his lip at the dreadful realisation that the dragon would attack them in the same way it had the German marines on the beach earlier.

## The Balance Between

'We must warn them,' he said, but realised that Baranor was in a very perilous position himself. He turned to the bear and hound. 'Tempus you must go with Baranor back to the house and explain to my mother that she must hide Baranor. It's the only safe place. We can't send you back through the arch until we know for certain that the olorcs aren't just waiting on the other side. I'll go to the army officers and warn them, but we don't have much time.' And before anyone had time to disagree, James was off.

'Number one gun reports ready to fire on the creature when it gets forward, sir.'

The foremost turret had swung around to bring its gun to bear. If it fired a shell at such close range everyone on the bridge would be deafened by the explosion, but there were few options remaining to the ship. The *Ausburg* was fighting for her life.

James ran around the dune and slammed straight into a soldier, sending them both sprawling.

'Please listen to me,' he said. 'I must speak with your officer.'

The soldier picked himself up and brushed the sand off his uniform. 'Now listen, sonny, this isn't a place for young lads like you. We've got to clear this area,' he said in a broad Geordie accent.

'Listen to me, I know what's been going on and your commanding officer will want to know. It's very important. People will die, they already have,' James felt his anxiety pass from him to the soldier as a blood-curdling scream cut the air. The roar of a large calibre gun replied.

'Right, sonny, follow me.' And the soldier doubled off with James running to keep up.

※

Tempus stood at the entrance to the house as the ladies bustled around the room paying no heed to the hound. In the time since the door had burst open and the soldier had been struck down, Lady Jennifer and Amanda had managed to get the housekeeper Polly to bed, so badly shaken were the poor lady's nerves. Now Amanda was busy filling a kettle to make tea while James's mother swept up the broken wood that covered the floor. The marines lay where they'd fallen.

'Excuse me, ladies,' said the dog.

Both women turned and stared down at the motionless body of the soldier.

'Did the soldier say something?' whispered Amanda to her aunt. They edged a bit closer to have a look.

'No, it was me,' said Tempus. 'I'm sorry to intrude like this but we need your help.'

Lady Jennifer glanced at the dog and then walked to the door and looked cautiously outside, patting the dog on the head to keep it quiet. 'Is there anyone there?' she hissed in a low voice.

Behind her Amanda set down the kettle and picked up the poker.

'Mmmm, that's nice. Yes there is, me. But as I was saying, we need some help. James sent us,' said Tempus as he revelled in the attention.

Lady Jennifer slowly raised her hand from the hound as she stared down at him in disbelief.

'You?'

'Yes. James sent us. You are James's mother, Lady Jennifer Kinghorn?' the dog enquired. Had it not been for the fact that Lady Jennifer had already had a day quite full of surprises and shocking occurrences, she may well have fainted once more. But her constitution was by now able to cope with just about anything.

'Yes I am,' she replied.

'My name is Tempus. It was me you saw at the window a short while ago. And you also met my friend Baranor. The one who doesn't use doors.'

## The Balance Between

'The creature that attacked the soldiers?' enquired Amanda, who was showing quite an ability to adapt to weird circumstances.

'Yes. He's a bear, a very good one at that. And now we need somewhere to hide him for the time being. James sent me to ask for your help. After all, it seemed unlikely that you'd accept an explanation from a bear.'

Baranor edged into the room and introduced himself to the stunned ladies. He offered to carry the unconscious soldier upstairs, where he put him in one of the bedrooms, then was shown to Amanda's bedroom where the bear lay out on the bed and dozed off. Tempus promised to return with help, but for the moment he was needed by James and dashed off, leaving the women quietly wondering what they were doing with a big black bear and a German soldier in bed in the house.

～⌒⌒⌒～

'Father!' James called as he saw Sir Philip striding through the long grass towards the beach. Sir Philip couldn't believe his eyes and ran to greet his son, throwing his arms about James, relieved at his safe return.

'James, you're alive! Your mother has been beside herself with worry. Where have you been and what's going on?' The sound of battle drifted over the dunes. The smell of cordite hung in the air.

James looked at the entourage of officers and civilians that accompanied Sir Philip. The boy doubted they would believe him. But they would believe their own eyes and ears.

'Father, we must be quick or things will get worse. Over the dunes, to the beach. Hurry!' And he led them at a run back to where the khaki-uniformed soldiers were just beginning to discover the terrible events.

'Order the artillery over here at the double,' Sir Philip said to the colonel of the regiment when he'd taken in what was happening.

## The Balance Between

Out to sea the *Ausburg* lay dead in the water. Black smoke rose from the triple stacks, but the ship was under siege to the enormous lizard that flashed blue and silver against the dull grey cruiser. On the beach the British soldiers were under strict orders not to fire, and they were busy rounding up the surviving German marines and tending to the wounded.

'Let's just pray that thing doesn't lose interest in the ship before we're ready,' said Sir Philip as he and James stood together among the dunes.

## ~ 18 ~

## A Farewell to Arms

The fight was a vicious affair. Once Bartholomew had stumbled over the rows of fangs and teeth that lined the dragon's mouth, he'd carried on, slashing in every direction with his sword. Siganatoris Bloodboiler had recoiled in a reflex reaction, attempting to spit the dwarf out. Her head snaked backwards and out of the tunnel and then her long neck convulsed into a frenzy of distortions as she tried dislodging Bartholomew.

Inside the gullet of the dragon, the dwarf found himself tumbling further into the body, losing his footing as he rolled with her frenzied exertions. His protective leather helmet flew off and the white asbestos suit he wore began to tear under the strain. He kept hacking around him in the dark, both hands gripping the sword tightly as he thrust and lunged, ripping his way out of the dragon's stomach and into the vital organs alongside.

Siganatoris Bloodboiler screamed in pain as she felt the wounds open up inside her. It was as if a parasite were slowly working its way through her, destroying her abilities by attacking her from within. She didn't feel her legs and wings give way. Her tail still thrashed vehemently and her eyes, ears and snout told her that the dwarf at her side, hacking at her with an axe, was a nasty distraction. But inside her, beyond the reach of her strength or power, unreachable by talons or jaws, something was slowly carving her heart out. She must act quickly with all her guile.

The ornamental lake glistened as the late sun caught the reflections of the disturbed water and the dragon saw that salvation lay there. She lunged at the water and sank deep, holding her jaws open and letting water flood down her neck. She would drown the noxious creature inside her. Drown it before she drowned herself.

Solomon waded in up to his waist, raining heavy blows down on the dragon with his axe, giant scything blows that started high above his head and swung pendulously down to cleave the armour of the serpent. No other blow would cut through its scaly skin. The dragon was oblivious to his efforts, and the wounds that he drew from the flank of the creature were shallow. Solomon knew that, inside the enemy, his brother would be fighting for his own life while seeking to end the dragon's. Solomon hacked on.

Bartholomew was on his back, squashed between two slippery muscular ridges of flesh. His sword lay embedded in a sheath of tissue that swelled and contracted rhythmically. At his side the digestive stones rumbled together in the pit of the stomach where he lay. Blood and digestive juices ran in his face and over his body. The dwarf had lost the protective headgear long ago and he kept his eyes firmly shut against the corrosive effects of the liquid. And then he was swimming, swimming for his life as his body cartwheeled and twisted in a sack of water.

Bartholomew dragged at the hilt of his sword, which anchored him to one place, but it would not budge. As his body surged forward with a new influx of water, his weight was thrown on to the blade and it sank further in. Realising he was running out of time, the brave dwarf made one last supreme effort. Fixing his feet where he found purchase, he gave a mighty shove on the hilt of his sword, pushing it deeper into the flesh, and striking at the dragon's soul.

The great dragon known for aeons as Siganatoris Bloodboiler, whose history stretched far back to the very first moments of Creation, died. As the last spark of life left that ancient and cruelly magnificent creature, her tail lifted once more and fell dead to the ground.

Solomon lay in the sloshing cold water with his back to the wall. He'd been knocked backwards by the dragon as its head flailed from side-to-side, and he'd broken a leg just below the knee. White bone stuck through a tear in his trousers, and the whole of Solomon's leg was crusted in blood. His axe lay useless by his side.

Siganatoris Bloodboiler lay by the ornamental lake, her body half submerged under the water, her great wings splayed out on either side of her, drying and hardening in the late afternoon sun. Dragon blood seeped from her mouth as it lay agape in the shallows, turning the water a sickly bile green.

---

Komargoran Monarchmauler completely destroyed the exterior of the vessel, her claws ripping up the teak decking and tearing down the radio masts. She gouged deep rents in the chimney stacks and twisted metal everywhere until the ship no longer resembled a warship. The gun turrets and decks ran with blood.

The dragon stood on the metal shielding of the forward turret and peered through the observation slit into the bridge. Her enormous eye blazed red and yellow, the elliptical pupil shifting from side-to-side as she held the humans in a trance-like state. She studied each of the naval officers and crew in turn, using her archaic powers of magic to look into their souls. She was hunting for the man with the weakest spirit, the one she could exert her magic on to do her bidding. Komargoran Monarchmauler was looking for a soulslave – like Herr Dorpmuller and the others whom she'd enslaved with magic – who would open the door into the bridge so she could finish them off. The piercing gaze of her eye settled on a terrified junior officer whose will could be quickly bent to her needs. The other officers and men on the *Ausburg* bridge were locked in her spell, unable to move.

Only the strongest will can resist the power of a dragon. In that moment, as Komargoran Monarchmauler was about to capture a soulslave, Captain Raeder found the strength to do just that, to resist. Shaking off the magic-induced torpor, he pulled a pistol from under the navigation table and levelled the gun. He shot a whole magazine of bullets into the dragon's eye.

Komargoran Monarchmauler screamed in abject pain and reared back, clawing desperately at her face to stop the agony that lanced through her head, and breaking off her assault on the warship in the process. Captain Raeder had saved his ship, for the moment.

Further out to sea three destroyers accompanying the armoured cruiser *Cressy* formed line astern, and the small squadron of ships closed with the coastline. In the distance they could make out the silhouette of the wrecked German warship as it lay mauled and wounded in the shelter of Beadnell Bay. The ships closed, crews at action stations and guns trained on the *Ausburg*.

Standing astride the vessel, the dragon thrashed her tail in pain and anger, dismounting the forward turret and sending it over the side. Despite her wound, Komargoran Monarchmauler looked up with her one good eye to see more of the enemy sailing towards her. Screeching her fury, she rose into the air to retreat back to the coast.

'Look out!' someone cried, and everyone's attention was focused on the great beast as it hurtled back over the water.

'Are the guns ready, Colonel?' Sir Philip calmly enquired. The beach was now a swarm of activity. Soldiers took cover behind every dune while, further inland, teams of horses were being unshackled from artillery pieces.

## The Balance Between

'They'll be ready in a few moments, Sir Philip,' the colonel replied, his voice a good deal less sure than that of James's father.

Sir Philip looked down at his son. 'I don't suppose there is anywhere safer that I can pack you off to,' he said with great affection. 'Your mother would be horrified to know what danger I've placed you in.'

James looked seriously at his father. 'Actually, father, it's me that has put us all in this trouble. That dragon is my problem, really. I don't think the army will stop it. Not with what they have here.' He looked around at the six artillery pieces.

'Get down!' screamed a voice that cracked in panic. Sir Philip and James threw themselves on to the ground as an enormous shadow passed over them. James felt the down-stroke of Komargoran Monarchmauler's wing beat. The dragon wheeled overhead, each hind foot grasping a khaki figure.

Already the guns were useless, unable to bear on the rapidly moving target. The men milled around the ordnance unsure of what to do. Komargoran Monarchmauler struck down, ripping a gun from its mounting and sending it flipping end over end into the scrub before the barrel buried itself in the soft sand. The horses bolted as another artillery piece went careening into the next one in the line. Sporadic rifle fire gave way to sustained volleys, but it only served to goad the dragon further.

'This is hopeless,' Sir Philip called to the colonel who lay sprawled nearby. 'We'll have a massacre on our hands before that creature is done.'

James looked up the beach to where the Sea Arch stood unobserved. Suddenly he recalled the words of Sibelius.

'Maybe, just maybe,' he said to himself. Without a moment's hesitation he picked himself up off the ground and began to run.

*The Balance Between*

'Aagh.' Bartholomew had placed his hand in yet more slime. He crawled over the ridges lining the slippery oesophagus, heading towards the light. Extricating himself from the insides of the dragon was a totally new form of orienteering. First he'd had to hack his way out of the dragon's body and into its throat. When he'd reached the mouth cavity the dwarf then used his sword to lever the jaws wide enough to crawl over the teeth and escape, tearing his asbestos suit until it hung in tatters. That was when he found Solomon lying beneath the dragon's tail.

'Brother,' was all Bartholomew could say as tears streamed down his face. He knelt next to Solomon, gently lifted his head and shoulders, and held him in his arms. Solomon lay limp, his body broken asunder by the final fall of the dragon's tail. A little blood escaped his mouth. His eyelids fluttered open but his eyes had a glazed, faraway look as if they were glimpsing a place no one else could see.

'Did you succeed, Bartholomew?' He coughed gently, more bubbles of blood coating his lips. 'Did you kill your dragon?'

Bartholomew wiped his eyes and caught his breath. 'Yes, we got our dragon, Solomon. Together.'

'Good. And now we'll live on forever in legend, the Broth–'

'The Brothers Bandamire.' Bartholomew choked back the sadness that welled up. 'Slayers of the dragon Siganatoris Bloodboiler and Deceivers of Dragons. That's us. We'll be famous, Solomon, you and I.' And then Solomon was gone.

※

James ran as fast as his legs would carry him, over the last sand dune and down to the foreshore. He didn't hear the shouts and gunfire behind him. Only the sound of the sea and the beating of wings registered in his mind. He didn't look back but he knew the dragon was closing on him, swooping low to pluck him from the ground in its cruel talons. He was almost at the Sea Arch.

## The Balance Between

Komargoran Monarchmauler extended her hind claws, reaching down to grind that little boy into mince. She stretched out her wings as flat and as wide as possible, allowing her to glide in for the kill. She dropped out of the sky, one hundred feet, seventy-five feet...

'Fire,' the artillery officer ordered, and the last working gun flung a shell over the dunes straight at the dragon.

The solid shot tore the innermost talon from the right hind foot of Komargoran Monarchmauler and knocked her sideways in the process. The dragon pulled in her legs in reflex, the pain already coursing through her nerves and screaming into her head. Instinctively she wheeled out of the way, overshooting and missing the boy as he ran along the beach.

James felt the blast of the solid cannon shell as it flew overhead and was immediately knocked down as something thumped into his back. He rolled over as he hit the ground and saw the wicked talon claw sticking out of the sand. Without thinking he grabbed it and got to his feet. Out of the corner of his eye he saw the enraged Komargoran Monarchmauler wheeling above him preparing to strike again. James was only feet away from the Sea Arch.

'You will not escape this time,' she bellowed out, her voice igniting into a gout of flame that licked the sand, turning it instantly to glass. James ducked behind the Sea Arch just in time. The dragon wheeled around the top of the Sea Arch and fell towards James. He only just managed to push open the gate and scramble through.

Sir Philip jumped to his feet and watched in disbelief as his son raced off over the sand. James was running towards the Sea Arch that only the two of them were able to see.

'He must have a plan,' he said to himself.

'Yes, he will have a plan,' said Harrington, who had come to stand next to James's father and watch.

*

*The Balance Between*

The Colonel stared after the dragon. It had ceased attacking his soldiers and was now about to pluck the boy off the sand to his death. Behind him the gunnery officer was exhorting his men to make haste for another barrage. He watched as the flames licked the sand and the boy attempted to dodge the beast. It was futile. The child was as good as dead. Then, miraculously, the boy simply vanished into thin air. The Colonel's jaw dropped.

Komargoran Monarchmauler watched as the boy slipped through the ornamental gates. Anger welled up in her and the bloodlust returned, crashing through her brain and all but blinding her sight and reason.

'How dare this little worm of a human continue to evade me, Queen of all dragons,' she cried out to herself. Fury consumed her and she arrowed straight down at the gates, intending to knock them from their hinges and crush the cursed whelp for good. 'Die, you spawn of the soulless! Die!' she screamed and flew through the gates.

James lay on the long grass where he'd fallen and looked back between the open gates at the dragon. Komargoran Monarchmauler hung there, trapped in the portal's magic. The great blue and silver beast writhed like a worm caught on a hook. Her jaws snapped open and shut as she sought to break the powerful field of magic that held her in check. Her tail thrashed and her wings beat furiously, but the only thing to pass through the sea gate was the terrifying noise that detonated like a hundred guns all at once. James watched as the oldest life that Creation had set upon Earth was drained of its magical powers by the portal. And as Komargoran Monarchmauler lost her powers, so too her soul drained away, and she was gone.

On the beach there was almost as much pandemonium when the dragon spectacularly disappeared as when the soldiers and officers had first laid eyes on the creature.

Sir Philip turned to Harrington. He was mentally and physically exhausted from the recent events, but his anxiety kept him from collapsing. 'Harrington, what the devil happened? Did they both go through the Sea Arch?' he asked.

Harrington shook his head. 'I don't know, Sir Philip. I understand that no magical creature may pass through a portal. Dragons, like elves, possess magic. Therefore it is probable that the dragon could not make it to the other side. But there's no one who can say.'

Sir Philip turned to Corrick. 'You've been through a gateway before, Corrick. You could go after him.'

Corrick shook his head. 'Sir Philip, I am sorry. I am like the rest of the men on this beach. I cannot see this gateway,' he said apologetically.

'Then perhaps this is the reason why I can see the Sea Arch,' Sir Philip thought. 'It's me who's meant to go after James.' Sir Philip started to run down to the Sea Arch.

James picked himself up off the ground and looked about. The sun still had a while to go before it set. He knew where he was. 'No surprises there,' he said aloud.

Then he heard a howl from further up the valley, behind the Sea Arch. He spun around, his hand going to the hilt of the dagger. There, beyond the arch, James briefly caught a glimpse of a big grey werewolf slinking into the glade before turning and running as fast as he could.

He was no more than fifty paces from the Sea Arch when the great loping body of the dog raced out from the dunes. Sir Philip didn't know what it was, but it was running straight for him and he felt fear grip him. He glanced around and spotted a rifle discarded by one of the German marines. He veered off and lunged to grab it. Lifting the stock to his shoulder, he swung the rifle in an arc, trying to get a bead on the moving animal. Too late! The dog bounded up and brushed Sir Philip to one side, sending him sprawling to his knees.

'Stop! I'm a friend of James.' The voice seemed to come from the hound. 'James has gone back through the Sea Arch. We must help him.' And with that the dog turned and ran through the open gates. Sir Philip levered himself off the ground and followed.

'Damn my eyes. What the hell has happened to Sir Philip?' The Colonel garbled out the question. Other senior officers milled about, equally perplexed. Elsewhere the good sense of junior officers and NCOs ensured that the wounded men were being attended to.

Sir Philip found himself in the glade where James had lain only a short while before. The hound stood quietly scenting the afternoon air. Sir Philip moved to stand beside it.

'James was here,' said the big silver-grey hound, 'but he quickly moved off down the valley. He's not the only one.' The dog sniffed again. 'Werewolves. Maybe one, maybe a pack of them, I can't tell.' Tempus stood quivering from nose-tip to tail-end. Sir Philip didn't know whether it was excitement or fear. Sir Philip knew what was making himself shake, and it wasn't just the effect of having passed through the portal. The prospect of werewolves was quite appalling.

'We'd better get going. James may be in trouble,' said the hound and they set off down the path together.

☙❦❧

Sibelius gazed down at the pool of water that lay in the centre of the vallmaria. He had watched the water ripple once and then twice more. But he had also seen it suddenly flash with brilliant light; the vallmaria had registered something remarkable. He interpreted the three ripples as three individuals passing through the Sea Arch. The other flash of light he couldn't explain. His reading of the vallmaria was limited. He'd need to redouble his efforts to relearn the lost magic of the elders. Time pressed in on the old wizard. 'There is so much to do, so much to lose,' he said to himself. 'And yet there is still much to gain.'

Sibelius spun round and found the Lady Orlania standing at the top of the flight of steps leading to his observatory. 'Lady Orlania, I was not aware of your passing through the dream generator.'

'No, my good wizard,' she said with a smile, 'and I intended you not to know.'

'I was thinking aloud. Forgive me,' Sibelius said. He watched as the Elven princess strolled around his room, her fingers brushing objects at random. 'I see that you still practise the art of resonant memory, my Lady.' Her hand withdrew behind her cloak. She was adept at resonant memory, an ancient power that allowed a user to learn of events simply by touching artefacts present at the time of the event occurring. Lady Orlania could read the room like it was a book, and for this reason the wizard was less than pleased whenever she visited him. He preferred to meet with other sorcerers and magi beyond the confines of his observatory.

'Sibelius, I know that crucial events pass Eldaterra by without our world knowing of them. I know your position as Master of the Shadows places greater knowledge and power in your hands than anyone else in the world. Yet these events affect us all, and we know nothing of them.' Her voice carried a hint of accusation. 'That boy James, for instance: what has become of him? You plot and you connive for the good of Eldaterra, I have no doubt. But still you plot and connive, traits that I do not fully appreciate in anyone, let alone a wizard.'

'My lady, I am most flattered. But my knowledge of events is ever incomplete, and my labours often come to nothing.' He walked towards his desk and picked up a small silver object. 'I fashion devices such as this that are merely facsimiles of the tools of the ancient wizards and sorcerers of the Guild. I know not how they work, but I seek to unlock their secrets. Should I inform everyone of what I do, when I know not myself?' He replaced the item on the desk. Lady Orlania remained silent and Sibelius continued. 'You ask of James. I know that at this moment he has passed through the Sea Arch into Eldaterra. I do not know if he succeeded in his fate, or indeed what that fate held. But I do know that he may yet perish, whether the task is done or not. If he succeeds and he survives long enough to reach the Western Tower I will learn more. If he does not, then I will be required to renew my efforts, through plotting and conniving, to discover the enemy's intent.'

'And will you not save James?' she asked. 'He lies within Lauderley Forest and therefore within your protection,'

The wizard's head shot round and his eyes bored into those of the noble elf. 'With every use of my power, the enemy learns more. He learns of our limitations. He learns of our weaknesses and he learns of our divisions. I cannot risk everything for one life, regardless of our feelings.'

Sibelius's words struck home. Colour came to Lady Orlania's cheeks and her eyes flared in anger, but Sibelius caught a glimpse of the tears she blinked back.

'Lady. I understand,' he said, his voice soft and sympathetic. 'We all must walk the harder path.'

She turned and departed without another word.

---

James heard the crunch of twigs and leaf litter beneath the silent padding paws that stalked him. He lay behind a bole of roots that offered protection on three sides. Above him the pine tree swayed quietly. The branches were too high off the ground to enable James to climb out of harm's way, and he couldn't outrun the werewolf. He decided to stand and face his attacker rather than be jumped from behind as he fled through the forest. Now he sat and waited, peering over the root and back up the path. It was only another few seconds before the werewolf broke cover.

Its nose was to the ground, following his scent. With a long pointed head and rigid ears it looked almost like a bat. Behind the head a shaggy mane of grey fur sprouted unevenly and continued along the spine of the animal's long back. The legs and body were sinewy and the limbs moved as if the werewolf used a minimum of effort. Its gait was relaxed, yet deceptively fast. Its teeth and claws reminded James of the dragon.

The animal stopped a short way up the path. It sniffed at the ground, hesitating, as if it knew something was wrong. James had sprinted down the path before doubling back to where he lay hidden, hoping to ambush his pursuer. Now it looked as if the creature's cunning had found him out. He stopped himself shaking as the werewolf scratched and mulled a while longer. What was it waiting for?

Tempus leapt from behind a pine tree and gave a warning bark that caught the werewolf unawares. It hadn't expected to find itself pursued. It walked towards Tempus and sized the hound up. The bearhound was indeed no match for a fully-grown werewolf, and this one was enormous. Nonetheless Tempus held his ground, challenging the werewolf to attack. The werewolf's hackles rose and its jaws fell open, drool spilling from its mouth.

Now James jumped up to draw the werewolf's attention away from Tempus and allow him to escape. 'Hey, over here,' he called. The werewolf turned in James's direction, confused that the hunted had turned on the hunter. Tempus barked again and this time the werewolf decided. It leapt at Tempus.

Crack! A bullet caught the werewolf in the chest and flung it to the ground, dead. Sir Philip stepped out from behind a tree, the gun still at the ready. James and Tempus moved cautiously to the inert body, but it was a clean kill.

'Father,' James said, and hugged him.

☙❦❧

Captain Raeder gave orders to clear the ship and attend to the casualties. Smashed guns and wreckage were heaved over the side. In truth the ship was a smouldering hulk, hardly recognisable as a serviceable warship. He left the ship in the charge of his first lieutenant, clambered into a canvas dinghy, the only seaworthy boat to have survived the onslaught, and was rowed to the beach.

'Good day, Colonel.' Captain Raeder gave a stiff salute to the senior British officer before him. 'My name is Captain Raeder of Kaiser Wilhelm II's Imperial German Navy. I command the warship *Ausburg* you see moored in the bay.'

The colonel eyed the German suspiciously. Sir Philip had left word for the colonel to be advised by the civilian Harrington in matters concerning the sovereignty of Great Britain. Apparently this chap Harrington was a Foreign Office official attached to the War Office.

'Good day, Captain Raeder. I am Colonel Smythe-Whitely of His Majesty King George V's Army, fourth battalion of the Royal Northumberland Fusiliers, and this is Harrington of the Foreign Office. It seems we've had quite a show today, one way or another.' The colonel slapped his walking cane against the top of his boot as if to accentuate the fact.

'Colonel, the unfortunate events that we speak of necessitated me bringing my ship within the sovereign territorial waters of Great Britain. You will see that from the state of my ship –' He turned and looked back at the *Ausburg*. Captain Raeder visibly blanched when he saw for himself the catastrophic damage that his ship had suffered. He struggled to regain his composure and continued. 'We've been sorely damaged.' It was clear Captain Raeder was searching for an explanation of events without having to describe it as an attack by a dragon. Such a report would lead directly to dismissal on the grounds of insanity.

'Captain Raeder,' Harrington began, catching the colonel's eye. 'I understand entirely how you may have been obliged, at such short notice and under the difficult conditions you found yourself in, to make for the protective anchorage that this bay offers. Observing your ship one might imagine that it suffered from rather a bad crossing of the North Sea?' he offered.

The captain took the cue and responded positively. 'That is correct, Mr Harrington. My ship was caught in a most savage storm that wrecked communications and did extensive damage throughout the vessel. Sadly it resulted in the loss of a good many lives.'

'And so, Captain Raeder, you were obliged to put men ashore while repairs were carried out?'

'Exactly.'

'Well then, Colonel,' Harrington said as he turned to the army officer. 'I believe the Foreign Office will be satisfied with the description of events I will be reporting on. It only now requires a decision as to how events will be presented to the War Office.'

The colonel looked at both men and said, 'I believe that it was most unfortunate Captain Raeder's enforced evacuation took place on a stretch of beach used for live ammunition practice. That will account for the dead and wounded on both sides, with a little bit of work.'

## ∽ 19 ∽

## The Truth about Everything

Tempus moved upwind of the dead werewolf and thrust his nose into the faint forest breeze. 'It's as I suspected. This one was the lead beast. The pack follows, and they're not far behind. We must hurry.'

James and his father turned to follow the hound down the path. They went as quickly as they could, but the pack would still be gaining.

'If we can make it to the hunting lodge we can hole up there for a while,' said Tempus as he ushered them down the path. A terrible howling rent the forest. The werepack had discovered their fallen packmember.

'They'll be coming even faster now they seek revenge,' said the bearhound.

They raced on and, in the distance, the lodge lay squat in the meadow, its windows, thankfully, shuttered. Behind them the forest muffled the noise of the rapidly closing pack until it burst onto the trail. There were perhaps twenty werewolves, all with long salivating jaws and cruel intent in their eyes.

'Don't stop!' yelled Tempus and he fell behind to delay their pursuers. James and his father didn't look back but pelted the last few yards to the broken door, throwing themselves through the opening and into the gloom beyond.

# The Balance Between

Tempus wheeled about and stood, legs spread wide, jaws set, and growled a deep, dangerous warning to the werewolves. The pack was taken by surprise by this sudden show of resistance and slowed to a halt just yards from the bearhound. In a line across the path they studied him with contempt. Snarling and clashing their jaws they paced slowly forward, moving in for the kill.

*Crack.* A large and fearsome werewolf sank howling to the ground, its rear legs useless. The other creatures faltered, unsure of what was going on. Tempus span and fled, gaining a good lead over the pack. *Crack*, a second werewolf fell stone dead as Tempus reached the broken door and sailed through it with a mighty leap.

---

Much of the clearing-up work on the beach had been done by the time Lady Amanda Brightmere marched over the rough pasture land that separated the farm from the beach. She held her long skirts up to avoid trailing them in the mud and sand.

'Excuse me, gentlemen,' she began as she approached a group of army officers and civilians, 'I am looking for Sir Philip Kinghorn. I am his niece, Lady Amanda Brightmere.'

The men raised their caps in salute and several bowed. An older man stepped forward. 'Lady Amanda, my name is Harrington. I accompanied your uncle from London this morning. Sir Philip is indisposed at present ... Is there any way I may help?'

Amanda looked at Harrington keenly. If Sir Philip had travelled down from London with this man, then one could assume they were both here for the same reason.

'Mr Harrington, my aunt, Lady Jennifer, and I are staying in the farmhouse you can see in the distance. We have wounded guests that you should know of.' Her eyes glanced at the wounded lying on stretchers awaiting evacuation. 'If you would care to accompany me back I would be much obliged.'

Harrington agreed immediately and requested the colonel to

arrange transport for the wounded. Then they set off back across the fields.

When they reached the farmhouse Harrington looked down at the fallen soldier outside. 'Done for, I'm afraid,' was all he said. Amanda led him into the house, noting his reaction to the destroyed door. Once inside, Harrington heard the sound of movement coming from upstairs.

Lady Amanda turned to him. 'Mr Harrington, what precisely do you know of events?' Her eyes locked on to his and Harrington had the erudition to realise it was a trick question.

'I know as much as Sir Philip, and a good deal more, Lady Amanda. He and his son are together, and they are accompanied by the dog.' Harrington prayed that this would answer the question at both levels.

'Mr Harrington, we have a wounded German soldier upstairs as well as the housekeeper in her room at the back of the house. But there is also one other guest and I am not quite sure how to put this . . .' Amanda left the statement unfinished.

'Perhaps if I may see the guest myself?'

Amanda pushed open the door to find Baranor with his head in a bucket, sitting on the bed. Lady Jennifer sat next to him. She turned and smiled. 'I made our good bear some soup. He was hungry.' The bear ignored the new visitor and polished off the broth.

❦

Herr Dorpmuller had searched through the endless empty corridors and caverns to no avail. The entire workings had been deserted. By chance he'd come across a doorway not indicated on the map and this had led him upwards, closer to the surface. In these levels he had been appalled to see the vilest creatures one could imagine: great hulking monsters with thick arms and shoulders and heads like mastiff dogs with cropped ears. After succeeding in communicating with these creatures one of them escorted Herr Dorpmuller into the chambers of General Balerust. He was shocked to see the General resembled a human, an old, dark, oily-skinned human, with disfigured features and grotesque in body, but a human nonetheless and quite unlike what Herr Dorpmuller had been expecting. He was also surprised to see the cruel-looking olorcs treat the general with comparative gentleness, compassion even, setting a pitcher of black wine close to hand for their charge and trimming the torches that guttered in the wall brackets.

'General Balerust, I am most pleased to make your acquaintance,' Herr Dorpmuller began tentatively.

The general looked up at him with rheumy old eyes. He spoke with a quiet, frail voice. 'I believe you must be Herr Dorpmuller, yes? Freislung has told me all about you.' He coughed, his breath wheezing in his chest.

'As he's told me of you, General, though in the circumstances I was led to believe –'

'Yes, Herr Dorpmuller, you were led to believe. Did you not think that a man you bought for his treacherous services couldn't be corrupted a second time? Your Herr Freislung was as happy to collect payment from me as he was from you.'

Herr Dorpmuller hesitated, his mind speeding like a locomotive's wheels with no rails to grip. 'You mean ... you mean to say there is no army assembling for the invasion of the New World?' Herr Dorpmuller asked incredulously.

General Balerust smiled and gave a little nod of his head.

The enormity of the situation was simply too much for Herr Dorpmuller to bear and he collapsed into a chair. 'After all these years, all Frau Colbetz's plans –'

'They were simply wishful dreams on her part, I am glad to say. I simply fed your servant Freislung the story that you wanted to hear, until the end, when he became ... unnecessary.'

## The Balance Between

Some minutes passed while Herr Dorpmuller came to terms with this news. The old general sat patiently. Outside the closed door, the faint noises of activity could just be heard.

Herr Dorpmuller looked up. 'But the creatures that came through the Sea Arch?'

'A diversion that was not of my making, but fortuitous nonetheless. There is no alliance, no invasion army, no one.' General Balerust's voice trembled with age. 'No one to lead them.'

The full implications of what he'd heard slammed into Dorpmuller and his self control snapped, his despair transforming into rage in a matter of seconds. 'You, you,' he said accusingly, 'you are *not* General Balerust!'

'Oh, I suppose after fifteen years I am. Certainly the olorcs believe me to be,' replied the old man from behind the desk. 'I have eaten the black substance they call shol and it's transformed me so that I have come to resemble them.'

Herr Dorpmuller felt utter resentment rising from his black guts, clamping over his heart and crushing his chest. This pathetic, wizened old fool had interfered with the plan that he had so carefully devised, a plan that would have changed the face of the world forever. He, Herr Dorpmuller, could have had everything, power, wealth, the love of a dragon as his bride-queen, even an empire, but for this decrepit and meddlesome schweinhund. Dorpmuller flew out of the chair, sending it crashing to the floor behind him. His hand scrambled at the holster by his side as he grabbed his pistol and pointed it at General Balerust.

The old man smiled again. 'We destroyed the dragon birthpit long ago. Tell your mistress she will never breed. And she will never rule.' He looked at the gun. 'It will be a welcome release from fifteen years of servitude, offered to me as my fate. Please, Herr Dorpmuller, pull the trigger.'

And Dorpmuller, in his hatred and anger, did just that.

## The Balance Between

Sir Philip and James barricaded the doorway with the upended table and backed it up with a large chest of drawers rammed behind it. Night had fallen and the werewolves were growing bolder in the darkness.

'They will attempt to break down the door,' Tempus said, the inevitability of it making his voice sound weary. 'They are driven by the dark powers. They must obey, or die trying. Don't let them get near you. The teeth of a werewolf are especially dangerous because a single bite can kill from blood poisoning.'

Sir Philip checked the rifle. The magazine had only two bullets remaining. Once these were used he'd reverse it and wield it like a club. James still had his dagger. Together they set about building a fire in the hearth with the wood the brothers kept ready for use.

The howling started up in earnest when the yellow moon rose in the east. Father, son and hound waited.

The attack, when it came, still took them by surprise. All at once half-a-dozen bodies thudded against the barricade, shifting it. Sir Philip raised the rifle but James called out, 'No, Father, not yet. Wait for a clean shot.' And the young lad leaped forward, his dagger in his hand, and slashed at the nose of the first werewolf pushing its snout into the room. The creature gave a yelp and the head disappeared. Blood ran along the blade. A second head replaced it, the werewolf attempting to shoulder its way past the obstruction. Sir Philip brought the stock of the gun crashing down on the animal's head, crushing the thin skull with the blow. The body sank down, only for another werewolf to leap on it and scramble into the gap that was slowly widening.

'Stop the table shifting, Father,' yelled James, slashing again at the intruder. Sir Philip thrust his full weight behind the table. At the same time he brought the rifle level, stuck it in the throat of the werewolf snapping at James's blade and pulled the trigger. The creature was blown out of the gap. James threw his weight behind that of his father and the table eased back, closing up the hole.

Outside, the werewolves howled with rage and tore at the bodies of their fallen.

Sir Philip dragged more furniture from the far end of the lodge to reinforce the doorway. All the windows were shuttered, they would be more than sufficient to keep the werewolves out. James poked around in the kitchen and found a few meagre morsels to take the edge off their hunger. They kept the fire stoked and eventually dozed off, leaving Tempus to guard them while they slept.

༺❀༻

Baranor sniffed the man.

'Elf,' the bear said matter-of-factly. Lady Jennifer and Amanda looked puzzled. Harrington gave them a polite smile but said nothing.

Baranor waited in the locked bedroom while the soldiers came and collected the wounded German and his dead comrade. Harrington sent a request back to the colonel that a lorry be made available at the earliest opportunity for Lady Jennifer's belongings. This ruse was necessary to transport Baranor, who'd explained briefly to the humans the events that had taken place at Cragside. Since the dwarves hadn't caught up with James, Tempus and Baranor, it looked suspiciously like they'd fallen into some sort of trouble. Baranor wanted to return to Cragside quickly to see what could be done.

When the lorry arrived, the driver was ordered to back up to the doorway and, while Lady Amanda distracted the young man – an easy enough task – Baranor slipped out of the house and climbed aboard, into the canvassed rear, the lorry's suspension sagging under his weight. Harrington and Amanda climbed into the cab, leaving Lady Jennifer to await the return of her husband and son.

They drove south-west to Alnwick and then down the Rothbury road, turning onto the estate's gravel drive as the sun sank.

*The Balance Between*

Baranor called from the back for the driver to halt, and Harrington ordered the driver to wait there for them. He and Amanda climbed out of the cab, opened the back and followed the bulk of the bear as it sped through the wrecked gardens.

Baranor could smell the dragon down by the lake. The remaining dragons who survived had fled, taking the precious magic-soaked carcasses of their breathren to dine on, and renew their magical powers. When they reached the lake, Baranor padded over to where the two dwarves lay embraced. He snuffled in the ear of Bartholomew, and the dwarf opened his bloodshot eyes.

⁂

Tempus gave a yelp of surprise that woke Sir Philip and James instantly. The room was full of flying sparks and burning wood scattered across the floor. In the hearth a werewolf fought to disentangle itself from the grate, the fire singeing its flesh and filling the air with a sickly odour. Like a rabid animal the werewolf leapt forward, its jaws snapping at the pain in its scorched flesh. James scrambled over the back of his chair to escape. Sir Philip reached for the gun standing by the side of his chair, but he was too slow. The werewolf had already launched itself at the boy.

The bearhound sank his teeth into the neck of the werewolf and locked on, his weight dragging the werewolf down and away from James. But the bearhound was no match for its enemy. The werewolf was at least twice the size of Tempus and it craned its neck to sink its own jaws into the dog. James rounded the fallen chair, his dagger held ready, and lunged, sending the needle-sharp point deep into the chest of the beast. The werewolf, with its last dying attack, snapped at James, catching him with a fearful bite on his forearm.

Even as the beast sank lifelessly to the floor, Sir Philip and Tempus stared in shock at James, aghast at the wound and its consequences. James felt his head get lighter as the room started spinning, and sank to the floor beside his attacker.

※

Herr Dorpmuller slipped away, back into the abandoned caverns below. Crawling through the darkness, it was many days before he made his way to the gateway. The portcullis stood open and Herr Dorpmuller slipped out of the Old World. Had he stopped and examined the brass plaque he would have noticed an inscription. It read:

> *Assassin cried the righteous dead*
> *Who locked in fate here must lie*
> *Leave this world by cautious tread*
> *For in it none the fates defy*
> *Walk the darkness of your world*
> *Free to choose the cruellest road*
> *And the banners yet unfurled*
> *Lead to evil you have sowed*
>
> *An endless time yet still to pass*
> *When men shall harvest men*
> *With the turning of the glass*
> *Stirs the evil from its den*
> *An angel of the wrongful kind*
> *To stalk the worlds and deep*
> *First a science they must find*
> *And breach the walling of the keep*
>
> *Your fate awaits you in the dark*
> *And the magic fails before you*
> *But as the hounds of war do bark*
> *Recall those you come to bow to*

## The Balance Between

*For your second revolts anew*
*Marked it well as a subtle lie*
*For your third you finally threw*
*The crooked cross and live to die*

☙⁂❧

Baranor helped Bartholomew to lift his brother gently into the back of the darkened lorry. Harrington collected the fallen weapons and followed. Over on the far side of the park, Amanda shared a cigarette with the driver, his attention still diverted. Presently they drove back to the coast in the darkness, the headlamps playing on the road ahead.

When they arrived at the coast, Harrington delegated the lorry driver to assist with the last of the clearing up operations on the beach. Lady Jennifer and Amanda made the upstairs room presentable and Solomon was laid down to rest. The remainder of the party stayed downstairs. Lady Jennifer had already sent Polly the housekeeper back to London. She'd developed quite a nervous disposition and the presence of a dead warrior dwarf was unlikely to improve it.

☙⁂❧

The sound of hammering on the barricade awakened James. Rolling his feverish head to the side he could just make out his father and Tempus defending the doorway, but his eyesight failed him and he drifted off in a delirium.

Sir Philip pulled the barricade to one side and a dismounted rider strode in. He explained that a troop of cavalry stood guard outside and that Sir Philip should get the boy and prepare to ride with them immediately. Sir Philip lifted James from the blankets where he lay and, with Tempus by their side, they left the place, escorted by the cavalry.

☙⁂❧

When James next awoke it was dawn. For twenty-four hours he'd been at the threshold between life and death. Only the skills of Sibelius and the Lady Orlania saved him. He lay in the bed that he'd woken up in almost three weeks ago when he'd first arrived at the Western Tower. Lady Orlania stood next to his bed, smiling down at him. 'So our young warrior has returned,' she said, and placed a hand on James's arm.

James smiled up to her and asked, 'Are my father and Tempus all right?'

The Lady smiled again just as the door opened and Sir Philip walked in accompanied by Sibelius. James looked around for Tempus.

'Your four-legged friend returned through the Sea Arch to bring the others home. A detachment of cavalry stands at the arch awaiting their return,' said Sibelius.

James's father sat on the bed and took his son's hand in his own. 'James, I am so proud of you,' he said. 'Sibelius has told me what he knows of your undertaking, and with what I learned from Tempus, it is beyond belief. Your mother and I could never have wished for such a son.' Tears sprang up in the corners of Sir Philip's eyes, and James watched as they rolled silently down his face, unseen by the others. James felt his eyes burn in reply.

'I think, Lady Orlania, that we are expected elsewhere,' said the wizard.

News of the return of the Bandamire brothers and Tempus was greeted with a mixture of excitement and remorse. Solomon was laid out in the temple of rest where Lady Orlania and her maids saw to his last requirements. Bartholomew and Tempus came to visit James, but despite the warmth of reunion, it was evident that they mourned their brother and master. James too felt the loss of his friend deeply, and cried when he heard the news. Together the surviving company comforted one another and consoled their spirits. Despite the sad news, James made a good recovery and was out of bed on the third day.

'James,' his father said, 'we will stay for the funeral of your worthy friend, Solomon. I asked Tempus to take a message to your mother saying that we'd remain here until you were healed – I didn't mention that you were actually at death's door – but it's appropriate that we stay a little while longer.'

'Father, will everything be all right?' the boy asked.

Sir Philip sighed. 'What I've learned from Sibelius in these few brief days is discouraging. Enemies without and discord within beset Eldaterra. Wizards such as Sibelius labour to keep this world in order and yet they lack much of their predecessors' magic. As I understand it, the Old World is losing its magical powers and slowly sinking. One day it may become as our world is. Then all this will be lost.'

James thought for a moment. 'Did Sibelius tell you of grandfather?'

'Yes, James, he did,' replied his father. 'Sir Neville was on board the *Parsimony* the day she was lost off the Essex coast. I believe he was secretly evaluating the possibilities of a governmental restructuring plan. The *Parsimony* was sabotaged in an effort to discredit your grandfather and his plans. When it led to the loss of the crew and apparent disgrace and disappearance of Sir Neville, the blame was shifted on to me. How ironic that they should have been obliged to use me as the scapegoat. I was expected to shoulder the blame, but my career was saved when I was asked to join the War Office.'

'Do you know who was behind the sabotage, Father?'

'Yes, I do, but there is nothing we can do about it now.' His voice lost its confidence. James wanted to drop the conversation but Sir Philip went on. 'James, I know Sibelius told you your grandfather was still alive when you were last here. Unfortunately the wizard has since learned Sir Neville is no longer alive, killed it is believed, by someone from our world.'

James knew who the murderer was. 'Herr Dorpmuller,' he said. 'I read about it in a book. He left on the warship bound for somewhere. Probably to send the invasion army Frau Colbetz was expecting.' James thought about his grandfather who he'd never met and now never would.

Sir Philip patted his son's arm. 'Sibelius tells me that your grandfather was chosen by fate to remain in this world. Sir Neville survived for fifteen years as a Shadow – a spy – working for Sibelius. He took over the identity of a General Balerust, and for fifteen years deceived the enemy into thinking he was overseeing the dragon's plot and preparations for an invasion army to conquer our world. In those years he did more to protect the Old and New Worlds than any man could ever hope to achieve. Sibelius says he was a truly great and uncorrupted man.'

---

The little dinghy moved slowly in the gentle morning breeze, inching its way up the Essex coast. Rawlings tacked the boat and ran with the breeze, running the small craft up the beach until it gripped. He jumped out and hauled it higher out of the breaking tide. Although his work for Sir Philip was finished, something still tugged at his subconscious. Instinctively he had come back to this place, hoping and expecting to find something that linked the whole plot together, the *Parsimony*, Sir Philip and Sir Neville. Something worth killing for. But there wasn't anything. Looking about him he could see nothing but flat beach and low-lying tussocks of grass. He walked awhile, enjoying the sun on his face if not the quiet solitude. Then he turned and headed back to the boat. There was nothing here after all.

'Halt,' called a voice. Rawlings stopped. 'Turn around, slowly,' the voice commanded.

Rawlings turned and found himself looking at a bedraggled foreign-sounding gentleman pointing a gun at Rawlings's chest.

'I need to get off this island. I will pay you for your assistance,' the man said, a hint of desperation in his voice.

'I can take you to Shoeburyness,' Rawlings offered. 'But the charge is five pounds,' he added, gauging the man's predicament perfectly.

'The price is no matter. But you misunderstand me. I need to get off this island of Great Britain.'

'Then the price will be considerably more,' Rawlings smiled coldly.

~~~~~

The funeral for Solomon Brunel Bandamire was over. He'd received his hero's send-off – the whole population of the Western Tower turned out to stand in silence as the pyre burned into the night. Above them a comet streaked across the midnight sky and some called it an omen. Sibelius and Sir Philip, the wizard of magic and the man of science, did not offer their own interpretations.

After that James went to talk with Sibelius alone. Among the many things they talked about, the old wizard touched upon the Drezghul. 'I know little of this thing that you and your friends faced. It is a cause of grave concern that such dark magic should be within the reach of the enemy. It will require study, in the hope that we may one day learn the secrets of the Warkrin's dark arts.'

'And what about my vision, Sibelius? The three princes and the boy in the shadows, the one I saw when I looked at the Drezghul?' James asked.

Sibelius shook his head as he replied. 'Twice, James, you have seen a future, once in the eyes of the enemy and the time in the dream generator.' This last piece of information brought a frown to James's brow as the wizard explained. 'That was not your father standing by the king, it was you. So the dream was your future, not your past. But how ... I do not know. The dream generator isn't an oracle. That future knowledge came from you. This leads me to believe the image you saw when you looked at the Drezghul is also in the future, but I do not understand the meaning of the three princes, nor their horrible deaths. That is for time to reveal.' They fell silent awhile, contemplating the implications of these words.

Then James handed over a bag containing the two gifts that Sibelius had given him, saying: 'They are magical devices, Sibelius. They deserve to stay in this world.'

Sibelius nodded a silent agreement. He placed the Antargo stone on the workbench and opened *Talmaride's Answers to Questions*. There he found the last question James had asked the book: 'What use is a dragon talon?' The book had replied:

*A dragon talon is one of the rarest of all magical artefacts used by wizards and sorcerers.*

*Its importance is in the provision of a range of magical properties that reside exclusively within the domains of dragon magic.*

*Its rarity has been brought about by the fact that only on one previous occasion has a dragon talon been taken from a dragon, and the talon was subsequently lost to the dark powers.*

*The exile of the dragons in 10,996 BC (local time) led to an Old World shortage of dragon talons that was never corrected.*

At the bottom of the bag lay the dragon talon.

However, with every gain there is a loss. When Sibelius learned of the rifle that Sir Philip had inadvertently left back at the upper lodge, he despatched troops to retrieve it, but to no avail. It was gone.

# ~ Epilogue ~

## Old World, New World

Colonel Smythe-Whitely ordered the last of the wounded and fallen German marines to be returned to the *Ausburg*. They were ferried aboard with cutters manned by sailors from His Majesty's warships that stood inshore next to the wrecked cruiser. When every member of the compliment had been accounted for, Captain Raeder ran the Imperial Eagle up a makeshift masthead and the *Ausburg* steamed slowly back to Kiel under escort of *Cressy* and her attendant destroyers.

Harrington made one final request of the army and, together with Chief Inspector Corrick, he made the trip back to Cragside with a squad of soldiers. Harrington supervised the loading of a dragon carcass onto the flat bed lorry, had it covered in tarpaulin and despatched to the local railhead. Curiously, no witnesses to this survived the Great War.

Some weeks later, the carcass arrived at its destination, The Natural History Museum, London, and was accepted into storage on the orders of someone from the Foreign Office, and promptly lost.

James and his father said their farewells to Sibelius and Lady Orlania, while Bartholomew and Tempus escorted them to the Sea Arch. It was a strange goodbye, with Bartholomew and the hound standing together, drawn closer in their sadness, somehow incomplete without Solomon.

Bartholomew, his eyes filled with sorrow, said, 'I've lost a brother, and now I feel I'm losing a friend.' They shook hands and embraced.

As James and his father passed between the stone pillars and wrought iron gates, they both felt a sense of finality. Walking up the nearest dune, they turned to look back at the Sea Arch. And as they watched, it slowly began to fade until it was gone. Father and son turned and walked across the open countryside to the farmhouse, where they found Lady Jennifer and Lady Amanda waiting for them. The women greeted the men with tears of joy, and the four of them sat down to tea on the rough garden furniture as the afternoon sun gently gilded the clouds in gold.

James told his story from start to finish, with his father, mother and Amanda interrupting to add their own parts in the adventure.

They stayed on another day to tidy up and then set off for home. On the way to London, Amanda confessed to her aunt that she would not have missed these past weeks for anything, to which her aunt confided, 'That lovely bear Baranor presented me with a tooth that dislodged when he'd been fighting.' It was a magnificent two-inch carnasic.

※

The *Ausburg* eased into harbour in the dying moments of the day, under strict security. Once the casualties and dead had been disembarked, the remainder of the crew and officers were taken for debriefing. Captain Raeder was escorted directly to the Kaiserliche Marine Headquarters in Berlin, accompanied by the sample taken from the beach that day. Some months later the *Ausburg* was quietly struck from the Imperial Navy's list and, after a long refit, the vessel was re-dedicated as *Bremen*.

~~~~~

James spent a further week in London before returning to Drinkett College. There he discovered his absence had been explained as a bout of whooping cough that had confined him in a boring sanatorium for the duration. He never told anyone of his adventure.

Sir Philip returned to the War Office and was forced to endure the machinations of the Secretary of State for War for a further three months before Prime Minister Asquith called elections in November. This resulted in the removal of Mr Thomas Audrey, who did not receive the customary knighthood.

In the following year Sir Philip took his leave of the War Office, standing down when Richard Haldane, Viscount of Cloan, left office for the second and last time in April 1912.

~~~~~

News of the dragon talon travelled fast. The Guild made a formal request to Sibelius for the item to be delivered into the hands of the central committee, but Sibelius declined, bluntly saying that it was a personal gift to him from a friend.

The High Counsel of Elves also made representations for ownership of the dragon talon. This Sibelius flatly refused, not least because the Elven nation chose not to participate in the alliance against the dark powers of the Warkrin.

Sibelius redoubled his efforts to rediscover the lost powers of the Old World. In both worlds, events were moving towards another confrontation at some point in the future.

~~~~~

The existence of the Sea Arch remains closely guarded. The time and place of the next portal opening remains at the discretion of the portals.

※ ※ ※

The Natural History Museums in London and Oxford have never put the specimens of the dragon or the dragon new-born on display. All enquiries have so far been ignored.

※ ※ ※

Cragside had to be largely rebuilt, as a result of a fire. It exists as a National Trust property open to the public.